PLOUGHSHARES

Fall 1999 · Vol. 25, Nos. 2 & 3

GUEST EDITOR
Charles Baxter

EDITOR
Don Lee

POETRY EDITOR
David Daniel

ASSISTANT EDITOR
Gregg Rosenblum

ASSOCIATE FICTION EDITOR
Maryanne O'Hara

ASSOCIATE POETRY EDITOR
Susan Conley

FOUNDING EDITOR
DeWitt Henry

FOUNDING PUBLISHER
Peter O'Malley

ADVISORY EDITORS

Russell Banks
Ann Beattie
Anne Bernays
Frank Bidart
Robert Boswell
Rosellen Brown
James Carroll
Madeline DeFrees
Mark Doty
Rita Dove
Stuart Dybek
Carolyn Forché
Richard Ford
George Garrett
Lorrie Goldensohn
Mary Gordon
David Gullette
Marilyn Hacker
Donald Hall
Paul Hannigan
Stratis Haviaras

DeWitt Henry
Jane Hirshfield
Fanny Howe
Marie Howe
Justin Kaplan
Bill Knott
Yusef Komunyakaa
Maxine Kumin
Philip Levine
Thomas Lux
Gail Mazur
James Alan McPherson
Leonard Michaels
Sue Miller
Lorrie Moore
Jay Neugeboren
Howard Norman
Tim O'Brien
Joyce Peseroff
Jayne Anne Phillips
Robert Pinsky

James Randall
Alberto Ríos
Lloyd Schwartz
Jane Shore
Charles Simic
Gary Soto
Maura Stanton
Gerald Stern
Mark Strand
Christopher Tilghman
Richard Tillinghast
Chase Twichell
Fred Viebahn
Ellen Bryant Voigt
Dan Wakefield
Derek Walcott
James Welch
Alan Williamson
Tobias Wolff
Al Young

PLOUGHSHARES, a journal of new writing, is guest-edited serially by prominent writers who explore different and personal visions, aesthetics, and literary circles. PLOUGHSHARES is published in April, August, and December at Emerson College, 100 Beacon Street, Boston, MA 02116-1596. Telephone: (617) 824-8753. Web address: www.emerson.edu/ploughshares.

EDITORIAL ASSISTANTS: Elizabeth Dresner, Colleen Hubbard, Carolyn Rathjen.

FICTION READERS: Nicole Hein, Kris Fikkan, Amy Shellenberger, Nicole Vollrath, Darla Bruno, Laurel Santini, Emily Doherty, Eson Kim, Joseph Connolly, Kathleen Stolle, Elizabeth Pease, Billie Lydia Porter, Michael Rainho, Karen Wise, Tammy Zambo, Debra DeFord, and Wendy Wunder. POETRY READERS: Brian Scales, Christopher Hennessy, Renee Rooks, Tracy Gavel, Jessica Purdy, Jennifer Thurber, Michael Carter, Paul Berg, Michelle Ryan, Aaron Smith, January Gill, and Tom Laughlin.

SUBSCRIPTIONS (ISSN 0048-4474): $21 for one year (3 issues), $40 for two years (6 issues); $24 a year for institutions. Add $5 a year for international.

UPCOMING: Winter 1999–00, a fiction and poetry issue edited by Madison Smartt Bell & Elizabeth Spires, will appear in December 1999. Spring 2000, a poetry and fiction issue edited by Paul Muldoon, will appear in April 2000.

SUBMISSIONS: Reading period is from August 1 to March 31 (postmark dates). Please see page 232 for detailed submission policies.

Back-issue, classroom-adoption, and bulk orders may be placed directly through PLOUGHSHARES. Authorization to photocopy journal pieces may be granted by contacting PLOUGHSHARES for permission and paying a fee of 25¢ per page, per copy. Microfilms of back issues may be obtained from University Microfilms. PLOUGHSHARES is also available as CD-ROM and full-text products from EBSCO, H.W. Wilson, Information Access, and UMI. Indexed in M.L.A. Bibliography, American Humanities Index, Index of American Periodical Verse, Book Review Index. Self-index through Volume 6 available from the publisher; annual supplements appear in the fourth number of each subsequent volume. The views and opinions expressed in this journal are solely those of the authors. All rights for individual works revert to the authors upon publication.

PLOUGHSHARES receives support from the Lila Wallace–Reader's Digest Fund, the Lannan Foundation, the National Endowment for the Arts, and the Massachusetts Cultural Council.

Retail distribution by Bernhard DeBoer (Nutley, NJ), Ingram Periodicals (La Vergne, TN), and Koen Book Distributors (Moorestown, NJ). Printed in the U.S.A. on recycled paper by Edwards Brothers.

© 1999 by Emerson College

CONTENTS

Fall 1999

INTRODUCTION
Charles Baxter 5

FICTION
Jill Bossert, *Remaining in Favor* 9
Michael Byers, *The Beautiful Days* 20
Peter Ho Davies, *The Hull Case* 46
Doug Dorst, *Vikings* 61
Emily Hammond, *Back East* 79
Mabelle Hsueh, *Spillage* 96
James Morrison, *Stalker* 104
Antonya Nelson, *Palisades* 124
Stewart O'Nan, *Please Help Find* 140
Hilary Rao, *Every Day a Little Death* 150
Elwood Reid, *Buffalo* 160
Joan Silber, *Commendable* 174
Elizabeth Tippens, *Spring* 190

ABOUT CHARLES BAXTER *A Profile by Don Lee* 210

BOOKSHELF/EDITORS' SHELF 218

POSTSCRIPTS *Cohen Awards* 226

CONTRIBUTORS' NOTES 231

Cover painting: *Fossil* by Rob Evans
Mixed media on paper, 27″ x 38″, 1997
Collection of Bill and Mandy Strum

Ploughshares Patrons

This nonprofit publication would not be possible without the support of our readers and the generosity of the following individuals and organizations.

COUNCIL
Denise and Mel Cohen
Eugenia Gladstone Vogel
Marillyn Zacharis

PATRONS
Anonymous
William H. Berman / Houghton Mifflin
Jacqueline Liebergott
Estate of Charles T. Robb
Turow Foundation

FRIENDS
Johanna Cinader
In Memory of Larry Levis

ORGANIZATIONS
Emerson College
Lannan Foundation
Lila Wallace–Reader's Digest Fund
Massachusetts Cultural Council
National Endowment for the Arts

COUNCIL: $3,000 for two lifetime subscriptions, acknowledgement in the journal for three years, and votes on the Cohen and Zacharis Awards.
PATRON: $1,000 for a lifetime subscription and acknowledgement in the journal for two years.
FRIEND: $500 for a lifetime subscription and acknowledgement in the journal for one year.
All donations are tax-deductible.
Please make your check payable to
Ploughshares, Emerson College,
100 Beacon St., Boston, MA 02116.

CHARLES BAXTER

Introduction

It's probably a shame to say so, at least at the outset of an introduction to this issue of *Ploughshares,* but I may not be a particularly good or efficient reader of other people's fiction. By nature I am somewhat distractible. And although my distractibility is matched at times by my ability to concentrate, these two qualities create certain difficulties in judging and editing a group of stories.

For example: a few days ago, I returned from taking some cash out of an automatic money machine near the University of Michigan campus in Ann Arbor to find that the meter lady (actually, I believe her title is "parking enforcement official") was writing out a ticket in the spot where I had parked. Thanks to a cold downpour, I was both soaked and irritated. Standing near the driver's-side door, I informed her that, after all, I had only been gone for four minutes. (Actually, it had been longer than that; I had been distracted—again!—by the almost-invisible automated camera behind a tiny square of glass hidden away on the upper-left-hand corner of the money machine. I was doggedly wondering about who, if anyone, *looks* at these pictures—and, for that matter, when. Where does all this surveillance information go? I obsess about such things.) I told the parking enforcement official that, as she could certainly see, I was back now. I told her that I was now going to get into the car and leave. I told her that since she obviously hadn't finished writing the ticket, it would now *not* be fair to lay it on me, since I *had* returned and was presently about to drive away. She, too, was irritably soaked, and from the bored and offended expression on her face, I knew that she was all too accustomed to similar forms of lawyerly back talk from irascible motorists. She turned, walked down the street, and disappeared around the corner. Excellent!

It was only after I had tried to put the key in the door lock that I realized that the car next to which I had been standing, that I had been defending from attack, was not, in fact, mine. That the ticket that the parking enforcement official had been writing was not intended for me, but for someone else. My car was two spaces away, ticketless. The color of the two cars was similar, but they weren't the same brand, the same model, the same anything, otherwise.

This tendency toward obliviousness is, perhaps unfortunately, characteristic of me. As a reader, a writer, and a human being, I tend to be distracted by the actual and metaphorical trees, which in this case may be an immediate task such as talking off the meter lady, and I have a way, sometimes, of losing track of the overall shape of the forest, at least the first time through. This trait can present analytic or even perceptual problems for anyone, but it can be a particularly grievous fault in editors. I am as a result a slow reader and usually have to read everything twice. Acts of analysis and of creation tend to require a balancing-off of parts against the whole, and, in the case of the short story, that process may involve noting how the story's apparent theme or subject—what it's about—is voiced and dramatized by its tonal, imagistic, and associated dramatic elements, and I can almost never do that the first time through.

What I am saying is that each of the stories in this issue often had a detail or set of details that was so remarkable that, for moments at a time, I forgot what the story was about and was transfixed instead by an image, a tone, a dramatic action, or a statement by one of the characters. The contemporary stories that I tend to love are the ones that stop me dead in my tracks, not through surprise, exactly, but rather through an effort of supreme focused concentration. They distract me in the way I want to be distracted; they play to my weakness for stillness and wonder.

I have noticed lately that students in my workshops have gotten into the habit of complaining about certain kinds of stories as "slow." How is this story? What is it like? *It's real slow.* How was the movie? *Well, it was kind of slow.* This adjective, once descriptive, has now become part of an inventory of complaint. Out of a certain perversity, or perhaps a feeling that very serious matters of aesthetic judgment are on the line, I find myself these days complaining at some length about the opposite problem. Most of the movies I go to at the cineplex are much too fast; events have happened before you have a context for figuring them out, and you feel as if you have been given the narrative equivalent of a shell game. The pacing is often, and too literally, breakneck. You feel as if you're being sold something that basically won't stand up to any intensive or serious scrutiny, that doesn't, in fact, make any sense and that doesn't care to do so, sense not having been part of the project at any point in its conception or execution.

Years ago, James Agee, in a fit-to-be-tied defense of Carl Dreyer's somberly beautiful and by now classic film *Day of Wrath*, defended its pacing against an attack from a rival critic, Bosley Crowther, who had complained of its slowness, by saying that such a charge against a serious work of art is absurd. It would be, Agee wrote, like complaining that Beethoven's adagio in the slow movement of the "Archduke" Trio was too slow. Slow music isn't bad *because* it's slow. If it's bad, it's bad for some other reason. The problem is never one of pacing but of focus and concentration. He had a point, and I wish he were still around to make it again, only with more vehemence. Too much recent fiction, I think, has been written as if for the movies, and the resulting rhythms are often too staccato or too breezy. Such fiction gives off a nervous and impatient air, a feeling of stage fright, as if the story had to get its business done in a hurry and had no right to exist if it didn't.

This is, just possibly, an aesthetic spillover effect from the age of data processing, whose primary adaptive virtues include efficiency and speed. But perhaps it should go without saying that writing fiction, including short stories, is not data processing and never has been. This art does not need to be done quickly or consumed quickly; it just needs to be well-made, by whatever means, in communicating its experiences, emotions, and meanings. The late (and, by me, lamented) American novelist, essayist, and short-story writer Wright Morris used to go on at length in his essays defending slow reading, reading transfixed by wonderment, by the perfect image and detail. His own novels are typically slow reads. They invite a certain kind of reverie, and like his photographs they also invite solitary contemplation of the timeworn objects within them, often touched by what the Japanese call *sabi*, a quality of noble shabbiness.

As Flannery O'Connor says in "The Nature and Aim of Fiction," there is "a certain grain of stupidity that the writer of fiction can hardly do without, and this is the quality of having to stare, of not getting the point at once."

The stories I chose for this issue typically made me slow down rather than speed up. They required multiple readings. I found them arrestingly beautiful in both the part and the whole. I feel as if I have been the curator for an exhibit of wonders: for example, those semicircles of steam from two coffee cups just beneath the car windshield in Peter Ho Davies's "The Hull Case," or the three-paragraph scene in the Tuileries in Jill Bossert's "Remaining in Favor," or the miraculously cool and slowly darkening twilight paragraph at the end of Stewart O'Nan's "Please Help Find." A Chinese herbal doctor, possibly a quack, holding out his hand compassionately in Mabelle Hsueh's "Spillage," a character saying, "Stop we must," in Joan Silber's sweet and beautifully creepy story "Commendable," the runaway parents in Hilary Rao's "Every Day a Little Death," the spots of blood on a dirty mattress in Antonya Nelson's "Palisades," the methodical stalking prose in James Morrison's "Stalker"—well, I don't mean to do an inventory of these or the other wonderful stories here, only to suggest that such moments, tonally, thematically, or imagistically, provoked in me a sense of formal cared-for beauty in the work, something so well cultivated that its effect was to make the other world, the one I actually live in, disappear for a moment and give way to the reverie-inducing one represented by the words on the page.

Reading these stories will not be a job for you any more than it was for me as I gathered them together. For your own good, your skills of efficient speed-reading—if you have them—might well be, as we say now, disengaged. Some pleasures, usually the best ones, take their own sweet time, and although literature has no traffic cops, if it did, and I were one such cop, I would be stopping the graduates of the Evelyn Wood Institutes to ask, "Hey. What's your hurry?" What is profound or psychically consequential often allows its pivotal elements a kind of suspension in the midst of an onward narrative flow, and each one of these stories has that power to suspend itself, like a trapeze artist who flies off into the air and somehow, despite the forces of gravity (and of time), manages to stay transfixed, by us, above the net.

JILL BOSSERT

Remaining in Favor

"Let me ask you, have you ever, you know, faked an orgasm with me?" Frank asks Lise. They're in a crowded restaurant just off Madison. Lise looks up from her softshell crabs to see if the diners at the nearby tables are staring. This question is unlike Frank; it's direct and uncharming. "Well, when we were first together, maybe," she says.

Frank, in cool seersucker, asks, "Do you mean the first time, well...since?" meaning the first time since his marriage.

"No, no, when we were in our twenties."

"Oh, well, that was nearly twenty years ago." He looks at the ceiling, calculating. "Nineteen, in fact." Frank is dismissive of the lovely eager boy who had taken her in a flurry, still in her cotton nightgown with the eyelets. "But not now?"

"No, my darling," she says and touches his hand. There is no other answer, regardless of the truth.

Less than a week later, Frank comes to town unexpectedly. Unable to get him a reservation at his regular hotel, his new secretary has booked him into a horrible one on Third Avenue. After a long dinner, he and Lise are too tired and too excited to change hotels. Once they're in the room, Frank sees a pubic hair on the pillow. "Like a mint," Lise says, and they laugh, gag, and strip the pillowcase. Then, just as they've stripped off their clothes as well, his wife calls, and Lise lies still on the bed.

"What did the mechanic say?" (As if you knew a thing about cars, Lise thinks.) "Well, when?...Um, um. Did Victor call? Good. Wait, hold on a minute, I gotta get a pen." He makes a writing gesture, and Lise gets off the bed and goes into the bathroom, leaving him to scramble, naked, stretching the phone cord. She is furious about this Victor fellow who has suddenly appeared in the room with them, this man from Frank's other life. She turns on the shower.

* * *

On Wednesday Lise goes to the Frick Reference Library. She's been researching the work of a little-known American Impressionist for a client who owns several of his later paintings. It's nice work; the more Lise learns about the man, the more she sees in his art. Under the coffered ceiling, with her elbows on the burgundy felt mats that protect the books and absorb sound, she looks at lush reproductions of paintings by John Singer Sargent, a contemporary of the artist she's investigating. She focuses on the dexterity of Sargent's talent: four wild brush strokes in four distinct colors perfectly depict a sleeve of weightless organza around the pink flesh of Mrs. Henry White's arm. She reads about his frustration with his own facile skill, his sense that it's robbed him of some finer, harder won truth.

The next time Frank's in town, there is no mistake, and they go to the nice hotel, their usual hotel, where they always get a suite. Lise's skirt is rucked up to her waist, and the sweat courses down Frank's long nose, his seersucker pants an accordion at his ankles; after all these years they still can't wait.

Later, when they're in bed, showered and cozy, they settle down to talk. They entertain one another, they don't talk about plumbers. Lise tells Frank a story about the third wife of the Sultan of Brunei.

"No one has ever seen her. She doesn't go out, ever; no one's allowed to 'gaze upon her.' Anyway, this wife, when she comes to Paris to shop, she takes over an entire floor at the Plaza Athenée."

"*This* is what Favored Nation is for?" Frank says, sitting up to get a glass of Perrier from the bedside table.

"So, all the fashion houses send over dozens of complete outfits—ones she picked out from books of photos and from videos; they're all numbered. She looks over everything, the dresses themselves, then all the hats, gloves, scarves, jewelry, shoes..."

"Does she *take* everything, the Sultan's third wife?" Frank asks. He turns his back on Lise when he leans over to put the glass back. Absently, she starts tracing circles on his skin with her fingernail. He doesn't move while she's talking.

"Mostly. The rejects are returned to the couturiers. Then a bill is sent and paid for. No fittings, just tons of clothes. Literally tons."

"But no one sees this woman?" Frank says softly, his eyes closed, as Lise scratches patterns along his shoulder and up his neck.

"Except *him*! That's the thing. He's the only one who gets to see these unbelievable clothes."

"For as long as she remains in favor."

Lise dreams: She is in a house so close to the ocean, the waves rise to their highest point right outside the windows—tall, wide, Victorian windows, heavy moldings. The spray comes in sometimes, and it only makes her laugh. A wall of blue-green water rises and rises above the house, and she is not afraid. A storm breaks, and lightning strikes the sea and strikes the house. She laughs to feel the electric charge as it plays between the plaster ceiling and the parquet floor. Lise wakes up, and someone is lying there, his back a freckled wall, and suddenly she realizes: It's Frank. So rarely is he there to catch her dreams.

Each July, Frank would go away to his big summer house on Cape Cod, where he entertained friends and had begun teaching his small children about boats. To Lise, the picture of Frank's life held little appeal. Frank has become middle-class—Frank with his flippy turn of mind. She imagines him railing against the capital gains tax, debating the location of the best bone fishing in Belize, taking orders from his wife. As far as she knows, she's his only perversion, Lise—in hotel rooms, where she throws her garter belt over a chair and laughs until her ribs hurt.

Once, at a party, a man who knew Frank but was innocent of his secret liaison with Lise referred to him as "henpecked." At the time this remark embarrassed Lise, on Frank's behalf and on her own as his lover. Sometimes, when she can't help thinking about his life without her, she is reminded of the phrase. She imagines tiny spots of blood in clusters on his skin where a sharp beak has broken through. Peck peck peck. Quick holes. Then scabs.

When they were young, Lise had had idiot dreams of her future with Frank. She'd imagined herself in Europe with him, in a villa above Florence, a house of terra-cotta walls and an old couple who looked after them. She would do charcoal studies of Michelangelo's slaves, he would read Dante aloud to her in the original. Their friends would compose plays on the spot, and they'd all sing around a grand piano. And there'd be happy children speaking many languages. Children with her long legs, his strong jaw, and their blue eyes.

After they'd begun sleeping together—nicely, but without a lot of flourish—she had often thought of their children. Once, she'd asked him, "What would you do if you had a stupid child?" They were both silent for some time.

"Love it," Frank said finally. Lise was young enough then to be proud of him for this lie.

In early September, Frank returns from his summer on the Cape. In their hotel, he reads aloud to Lise from an English magazine dedicated, it says, to "strange phenomena, curiosities, prodigies, and portents." Lise cannot imagine him reading it to his wife. Frank laughs all the while, and Lise giggles with him. In truth, she's fascinated but unsettled.

One article is about a man who was tried on five counts of outraging public decency in Hereford. He had been found face-down on the sidewalk with his pants around his ankles. Children watched him humping up and down. They watched him attempt to mount an underpass. Then there was the man in a bulletproof vest who shot himself in order to achieve orgasm. And the man who swallowed Barbie doll heads at the moment of release.

After he finishes reading aloud, Frank says, "These are true stories."

"I believe it. Now. There was a time I wouldn't have. A long time ago, though," Lise says in a quiet voice, curving herself into a spoon around Frank.

"Did you bring your Barbie heads?" he says, turning to face her, the sheets twisting under him.

"I'm afraid I had them for lunch," she shifts her mood to fit his.

After he smiles and throws the magazine down, Frank grabs her rear, pulls at her satin panties. The thigh-high stockings do their dirty work. That edge of him inside her, the dark beauty of this act, successful, in part, because it is dirty—this has the power to break her down, to accept him blindly and on his terms. She is fearful and excited by the shift within her, the friendly silliness that switches in a moment to this dark meeting.

* * *

More than a month later in the hotel, after Frank hasn't bothered to make even a feeble excuse for this longish absence, Lise asks him, "Why didn't you marry me?"

"You were living with Jim then," Frank says, covering his body with the sheet.

"Before that. Before Jim. Before you got married."

"I don't know."

"You don't know," Lise says, flatly.

"That's right, I don't know. Too young, I guess." There's an edge in his voice.

That's as far as she dares to take it. The question of her life. Years before, a friend had said to her, "Frank told me that the biggest mistake he ever made was not marrying you." Now Lise wishes she'd never heard those words. She has allowed them to break her down with possibility.

Later, after they've made love again and she's cuddled up under the sheet to warm her cooling body, Frank says, "Remember when we had that fight?"

"When I socked you?" Lise says, remembering their one and only bad quarrel. Charmed by their past, they'd run through this memory before, up to a point.

"It hurt!"

"Well, the evidence, those earrings under your coffee table—it was your little apartment on 10th Street, just before you moved? You deserved it. But it *was* amazing, that I'd hit you..."

"We just burst out laughing!"

"Well, it stopped the fight, all right. And we were so relieved to be friends again," Lise says. "See, you were cheating even then."

"But we weren't sleeping together yet!"

"Oh yes, that's when our love was pure." Lise laces her fingers under her chin, tips her head, and flutters her eyelashes at Frank.

"God, that was weird, considering everyone was screwing around like mad—it was even before herpes." Frank is looking straight ahead and hasn't seen her innocent act, so she puts her hands down. "But weren't you sleeping with that guy...what was his name?"

"Peter. Pete."

"What a creep."

"Not really."

"So why did you hit me, anyway, if you were sleeping with someone, too?"

"You didn't know at the time, you know, about Pete."

"So?"

"So, our love was pure."

"I'd say it was a case of reverse double standard," Frank says.

"Yeah, well, that's the name of the game with us," Lise says. She adjusts her body away from Frank. "I never would have married you, anyway. You'd have been unfaithful to me."

"You'd have never known. I've learned not to leave earrings lying around, thanks to you," he says, moving over to her and nuzzling her neck.

"I would, too, know."

"She doesn't."

"*She* doesn't want to."

"*We* have nothing to do with her," Frank says and stops nuzzling.

"*Every*one in this stupid situation says that. But you're wrong. *We* have everything to do with her. You like to hoodwink people. You hoodwinked me."

"Hoodwinked? Is that what I did?" Frank pulls the sheet over his head, then pulls it aside to expose one eye.

"Shut up, this is serious."

"I don't want to talk about it anymore," Frank says, pulling the sheet off, sitting up straight, and plumping the pillows behind him. "If you don't like the *situation,* you just say the word."

Lise knows that Frank hates confrontations and messy emotions. That he could live without her is something she doesn't want to test.

When Frank goes on a month-long sail to the Caribbean with some friends, Lise doesn't expect a call. How could he call her? Even if he found himself separated for a moment from his shipmates, the unfamiliar phone charges would be evidence. It's not worth the risk. After all this time, it's no big deal.

While Frank is away, Lise goes to Paris to visit friends, to meet with a few dealers, to be away from New York. She has never been to Paris with him. She has been on a boat with him, watched him maneuver the craft through wind and water with a knowledge learned in childhood, squinting up to check the sails or the little flag that signals the wind's direction. Where she was all knees and elbows, unaccustomed to the compressed space and sharp angles at odd heights, he was grace. His turned-out walk held him steady on the bow. Watching him, she'd hit her head on the gangway door.

In Paris without him, she maneuvers through the streets like a Shield—a sleek, perfect racing boat. Cities are her element. She imagines Frank, confused in the Musée d'Orsay, turning the map around and around. He'd like Courbet's complicated allegory, *Interior of My Studio,* because the dog in the picture reminds him of Tibby, his long-dead spaniel. But then, she's never gone with him to the Musée d'Orsay, or the Louvre, or the enchanting Rodin Museum. Never been to the Met, or the Frick, or the Morgan Library. Never been to her favorite place in the park, Conservatory Waters, where the views haven't changed very much since William Merritt Chase painted them at the turn of the century. Frank doesn't know William Merritt Chase. The trees are taller now.

Lise stays with friends on the rue Jacob. She goes out every night, she goes out every day. Into the streets, out with people, to art openings and little dinner parties in the newly fashionable arrondissement near the Bastille. She falls in love with Paris again, its cream and golden buildings, its wide romantic vistas. She cannot imagine being with Frank on the Left Bank. They'd be staying at the George V, they'd go to the Louvre and tire quickly, they'd meet his American friends in restaurants on the Right Bank, where they'd drink and laugh. Frank would complain about the snotty attitude of the French, and she would not point out a little girl on the stern of a bateau wearing a perfect white dress. They'd make love in rooms with long windows. Sheer curtains would billow in and change the light. They'd enjoy Paris, but she wouldn't have time to hold it close.

One day, following a lengthy visit to the Louvre, Lise goes into the Tuileries and sits down. Not long after, a woman in her mid-fifties drags one of those green-backed slatted park chairs from its accustomed place and sets it down in the middle of the golden gravel path. She wears one black hose with a seam, the other leg bears a drawn-on line. She carries what looks to be a good but worn crocodile bag. She wears carefully applied but heavy make-up: very black brows, very red lips. Her dyed black hair is not well cut but approximates a sophisticated, severe style, straight to the ears and with deep bangs. Taken with her odd glamour, Lise thinks the woman was probably beautiful once.

Lise watches as the woman drags another green slatted chair near the first one. Their positioning seems important to her, but she struggles to avoid running her remaining stocking. Her bag keeps getting in the way. Lise feels a small impulse to help her, it would be so easy. But, of course, she only watches. Finally satisfied with the arrangement of the chairs, the woman sits down on one, spreads her legs quite widely apart, then places one knee up on the other chair. Uncomfortable, Lise looks away for a moment but can't resist turning back.

When she does, she sees a man standing directly in line with the angled chair in which the woman sits. He wears a good camel-hair coat. His hands are at work under it, as he watches the black-haired woman with her legs spread. Lise, fascinated, looks directly at the woman's face. Her head is tilted back slightly; sickle-shaped shadows cut arcs beneath her heavy brows. Her nose casts a short dagger of shadow to her very red and not quite parted lips. Lise looks over at the man again. He finishes his business, turns his back away from the path, and disappears. The woman composes herself and returns the chairs to their rightful places, then walks off. Lise sits dumbfounded, then she puts her hand up over her mouth and laughs. This is one for Frank.

Lise wanders through the little streets near boulevard St. Michel. The buildings, now steam-cleaned white, she recalls from her earliest visits as being tobacco-colored and soft gray-green. She stops at a café and buys a copy of the *Herald Tribune.* She checks out the weather page. There are storm warnings in the Caribbean; the black concentric lines on the map alarm her. She worries about Frank in the waters off Bermuda, mixed up with halyards and jib sheets and great tossing waves. She thinks of the

Triangle. Then, quickly, she computes the time change and tries to imagine him cozy in his cabin or drinking coffee with his shipmates at dawn.

That night in bed, to help her to sleep, Lise replays the memory of the first time she and Frank made love. Like a lullaby, the memory is sweet and ends happily. The pictures in her head are clear and never changing. And though she no longer trusts their accuracy, they never fail to make her think tenderly of Frank. Details stand out in sharp focus against a blurry background: his fingers on a button pulling the thick blue fabric of his shirt, his ear flat against his head and the sharp long line of his jaw, the white lace of her cotton nightgown stuck to his smooth chest. She pictures her own arms around his curving back, the freckles on his shoulders. She recalls how he'd cried out sharply when he'd come so swiftly, and how he'd laughed with embarrassment a moment later. She thinks of the weight of his arm across her hip and his purplish eyelids and the slight whitening at the bridge of his nose and his breath just inches from her face.

The next day, in the fragrant dark of Notre Dame, Lise sees an ecstatic woman perched on her knees on a shallow step in front of a crucifix. The woman wears a plain shirtwaist dress, an ugly modern dress that scarcely accommodates her bulk. Her purse, square and black with a short strap, swings at the crook of her elbow. Her hands are lifted, palms together in prayer, as she kneels before the crucifix. Her toes, in clunky shoes, barely touch the stone step. Her weight is centered in her thick body, held with perfect poise. Struck by the woman's unblinking eyes, her unmoving muscles, Lise watches for a long time. She even thinks of moving on, but is held there. Kneeling in her ill-fitting clothes, transfixed before that cruel symbol, a man impaled, the woman is frozen except for the slight swinging of her purse as it moves to the pulse of her heart.

Lise is humbled. Devotion like this, if someone described it to her—as she imagines she will describe it later to Frank—would sound foolish. But here in the smoky, fragrant church, faith has presented itself to Lise through the gesture of the praying woman. The Margaux, so rich and mellow at lunch, is sour in her mouth.

She is not blessed, and she knows that her knees will never balance her in painless exaltation. She walks quickly out of the cathedral, runs across the street through the crowd of gaudy tourists and respectable Parisians in their somber clothes. She runs, and her heart thuds in her chest.

Lise returns to New York and tells her friends how wonderful her trip had been. There are no messages from Frank, who should have been back for nearly a week by now. At first she's not bothered, they are not new lovers needing to know one another's every move. They simply are. Yet, there is a tacit understanding about time and its significance. And there are needs.

It has now been two weeks and a day since Lise's return. Tired of looking and looking at the phone, she picks it up and calls a nice man she met during the intermission of a bad play. Each of them had received tickets from friends in the production. He had given her his card just as the lights signaled the start of the long second act. Now, Lise makes a date for dinner with him, and even before the phone is in its cradle, she wants to cancel. She doesn't want to talk to this man. She wants to talk to Frank. Before she goes on the date, she buys a new pair of shoes from Manolo Blahnik. They are beautiful, but they hurt her feet.

The man chastely dines with her and never flirts, but holds her wrist from time to time, to emphasize a point. Watching her hands describe an abstraction, a narrowing idea widening out, he says, "What a beautiful gesture!"

The next day, Derrick, an old friend, calls.
"God, Der, it's been forever. How the hell are you?" Lise smiles, standing by the bed in her coat, about to go out.
"I'm great, great," Derrick says. "In fact, I'm in town to direct a fundraising film for the Episcopal Church. You know, tasteful, with a little MTV."
"Sounds about right. How's Susie?"
"She's good. In fact she's coming in on Friday at the end of the shoot. And we thought, kinda after Twig called about poor old Frank, that some of the old gang might get together, you know..."
"Frank?" Lise sits down on the bed.

"Oh, jeez, maybe you didn't hear about it? Have you been in touch with Frank at all?" Derrick says, his voice all wound up now.

"What about Frank?" Lise says, trying to keep her breathing even. She's slipping down a hollow black tube.

"Oh, Christ, well, it seems he was sailing with some of his business buddies, you know Jack Lukins and Davey Armstrong, those guys. And well, apparently there was this weird squall, like some sort of tornado out on the water, some spout thing, just awful. And they all bought it, the crew, everyone. Busted up the whole boat, the, the..."

"*Poseidon*," Lise says.

"Yeah, the *Poseidon*. What a bitch. Do you think you'll go to the memorial service? Twig said it was going to be at..." Lise has stopped listening. She would not be going to any memorial service. Derrick's voice disappears as she puts the phone down.

Lise gets up off the bed. She goes down the hall. She walks around and around in a circle in the living room. She sits down on one chair after another. She walks back to the bedroom and lies down and gets up again. She doesn't take her coat off. There is nothing to do. No one to call.

It's been over a month since Frank's memorial service. Lise visits the Met, her favorite museum. She stands in front of the three Vermeers in salon 12. She starts to cry. It is the tender light through the wimple on the woman in the painting on the right, *Young Woman with a Water Jug*. It is the ewer and the flat bowl in which it stands, and the perfect mirroring of the Persian rug beneath it. Calmer, but with tears still hanging off her lashes, she stares at the woman playing a lute in the picture on the left and at the unearthly translucence of her brown hair, its feeling of double exposure. It shimmers and sets the woman's quiet vitality against the flawless rendition of objects and their reflections: a chair with carved lion heads, the map of Europe—a difficult thing to do, paint a map so it feels like a map. Lise stands motionless in front of the picture. She recalls the suspenseful moments before Frank would arrive, and how, really, there were so few. She knows why the woman with the lute is watching out the window, watching so intently with a play of a smile, a little push of pleasure in the muscles of her mouth. A woman waiting to please.

MICHAEL BYERS

The Beautiful Days

In the days of his youth, Aldo often found himself—as many of us did—in a state of grace, and the sensation in his boundless filling heart resembled, to his mind, the transports of love. His Midwestern college, set down in the middle of a cornfield and isolated from any big city by fifty miles of empty, cold-roughened highway, seemed a basin of happiness in which he had been permitted, by some heavenly dispensation, to swim. Elms, dead elsewhere, had somehow survived in this town, pointing their great forked limbs at the sky. The quarry south of campus, hidden in its fringe of college-owned forest, echoed with the autumn shouts of naked swimmers; and in the frigid winters, skaters hiked the long way through the trees and picked their way carefully down to the ice. The rural sky was a comforting black infested with stars, and though he bruised himself when he skated, the cold Ohio air acted as a sort of balm, or at any rate it numbed him until later, when, in the heat of the town's one diner, he could examine his empurpled knees, not without some pride.

Small towns were new to him. The daily goodness of the Ben Franklin on College Street, offering its yarn and Bic lighters and artificial plants to whomever happened to walk through the swinging glass doors, swelled his soul. The tiny bank employed two tellers, both named Marie. The movie theater with its red velvet seats ran only the most second-rate films, and the screen was stained near the upper-left-hand corner; but this became visible only in outdoor scenes, when the stain resembled a small rain cloud. Despite the bad acting and ridiculous, juvenile plots, Aldo usually left the theater in a haze of goodwill, while around him the town disappeared into darkness down its two main streets, streets which carried their heavy freight of brick and ironwork as they had for a hundred and sixty years. He loved the town and the college, both lit with a stage-set perfection. Naturally, like many other students, he was often tired and fretted over his schoolwork, and his romances were only middlingly satisfying. He was poor, and had grown chubby on dormitory food. But even when he least expected it, he would be visited with a new gust of this unnamable generosity of spirit, when the world seemed nearly Platonic in its perfection. At these times he loved the world with such a passion that he worried he would one day lose his way to this grace, that its sources were more mysterious than the town around him: the pharmacy, its Valentine hearts illuminated in the window display; the dense tarry air in the Army-Navy store. The sensation that he was one among many—and yet still one, an individual being set loose on the planet—and that so much beauty abounded, on all sides, in every form, for him to encounter—all this combined to lift his heart above the ordinary, and made him, when it came, inexpressibly joyful. He was not religious, but such moments drove him to believe that something indefinite stood behind the bright curtain of the world—some great moral idea, some brilliant distillation of planetary consciousness that ringed the earth like a second atmosphere—something. It had come on him slowly in his three years here, this feeling, but now he sensed it defined him, and if he lost it, he feared, it would be like dying. Superstitiously he avoided thinking of it, as much as he could. Grace examined was—he suspected—grace denied.

His apartment off-campus Aldo shared with two relative strangers: a woman pianist named Eleanor, who used her long fingers as leverage to open difficult jars; and Bram, a dull, thick-chested economics major. Eleanor the pianist was taller than he, with a great pianist's wingspan, and irritatingly left behind in the shower's drain trap her short brown hairs. Though pretty she was a poor housekeeper, and her dirtied knives and half-eaten lunches lingered on the brown Formica counters for days. Beneath the window of her long bedroom she kept a sleek Japanese keyboard, futuristically black and technological; wearing headphones, she tamped its keys with great passion. Bram, who had an almost perfectly cylindrical head—except for his jutting nose, it looked as though it had been painstakingly lathed—strenuously lifted barbells in his small room beneath the eaves, filling the hallway with a sweaty stink. Strutting to the shower after these sessions, he wore bikini underwear, his blunt uncircumcised penis visible in outline beneath the fabric. A girlfriend could be heard in his room late at night, though she never stayed till morning. As for Aldo he had his metal shelves and rickety desk, his Greek and Latin dictionaries—he was a classics major—and his shoeboxes full of vocabulary flashcards. In the mirror he was a plumpish, curly-headed version of his father, shorter by three inches and with his mother's large sorrowful Italian eyes fastened, somewhat incongruously, above his father's looming, cavernous nose. While not vain exactly, he liked his own looks, and was bothered only by the troublesome way his eyebrows met in the middle, giving him a sort of primitive appearance. He had slept with four girls—women—since his freshman year, when he had lost his virginity to a slim and fragile-feeling poetess who had since dropped out of school and gone home to Columbus. Such were the facts of Aldo Gorman's life at twenty: sexually adequate, though unremarkable; interesting-looking, and handsome in the manner of most youths; periodically filled with an inexplicable grace which, when it faded under some daily pressure, he feared would never come again; and, not unimportantly, devoted to two dead languages, great sloppy tubs of vocabulary and syntax he hefted alternately—Greek four times a week, Latin five. And also, that winter, there was a girl he loved who did not love him back. Her name was Miranda Lowe.

She sat beside him one day in his glaciology class—a gut, to complete his science requirements—and she had forgotten to bring her book; would he mind if she looked on at his? "Oh—no," he said, surprised.

"You'd think, with all this snow," she said, almost whispering, "we wouldn't need a class on glaciers."

"You'd think," he agreed. "I felt like Amundsen this morning."

She smiled. "I know what you mean."

"Without the dogs."

"I don't think he used dogs," she said. "I think he used ponies."

"Oh," he said. "Really? Ponies?"

"One of them did."

"Actual ponies?"

"I think so," she said, glancing at him shyly, "and then I think they ate them."

"Oh," he said again. In the cold classroom full of melting boots and wet wool, she wore only a thin-looking white cotton sweater imprinted with black dots, as though her own heat were enough to keep her warm. Brown hair, brown eyes, pretty, with a fine long nose: in many ways she was a conventional sort of beauty, but what seemed to be shyness—she wouldn't meet his eyes—distinguished her from any of a hundred beautiful girls, as did, seen this close, the ghostly blond mustache on her upper lip, which he imagined another girl might have eradicated in some way. She seemed, like him, mostly innocent, and it was this that twanged at his heart, producing not love but its disreputable cousin, desire. "Okay?" he asked, before turning the page. "Mm-hm," she answered. A tiny feather, released from his puffy down jacket, lifted into the air between them.

But she would not have him. She was from New Mexico, and was already engaged—unusual in their generation, but she had the ring to prove it. In the library she held it out, where, under the fluorescent lights, it seemed a pale, fragile thing. "Two years ago," she said.

The news disappointed him, but it wasn't exactly a surprise. "You see him much?"

"At breaks."

"What's his name?"

"Oh...I'll tell you, but you can't laugh."

"All right."

"It's *Elmer*. But he's not what you think!" A flush of embarrassment colored her cheeks, and the sight weakened Aldo's heart. "He's very tall, and he doesn't hunt rabbits. And he talks like a normal person."

"He in school?"

"He's doing his residency now."

"He's a doctor?"

"Yes." She hesitated. "Or—almost. He's got a year still."

"And he's back in New Mexico?"

"No," she said. "He's at Harvard."

"Oh."

"He's going back to New Mexico when he finishes, to work on the reservations." She touched his arm, laughing. "He's not at all snobby."

"I didn't say anything."

"The way you said 'Oh.' It was suspicious."

"Elmer."

"Yes: Elmer Grand," Miranda said. And she pronounced the name with such firmness and resolution that Aldo understood at once he had no chance at her. The name as she spoke it seemed a brand of fine paint, or an excellent, old-fashioned toothpaste—something common, decent, thoroughly goodhearted. Like the glue, he thought.

A junior, Aldo was the only student studying Herodotus that year, under the direction of Larry Feingold—a short, skinny man in his seventies whose two front teeth rested endearingly on his lower lip, like a rabbit's. He seemed happy among his decades of books, with the radiator ticking cozily under the snowy window, and despite his age Feingold had a round, childish head and a great shrubbery of curly black hair; settled back in his worn chair, with his tiny brown shoes propped nimbly on the desktop, he looked more like a boy than anything. When Aldo stumbled, Feingold corrected him with a high cackling giggle—it was meant to be encouraging—and then, with a flourish that seemed showy from so small a man, he would lean forward and take over, speaking first one language and then the other, as though playing tennis with a second, equally agile version of himself.

By January they were skipping around in Book Two and had reached the material on Egypt. "When an Egyptian committed a crime," Feingold said, "*adikema*, it was not the custom of Sabacos to punish him with death, *thanatou*, but instead of the death penalty he compelled the offender, see that? Compelled, in the aorist"—he rolled his eyes with the pleasure of it—"to *raise the level of the soil* in the neighborhood, *geitoniai*, dative of location, of his native town, yes, or home, or—well, yes, *native town*, let's say, for simplicity."

"Raise the soil?"

"Yes," said Feingold. "Hm. I think, in other words, to build a levee. Against the Nile."

This seemed plausible. But down the page, an entire town had somehow been lifted high above the river, houses and all. Had the buildings been somehow propped on jacks, and soil shoveled beneath them? Or were they collapsible structures that one could take down and put up at will, like tents? And where did the extra soil come from? "No," said Feingold, puzzling, "it's just a levee. See? *In the neighborhood* of his native town." He chewed with his rabbity teeth on his lower lip. "But, hmm. The temple stands in the center of the city, *tou polou,* and, since the level of the buildings everywhere else has been raised, *anaskanomai,* one can look down and get a fine view of it from all around. Now that seems to say..."

"But the temple's on the river."

"Oh, that must be it. So, the temple is down *there,* on an island essentially in the middle of the river. The town is up *here* on the riverbanks. They look down on the temple."

"But they did raise the buildings, he says."

"Yes... well, fanciful, maybe. It's hearsay, at least. He gets it from the priests, after all. Or maybe he doesn't mean *buildings* really." Feingold read on. "Oh, but look at this, here. The road is lined, *grammatos,* yes, *lined* on both sides with immense trees, so tall that they seem to touch the sky."

"So...?"

"Oh, nothing," said Feingold. "Just those trees. Ancient ancient trees that were *there* once, on the road to the temple. Dead twenty-five hundred years, and yet there they stand. God bless the man for that."

Grace was to be found in the library as well, in the long free weekend mornings, when the sun was out over the snowy fields. From the top-floor windows the little town could be seen huddled under a Saturday morning's icy calm—Aldo might be in the library as early as eight—while light, the cleanest, brightest illumination he had ever seen, poured down from the tiny, wintry sun and, after caroming off the snowy lawns, went flooding back into the empty sky, to fill it more with light. The world, though cold, was illuminated as though by the gods, in a way that seemed somehow removed from time; and the leathery odor of the hundreds of thousands of books—among them his own Greek lexicon, the paper soft with wear—gave even this modern concrete building a gratifying, antique atmosphere, as though he had sat here for a hundred years, and would sit here a hundred more, until the winter's light consumed him.

But he could not forget Miranda Lowe, and she seemed unable, for her part, to leave him alone. Without meaning to, he had become something of a companion to her. They studied together. She was an English major, and he watched as she beat her way faithfully through *Pamela,* the book's polished black cover becoming creased and scuffed and its spine acquiring a series of white cracks. She *used* the book, writing in it heedlessly, while he, beside her, filled notebooks with long columns of writing, leaving his texts clean, unblemished, as though they had never been read at all. Necrophilic, he supposed. Orderly, at any rate. This contrast between them pleased him, though he couldn't say why, exactly. He enjoyed her teasing, maybe. Pacing restlessly the night before an exam she read the dictionary, folding back page after page. "Megrims," she said. And then after a pause, "Mephitic."

Spending so much time with Miranda allowed him to watch her move around in the world. She had long graceful arms, and though her legs were unremarkable, her feet, when she slid her shoes onto the checkered carpet, were shapely and even-toed. Small, compact breasts. He was not alone in thinking her beautiful. She had dozens and dozens of friends, far more than Aldo, and many of them were admiring men who, after talking with Miranda, would look him over querulously. He permitted himself to feel some pride at such times, though he knew she considered him a sort of eunuch, not to be feared. This was wounding; but there she was, sitting with him, while the other men had to drift away into the stacks. She did talk endlessly about Elmer, which grew tiring; but to her credit she knew it. "I don't want to," she said, "but he's all I think about sometimes."

"It's understandable."

"You'd like him, I think."

"I think maybe I would."

"*Maybe.* Listen to you. He's such a good guy."

"If he's so good, what's he doing away from you?"

"Oh, stop, he is good. He's always talking about *helping* people. Which is, you know—it's good. But he can actually *do* it, and it's what he wants." She touched his books. "Unlike the rest of us. Like me. I'm so *not* good it's not even funny."

He didn't know what to say to this. "You could teach."

"But I don't like kids. I don't know *what* I'll do, I'm so selfish.

He's just so *good*, just categorically good. At least in that particular way."

"Good is good."

"But the thing is, he's *too* good sometimes. In that way. *Socially* good. It's like an act sometimes. Especially..."

He waited. "Well, badness is good, too, now and then."

"For a change," she said.

"Exactly."

"Mostly he *is* good," she insisted, "and he can't help it. So don't make fun of him."

"I'm not."

"Yes, you are. You always do. It's because of his silly name."

"Like I'm one to talk."

"I like your name. It's exotic. Not like *Elmer*."

"Forget his name for once."

"But I can't!" she cried. "Elmer Grand!"

Neither had a car, but when a friend of hers drove to Cleveland after Valentine's Day, Aldo came along, squished in the back seat beside Miranda, their arms mashed together and their legs touching from the hip down. For comfort's sake he extended his arm along the back of the seat. They could almost have been a couple. And her beauty, despite his familiarity with it, had not faded. In fact, under the red neon of the Flats bars, he could hardly look at her. But she talked constantly of Elmer, and her frail ring darted in and out of the light. She irritated him. And he wondered what he was doing here, in the racket of the bar—what he hoped for. Nothing, plainly, would come of any of this. It was foolish to think otherwise. She got up to dance, and Aldo, unable to watch, stayed at the table.

But she sat happily beside him on the way back, smelling of cigarettes. "I forgot to tell you," she whispered, her mouth close to his ear, "Elmer's coming to visit."

"Good," he said. "Have a good time." Outside, the flat, frozen landscape sped past in darkness, and the warm air in the car had taken on a beery, hopeless sort of stink. Drunk, he began to feel a little sick. Jacqueline, on the other side of Miranda, slept, her skull rolling against the window.

"I want you to meet him. You've got a lot in common."

At least one thing, he thought. "I'll look forward to it."

"You'd like him."

"Okay."

"You sound reluctant."

"Let me know when he's coming."

"Why? So you can get sick, I guess."

"No, so I can leave town." Daringly he added, "And take you with me."

In the darkness she said, "Very funny."

"I mean it."

"If you really meant it," she said, "you wouldn't be sitting here."

"I wouldn't?"

"No. You'd be somewhere else. Alone with me."

"I've always figured that was impossible."

"I know you have." She put a hand on his leg. "That's what I like about you."

"No, what you like," he said, "is that I hang around and adore you, and don't make things awkward by making passes at you, which you would be duty-bound to deflect."

"Oh, duty," she said. Spitefully she removed her hand from his thigh. " 'New occasions teach new duties.' "

"You can keep that there."

She turned to look at him, her face dark in the darkened car. Her lips were close to his. "I thought I was duty-bound."

"You've always thought so until now."

"How do you know what I've thought?"

"I know what you tell me," he said.

"Oh—you won't get far that way. Being good." She leaned and kissed him carefully, just once, and sat back again, hand on his leg. Then she took her hand back. No one had noticed. The car motored on dumbly into the night.

"I—" he began.

"No, I'm sorry. I won't do that again," she said, her face turned away.

He leaned to kiss her, but caught only the side of her cheek.

"Please don't," she said. "Please."

He tried again.

"Please, Aldo. I'm sorry."

Touching from hip to calf, they rode the rest of the way home in silence. Drunk, he thought. But still, this was unfair. When he climbed alone from the car, the first to get out, he called his goodnights to everyone, but Miranda said nothing: she merely slid over away from Jacqueline, glanced up at him with her apologetic, beautiful eyes, and closed the door.

After this, she stopped returning his calls. When he encountered her by chance in the library, she seemed always to be idling—killing time. She was still as lovely as ever, but she appeared, to his eyes, preoccupied, as though she had been caught in the dragging middle of one of her gigantic novels. He felt he had missed some opportunity—that had he been more forceful earlier, been more daring, he might have won her, and he regretted his weeks of inaction. But he had only been behaving decently, he told himself, and no one could blame him for that. On the other hand, hadn't he been waiting, vulture-like, for the engagement to be miraculously broken off, so he could snatch Miranda before she touched the earth? And how could that be considered decent behavior? In fact, wasn't he both timid and sleazy—and who would ever bother over a man like that?

By the middle of April the winter had rounded nicely into an early spring, and the elms, so long dormant, had begun again to bud, acquiring a faint green haze. Elmer Grand had come and gone sometime in March, or so Aldo heard: he had fallen that quickly from her circle. He continued to avoid Eleanor and Bram, and in the meantime Cambyses invaded Egypt from Persia, crossing the Arabian desert to engage Psammenitus at the mouth of the Nile. Years after the battle had been fought, Herodotus walked the battlefield, the dry bones of the fallen still divided, as the bodies had been, into Persian and Egyptian camps. "Yes," said Feingold, "the *skulls,* exactly, of the Persians, are so thin that the merest touch, *epaphes,* with a pebble will pierce them, but the skulls of the Egyptians are so tough..."

"...that it is hardly possible..."

Feingold put a narrow hand on the back of his head. "Wait," he said. A look of concern crossed his face. "The skulls..."

"That it is hardly possible," Aldo continued, "to break them with a blow from a stone."

"Yes," said Feingold, puzzled.

"Right?"

"Oh—yes," he said again. "Do you know what I was thinking? How much I would like a drink just now."

"Now?"

"And I don't drink," said Feingold. "I haven't for years. I quit twenty years ago, and since then I've been clean. And now suddenly I need a gin and tonic. Out of the blue." He laid his text gently on his desk. "I was a terrible drunk, you know."

"No."

"Oh, I was. Terrible. I stopped because I nearly killed myself. My liver was calcifying, or whatever it is that happens to livers. Lithifying. And I was just careening all over the county." A look of great distance had entered Feingold's eyes. "I never thought I'd get to be this old. I'm seventy-one." He narrowed his expression. "You're a calm boy."

"Calm," said Aldo. "I guess so."

"No, that's good. I don't mean to put you on the spot. I *wasn't* calm, is what I mean."

"But here you are."

Feingold nodded, once. "Yes, here I am. And almost dead, anyway."

"No getting around it."

"No. A cruel thought, but true. Are you a Jew?"

"Me? No," said Aldo. "I'm not."

"No? I thought you and I . . ." Feingold in his sky-blue jacket shrugged. "A Christian?"

"No."

"Nothing at all?"

"I guess not," said Aldo.

"Do you believe in an afterlife?"

"Not really."

"But maybe a little bit?"

"I would like to," he said, "but it seems a little delusional."

"Awfully attractive, though, isn't it? Imagine."

Aldo hesitated. "I believe in grace."

"Oh: grace. Are you Catholic?"

"No, just"—it was inexpressible—"happiness."

"Oh. Well, good. Happiness is good."

"But not *only* happiness... *grace*," he said, ferociously. But worryingly he had not felt it in weeks, and it felt like bad luck mentioning it out loud. "It's the only word. When you know your place in the world."

"Yes; I remember the feeling."

"The beauty," said Aldo. "Something about all..." He gestured. But it was eluding him. "Everything being *where* it is, in *time*, in the right proportions. *Beauty*. When things are perfect."

"That which is immortal in us."

"Well—"

"That's grace. And then you get to sin: the sullying of that goodness. But to begin with, starting out, *now,* say, for you, that which is immortal is inherently good, by definition."

"But not all goodness is immortal."

Feingold picked up his book again. "I believe in an afterlife," he said, "because it gives me solace, and because so many people have believed in it before me. If it is a delusion then it is an old and very decent delusion. But people are starting to come back now, with this new technology." He looked away. "That tunnel of light."

"I've heard there's a biological explanation for it."

"Well."

"Dopamine, or something."

"Well, go fuck yourself, Aldo," said Feingold, mildly, "if you can't let an old man believe what he needs to."

"Sorry. That's what I've read. It's all biological."

"Well, go fuck yourself, anyway," said Feingold, with more force. He closed his book. "Just wait till you're my age. Then you'll be happy? I don't think so."

"I'm sorry."

"You should be." Feingold reclined, looked away. "There are other people in the universe, Aldo," he said. "Pay attention."

That afternoon, feeling guilty and ashamed, and sickened by Bram's grunting, Aldo called Miranda. She picked up immediately. "Why, it's Aldo," she said, surprised. "The long-lost stranger."

"Ha," he said.

"Why haven't you been calling me?"

With some irritation he said, "I have been." And he had: once a week at least. Never home. Always got her housemates. "I've left messages."

She sighed. "I don't always check the machine."

"Well, I've been calling."

"I've got something to tell you, actually, Aldo. A little surprise."

"You do?" She'd broken it off, he thought. "What?"

"I think it's better said in person."

"Okay," he said. "There's a movie tonight."

"Fine."

"I won't do anything," he said. "Scout's honor."

"Oh, I wouldn't know a Boy Scout if I stepped on one."

"Really. I won't do anything."

"Fine," she said.

"Just so you know."

"I know, all right?"

"Good."

"So stop talking about it."

"I can't just not bring it up."

"Look," she said, "I'm sorry I didn't call."

"I was wondering about that."

"It was a stupid thing to do," she said. "I mean in the car. But I do like you."

"I know you do."

"Christ almighty," she said, and laughed. "You're so *somber*."

Though he knew he had no right to be hopeful, he couldn't help it. With great devotion he shaved the smooth planes of his face in the befogged mirror. Flecks of white foam dotted his earlobes. Cowardly, he was. It was cowardly to see Miranda again, rather than forget about her. Or, if not cowardly, then indulgent. He was purposefully fooling himself. Lying.

But he lied all the time. Despite his protestations to Feingold he did believe—didn't he?—in something like an afterlife; but what an embarrassment to admit to it! Though if he believed in the soul, as he thought he did, then why not? The soul takes nothing with it into the next world, said Plato, except its education and culture. That was a gratifying thought. Silly and unscientific, but gratifying. The springy air puffed through the bathroom window, drying his hair. On the twilit walk across campus through the daffodils, he felt a little shimmering—a faint suggestion of the old feeling—though by the time he met her at the theater it had gone away again. He didn't mind, really. She was lovely, as she always was, waiting for him under the marquee in a yellow dress, holding a magazine, and abruptly he had the sensation that he was exchanging something—trading in, somehow, the ineffable for the tangible. The loose weave of her dress. "This won't be very good," she said.

"I suppose," he said, "we could go elsewhere."

"Like?"

"I don't know. Valentine's? No."

"So, look." She held out a hand. "I have a new ring."

It took a moment to understand. "You're married."

"We did it when he came in March. Downtown."

"Oh. Congratulations." A bitter disappointment rose in him. "That's the surprise."

She smiled. "I didn't want to tell you over the phone."

"He's a lucky man."

"I tell him that, too. We're doing the ceremony this summer, if you'd like to come."

"Maybe I would."

"You and your maybes. *Maybe* you would." They bought tickets.

"It might tear my heart out."

"Oh, Aldo, don't say that."

"You know it would. I don't think that's a secret."

"Well," she said, "I need my friends to be my friends."

"I'll do my best." He followed her down to their seats.

"You did promise."

"I know I did."

Her eyes were weak, and she disliked wearing glasses, so they sat near the front, leaning back in their seats to watch. The movie was bad, and to pass the time Aldo watched the lit-up clock over one of the exits, the second hand patiently sweeping the minutes away. The stain on the screen appeared and disappeared, and he watched it idly. Now and then their arms brushed. Her lovely arms, bare, shone in the white cinematic light. At last, hopelessly, he took her hand. Married, he thought, guiltily. But she allowed it. In the dark he studied the architecture of her fingers. Each one was long and finely articulated—like Eleanor's, he realized. The knuckles were boxy, like dice under the skin. The palm was slender. He heard her breathing beside him, little puffs through her nose. She whispered: "You promised."

"You don't mind," he replied.

"You're being bad."

"Yes I am."

"So am I, I guess."

He clasped her hand more tightly. He touched her wrist: his fingertips against the soft skin.

"I'm married," she told him.

"Big deal." He put his hand on her thigh. "This doesn't count."

"It doesn't?"

"No. We're just friends." He leaned and kissed her ear. "Doesn't count," he said. He had a terrific erection which pushed uncomfortably against his fly. He kissed her again. "Doesn't count."

"No," she said. She kissed him back, her lips narrow and firm.

When the movie ended they sat together and watched the credits. He counted names: three hundred sixty, and he could stand up and in the darkness rearrange himself without much embarrassment. Then she took his arm and led him through the rear exit, which opened onto the brick-walled alley. Against the wall they began kissing again. That he should be this close to her lovely face—that she should allow it—that she allowed his hands to travel unimpeded over her hips—all this was wonderful to him. At the same time he knew it was a crappy thing to do, and could lead to no good. In fact it was a very bad thing: but he didn't care.

"Miranda—"

"We shouldn't be doing this," she said.

"But you want to," he said, kissing her throat, "and I do, too."

"I almost told him no," she said.

"Don't talk."

"This is why I never called you."

"Good thing I called *you*."

"I can't do this," she said, and kissed him again.

Presently they separated and walked hand-in-hand down the alley; when they reached the sidewalk they let go and walked hurriedly through town. It was balmy still, and though the sky was clear the horizon flashed with heat lightning, and the elm trees moved their limbs about in the warm wind.

"Come back to my place," he suggested. "It's a nice night."

"I shouldn't." She clasped her bare arms to her sides. "I shouldn't be doing any of this."

"But you want to," he said.

"All right. But we can't do anything."

"Fine," he said, blithely, "we won't."

"We will." She clasped his elbow. "I know we will."

"Not if you don't want to."

"It's not that," she said, "it's not that at all. Obviously."

They kept walking. As they reached the dark side streets, she took his arm again.

"So," he said.

She stopped abruptly. "I left my magazine back there."

"You want to go back?"

"Yes—no," she said. "Never mind."

Three blocks down they came to his little house sitting on its sloppy lawn. Lights were on inside. "People are home," he said.

She had grown momentarily timid. "That's all right."

He lifted the creaking screen door open. Upstairs, Bram had filled the hall with his sweaty stink, and Eleanor could be heard tamping away at her keyboard. "My housemates," he said, and ducked with her into his bedroom, and locked the door.

"What are their names?"

He told her. "Hear that?" He tipped his head at the wall. "He's lifting weights."

"So neat," she said, glancing around. "It's like a guest room."

"He does it all the time," he said.

"Who?"

"Bram."

"Why doesn't he go to the gym?"

"I don't know. They're actually both sort of gross."

She examined his bookshelf. "That's not very nice of you."

"I mean—I was late with the housing thing. I wouldn't have chosen them."

"That's not very nice, either."

"I'm being bad."

"No," she said, "you're *not* being *nice*. It's different."

He came up behind her and spoke into her ear. "It's not so different," he said. He put his hands on her hips.

"This is the only time this is going to happen," she said, turning to him. "We'll just get it out of our systems."

Bram set down something heavy on the floor. The screws in the bookcase jingled.

She reached behind him to turn out the light. He opened the buttons on the back of her dress: the material was a light cotton, warmed by her skin. He took down her shoulder straps and the dress settled to the carpet. In her white underwear she was much slimmer than he had imagined: the points of her pelvis rose in little knobs. He helped her with his shirt, which slid off him easily, like a jacket off a book. A shaft of orange light from the street entered through the uncurtained window and marked a square on the wall.

"You're so quiet," she said.

"So are you."

"I'm just—I feel like—" She threw out her arms. "Ta daa." Her little breasts bounced in her brassiere. "Such a performance this is."

"Well."

"So I'm proving something," she whispered, "and I know it, and after this it's forget it, right?" She set her jaw and peered at him. "Right?"

"Right."

Abruptly she reached behind her, unfastened her bra, then stepped out of her underpants. "Okay," she said, and stood naked. "You like this?"

He found it difficult to speak.

"So somber," she said again.

"I," he said.

She took off her ring, set it on the dresser. "Is that better?"

They climbed into bed together. He kissed her and took her breast in one hand, the nipple firm in his palm.

"What if I told you I wasn't married?"

"It wouldn't matter to me." Not true, exactly.

She was disappointed. "Not at all?"

"No. Maybe. I don't think so."

"Isn't it more fun if we're—if I am?"

"We should be quiet," he said, and turned on the radio. "The roommates."

"You care about them?"

"No—"

Her nakedness had surprised him with its loveliness, the sweetness of the curve beneath her little white breasts, the inward dip of her flat, pale stomach, the fine wiry hair in unexpected abundance between her legs and across her lower belly. Beside him it tufted pleasantly against his leg.

"Well," she said, "your move."

"It matters to me that you're married," he said, "because I can't marry you."

"No, you can't."

"But that's all."

"He made me," she said, kissing his throat. "He said he'd leave me if I didn't do it. But this is showing him."

He didn't believe her; it didn't much matter. Still. "Don't do this for me."

"I wouldn't."

"You wouldn't?"

"No. This is for me."

"What if you weren't with—? Would you—would I—"

"Oh, don't ask me that," she said. "Please."

Hesitantly, he asked, "Do you use any—are you on—?"

"Yes," she said, blinking. "Yes, yes, yes."

Stupidly he felt as though he might cry; but he stopped it, and turned up the radio, which crackled with the approaching lightning. Shifting his weight, he moved atop her. "Just—?" he asked.

"Aldo," she said.

His name in her mouth thrilled him. "What?"

"Nothing."

"What?"

"No," she said, "I just wanted to say it."

"Say it again."

She did, and he slid easily into her. Smooth and easy, all the way to the bottom.

"There." She smiled up at him from her tousle of hair. "Feel better?"

"*You* do. Don't lie."

"Yes, I do," she said, *"Aldo."*

"Don't—" He felt himself letting go, pulled back.

"Your own name," she said. "What narcissism."

"Let's not talk."

"My voice?" she asked. "Or is it just your name?"
"No."
"Which one?"
"It's neither."
She laughed, "Aldo!" Loud enough to be heard.
He would make her stop, he thought. "Elmer," he said.
"Okay," she said, wincing. "Don't."
"Don't? Elmer Grand."
"Oh—truce."
"Elmer Grand."
"Truce!"
"Truce," he said.
"You're terrible." She shifted beneath him, locked her legs at the backs of his knees, and pressed upward. "You're so terrible—so bad."

He supposed he was. And if that was what she wanted, then he would say so. "Both of us. You're bad, too," he said. "You're so bad."

"I am?"

"So bad," he said.

"Oh, yes—yes." She grimaced menacingly, eyes shut. "Fuck," she said, "fuck, fuck, fuck—"

Slipping in and out of Miranda he felt—as he had felt before, with other women—that he was exploring a city, an ancient clay-walled town, through the narrow streets, where various flags were hung out... She was very firm, and he fit her with a great precision. They sweated a good deal, and their bodies, in the humid room, smacked together like fish hitting a countertop. If it was really to be only one night—and he did not believe this, either—then they were making the most of it. The storm that had stood on the horizon hours ago had come across the countryside and now walked slowly through town, delivering five or six great crashing bolts of lightning which illuminated the room—enough to see Miranda, above him, working in a pose of great determination, gazing down not at his face but at some spot near his sternum. Why, he wondered, had she agreed to this? What did she want to prove? That she was desirable?—but no, that was only too plain. That she was unpredictable? This was closer; but he didn't know, and to his surprise he found he didn't know her well enough to guess.

"Let's do something," she told him, past two, "you've always wanted to do."

"This is about it," he said.

"Something else."

"Oh—"

She propped herself up on an elbow. In the darkness the whites of her eyes flashed. "Think," she said. "Out of our systems."

"Well—"

"That's the deal," she said. "We agreed."

"I know."

She sighed, lay back. "Do you want to tie me up?"

He laughed. "No."

"Do you want me to tie you up?"

"Not really."

"A little bit?"

"No," he said.

"What, then?"

"I don't know."

"I won't tell anyone," she said.

"How about—just—" he motioned, downward.

"Except that," she said.

"Not bad enough?"

"No, it's not bad at all," she said, "I just don't like it."

"Just a little," he said.

"I don't like it."

He said, "You should have said so."

"Maybe."

"Just a little."

She said, "A little."

"Okay, a little."

"Just once," she said.

"Okay."

Grimacing, she made her way down his abdomen. He was sore, slightly, and he flinched when she began, taking him half-erect into her mouth. And he felt it *was* dirty—particularly since she didn't like it. The thought excited him, very suddenly. He held her head. She twisted once, stopped. Quickly he came in her mouth. Extracting himself, he pressed his hand over her lips, over her nose. "Swallow," he said.

She twisted again.

"That's what I want," he said. It was. He knew it as he said it.

She made a sound. Spitting, she bit his hand. "Asshole," she said, hitting him.

"That's what I want."

"Asshole," she repeated. Freeing herself, she spat at him, wiped her mouth on his discarded shirt. "Fucking shithole asshole." Spat again, wiped.

He sat up. "I just thought of it then," he said.

"You incredible fucking asshole." She dressed, retrieved her ring. "Fucking shithole. Jesus."

"I just realized it," he said. What had compelled him? He put on his underwear.

"*Don't* say anything." She pulled her dress over her shoulders. "I can't believe you."

"That was—"

"*Don't* say anything."

"I'm sorry—"

"You're supposed to *know*," she said, "how to *behave*."

"Stay."

"Oh, you fucking asshole," she said, loudly. "You unbelievable fucking asshole."

"Don't—they'll hear—"

"He hates you," she shouted, "he hates you both." She swung, hit him with the sole of her shoe. "Prick," she said. Barefoot, she walked downstairs. The screen door creaked and slammed.

After a moment Bram appeared in the hallway, dressed in his bikini underwear. He filled the corridor, huge.

"Sorry," said Aldo.

"Friend of yours?"

Aldo stepped back into his bedroom, closed the door.

Bram knocked. "Sounded bad," he said, through the door. "Woke me up."

"Sorry."

"Guys were loud."

"What about you and your weights?"

"You should try it. Lose that chub."

"Thanks."

Bram opened the door a crack. "Want to borrow them?"

"Not right this second."
"Whenever," said Bram. "You want a beer?"
"No."
"They're half Eleanor's," he whispered.
"No thanks."
"Say the word."
"Goodnight," said Aldo.
"Okay," said Bram, "goodnight."

It was essentially the last he saw of Miranda. He was ashamed of what he had done, and he was happy to avoid her when he could. He caught glimpses of her around campus, but they never spoke. Her friends eyed him unpleasantly. For the second time, she vanished from his life. Embarrassed and contrite, Aldo kept to himself. It was a terrible thing to have done, and he had done it, and couldn't forget it. All the talk about goodness, and *things being right,* and grace, seemed so much crap. And Feingold, though still genial, also withdrew.

After graduation Aldo moved back to Portland, believing he was only taking time off from his studies, that he would return soon enough, but he landed a job teaching Latin at a boys' school in town, and the pleasures of this, and a certain lassitude, kept him from leaving. The corridors smelled of wax and the heated air that came forced through vents in the floor. His classes, full of the sons of the rich and happy, were sedate, and the boys were, as a rule, at least well-informed about things, if not always interested or original. When he turned them loose at vacations, Aldo was sorry to see them go. "Goodbye, Fitch," he said, standing at the door, "and Gerard, and Lumber, and Poole, and Regent, and Franklin, and Vinton, and Chillingham," and they would ceremoniously shake his hand as they went out, loosening their ties. He was liked. The custodial staff knew his name, and Mike seemed genuinely affectionate when he arrived in the afternoon to sweep and empty the trash.

"Mr. Gorman."
"Mike."
"Not bad weather."
"Little sun," said Aldo.
"Oh, a little sun, not bad. Not bad at all."

But it was nothing like the grace he had known: no, that had gone, seemingly for good. He was essentially friendless in the dark, gloomy city, and he remembered his college days with a mixture of nostalgia and shame, a complicated shame that had to do with, first, not going on with his education, and second, with the way he had behaved that night with Miranda. He was not civilized, not at heart. No, he was not at heart a good person, and he had proved that. And as if in punishment he had been shunted onto this side track, a track occupied by others like him: Mr. Toobman, who taught history, a sour, balding homosexual who smelled of his lemony soap; Mrs. Graven, the shy, aged mathematics instructor whose throat was peppered with protuberant moles. Even Aldo, old before his time, had grown a gut and developed a persistent phlegmy cough. He was sick all the time. Some weeks he was mostly well, other times the cough racked him, and he would run a fever, which gave him harrowing dreams in which he grew to a terrific size, then shrank away to nothing. His heart raced, then beat lopsidedly, as though on three legs. Hacking into his handkerchief, he graded his exercises: *That friendly king did not remain there a long time. Our mothers had not understood the nature of that place.* He began to drink more, and thought of Feingold when he did. If this was his punishment, it was not the worst he could imagine; and at any rate he felt he deserved it. And at the same time he knew he was being stupid: that holding on to a little guilt in this way was a waste of time. Forget it, he told himself. But he didn't.

His cough worsened that spring, grew painful, and one weekend the fever knocked him down entirely. In his chilly Saturday apartment he poured sweat terribly into his sheets. From bed he watched the sky change through its stages of gray, one layer of cloud sliding aside sluggishly to reveal another, each darker than the last. It seemed a vision of terrible unhealth, and he grew afraid. Sleep came abruptly around noon, and he woke in darkness, in what felt like the middle of the night, with his heart racing. A gurgling escaped his lungs. He had no one to call. Next door his neighbor was hammering a nail into the plaster. Sitting up in bed he gasped for breath. It was just past dinnertime. Teetering against his dresser, he buttoned his pants with trembling hands. Outside in the parking lot the wind had picked up and blew through his hair, wind that smelled pleasantly of the river. It would not be so bad—he could take a week off. And he was not all that sick, really. But his fingernails on the steering wheel were so purple they looked bruised—and this frightened him—as though he had grasped too eagerly at something, and had it snatched away.

The clinic was empty, and he was seen almost at once by a doctor whose large masculine hands, covered with red hair, pressed the glands in his throat, his armpits, his groin. The doctor looked young, not yet thirty: Dr. Grieve. "Harvard," said Aldo, sighting the diploma.

"Yes."

"What're you doing here?"

"This is where I live." He peered into Aldo's eyes. "Do any drugs?"

"No."

"Drink?"

"Not much."

The doctor sighed. "Why do you ask? You know someone there?"

"Elmer Grand."

"Oh—Elmer Grand," said Dr. Grieve. "I know Elmer Grand."

"Really?"

The doctor peered into his ears. "Friend of yours?"

"No—I don't know him. I used to know his wife."

"Miranda?"

Startled, Aldo croaked, "Yes."

"Miranda. Breathe. In. Now hold it." He applied the stethoscope to Aldo's sternum. "Quite a girl."

He nodded.

"Out." There came a long pause. "Bronchitis," he said at last, "and sounds like pneumonia."

"How is Miranda?"

"Oh, well, fine," said the doctor. "Last I heard."

"No news?"

"Not that I know of. It's only a Christmas card sort of thing."

"Not—they're still together?"

"They were at Christmas."

"No children?"

"I don't know. I don't think so."

"Well," said Aldo.

Ruefully, Dr. Grieve said, "Elmer was a hound. Anything that walked."

Aldo said, "Really."

"Really. And I imagine she must have known."

"She never—I don't remember her mentioning it," he said.

"You knew her well, then."

"Pretty well. For a while."

"You're pretty sick," said Dr. Grieve. "This cough, how long?"

"I don't know. Months."

"Months? Two? Eight?"

"Six."

"Any blood?"

"No."

"What about your heart?"

"My heart?"

"This kind of long-term infection, it can get lodged in the heart valves. We see that now and then."

"It's been fine," he said.

"No palpitations? No irregularities?"

"Oh—" he said, "no." A current of dread moved through him.

"You're lucky, then."

"Okay," said Aldo. "Good."

"So: Elmer Grand."

"How many—" Aldo stopped. "He did it a lot, then."

"Slept around? Oh, all the time, Jesus. Sleep-deprived and still he'd be after it."

"But—"

"That's what he liked. Likes, still. Probably."

"So," said Aldo.

"You should take a week off. Keep warm. Get these filled. You'll feel better."

He hesitated. "And the heart—?"

"If anything unusual comes up, come back." He helped Aldo off the table. "Okay? All better."

And he did get better, more quickly than he imagined possible. His lungs cleared. His heart beat normally again, in sequence. His sleep, for the first time in months, was seamless. And by Thursday he was back at school. *"Copia?"* he asked.

"Abundance," said the class.

"Yes; *ratio?*"

"Judgment," they said.

"Yes; *duco?*"

"To lead," they said.

Well, it was something, these voices. Always answering. They hardly asked anything of you; and what they did ask, you could give. It was not the life he had wanted; but it was close, in some ways. He had his languages, and he had the afternoons to himself. He thought of Miranda now and then, but less often as time went on. He had lost his way to grace, that was true. Sometimes—driving over a high bridge, say, or waking up early on a bright Saturday—he felt a sort of echo, from what might have been his soul, and then he was sorry for what he had lost. But more often he felt sorry for that old figure of himself, waiting for grace to descend, afraid when it left him. No one could live that way, not forever. It was too much to expect of life. Always waiting. No; but he could work. A cedar tree outside the classroom window broke the sunlight, and the confetti of broken light played on the back wall of the room, where he could watch it in the afternoons. Doors closed, here and there, in the empty cavern of the school. The waxing machines murmured up and down the hallways. When Mike put down the trash can, it made a nice, hollow bonging sound; always he put it down on the wrong side of the door, and Aldo, before he left for the night, would put it back where it belonged.

PETER HO DAVIES

The Hull Case

> *Of modern North American cases one of the earliest and most widely reported abductions occurred in the early sixties to a mixed race couple in New Hampshire...*
> —K. Clifford Stanton, *Taken: 12 Contemporary UFO Abduction Narratives*

Bessie is telling the colonel about the ship now, and Bernie, sitting stiffly on the sectional sofa beside his wife, can't look up. He stares at the colonel's cap, the gold braid on the rim, where it rests on the coffee table next to the latest *Saturday Evening Post* and the plate of tuna-fish sandwiches Bessie has laid out.

"What color were the lights, Mrs. Hull?" the colonel wants to know, and Bessie says, "Blue."

The colonel makes a checkmark.

"Baby blue," Bessie adds. She looks at Bernie, and he nods quickly. He thought the lights were a cop at first.

"Baby blue," the colonel repeats slowly, his pen scratching along. He's resting his clipboard against his khaki knee. His pant leg is crisply ironed, and his shoes glint. Bernie wishes he could see what the colonel's writing.

"Is that usual?" he asks. "Blue lights? In these cases, I mean?"

"I'm afraid I couldn't say," the colonel says.

"'Cept I believe aircraft lights are usually red and white."

"Yes, sir."

"Then this wouldn't be an aircraft?"

"That's what we're aiming to determine," the colonel says. "Sir." His smile reminds Bernie of Richard Widmark.

There's a pause, and then Bessie asks, "Won't you have a sandwich, Colonel?" and the colonel says, "Thank you, ma'am. Don't mind if I do." He takes one and lays it on his plate, but doesn't take a bite.

Bernie thought the lights were a cop at first. They'd already been stopped once on the drive back from Niagara. He could have sworn he'd been doing less than sixty. The cop had shone his flashlight in Bernie's face—black—and then Bessie's—white.

"Any trouble here, ma'am?"

"Not at all, officer," she told him while Bernie gripped the wheel with both hands.

It was meant to be a second honeymoon. Not that they'd had a first, really. They'd been married for seven years. Bernie had been serving in Korea, a corporal in the signals, when he'd been caught in the open by a grenade. Bessie was his nurse in Tokyo. He'd heard some of the white nurses refused to touch the black GIs, but she didn't mind. The first day she gave him a sponge bath, he tried to thank her—not sure if he was more embarrassed for her or himself (he felt an erection pushing at the slit of his pajama pants)—but she told him not to be silly. He always remembered that. "Don't be silly." Like it was nothing. "I'm just saying I appreciate it," he said, a little stung. "The nature of the race matter and all."

"The race matter doesn't matter to me," she told him briskly. "And it shouldn't matter to you." Later she came back, and he asked her to scratch his back, below the shoulder blade where it itched him fiercely, and she did.

Perhaps it was the thought of losing his arm. He was so relieved when she told him they'd saved it. She'd been changing the dressing on his hand, unwinding the bandages from each fat finger. He whooped with joy. He asked her to have a drink with him. She said she didn't think so, and his face had fallen, but then she'd laughed, her teeth as bright as her uniform. "Oh," she said, turning his hand over to wash it. "You mean after your release? Why, of course. I'd like that. I thought you meant now. You shouldn't be drinking now, not with your medication." And then she wound his hand up again in fresh white bandages.

Her tour had finished three weeks later, but she'd stayed on in Tokyo, and by the time his disabled discharge came through, they were lovers. They ate sushi together, and she wore beautiful multicolored kimonos, and it all seemed perfectly natural. He'd been in the Army for nine years so he hung on to her now as the next thing in his life, and one night after a fifth of whiskey—"Why, Bernie Hull, you're stinko"—he asked her to marry him. "Of course," she said, and he'd laughed out loud. *"Of course!"* They'd gone back to New Hampshire, where she had a job in a hospital in Manchester. He'd found work at the local post office, and they'd been married within the month.

They'd made a good life together. Bessie's parents had been kind to him after some reservations. "They know better than to try and stop me when I want something," Bessie told him. Her brother called Bernie a hero and a credit to his race at the small reception after their wedding at the town hall. Bernie appreciated it, but it only reminded him that he was the one black man in the room. His own parents were long since dead, and his sister, Bernice, back in Summer Hill, had refused to come when she heard Bernie was marrying a white woman. "What for?" she wanted to know, and when Bernie said, "For the same reasons anybody gets married," she told him no, she didn't believe it.

Bernie didn't know what to say to that. He could hear her kids, his nephews and nieces, in the background, yelling, and then a baby's sharp, sudden sobs.

"I gotta go," Bernice said. They hadn't talked since.

His brother, Roy, had been more sympathetic. "You and me been dreaming about white girls since we were boys. Bernice thinks that's all wrong, and maybe it is, but a man's got to follow his dream. 'Sonly natural to want what you can't have." But Roy hadn't come, either.

He and Bessie did have a good life, though. Decent friends. Enough money. Bessie had even taught him to skate. He liked his job, was proud of the uniform, and Mr. Rhodes, the postmaster, treated him well. The first week, when there'd been a little trouble over Bernie eating at the local sandwich shop, Mr. Rhodes had stepped across the street and told the owner that none of the postmen would be eating there again if Bernie didn't. And just like that the shop integrated, although Bernie told Bessie he wouldn't have made anything of it himself.

"Why not, for Pete's sake?" she'd asked him, and when he shrugged she'd exclaimed, "You're too darned dignified for your own good sometimes."

He was the only black man he knew in Manchester, but he followed the news of lunchroom sit-ins and the freedom riders and joined the NAACP, although he was a lifelong Republican, like his father and his grandfather before him. He met more Negroes, but they all seemed a little shy of each other, almost sheepish. "Far as civil rights goes," one of them pointed out to him, "New Hampshire ain't exactly where it's *at*."

What nagged Bernie was that it was all too good, unreal somehow, more than he deserved. He thought of his brother and sister and all the kids he'd grown up with. Why had he been the one singled out, plucked up by life and set down here? It made him a little scared to have something. Bessie said he was just being superstitious, but he couldn't shake the idea. He thought one day he'd wake up, or someone would come along and take it all away. When Bessie'd miscarried for the first time the spring before, along with the worry for her, he'd felt an awful relief that finally something terrible had happened. He'd been so ashamed he hadn't known how to comfort her, except to keep trying. But when she miscarried for the second time that summer, he'd decided they couldn't go through it again. They'd been distant these last few months—Bessie insisting she still wanted a child, had always wanted one, Bernie doubtful, thinking, *She wants one more now she maybe can't have one*, wondering if this is how she once wanted him, wondering if he was no longer enough for her—which was why the idea of a trip to Niagara felt like such an inspiration.

Bessie had laughed and called him a romantic, but took his hand across the dinner table.

The colonel wants to go back over the details again as if he's trying to trip them up. "I thought you said it was cigar-shaped, Mrs. Hull?"

"From a distance," Bessie says impatiently. "Up close, you could see it was a disk." She looks at Bernie for support.

"We had a pair of binoculars along for the trip," he says. "I thought it might be a star at first. But when I pulled over at a lookout and used the glasses, whatever it was was definitely moving." The colonel is silent so Bernie hurries on, a little breathless but feeling more is required of him. "A little later it came to me that I'd left the car running the first time while I leaned on the roof with the binocs. I thought the vibrations from the engine might have been the problem, see, so I pulled over again, stepped away from the car before I put the glasses on it. And it was still moving."

Bernie wants the colonel to write this down, but his pen doesn't move. The colonel doesn't even ask him about the binoculars—his service issue 10 x 42 Weavers.

"Spinning," Bessie says. "Don't forget it was spinning. That's what gave it the twinkling effect."

"Right," Bernie says. "The lights that looked like they were moving across it from a distance were actually fixed to the rim." He makes a circling motion in the air with his index finger while the colonel stares at him.

"Did you write that down?" Bessie asks, and the colonel blinks and says, "Yes, ma'am. I got it. 'Twinkling was spinning.'"

They had agreed before the colonel arrived that Bessie would do most of the talking. Bernie hadn't wanted them to tell anyone about what they had seen right from the start, but Bessie insisted on calling her sister, Marge. Hadn't Marge seen a UFO herself in '57? Bernie shrugged. He'd never believed Marge's story, but he knew Bessie needed to tell someone, and Marge at least wouldn't make fun of them. But it hadn't stopped there. Marge put Bessie on to a high-school science teacher she knew, and he told her they should really notify the Air Force. Now here was the colonel with his clipboard. Bernie hadn't wanted to meet him, but Bessie'd had a conniption fit.

"Bernie Hull! How's it going to look," she said, "if I'm telling this story and my own husband won't back me up?"

Bernie told her it wouldn't make any difference, but what he really thought was that nothing he said would help her, might even make her less believable. "You're a white woman married to a colored," he wanted to tell her. He didn't think anyone would believe them, but Bessie wasn't having any of that. "Of course they'll believe us," she said. "So long as we tell the truth. We have to try at least. You've no gumption, Bernie, that's your whole trouble." It seemed so easy to her, but Bernie'd had to work hard to be believed most of his life.

Now he can see Bessie is getting tired of going over the same story again and again.

"I'm not telling you what it means," she says. "I'm just telling you what I saw. We were hoping you could explain it to us."

But the colonel just spreads his hands and says, "Sorry, ma'am."

"You act like we're lying."

"No, ma'am," the colonel says quickly. "I assure you."

Bernie knows what's coming next. Bessie wants to get on to the part inside the ship, the stuff Bernie doesn't remember. He's asked her not to talk about it, but she told him she couldn't promise. "What if it's a matter of national security?" she said. "It's our duty, isn't it? Think what it could mean for the future of everyone." So now she explains to the colonel how she only remembered this part later, *in her dreams*. Bernie feels himself shrink, but the colonel just makes another scratch with his pen, and Bessie starts to tell him about the aliens—the short gray men—and their tests.

"Gray?" The colonel looks from Bessie to Bernie, Bernie to Bessie.

"Gray," she says, and he writes it down.

"And short," she adds. "But not like dwarfs, like children."

In her dream, Bessie says, she remembers them scraping her skin with a strange metal instrument. "Like a dentist might use, only different. It tickled," she recalls, without a smile. Then she remembers them pushing a long thin needle into her navel. "That really hurt," she says, "but when I cried out they did something, and the pain stopped at once. They seemed sorry. They told me it was a pregnancy test."

The colonel, who has been taking notes with his head down, not looking at them, now glances up quickly.

"Oh, of course, I'm not pregnant," Bessie says brusquely, and Bernie sits very still. This is what he feared all along, that they wouldn't be able to keep their private business out of this.

"Have you ever heard of anything like it?" Bessie asks. The colonel tells her he hasn't.

"You have no memory of this?" he asks Bernie, who shakes his head slowly. He's racked his brains, but there's nothing. Bessie can't understand it. "How can you not remember?" she cried the first time she told him, as if he was the one being unreasonable.

"Bessie tells me I was in another room on the ship, drugged or something, but I don't recall." He wishes he could support her now, but also in the back of his mind, he resents her dream, his weakness in it.

Bessie presses on. She says she knows how it sounds, but she has proof. "I'm just getting to the best part," she says. "The part about Bernie's teeth."

"Teeth?" the colonel says, and this time Bernie sees a twitch to his lips that makes him feel cold inside.

"That's right," Bessie says, and Bernie can tell she's seething now. The aliens, she explains slowly, as if to a child, were surprised that Bernie's teeth came out and Bessie's didn't. "They didn't understand about dentures," Bessie says. Bernie feels his mouth grow dry. They have argued about this part. He didn't want her to tell it, but Bessie feels it's the clincher. "How could we make that up?" she asked him last night. "Plus there's the physical proof."

"This was after the other tests," Bessie says. "They were as curious as kids. I'm jumping ahead a little, but don't mind me. Anyway, after we were done, the one I think of as the doctor, he left the room, and the *grayer* one, the leader, he told me they were still finishing up with Bernie. Anyhow, a few seconds later the doctor runs back in. He seems very excited, and he asks me to open my mouth. Well, I don't quite know why, but I wanted to get this over with, so I obliged, and before you know it he'd pushed his little fingers in my mouth, and he was pulling on my teeth. Well! You can imagine my surprise. I slapped his hand away quick as I could. He was pulling quite hard, too, making my head go up and down. 'What do you think you're doing?' I said, and then he held out his other hand, and can you guess what he had?"

The colonel shakes his head slowly.

"Why, Bernie's denture. There it was sitting in his little gray hand. Well, I snatched it back at once. I don't know what I was thinking. It made me so worried about Bernie, I guess. That and the fact that he's always losing them or pretending to lose them, anyway."

She pauses, and Bernie thinks he should say something.

"They pinch me," he mumbles. "And they click. I don't like them so good."

Bessie laughed. "I tell him he looks like such a fool without them, but he doesn't care. He has such a fine smile, too."

Bernie looks away past the colonel's shoulder out the picture window. He does not smile. It's October, and the first snow is beginning to fall in the White Mountains.

"Anyway, I snatched them up, and then the leader started in about why my teeth were different from Bernie's, so I had to explain all about dentures, about how people lose their teeth as they get older or like Bernie here in accidents. I thought it was funny they were so flummoxed by dentures, but you know now that I come to think about it, I don't remember seeing their teeth. They had these thin little slits for mouths, like I said before, and when they talked it was as if they didn't move their lips."

"Did they speak English?" the colonel asks. "Or was it more like telepathy?"

"Maybe," Bessie says. "Like voices in my head, you mean? That certainly could explain it."

"And their fingers?" the colonel asks seriously. "Would you say they had suckers on them? Small pads, maybe?"

Bessie pauses and looks at him hard. "No," she says very clearly. "I would have remembered something like that."

There is an awkward pause before she goes on more brightly.

"Anyway, to cut a long story short, I thought the whole thing about the dentures was funny, and I remember laughing, but it must have been one of those nervous laughs because afterwards when I looked at my hand, where I'd been gripping them, I'd been holding them so tight that the teeth had left bruises." And here, Bessie holds out her hand to the colonel. He leans forward and takes it and turns it to the light. Bernie can just see the crescent of purpling spots in the flesh of her palm.

Bessie nudges him. Bernie doesn't move for a moment, but then he decides. She's his wife. He'll try and help. He holds a handkerchief over his mouth and slips his plate out. He passes it to her, and with her free hand she places it in her palm so that the false teeth lie over the bruises. The denture glistens wetly, and Bernie looks away in embarrassment.

"See," Bessie says triumphantly. "Now that's evidence, isn't it?"

"It's something, ma'am," the colonel says peering at Bernie's teeth. "It's really something."

Bernie has tried his damnedest to remember what Bessie's talking about. But he can't do it. It's the strangest thing, he thinks, because he recalls the rest of the trip—start to finish—vividly.

They'd got up at five a.m., packed the car, and been on the road to Niagara by six. Bernie wanted to get a good start on the day. It was September, peak foliage. "What impossible colors," Bessie breathed, sliding across the seat to lean against him. "Better than Cinerama," he told her. He'd sung a few bars of "Oh What a Lovely Morning," and made her laugh, and she'd done her best Dinah Shore: "Drive your Chev-ro-lay, through the USA." She'd got impatient with him the evening before for simonizing the car, bringing out the gloss in the two-tone paint job. Now, he saw, she was proud.

But when they stopped for brunch at a diner in upstate New York, Bernie felt uneasy. The din in the place died when they entered, and the waitress seemed short with them. He ordered coffee and a doughnut, but Bessie had the short stack and took her time over her coffee. When he called for the check, she looked up and asked what his hurry was, and he said they still had a ways to go. Didn't he know she had to let her coffee cool before she could drink it? "Have a refill or a cigarette," she said, pushing the pack of Chesterfields across the table, but he told her a little sharply he didn't want either. He felt people watching him. Bessie finished her coffee and went to the bathroom, leaving him alone for five long terrible minutes. He could hear a child crying somewhere behind him, but he didn't turn to look. When she came back, he hurried her out, before she could retie her scarf, leaving a big tip. He had to stop to urinate fifteen minutes later, and she made fun of him for not going earlier. "You're like a little boy," she said, and so he told her how he felt in the diner.

"Oh, Bernie," she said. "You were imagining it."

It made him mad that she wouldn't believe him, wouldn't take his word for it, but he didn't want to spoil the trip with a fight, and he let her half convince him, because he knew it would make her feel better. He played with the radio, pushing buttons until he found some Harry Belafonte. Bessie just didn't notice things the way he did. He loved her for it, this innocence, cherished it, though he couldn't share it (found his own sensitivity sharper than ever, in fact). That night when he drove to two motels and was told that they were full, he didn't make anything of it, and when she said as they left one parking lot, "You'd think they'd turn off their vacancy sign," he just let it ride.

"Must be a lot of lovers in town," she added and squeezed his thigh.

When they finally found a room at a place called The Falls Inn, she pulled him to her, and he started to respond, but when she told him she'd forgotten her diaphragm, he pulled away.

"It'll be okay," she told him. "Just this once." She clung to him for a moment, holding him inside her, before he rolled off. They lay side by side staring at the ceiling as if it were the future. After the second miscarriage Bessie had been warned she might not be able to carry a baby to term. "We can't take the risk," Bernie told her softly, but she turned away. "You're afraid." Curled up with her face to the wall, the knobs of her spine reminded him of knuckles. "I'm afraid of losing you," he said, at last.

He told her he'd go out and get prophylactics, but driving around in the car, he couldn't. He stopped outside one store and sat for fifteen minutes, waiting for the other cars in the lot to leave, listening to the engine tick as it cooled. He *was* afraid of losing her, he knew, though the admission, so abject and ineffectual, shamed him. But behind that fear was another—a dim, formless dread of his own children and what they might mean for the precarious balance of his marriage—that made him shudder. There was one more car in the lot, but before it left a police cruiser pulled in, and Bernie backed out and drove slowly back to the motel.

When they first married Bessie used to call him by a pet name, "Big," burying the tight curls of her permanent against his chest. He would stroke her neck and answer in the same slightly plaintive baby talk, "Little" or "Little 'un." It was how they had comforted themselves when they felt small and puny beside their love for each other, but remembering it now only made him feel hopeless before the childlessness that loomed over them. Bessie was asleep when he got in, or pretending, and he lay down beside her as gently as possible, not touching, but aware of her familiar warmth under the covers.

The next day had started better. They'd gone to the Falls and been overwhelmed by the thundering white wall of water. They bought tickets for the *Maid of the Mist*. Bernie bounced on the springy gangway and made her scream. They laughed at themselves in the yellow sou'esters and rain hats the crew passed out and then joined the rest of the identically dressed crowd at the bow railings. "Oh, look," Bessie said pointing out children, like miniature adults, in their slickers and hats, but Bernie couldn't hear her over the crash of the Falls. "Incredible," he yelled, leaning forward. He could taste the spray in his mouth, feel the gusts of air displaced as the water fell. Suddenly, he wanted to hold his wife, but when he turned to Bessie, she was gone. He stumbled from the railing looking for her, but it was impossible to identify her in the crowd of yellow slickers. He felt a moment of panic, like when she'd left him in the restaurant. He bent down to see under the hats and hoods of those around him, conscious that he was startling them, but not caring. In the end he found her in the cabin, her head in her hands. She told him she'd thrown up. She didn't like boats much in general, she reminded him, and looking at the Falls had made her dizzy. "I didn't want you to miss them, though," she told him, and he could see she'd been crying. He put his arm around her, and they sat like that until the trip was over. The other passengers began to file into the cabin around them, taking off their hats and coats and hanging them on pegs until only Bernie and Bessie were left in theirs.

They had planned to go on into Canada that afternoon, the first time they'd been out of the country since Korea, but instead they turned around, headed back the way they'd come. It was late afternoon, but Bernie figured they could be home by midnight if he got a clear run and put his foot down.

The colonel has a few more questions, and he asks if they'd mind talking to him separately. Bernie feels himself stiffen, but Bessie says, "Of course." He can tell she wants to go first, so he gets up and says he'll take a walk. He'll be back in about fifteen minutes. He steps out into the hall and finds his topcoat and hat and calls for Denny, Bessie's dog. He walks out back first, and from the yard he can see Bessie inside with the colonel. He wonders what she's saying as the dog strains at the leash. Probably talking more about her dreams. She thinks maybe the little gray men took one of her eggs. She thinks she remembers being shown strange children. They had agreed that she wouldn't talk about this, but Bernie realizes suddenly he doesn't trust her. It makes him shudder to think of her telling these things to a stranger.

When he takes Denny around front of the house, he is startled to find a black man in his drive, smoking. The young man drops the cigarette quickly when Denny starts yapping. He is in an Air Force uniform, and Bernie realizes that this must be the colonel's driver. He feels suddenly shy. He tells him, "You startled me," and the young airman says, "Sorry, sir." And after a moment that seems all there is to say. That "sir." Bernie lets Denny pull him up the drive, whining. The poor dog hasn't been out for hours and as soon as they're at the end of the drive squats and poops in full view of the house. Bernie holds the lead slack and looks the other way. When they walk back a few minutes later, the airman is in the colonel's car. The windows are fogged. Bernie knocks on the driver's-side glass.

"Would you like a cup of coffee?"

The airman hesitates, but his breath, even in the car, is steaming.

"I could bring it out," Bernie offers, and the young man says, "Thank you." And it's the lack of a "sir" that makes Bernie happy. He takes Denny inside and comes back out in a few minutes with two cups of coffee and climbs in the car with the boy. He sets them on the dash, where they make two twin crescents of condensation on the windshield. When Bernie sips his coffee, he realizes he's left his teeth inside with Bessie, and he's suddenly self-conscious. He thinks he must look like an old fool, and he wants to be silent, keep his mouth shut, but it's too late. The airman asks him how he lost them.

"A fight," Bernie says. And he tells a story he's never told Bessie, how he got waylaid by a couple of crackers when he was just a boy. They wanted to know his mama's name, but for some reason he refused to say. "I just call her Mama," he said. "Other folks call her Mrs. Hull." But the boys wanted to know her first name, "her Chrustian name." Bernie just kept on saying he didn't know it, and then he tried to push past them and leave, but they shoved him back and lit into him. "I don't know what I was thinking," he says now over his coffee, "but it was very important to me that those fellas not know my mama's name. Mrs. Hull's all I'd say. I knew it, of course, although I never called her by it or even rightly thought of her by it. But I'd be damned if I'd tell them, and they beat the tar out of me for keeping that secret."

"Yeah, but I bet those boys got their share," the airman says, and Bernie smiles and nods. He can't be more than eighteen, this driver. They talk about the service. The boy is frustrated to be a driver in the Air Force. He wants to fly. Bernie tells him how he was put in signals corps. "They liked having me fetch and carry the messages." The boy, Bernie thinks, is a good soldier, and he feels a flush of sudden pride in him. But then the coffee is finished, and Bessie is at the door.

"Bernie!" She doesn't see him in the car. "Bernie!" He feels suddenly embarrassed and gets out of the car quickly. "There you are. It's your turn."

Bernie ducks his head back into the car to take the empty mugs and sees the airman looking at him strangely. "Eunice," he offers awkwardly. The young man's face is blank. "My mother's name. Eunice Euphonia Hull. In case you was wondering." He closes the car door with his tail, moves towards the house. Inside, he hands Bessie the two mugs, and she takes them to wash up.

Back on the sofa, Bernie sees that his dentures are lying beside the plate of sandwiches, but he feels uncomfortable about putting them back in now.

The colonel asks him to describe his experiences, and Bernie repeats the whole story. They'd been making good time until the cop stopped them around ten-thirty, and even then Bernie had still expected to make it home by one. He explains how they noticed the lights a little after that and about twenty minutes later how they began to sense that the object was following them, how he had sped up, how it had kept pace. Finally, he describes it swooping low over the road in front of them and hovering a hundred yards to their right. He'd stopped, still thinking it could be a chopper, and got out with the binoculars, leaving Bessie in the still running car. But after getting a closer look he'd become uneasy, run back, and they had left in a hurry. They couldn't have been stopped more than ten minutes, but when they got home it was almost dawn, hours later than they expected.

"Mrs. Hull," the colonel says, "claims you were screaming when you came back to the car. About being captured."

Bernie feels a moment of irritation at Bessie.

"I was yelling," he says. "I was frightened. I felt that we were in danger, although I couldn't tell you why. I just knew this wasn't anything I understood."

He pauses, but the colonel seems to be waiting for him to go on.

"I was in Korea. I mean, I've been under fire. I was never afraid like this."

"These dreams of your wife," the colonel asks. "Can you explain them at all?"

"She believes them," Bernie says quickly. "Says they're more vivid than any dreams she remembers."

"Can you think of anything else that might explain them?"

Bernie pauses. He could end it all here, he thinks. He looks at his dentures on the coffee table, feels the flush of humiliation. He opens his mouth, closes it, slowly shakes his head.

The colonel waits a moment as if for something more. Then: "Any dreams yourself?"

"No, sir," Bernie says quickly. "I don't remember my dreams."

The colonel clicks his pen—closed, opened, closed—calls Bessie back in, thanks them both for their time. He declines another sandwich, puts his cap under his arm, says he must be going, and they follow him out to where his driver holds the door for him. The car backs out, and they watch its taillights follow the curve of the road for a minute. Bernie wonders if the colonel and his driver will talk. If the colonel will make fun of their story. The thought of the young man laughing at him makes him tired. But then he thinks no, the colonel and the airman won't share a word. The boy will just drive, and in the back seat the colonel will watch him. Bernie feels like he let the boy down, and he feels suddenly ashamed.

They stand under the porch light until the car is out of sight. "Well," Bessie says, and he sees she's glowing, almost incandescent with excitement. "I think we did the right thing, don't you?" He feels his own mood like a shadow of hers. Moths ping against the bulb, and he flicks the switch off. In the darkness, they're silent for a moment, and then he hears the squeal of the screen door as she goes inside.

It's not late, but Bessie tells him she's about done in. The interview has gone on for almost four hours. She goes up to bed, and Bernie picks up in the living room, carries the cups and plates through to the kitchen, fills the sink to soak them. The untouched sandwiches he covers in Saran Wrap and slides into the refrigerator. He drops his dentures in a glass of water, watches it sink. Then he goes up and changes into his pajamas, lays himself down beside his already sleeping wife, listens to her steady breathing, dreams about the future.

A few weeks later they'll receive an official letter thanking them for their cooperation, but offering no explanation for what they've seen. Bernie hopes Bessie will let the matter drop there, but she won't. She wants answers, and she feels it's their duty to share these experiences. "What if other people have had them?" They'll meet with psychiatrists. They'll undergo therapy. Bernie shows symptoms of nervous anxiety, the doctors will say, but they won't know why. Eventually, almost a year later, under hypnosis, Bernie will recall being inside the ship. He and Bessie will listen to a tape of his flat voice describing his experiences. Tears will form in Bessie's eyes.

"It's as if I'm asleep," he'll say on the tape. "Or sleepwalking. Like I'm drugged or under some mind control."

Under hypnosis, Bernie will remember pale figures stopping their car. He'll recall the ship—a blinding wall of light—and being led to it, as if on an invisible rope, dragged and stumbling, his hands somehow tied behind him. He'll remember being naked, surrounded, the aliens touching him, pinching his arms and legs, peeling his lips back to examine his gritted teeth, cupping and prodding his genitals. It'll all come back to him—running through the woods, the breeze creaking in the branches, tripping and staring up at the snowy trees. "Like great white sails," he'll hear himself say thickly as the spool runs out.

Afterwards, he'll tell Bessie in a rage he's finished with shrinks, but in the months that follow she'll call more doctors and scientists. She'll say she wants to write a book. Something extraordinary has happened to them. They've been chosen for a purpose. She'll talk to journalists. Bernie will refuse to discuss it further. They'll fight, go days without speaking.

Tonight, in his dream, Bernie wakes with a violent shudder, listens to his heart slow. He's lying in bed with Bessie, he tells himself. He can feel her warm breath on his back. She rolls over beside him, the familiar shifting and settling weight, but then he feels the strange sensation of the mattress stiffening, the springs releasing. He opens his eyes and sees his wife rising above the bed, inch by inexorable inch, in a thin blue light.

DOUG DORST

Vikings

We were almost out of money, so Trace went to steal us another bottle of something. We were celebrating. The holiday weekend was almost over, and the mechanic was due back in town the next morning. We'd finally be able to get back on the road.

I sat on the rear bumper of the van and waited. Smoke from the fireworks still hung in the air. Biggest display in the Mojave, the posters had promised. Maybe it was, but we couldn't tell. An hour before the show, the sky had curdled into a clump of fog. Fog, in the desert. First time in twenty years, someone said.

I watched the smoke and fog mingle and roll in lazy waves in and out of the orange floodlight of the gas station. All around me were junked cars parked at crazy angles, cracked windshields and fallen bumpers shining in the greasy light. Buicks and Chevys and Pontiacs, all chrome and disappointment. The dirt was speckled with pieces of broken glass. Every breath tasted like gunpowder. We were still thousands of miles from Alaska.

Trace was gone a long time, too long, and I wondered if he'd found a girl and gone off with her. It happened a lot. He'd picked up a girl at the bar the night we broke down. She was wispy and tan and blond, so good-looking that her red eyes and thick liquor-stink just made her seem game and fearless instead of sad. She said she was from San Diego, on her way east to divinity school. At last call, I saw her lift her skirt and flash Trace her tiger-print panties, and they spent the night in her motel room. I slept in the van. "I don't understand it," he said the next day. "I'm a fucked-up-looking guy, but I always get the beautiful ones." It was true. He was fucked-up-looking—short and puffy, with a half-closed eye and a nose that looked like it'd been hit with a bag full of nickels. And he did always get the beautiful ones, and he always seemed genuinely surprised by it. You could tell him to shut up and enjoy his luck, but that never stopped him from wondering out loud.

While I waited for Trace, I ran through the names of the places we'd drive through next: Tehachapi, Bakersfield, Fresno, Modesto, Lodi, Red Bluff, Redding. I'd studied the map, knew the route by heart. I wanted to see all these towns in the rearview, feel them as beats in a rhythm of places passed by, a rhythm as steady and soothing as tires thrumming over pavement joints.

When Trace came back to the van, he was carrying a baby wrapped in a threadbare beach towel. "Hey, Phil," he said. "Look what I got." He held it up like it was a carnival prize. The baby's eyes were shut, but it wrinkled its little fingers open and closed so I knew it was alive.

"Whose is that?" I said.

"Someone gave it to me."

"Who?"

"A woman. Outside the liquor store."

"People don't just hand out babies," I said.

"This one did," he said.

"Take it back."

"I can't," he said. "She drove away."

"We have to find her," I said. "People will think we stole it."

Trace carried the baby as we walked along the road into town. He hummed softly and rocked it in his arms. I kicked at the loose gravel. "The mother," I said, "was she fat?" The other morning, in the taco place, I'd seen a fat woman chew up a quesadilla and dribble it into her baby's mouth. Like she thought they were penguins or something. It was all I could do to keep my food down, watching. I wondered if this one might be the penguin baby. I didn't want any baby, but I especially didn't want that one.

"No," Trace said. "She was skinny."

"Even so," I said. "We have to get rid of it."

In the streetlight I could see the baby's eyes were open and coffee-brown. Its forehead and nose were bright red. The mother, whoever the hell she was, had let the kid get sunburned. Even I knew you're not supposed to do that. Still, the baby looked pretty happy. It wasn't crying. As babies go, this one was well-behaved.

We sat on the curb in the liquor store parking lot and waited for the mother to come back. The baby slept in Trace's arms. People walked by and looked at us suspiciously. No one recognized the baby. After a while the store owner banged on the glass and waved us away. I pointed to the baby, trying to explain, but the guy just shook his head and kept waving.

"I knew she wouldn't come back," Trace said.

"We should call the cops," I said.

"No," Trace said. "No cops."

He was right. Technically, we were fugitives.

"Let's go to the bar," he said. "I could use a drink."

I didn't have any better ideas. That's always been a problem for me.

We started walking again. "I wonder what its name is," Trace said.

"Is it a boy or a girl?"

"Either way, I'm going to call it Mo." Mo was his ex's name, short for Maureen. He loved her, but she was back in New York, shacked up with a guy who made millions riding the bench for the Yankees.

I knew what he was thinking. He was thinking that he could save this baby, that he was meant to save it. "We're not keeping it," I said.

"We could."

"We're giving it back." I was waiting for him to say something drunk like *This baby needs us*. This baby didn't need us. We were the last thing it needed. It needed anyone but us.

That whole year we'd been riding a crest of failure. In March, my girlfriend left me after I threw her shoes out the window, and then Mo and Trace broke up, this time for good. It had been Trace's idea to leave New York for Colorado. "We'll be river rafting guides," he'd said. "You get to help girls into their wetsuits." We got there, and the rivers were nearly dry. No snow that winter. So we bought the van and tried to start a painting business, but we never found a customer. It was easy to leave when the court dates started piling up. Alaska was his idea, too, and so far all it had gotten us was stuck. Stuck in a town that wasn't more than a crosshair of blacktop trained on the desert.

The bar was dark and narrow. Dim red light, like a darkroom. Red vinyl stools and booths. Two pool tables. A jukebox that played songs about trucks. I sat in a booth and told Trace to show the baby to the bartender. He held out his free hand for money.

"Drinks," he said. I took off my sneaker and gave him the ten I'd been keeping for an emergency. It was the last of the money for now, because Trace's sister would only wire us a little at a time. "I have my own kids to feed," she'd say. But usually she came through, wiring it in my name because she didn't trust him and because she liked me from when I was a kid. Trace and I had grown up together, watched our parents' marriages bust up at the same time, stayed close even after one strange summer when my dad was sleeping with his mom. Got closer, maybe.

The baby started to cry. Trace held up the bill and sniffed it. "For fuck's sake, Phil," he said. "The money stinks. You got trench foot or something."

What did he expect? I'd been walking around in a desert for four days without any socks. We'd had to pack in a hurry.

My head hurt. I leaned against the wall and stretched my legs out on the seat and tried to pretend I was somewhere else.

Earlier that night, Trace and I had gone to the fireworks show, which was held on a football field that looked like it hadn't been used in years. No goal posts, no scoreboard, just a rectangle of sandy dirt and rocks with scabs of turf. Lots of families sat on blankets out on the field. High school kids sat in the bleachers, and every now and then you'd hear a bottle fall on the gravel below or roll down the metal steps. We sat up on a little hill with some people from the bar. Trace had shot pool with some of them, and they liked us because he'd told them we were outlaws. They called us Butch and Sundance.

We drank and waited. Finally Trace said loudly, "When the hell is this going to start?"

A short, bald guy named Roy passed him a bottle of bourbon. "You got somewhere to go, Butch?" Roy said. Everyone laughed. They knew we were stuck. "They're waiting for the fog to blow through," Roy went on.

"It's not blowing through," I said. There was only the faintest breeze.

"It'll clear up," Roy said. "We're not supposed to have fog. We're not even supposed to have clouds this time of year." We'd met Roy our first night in town. He walked with a limp, told us he was wounded in Vietnam. Later we heard that Roy had never been farther than Barstow, that he limped because he took some shrapnel in his legs when the transmission in his VW exploded. So you didn't know whether to believe this guy when he talked about clouds.

"They should just cancel it," I said. "What's the point?"

Roy said, "Son, you don't cancel the Fourth of July. This is America."

Then the show started with a loud crushing thud that I could feel in my stomach and throat. There was the faintest glow of green from inside the clouds. People whistled and clapped, but I couldn't see why. More fireworks went up. Some were like thunderclaps and war-movie cannons, some were smaller, sharper, like cracks of the bat, a roll on a snare drum, popcorn popping. But it was just noise. Noise, and muted flashes of light just bright enough to remind you of how much you were missing.

"This place is killing me," I said.

Trace drank a long swallow. "We could steal a car," he said. He sat up straight. "I can't believe I didn't think of that sooner."

"We don't need that kind of trouble," I said. Although looking back, it probably was the best thing we could have done.

He lit a cigarette, nodding, and looked out across the field. "We'll be in Alaska before you know it," he said. He passed me the bottle. "Think of all the money we're going to make up there."

"We'll have to work hard."

"We'll save up and get our own boat, for next year," he said. "We'll get a boat with one of those Viking heads on the front."

"Boats are expensive," I said.

"I'll find a way. I always do."

"You can't steal boats."

"We'll get a fixer-upper," he said. Though neither of us was any good at fixing things. We'd proved that often enough.

Boom boom boom and clouds choking all the sparkles. It was unbearable, but there wasn't any point in leaving, either.

Around us people were talking. "They're changing the angle. Shooting lower." "Is that safe?" "Hope not." Laughs.

The new angle was no better. Just louder. Now and then I saw pinpoints of colored light leak out of the clouds and shine for an instant before they burned out close to the ground. By the end, the field was a big bowl of smoke. Trace and I would be blowing black snot out of our noses for days.

Trace came back to the booth. Somehow he'd gotten the baby to stop crying. He handed the thing to me and went back to the bar to pick up our drinks. I'd never held a baby before. I froze. It wriggled and kicked inside the towel, but its eyes were open, and it stared up at me calmly, like it wanted to learn what fear was by watching me. I just held tight and didn't move until Trace came back. I made him take it out of my hands. He sat down, cradled the baby in both arms, and sucked on his drink through a straw.

"The bartender doesn't recognize it," Trace said. "He said to wait an hour, see if anyone who comes in does. After that, he'll call the cops."

Trace held the baby up to his face and smiled. He rubbed noses with it. If Mo could have seen him like this, she'd never have left him. But it made me nervous.

"Seriously, did you steal it?" I asked.

"Call it by its name," he said. "Call it Mo." He unwrapped the beach towel. Underneath it the baby had on an old, faded green sleeper. On the chest was a cartoon duckling in a rain hat and boots, smiling. A happy, happy duck.

I ran my hand across the tabletop, which was gouged deeply with years of drunken attempts to leave a mark on the world. "Think about this," I said. "If we kept it, who would watch it while we were working?"

"Mo could. Big Mo, I mean."

"I don't think Mo is going to move to Alaska," I said.

"She might," he said. The baby slapped at Trace's glass, but missed. Trace moved the glass away. "Or Little Mo could come on the boat with us," he said. "Little Mo's a good luck charm. I can feel it. Fish will swarm around our boat."

"Fish don't swarm," I said. "They school."

"That's not the point."

"The point is," I said, "we have to find the mother."

We were almost done with our drinks when Roy the shrapnel guy limped over with a pitcher of beer. He put it on the table. "My treat," he said. "To make up for the fireworks. You picked the wrong year to get stuck here." Roy had been pretty nice to us. The other night he'd bought us a scratch-off lottery ticket, but it lost.

"Thanks," I said. You could smell the fireworks smoke on him. I guess it was on all of us.

He knelt down in front of Trace and the baby as best he could, with his bad legs and all. The baby gurgled and waved its arms in happy little ovals. "And what have we here?" Roy said.

"It's a baby," I said. "You know whose it is?"

"No," Roy said, but he didn't look at me. He kept his eyes on Trace and the baby. "Is it a boy or a girl?"

"We don't know," Trace said.

"There's an easy way to find out," Roy said.

"You're right," Trace said. "We should check." He moved his drink out of the way and laid the baby on the table.

"Don't," I said. "Not in the middle of the goddamned bar."

"What's the difference?" Roy said.

"It's no big deal," Trace said. "We ought to know."

"It's not right," I said. I thought the kid deserved better. "Don't do it, Trace," I said, in the voice I used when he took things too far.

Trace picked the baby up. He knew I only challenged him when I meant it.

Someone called Roy's name for the next game of pool. "The baby looks just like you," Roy said to Trace. With his thumb and index finger, he tickled the baby's chin. Then he tickled Trace's, which was thick with stubble. "Tell Sundance to lighten up." He shot me a look and walked over to the pool table.

"He's hitting on you," I said.

Trace shrugged. "I know," he said. "We need drinks, though." He smiled a smile that said he was in control, he'd take care of everything, he'd save the day all by himself.

Still, I knew it bothered him. It bothered him that Mo was probably in bed with her utility infielder, happy and horny after a Yankee win and postgame fireworks in a starry sky over the stadium, while Trace was dead-broke and stuck in the desert with Roy chucking his chin. So I wasn't surprised when, once the beer was gone, Trace went quiet and his droopy eye sagged almost all the way closed and he started looking around the place like he couldn't believe his life had come to this. And I wasn't surprised at all when he put the baby on the table and went to the phone to call her.

The baby waved its arms up and down like a drunk piano player, tiny fingers pattering on the table. I kept my hand on its legs so it wouldn't roll over and fall. My father once told me that when I was little, I'd fallen off a picnic table and hit my head on the cement patio. "Your mother was supposed to be watching you," he said. "It's her fault you're a fuck-up." He said this the day before Trace and I saw him necking with a teenage girl in the parking lot behind the bank.

The jukebox was too loud for me to hear what Trace was saying, but in the space between records I thought I heard him say something embarrassing like *We can be a family.* Then Patsy Cline started wailing, and Trace was smashing the receiver against the phone, which answered with cheerful pings. People looked over, then looked away. "At least do it on the beat," the bartender shouted, like he'd seen it a hundred times. Trace wound up and gave the receiver one more whack, then threw it down and left it to twist and swing. He came back to the table. I assumed she'd hung up on him, so I didn't ask.

"She wouldn't listen to me," he said. His face looked red, but it might have been the lights.

"Was the Yankee there?"

"Pinch-hitting sonofabitch."

"He's no star," I agreed.

"She didn't believe me about the baby," Trace said.

"You could have held it up to the phone."

"This baby's pretty quiet," he said.

"You're right," I said. "I wonder if something's wrong with it."

Trace picked up the baby, cradled it. He seemed to relax. "You have to support its head, see," he said to me. "It doesn't have neck muscles yet."

We needed more to drink, so Trace left to find Roy. I made him take the baby with him, to show it around. Right after he got up, a woman sitting at the bar turned on her stool and looked at me. I'd seen her in the bar before, and she'd been on the hill at the fireworks show, but I hadn't talked to her. She was forty, forty-five, thin, a redhead halfway to gray. She wore jeans and a faded black shirt with the top two or three buttons open and the sleeves rolled up. She walked over, pulled up a chair to the end of the booth, and sat down.

"I hear your name is Sundance," she said.

"It's Phil," I said.

She didn't offer her name, and I didn't ask. "I hear you're running from the law," she said. She had a long, thin nose that twitched when she talked.

"Not really," I said. "I don't think they're chasing us. We just have bench warrants. In Colorado."

She asked what we had done, so I told her. I told her about Trace's DUIs and Resisting Arrests and how he missed a court date because we were up all night drinking with two girls from the community college who, it turned out, were both hot for him. And about how I bashed the bail bondsman's guy with a two-by-four when he broke into our apartment a few days later. I didn't know they were allowed to break in. No one teaches you something like that until it's too late.

Trace came back to the table, balancing the baby and a full pitcher. A thin trail of beer wet the floor behind him.

"Whose beautiful baby is this?" the woman asked. She touched its nose, said something like *Wugga-wugga-woo,* and the baby made a noise that might have been a cough or a laugh.

"It's mine," Trace said. He sounded almost like he believed it.

"Four months?" she guessed.

"Three," he said, not missing a beat. "Little Mo's developing faster than most."

"Where's the mother?" she asked.

"New York."

"That's far away," she said.

"The mother," he said, "is a cold-hearted lying drooling bitch." Trace looked pretty drunk. I figured if he was, I must be, too.

"Some men think we all are," she said. I could tell she didn't like him at all. She looked at the baby like she felt sorry for it.

"I don't think he means that about you," I said. "Or about her."

"I don't mean that about you," Trace said. "I don't know you."

She turned to me. "How about you? Is there a woman in your life?" I watched her nose winking at me.

"There was," I said. "It didn't work out." I had been with her a year, and then one night, no warning, she told me it was over. *You want me to be just like Mo,* she'd said. *Well, I'm not Mo. It's not fair, and I'm sick of it.* She may have been right. It's just that Mo was a lot more likable. I told her so, and she threw her shoes at me, and I threw them out the window. One got stuck in a tree. It was still there when Trace and I left town.

The woman leaned back in her chair and undid her ponytail. Her hair fell in loose rings past her shoulders. "How old are you?" she asked. "Twenty-seven? Twenty-eight?"

"Twenty-three," I said. It occurred to me that my life was bleeding out of me even faster than I'd thought.

"I have a kid," the woman said. "He's eighteen." She sipped her drink. "He went to jail this week."

"What for?" I asked.

"Joyride. Took a car from the lot at the gas station."

"That's all?" I said.

"That bastard Chavez pressed charges."

"That bastard Chavez has our van," Trace said.

"We broke down," I explained. "We're waiting for him to fix it."

"He's a bastard," she said.

It would turn out that she was right. Chavez was a bastard. The next morning he would tell me and Trace our transmission was shot, and he wanted sixteen hundred to replace it. We'd say we couldn't pay that much, so he'd offer us a trade: the van straight up for a '79 Bonneville with no muffler and bad brakes and power windows that wouldn't go down. We'd take it. We'd need to get out of town in a hurry.

Behind me I heard a pool ball smack on the floor and roll away. The baby started to cry, but Trace jiggled it, and it stopped. Spit bubbled from its mouth. The woman finished her drink. I watched her neck as she swallowed. The skin around it looked a little loose, baggy. I'd never noticed that on anyone before.

"He didn't even steal anything good," she said. "Just an old VW, all rusted to shit. You'd think the boy would have some taste, at least."

"He's lucky to be alive," Trace said. "The transmission could have exploded."

She looked down at the floor. "The judge said I was a bad mother," she said.

"That's terrible," I said. "What'd he have to say that for?" But he could have been right, for all I knew.

She set her glass down on the table, hard. "I'm a good mother," she said. "A damn good mother." Her eyes got wet. It was like she'd been waiting a long time to say this, waiting to find someone who might believe her.

"I'm sure you are," I said.

"I have to take a leak," Trace said. "Can you hold my baby?" He held it out to her.

She sat the baby in her lap and bounced it up and down. "Hello, baby," she said. "What a big baby you are. What a bouncing baby." She kissed it on the top of its head, then smoothed its thin brown hair. Maybe she was a good mother. The baby looked like it was in heaven, eyes half-closed and dreamy. It drooled a little more, and she wiped its mouth with a cocktail napkin. Her eyes were still wet, but she'd started to smile. She was pretty when she smiled. I told her so.

"You should stop hanging around with that guy," she said. "I can tell he's holding you back."

I told her I knew that. It was what she wanted to hear.

The baby grabbed her nose, and she wiggled her head from side to side. "That's a nose you've got there," she said. "That's my nose." The baby let go, but kept moving its hand through the air like it still had a nose in it.

"When are you leaving town?" she asked me.

"Tomorrow," I said, "I hope."

"Where have you been staying?"

"In the van," I said.

Her knee touched mine. "Want to stay with me tonight?" she asked. She saw me look at her ring. "I have money for a room," she said.

I didn't even consider saying no. I swept the baby out of her arms, without thinking, without worrying, like I'd held a baby every day of my life, like I juggled babies in my spare time. That's when the smell hit me. The kid was ripe. She smelled it, too.

"Jackpot," she said.

I found Trace standing with Roy at the pool table, a fresh drink in his hand. I handed him the baby.

"Phil, this baby stinks," Trace said.

"You're going to have to change it," I said. "Maybe feed it, too. You got us into this."

He nodded, slowly. "I'll take care of everything," he said.

"For fuck's sake, Trace," I said, "why'd you take this thing? You could've said no."

He steadied himself against the pool table. "I was called," he said with a stupid smile. "I was called by forces we can't understand."

"Tell the bartender to call the cops," I said. "The mother's not coming in here."

"I'm going to give her some more time," he said.

"I'm leaving," I said. "I have somewhere to go."

"Where? Where is there to go?"

"The motel."

He looked surprised. Then he smiled that same smile again. "Have fun," he said. "I'll be fine here."

"I can't give you any more money," I said. "We're all out."

Roy lit a cigarette and draped his arm around Trace's shoulder. "Don't worry," he said. "Drinks for the daddy are on me."

"Yeah, don't worry," Trace said, smooth and cool. "Roy's buying."

I went back to the booth. She sucked the last ice cubes out of her glass, then whispered to me, lips cold and wet, that she would leave first and I should wait a minute before following. "It's a small town," she said. I doubt we fooled anyone. People turned to watch me as I walked out. She was waiting in the motel parking lot, money in her hand. She told me to get the room while she waited outside.

The lobby of the Astro-Budget Motel stank of curry. The desk clerk kept looking out the window like he expected something to come crashing through it. "What's wrong?" I asked him.

"There's a party going on," he said. "Lots of bikers. It may be trouble. It usually is." He gave me a room on the other side of the motel. I took the key and wished him luck.

She had her tongue in my ear before we got to the top of the cement stairs. We kissed outside the room, leaning on the metal railing. "Look at that view," she said, extending her arm like she was showing me a whole new world.

The fog had blown away, but all I could see was the motel parking lot, some scattered lights, dark desert. "There's nothing to see," I said.

"That's what I mean," she said, and she kissed me again.

I had to push her away to unlock the door. The room was decorated in sad shades of brown. Brown carpet and curtains, brown and orange plaid bedspread, two brown-cushioned chairs, a still life of a coconut on tan fabric.

The room was choking hot, and I said so. "It's the middle of summer, sweetie," she said, and I kissed her long and hard because I couldn't remember the last time anyone called me sweetie. She took off my shirt. Then she stepped back. "When was the last time you had a shower?" she said.

I counted back to the day we left Durango. "Five days," I said.

"Why don't you clean yourself up," she said gently. "I'll go get us a bottle."

In the shower it seemed like I could smell everything that was coming off me, layer by layer, a grimy scrapbook of our time on the road. Smoke from fireworks, cigarettes, and dope. Sweat from the heat and pushing the van and the booze and a dozen straight losing hands in Vegas. Road dust. And Jesus, my feet. I smelled like I was dying.

I got out of the shower without drying. I switched off the lights in the room. I turned the air conditioner on full and stood in front of it, naked, my eyes closed. At first it wheezed out warm air, but it gradually turned colder, just like I imagined the outside air would as we drove farther and farther north. I imagined me and Trace in Alaska, hauling in huge catches of salmon, wet and free and happy in the never-ending daylight and the cold ocean spray. And I imagined myself there in winter, when I'd have a wallet full of money and a head full of stories, ready to endure the long dark and the cold, a cold so deep that it would freeze out everything but your purest self, and suddenly you'd understand where things had gone so wrong. I stood there in the cold air, thinking, listening to the faint and soothing lilt of water drops on the thin carpet underneath the air conditioner's sputter and grind, feeling the goose bumps rise on my arms, then my legs, then along my scalp, until she came up behind me and skated her tongue down my spine, trailed it softly with a fingernail. We made love as much as anyone could in that town.

I was scared awake by someone pounding on the door. I sat up and looked around, my heart machine-gunning inside me. It was still dark, and I was alone. At first I thought she might be the one knocking, gone for ice or fresh air and trying to get back in. Then I heard Trace. "Let me in," he said, and in his voice was something that told me he knew she would be gone, and that I should have known, too. I found my shorts in the bathroom and put them on.

I opened the door. Trace stood there, wobbling, holding the wall for support. Roy stood back against the railing, holding a case of beer and a pizza box. "Come on in," I said, "but I'm going to sleep."

The door closed, and it was dark.

"I can't see," Trace said.

"Turn on the light," I said.

"I can't *see*," he said, his voice getting high and scared. "Oh fuck, I'm blind. I can't see."

I turned on the light next to the bed. Roy stood near the door, still holding the beer and pizza. Trace was lying on the floor on his side, his hands over his eyes, moving his legs like he was running. "I can't see," he said.

"Jesus, what's he on?" I said to Roy. "What did you give him?"

"The bikers said it was just crank," Roy said. "But I don't know."

I got out of the bed and knelt next to Trace. "Hey, buddy," I said, "it's me. It's Phil. It's all right." I pulled his hands away from his eyes. "You're going to be all right." I wondered if he was going to die, if I should call someone.

He stopped kicking his legs. For a few minutes he didn't say anything, didn't move, but I could see him breathing. Then he blinked and looked at me. "I got us some pizza," he said. He said it like he wanted me to say yes, yes, you sure did, you're a hero.

Roy sat on the edge of the bed and opened a bottle of beer. Trace pointed at him. "That guy wants to fuck me," he said. "He wants to fuck me in the butt."

I looked at Roy. He sipped his beer and shrugged. "Well, I do," he said. "It's no secret. I told him hours ago."

"Get out of here," I said.

"Cool it, Sundance," he said. "I paid for this stuff. I'm staying until it's gone."

Trace crawled over to the pizza box and took out a slice. "Have some pizza, Phil," he said, like he had it all under control. So I went and put on the rest of my clothes, took a slice, and opened beers for the two of us.

Trace and I sat at the table next to the window, and Roy sat on the bed. We ate and drank. Roy tried a few times to make conversation, but I didn't feel much like talking, and Trace didn't seem like he could. Roy gave up, leaned back, and watched us, smoking a clove cigarette. No one spoke, but the room was full of sound: the air conditioner grinding away, the alarm clock humming and flipping numbers on the minute, Trace and I chewing and swallowing, Roy exhaling long streams of smoke. We heard bursts of life from the biker party outside—running footsteps, laughing, a bottle smashed, a country song belted out in three-part discord, a man and a woman cursing each other. A Harley thundered alive and revved senselessly.

"They're from Bakersfield, most of them," Roy said. "They come through here a lot. Best parties this town ever sees." Then he leaned forward and said, "Bobbi's husband is down there right now, you know."

"Who's Bobbi?" I asked.

"The woman who brought you here," he said. "That girl gets around. So does her husband. I hope you used a condom." Of course I hadn't. I felt sick. I felt like I'd been in that town forever.

"Me, I never use them," Roy said. "I like to feel everything." Then rambled on and on about everything he liked to feel, and everything he wanted to do with Trace, and everything was *my cock* this and *my cock* that, and Trace just sat and ate and drank and smiled like it was the best joke he'd ever heard. Finally I got sick of it. I told Roy to shut the hell up and leave. "Look who's Mister Manly all of a sudden," he said. "I bet I could make you cry." He unbuckled his belt. "I could make you call for God."

That's when Trace threw a bottle at him. It shattered on the wall. Roy got wet from the spray.

"Settle down, Butch," Roy said. "I'm just kidding."

Trace took another bottle out of the case and threw that one, too. It barely missed Roy's head. "Leave Phil alone," Trace said.

Roy's mouth inched open, and he stared at Trace. "It was a joke," he said. He sounded scared, but he didn't move.

"Trace," I said. "Come on. Calm down." But Trace wound up

and threw another one, and this one thumped Roy in the chest. It made a dull, hollow sound. Roy cried out and jumped off the bed, limped toward the door. Trace kept throwing, and even as I was telling him to stop I found myself picking up a bottle and letting fly.

Roy fell once.

By the time he got the door open, there was blood on his face, but I don't know if we hit him straight on or if he got cut by a ricochet. For some reason he stopped in the doorway to yell at us. "You guys are insane," he shouted, his hands in fists. "You guys are sick." I picked up the pint bottle that Bobbi had bought, and I threw it. Roy ducked, and it sailed over the railing. I heard it shatter in the parking lot below. Then Roy was gone, his uneven steps pounding down the stairs, his undone buckle jangling.

We'd wrecked the room. The carpet soaked. The bedside light broken off the wall, dangling from its wires. The mirror hit dead-on, angry cracks snaking out from the point of impact. Blooms of beer seeping into the walls, into the fabric of the coconut print. I stripped the sheets and blankets off the bed, and Trace crawled onto the bare mattress, the only thing in the room not covered with glass.

"We should get out of here," I said.

"I'm going to sleep," he said. "I'm sleepy."

It was only then that I remembered the baby. I asked him if the cops had taken it.

"Oh, the baby," he said slowly, like he was remembering the night one frame at a time. "The baby."

"Where is it? Did you bring it to the party?"

"I gave it to someone," he said. He closed his eyes. "Mo would want to have her own."

Then he fell asleep. I didn't think that was a good sign. I thought his heart might be giving out.

I know I should have tried to find the baby. I may even have wanted to. But outside was a dark town with too many people I couldn't face alone. Inside was Trace, who needed me to make sure he kept breathing. I shook the glass off a chair and sat, watching him, trying not to think about the baby, trying not to think about myself. I watched for cops, but they never came. Neither did any friends of Roy's. No angry husband, no fucked-up bikers. No one. In a way, that made it worse.

Trace woke up just after sunrise, and we headed for the gas station, staying off the road. We waited inside the van for that bastard of a mechanic to show up.

We made it to Alaska, but we never got out on a fishing boat. Instead we had to work at the processing plant, keeping the drains clear underneath the giant waste pipes, twelve-hour shifts in a chill rain of fish guts. I only lasted a month. I caught pneumonia and had to go home to live with my father and his new wife while I recovered. At the end of the summer, Trace moved to San Francisco with some girl he'd met up there after I'd left. A year later, he would be dead. He hit bottom, and Mo—who'd married the Yankee—offered to fly him back to New York and pay for rehab. He hanged himself in the basement at O'Hare during the layover.

Who knew airports even had basements?

One night when we were in Anchorage, Trace won a storytelling contest at a bar. Five hundred dollar prize. He told the story of his first kiss—a story I'd heard the day after it happened. How he was eleven and she was sixteen, how this older girl had punched her tongue into his mouth and held it there, puffed up like an insult, not moving. How she'd just had lunch and he could taste everything caught in her braces: tuna salad, peanut butter crackers, banana. It wasn't so much the story as the way he told it, smiling and flapping his arms and dancing and shining with self-deprecation, offering every word like it was his last cigarette and he was glad to let you have it. He blew the five hundred in an hour, buying drinks for all of us in the house. Trace could be a hero. You just had to be watching at the right time.

Like the day we destroyed the house he grew up in with sledgehammers. His sister and her husband had bought the house from Trace's mom and wanted to redo the interior, so they hired the two of us to gut the place. I had to stop and rest, but Trace was like a machine, swinging the hammer harder and harder, grunting with every stroke, grunts that echoed louder as one by one the walls fell into rubble. I held the ladder for him as he broke apart the brick above the fireplace, where, for a few years at least, a whole family—mother, father, sister, and Trace—had hung their

Christmas stockings. I watched him as the chunks of brick and mortar flew under each stroke, and before long I picked up my hammer again, believing that this was the most honest work either of us would ever do.

EMILY HAMMOND

Back East

Uncle Lake and Aunt Bobette lived just off the La Loma bridge that crossed the Arroyo Seco. Right after the bridge, you made your first left—their house was classic Pasadena, a craftsman house with a low-pitched roof, exposed rafters, dark wood shingles, and a sleeping porch vined with wisteria and grape, drab green and idle in the approaching Southern California winter.

I used to baby-sit for them, before I could drive, so I had a lot of time to look out the car window, how beneath the bridge the arroyo was snake-dry, you could hear the grasshoppers chipping away at the sage and wild tobacco, the accidental ping of their exoskeletons against the thorns of the holly-leaf cherry that grew down there, too. Then just as quickly you entered the formidable silence of my aunt and uncle's neighborhood, old Pasadena homes so muffled by ivy, you had to wonder if anyone lived there at all.

My aunt and uncle's house was set back from the street, low patios aimed off the front and back of the house that featured my aunt's strange bonsai specimens, miniature chrysanthemum, pomegranate, juniper, and other odd Lilliputian plants on which she performed experiments, wiring branches, stripping bark.

She was a scientist, unusual in those days. A graduate of some Ivy League college Back East. Back East: it was how we oriented ourselves in the West, in Pasadena. People weren't identified by the countries of their forebears, not exactly. They might be referred to as English-Scottish stock or of French-German extraction (no one was pure anything, that was rare), but they were from Boston. They were from Philadelphia, New York, or Virginia, cities and states used interchangeably when you answered the question, "Where is your family from?" As if you originated from some Hawthornian manse located on the Eastern seaboard. Your people were buried there in a very old cemetery somebody saw once on a trip Back East.

Aunt Bobette was from Boston. I mean, she grew up there, unlike Uncle Lake who hailed from Altadena, back when it was chicken farms and orange groves, an auxiliary town to Pasadena. He grew up on some ranch with blood-splattered feathers floating around, and he thought nothing of throwing old baling wire or farm implements out into the yard. Or so I imagined. Actually I knew next to nothing about Uncle Lake's upbringing, only that he'd married my aunt, my father's cousin, and that *she* was from Back East, as they say. From money. All I really knew was that Uncle Lake grappled me into a kiss once, an open-mouth kiss, in the car as he drove me home from baby-sitting his twin sons. He made me kiss him, held his fist over the car lock until it was over. He was a heavy man, in khakis and a navy blue sport jacket, smelling of gin and cocktail nuts. The rogue society man, he fancied himself. As if a pig could join a country club. But this incident, the foul gin kiss, rooting fat tongue, salted lips, donkey teeth—this is not the point of this story. This story isn't even about Uncle Lake. I no longer care that I was forced to kiss him, after months of being cornered, twelve years old and skinny, undeveloped, whenever my aunt was out of the room. I don't care. It's unimportant now, it happened to so many girls my age, had always happened to girls our age, and by now we've either dealt with it or we haven't.

What this story is about is transcendence.

I baby-sat every Saturday night, arrived around dinnertime (driven by my father), delivered home around midnight. Uncle Lake and Aunt Bobette's twin boys were toddlers, thirteen months old, just starting to walk. Their names were Sid and Paul, and I had no idea what I was doing at first. I'd never baby-sat before, never even changed a diaper. Into my purse I'd slipped a copy of Dr. Spock, and on the subject of diaper changing, I followed the pictures. Sid was rather wiggly so the first time I got B.M. all over the place before I could wipe him clean. Getting a diaper back on him was a different matter: I gave up and let him run around naked until he peed on the carpet.

"Come on, Sid, help me out here." I got Dr. Spock, laid Sid out spread-eagled, unfolded the cloth diaper. The pins were what worried me. "Listen, pal, just don't move, okay?"

He gazed up at my face, eyebrows raised, as though I were a curious toy hanging above him in his crib. "Da?" he said.

"Da," I said, agreeing. Somehow I managed not to stick him with the pins, and the diaper, once I got it on him, didn't bag too much. "All right, now for the rubber pants."

By now his brother had come to watch, crouching before us in his diaper (still dry, I hoped), craning his neck as though watching TV. "Mama?" he said.

"She'll be back later, Paul."

Once I learned how to diaper, Sid and Paul were nice company. They laughed, talked in their own companionable language. "Ba? Da?" Sometimes they even said words I recognized, besides "Mama," words like "hi" or "bye," which didn't necessarily correspond to anyone's coming or going. They liked applesauce, mashed carrots, scrambled eggs, and their bottles, and when it was time for them to go to bed, I lay down on the floor of the sleeping porch, really their playroom, with a twin on either side. Paul was a mouth breather and usually left drool on my shoulder.

Sometimes Uncle Lake went away, on business trips maybe, although this wasn't clear, and Aunt Bobette would let me come stay for a weekend, as her mother's helper. I loved these times the most, not having a mother myself or any younger siblings. I could act out my favorite fantasy, silly for twelve, but I hadn't outgrown it yet: that my aunt was really my mother, the twins my baby brothers.

While Aunt Bobette tended her bonsai, the boys and I played on the lawn, a form of toddler football. They tackled me, whether I had the "ball" (a rubber duck) or not. I'd run, and they'd hurtle after me, crawling, rolling, creeping, staggering—arms in front like Frankenstein for balance, diapered bottoms sticking out.

My aunt would stop to watch us, a clay pot in each hand. "This is so good for them, Joan. You're really great with them."

"I am?"

"You are," she said in her Boston accent, words clipped at the end, different than the joke I'd heard, *Pawk the caw in Hawvahd Yawd.* "Would you mind giving me a hand with my plants, Joan?"

"Sure." I herded the boys into their playpen near the patio, then followed my aunt.

"Here's what you need to do," she said, handing me an eyedropper and a vial of what looked to be tea. "Give each plant five drops."

"What is it?" I said. She was always feeding strange concoctions to her plants—fish bones she'd ground up herself, fresh sheep manure. One time she even fed them blood, what kind I didn't know. Chicken blood?

"It's a new fertilizer I'm developing," she said. "Made of dehydrated milk and beef extract."

While I gave each plant five drops, she went along with a mister. As always I marveled over her slender fingers, hands, arms, her whole body as airy as her plants. She was pretty, too, dark hair swept back into a black velvet headband, green eyes, a dimple on her chin. I thought only men had dimples there, but on her it seemed the most feminine of attributes.

Once, when she was showing me around the house, the very first time I baby-sat, she had sneezed. The sound of a dainty hiccup. We happened to be in the bathroom so she tore off a single sheet of toilet paper and blew her nose delicately.

I'd stared. It was then that I knew I lived with men, my father and my much older brothers, whose sneezes detonated through the house; my father's alone could cause a roof to blast off. Not to mention the sound of him blowing his nose: like a typhoon, a gale, a cyclone.

"What kind of a scientist are you, Aunt Bobette?" I asked now.

"Botanist." She laughed. "But no longer. The twins, you know."

"Will you go back to being a botanist? When they're older?"

"Oh," she said. "I don't know. Perhaps."

I sensed resignation in her voice, regret, but not about giving up botany. It was something else.

There was much I would have liked to ask her. What was it like growing up in Boston, did she miss it, and why had she married Uncle Lake? Would she stay here forever and be my aunt, or would she depart in the night as my own mother had done?

My mother had fallen in love, that was her crime. I could tell from the way my father said it that he didn't quite believe it. It was a ruse, an act of childish spite. A mistake she would live to regret.

We had this conversation many times:

"Why did my mother leave?"

A leaden sigh. I hated to cause my father grief, but I couldn't *not* ask.

"Why?" he'd say, gradually warming to the subject. "I still ask myself that. Was it me? You kids?" That we could have anything to do with her leaving us—wasn't he supposed to avoid the very suggestion? But my father could be alarmingly open or, when he felt the need, covert.

"Well, the story is this," he'd begin. If we happened to be nearby a mirror, my father would pause to check himself in it. Odd, this habit of looking at himself in the mirror at such a moment. As if he were telling the story to himself or to a man who looked exactly like him. "I got up on a weekday morning, it was a Wednesday, I remember, because I had to take out the trash. I sat up in bed alone, thinking your mother must've gotten up already." If in front of a mirror, he might smooth a hand over his thinning hair. "Didn't think anything of it at first, figured she was in the bathroom, or out in the backyard. She liked to do that, you know. Garden, first thing in the morning. I started to get you kids your breakfast—that was always my job, you know. When I finally noticed she was gone was that your brothers didn't get up. That was her job, to wake you kids up. 'Where's your mom?' I asked them. They didn't know. Why would they?"

One of the strangest things about this story: my father never mentioned me. Maybe it was because I was still asleep that morning, or maybe unconsciously he felt I was colluding with my mother since I was a girl. Or was it that my father simply couldn't bear the thought of a mother abandoning her daughter?

"I started calling for her," he'd continue. "'Anne? Anne?'" My father would raise his voice as though calling for my mother at that very instant. As if she might actually answer him after all these years. Five years. Forever for a child. I'd often think when we got to this point in the story that it was cruel of him, to call her name like that, right in front of me, and inevitably, I never learned from this story what I really wanted to know: what was in my mother's character that she could desert her own children, and would I do the same to my children someday?

In later years I figured out, of course, that the story was merely a distraction: a story about the morning she left, not about *why* she left.

He should have been an actor, my father. Instead he was a bank manager. He should've acted on the weekends at least, in local productions, but instead he told this story or others like it. We'd heard all about growing up in the Great Depression, how a man paid my father's father money he owed him with a couple of dead chickens. Carried them into the house by their scaly feet and silently handed them over. Or he told us about men who, having lost everything, climbed the railings of Suicide Bridge and threw themselves off.

The rest of the story about my mother leaving went like this: finally my father figured out she'd left. This was later on in the morning after we'd left for school. That's when he found her note under his pillow (my father had the note memorized, naturally):

Dear Jack,
    I've left. I've fallen in love and we are moving Back East. I'm so very sorry to do this to you and the children. Tell them I love them, but that the world is not a forgiving place. It's better that we go off alone. I can't bear to say goodbye.
                                  Respectfully,
                                  Anne

She didn't leave an address. Didn't say she'd be in touch. Didn't say she'd send for us. Didn't mention me or my brothers by name. Signed her note "Respectfully." I expected my father to roar with bitter laughter over that one word; it would have been his style and his right to do so. Of all things to sign a note of abandonment with! "Respectfully"! As if writing a letter to the school principal or a withered old aunt. As if she'd gotten the idea for this letter out of a bad English novel.

But whenever my father got to that part, the word "Respectfully," his voice submerged to a cracked, angry whisper. His eyes glistened red, and he would turn away from me, away from the mirror if we were near one. "Goddamn her," he would say.

He was a patient father, his lack of ambition for himself a saving grace, it turned out. He relied on no nannies or relatives for our care. Once I was twelve and old enough, I came home from school and minded myself, but when I was younger, he had been there. He had been there when I was sick, when I needed a costume for school (he either struggled to sew it himself, rusty skills leftover from the Army, more suited for torn uniforms and canvas tents, or he hired someone to finish the job); he had fixed my hair in the mornings, and, in the last year, he had explained menstruation and the facts of life to me, although so far it was useless information.

I loved him, and I wondered why he did this for me, for us. He was similarly devoted to my college-age brothers, who liked it here so much they couldn't bring themselves to move out. They were copies of my father in many ways, devoted to me and to our family, yet my father had sworn if they weren't out by the end of the year, he would throw them out. They must live their own lives, he declared. Date more girls, go to parties, stay up late, learn how to handle liquor ("So you don't end up like your uncle Lake").

As for my father, he never did those things. He said he left such behaviors to young people and to fools like our uncle. "Pig-in-a-blanket" was what he called him. The Gut, The Lout, The Drunk, The Chicken Farmer. My father had a lot of names for Uncle Lake, none flattering; still, I couldn't bring myself to tell my father about the grapplings I'd had to endure. It'd been going on too long, for one thing—months. Why hadn't I said something before? At least that's what I feared my father saying. Mostly, though, I knew telling the truth would end my baby-sitting for Sid and Paul, that I'd no longer see my aunt, either. Our family would never see their family again. The most I could manage was to ask my father to come and pick me up, too, in addition to dropping me off, so that I wouldn't be alone in the car with Uncle Lake. I can't remember what reason I gave; I might have mentioned Uncle Lake's drinking, that he was weaving lanes and running red lights (which was true, but how much from drinking and how much from trying to grab me, I don't know). My father grumbled at first (Lout, Drunk, Chicken Farmer), but he was there every Saturday at midnight sharp. No questions asked.

Then one night my father couldn't pick me up. His car wouldn't start, and my brothers weren't at home; they'd finally listened to his advice and gone to a party. "You're going to have to ask your uncle to drive you home, Joan. I'm sorry. Is he too drunk?"

"I can't tell," I said cryptically. "Maybe."

"What about your aunt Bobette?"

"Asleep probably."

Uncle Lake eyed me while I talked on the phone, that glazed, sagging look he'd get, like pineapple upside-down cake.

"Dad, can I take a cab?"

"Sure, do that. Have your uncle call you one."

"A cab?" Uncle Lake said when I hung up. "No cab will come out this way, Joanie."

Joanie. What my father used to call me when I was little, now Uncle Lake's revolting nickname for me, but only when Aunt Bobette wasn't around.

He cornered me by the stove. I kicked at him, but he dodged at the last minute, and I missed. "Joanie," he said, red-faced, breathing hard, "how come you're so mean to me?"

I ran upstairs to Aunt Bobette, but she had fallen asleep, in her clothes still, on their bed. Probably so she wouldn't have to have sex with him.

"Joan?" I heard him call. "Time to go!"

I sat down beside her, touching her hand, small and so cold she might have been dead. "Aunt Bobette?"

Most Saturday nights ended this way, Aunt Bobette asleep before I even left. Maybe she was drunk herself. If so, well, who could blame her? Being married to Uncle Lake.

"Oh, Joanie!" he called up the stairs.

I picked up the phone and dialed my father.

"Joanie!"

The line was busy. Who was my father calling at this hour? I went downstairs before my uncle came up.

It was to be the night of The Kiss. If you could call it that. I fought but he pinned down my shoulders, all the while keeping his fist on the car lock.

"So you don't like riding with me anymore, Joanie," he said after it was over and he was driving me home, really driving me home now, in a hurry, it seemed. "What's the matter? Don't like kissing an old man?"

"Old, ugly, fat pig." I wiped my mouth on my sleeve again and again. Bile washed up my throat then went back down. "I want to go home."

"Maybe the real problem is, you don't like kissing men."

"I don't like kissing pigs," I said.

"Maybe you like kissing girls."

I tried to imagine kissing one of my friends, Sally Ortmeir, on the cheek. "What?" I said, my voice faint.

"Like your mom," he said. "Are you a lez like your mom? Running away with her *girlfriend*." He snorted.

It didn't register, what he was saying.

"I'll tell my dad what you did." This time bile backed up into my mouth; I had to swallow it. My eyes ran. I began to cry. I knew what it meant to be powerless, a beetle, the boot coming down, the beetle's hard shell crushed, what's left a white paste.

"I'll tell my dad!" I said.

"What, about that back there?" He jerked his head. The Kiss, he meant. "Or telling you the truth about your mom?" He hummed and drove as though nothing unusual had just happened—accelerating, braking, the tick-tick of the turn signal—my heart wrenched out of my chest, turned around backwards, and shoved back inside.

I didn't say anything to my father about what Uncle Lake had said, not immediately. I wasn't sure what I had heard, for one thing. A lez. It was what kids called our gym teacher in junior high, Miss Magda, a woman whose bug eyes seemed to appraise us when we showered, and who called us "gills," as in "Gills, two laps" or "Gills, line up in the gym." When we did line up, Miss Magda would go along with a clipboard checking off names. If you were having your period, you were supposed to say, "Special." This meant you might not have to run as much, or maybe not have to do anything at all if you uttered the magic word, "Cramps." Most of all it meant you were relegated to the special shower in the locker room, a private stall with a frosted glass door—a punishment of sorts if I were to judge from the shamed expressions of the "gills" who had to use it.

Miss Magda had a compact body and hairless tan legs, a whistle around her neck. Driven and lonely; was that why she stationed herself near the locker room showers? Was my mother like that wherever she lived Back East, an outcast, an anomaly?

What about the person she ran away with? Another woman, if

Uncle Lake were to be believed.

He was a lout, a pig, a drunk, but I didn't think he was lying.

My mother. I didn't like to admit to many memories of her.

She looked nothing like Miss Magda, for starters. She was tall and wasp-waisted, and she always, at least in my memory, wore nylon stockings. They were usually drying on the door of the shower, a pair or two of taupe, foot-and-calf-shaped flags, like transparencies of maps of Italy, the heel and toes several shades darker, like pubic hair on a pale female body.

I could picture my mother living Back East, where the women "dressed," as Aunt Bobette put it. That's what she had said when I asked her to describe it there, the weekend after The Kiss, when Uncle Lake had left on one of his many trips.

"The beach is here, Joan, here in California, but the *ocean*"— the word had the weight of an Amen—"is there, in New England. When I think of ocean, I think of blue-gray water, water that has depth and chill to it, not the green suds they have here, and that slimy seaweed that's always washing up onshore." She grimaced, her button nose wrinkling.

I was helping her carry out her bonsai tools, concave pinchers, tweezers, magnifying glass, copper wire, while in the playpen Sid and Paul rolled over each other, like bear cubs.

"Another thing," Aunt Bobette said, "the women dress there." I imagined a whole country of women, turned out in sheaths and evening gowns, my mother among them, in spectator pumps, a memory hat.

"It's a matter of culture, really," my aunt was saying. "There is no culture out West—"

"Do you know where my mother went Back East? Do you know where she lives?"

She stood perfectly still. "Oh, Joan, I'm sorry."

"I shouldn't ask," I said. "I know I shouldn't have asked."

"Nonsense, Joan. She's your mother, you have a right to know. I'm just surprised your father hasn't told you more."

"You mean that she—she ran away with a woman? I know that." Thanks to Uncle Lake. The pig.

"I somehow think," Aunt Bobette said, carefully arranging her tools, then looking straight at me, her eyes so green I wanted to cry, "that this is a subject you should discuss with your father."

"You won't tell me where she lives?"

"Please, Joan."

I thought of the note under my father's pillow. A crock. A lie. All to protect me, I should've guessed. Had everybody in the whole world known except me?

Still I didn't say anything to my father. He had seemed so happy lately, whistling and doing yard work on the weekends. It was spring, winter everywhere else in the country, winter Back East, but spring here. Plants which had kept their leaves all winter surged forth with bright green growth, while bulbs shot up and popped open, like speeded-up film—this wasn't like other places, where spring arrived cautiously. Here, overnight, birds sang, built nests, had babies; trees grew new limbs; flowers carpeted garden paths, vacant lots, twined their way up the sides of houses: a frantic display of spring before, overnight again, the weather would turn hot and smoggy, everything not hooked up to a sprinkler becoming gnarled, leathery and tough.

My own torpid body—flat nipples like blighted seeds—seemed impervious to the lure of spring. I turned inward, read a lot of books, read everything—backs of cereal boxes, return addresses on mail, clothing labels. I avoided going outside, pained by all that fervent growth, left out, bereft.

Even my brothers carried on like randy elk. They had fallen in love with pretty college girls, each of them, and now neither one was around much, neither available to answer questions about my mother.

When I wasn't reading whatever was in front of me, I immersed myself in the junior high chorus, me and twenty other girls exercising our vocal cords, our mouths opened as pitifully as the baby birds that spring—as if we were pleading for nourishment. I couldn't help noticing most of us were frail and flat-chested, our skin bluish and chalky. We sang like frightened calves about to be slaughtered for veal, which is to say we sounded awful, except for Val Vossman, who sang longingly in her woman's voice, *"Oh, my heart is back in Napoli, oh Napoli, oh Napoli, and I seem to hear again in dreams, your melody, your sweet melody."* She appeared ten years older than she was, her body, not her face. She was Mormon. She wore no makeup. Val resembled Jane Russell in the bra commercials (the meaner girls, the "developed" catty girls, called her Va-Va-VOOM), yet Val dressed conservatively in dresses, never skirts or culottes, bobbie socks, and navy blue Keds; in chorus, her breasts heaved incongruously just below the white of her starched Peter Pan collars.

Mormon. I thought this meant all kinds of secret rituals involving immersion into marble bathtubs in hidden, windowless rooms in the backs of houses, people with veiled, downcast eyes, nonetheless watching you. Constant spiritual surveillance. Praying for your soul. Val was tight-lipped on the subject; I know because she became my best friend. We were drawn together as kids that age are, often because of some similarity, or infirmity, usually physical: blond hair, athletic ability, or the need to wear glasses. Val and I weren't similar physically, of course. She towered over me, voluptuously, while I hopped along beside her, two steps for her every one, always wearing my cardigan sweater from fourth grade that still fit me—I was constantly cold, I had no body fat whatsoever.

Our affinity was mothers. Neither of us had one anymore, hers dead, mine gone. We talked about it all the time, what it felt like to grow up without a mother. I told Val about being in a school play, another girl patting my shoulder for the briefest moment, how I wanted to prolong that moment forever—how much I looked forward to rehearsals just for that. How embarrassed I felt.

"I know," she would say. "I actually liked it when I got my first bra and the woman at Bullocks fitted me for it. She had to touch me to do it—the measuring tape, adjusting straps. I was in heaven, but sad, you know?"

I nodded, we both sighed, me with worry: this hunger for touch, did it mean I was attracted to women? Or did it mean I simply missed having a mother? And what was Val talking about, a woman touching her. Did this mean she was a lez? That we both were?

I became terrified that Val would drop me, that she would see something unsavory in me—there might be some Mormon commandment about my kind of loss, that I was damned because of my mother. I felt damned. Val's mother, at least, had not left town in disgrace; she died of cancer and left Earth a beautiful angel, a mother whose memory a daughter could cherish.

Then one night I stayed over at Val's. Though no one said as much, we couldn't do it the other way around, I think—a good Mormon girl staying in a mostly male household. Val had sisters, albeit younger sisters; she was the oldest. Her father mostly stayed in the living room while we cared for the sisters, three of them, all with their hair done up in braids, buns, ribbons. We gave them baths, we redid their hair, we read them stories, we put them to bed.

At last it was time for us to go to sleep. Val wore a long white nightgown with a high neck; I had on my PJs (with teddy bears on them, also leftover from fourth grade). She had twin beds in her room, but after lying there in the dark for a while, I asked if I could come to her bed.

"Sure," she said.

I felt more peaceful there, and safe. I wondered if this was because Val was Mormon—if I should become Mormon. Would it wash my sins away, the sins of my mother? Would I become as pure as Val?

"When you grew bosoms," I asked her (I didn't know what to call them, what the best technical term was), "breasts, I mean, what did it feel like?"

"What did it feel like?"

"Not what it felt like exactly, but when you touched them, did they feel a certain way?"

"Like how?" she said.

"Well, all of a sudden I have these bumps underneath. It's like there's some fat on top and then something harder underneath."

"Sort of like cartilage?"

"Yeah, maybe. Would you check them for me?" I blurted out.

"What?"

"Could you—you know—see if they're normal?"

"Well, okay." She didn't sound so sure.

"You don't have to," I said. "Forget it."

"No, I will." She got up on her knees and turned on the reading light. "I know. I'm pretty sure I felt that way, too—"

"Nobody to ask," I said. "I can't ask my father!"

"Lift your shirt," she said.

I did.

"Normal as far as I can tell. You're growing breasts! So are you glad?"

"I guess. It's sort of weird. Is it normal to have that cartilage stuff? Like a ridge, kind of."

"Do you want me to feel?" she said, her fingers poised.

"All right."

She probed around, as if she were a doctor. She yanked down my top, said I was fine, I was just growing, and what sort of bra was I going to get? "It's a little early for that," I said, suddenly sleepy. I didn't move back to my bed but rested my head on her shoulder, part of her breast yielding to my chin. I gazed up at her face in profile, an ethereal face, Botticelli hair; she could have been stepping out of Venus's clamshell, into thin air. She might have been a departed angel herself. Thankfully I felt nothing besides that, except love.

I dreamt of my mother that night, dressed in something coarse and ragged. She was trying to write me a letter but kept crumpling it up and starting over again. I stood by her desk to read what she was writing, but I couldn't make it out.

* * *

Dear Joan,

Writing this is like talking into the wind.

I'm sorry I left. I didn't have a choice. I left because I'm different—I was supposed to love your father but I couldn't. I am attracted to women. Do you know what that means? It means I can't love your father, though I respect him.

I want to see you again. How about if you came Back East to visit me next summer? We'd have a lot of fun! There's so much to do here that you would enjoy—the swan boats at the Public Garden, tea at the Parker House, Paul Revere's house.

I handed the letter to my father, my shoulders sinking into my rib cage, as though I were collapsing inside myself, bones, muscle, gristle.

"What is this?" he said, wiping his face with the T-shirt he'd tossed aside earlier. He'd been gardening bare-chested, and he smelled of sweat, man's sweat. I wondered if such a smell disgusted my mother.

"Read it," I said.

With my eyes, the only part of me that felt alive, I imagined I saw our old pet turtle lumbering around, plowing at the ground stiffly, in slow motion, his ancient, reptilian legs so thick he felt nothing.

"This is in your handwriting," my father said. "What is this?"

I could not lift my shoulders, not even to shrug them. "A letter from my mother."

"You know that's impossible. This is in your handwriting, and you don't... Who told you about your mother?" My father emerged from his thicket of rhododendron, pulling his shirt on over his stinking, hairy chest. "We need to talk about this, Joanie. Now. Let's go inside."

Joanie. He hadn't called me that in a long time, only Uncle Lake had; the name was poison, all the horrible things that had happened since my mother left five years ago, in one bad word.

Numbly, I followed my father to our kitchen. We sat down at the kitchen table. He smoothed out the letter in front of him. I'd crumpled it into a ball so many times, it was soft, like velvet.

"I was planning to tell you, Joan, of course." My father wagged his head, confused. "I don't even know where to start. Who—"

I snatched up the letter and ran for the front door, hollering, "Why didn't you tell me? Why the hell didn't you tell me?!"

He caught up with me a block away, in front of the Nelsons' house, who probably knew all about this, anyway. My father reached out, grabbed my arm, and got me into some kind of straight-jacket hold. Panting, he spoke softly in my ear. "First, Joan, I'm sorry. I'm so sorry. You're right to be mad, I should've told you. I wanted to protect you, keep you a child a while longer. Secondly, I have to ask, I have to know: who told you?"

"What difference does it make, the whole frigging town knows!"

"Who told you?"

"Not you, that's for damn sure." My second curse word, and he didn't say anything.

I didn't wait for him to ask again.

"Uncle Lake told me," I said. "That and a lot of other things I shouldn't know." I stopped flailing, but my father didn't let go of me. The same old bile backed up into my mouth, as if it'd been waiting there all this time.

He turned me around slowly to face him. "What are you talking about, Joan?"

I coughed, sputtered really, and threw up on the ground between us.

Everybody came to our spring concert. I was surprised that twenty girls could have so many relatives, and as usual, I felt at a loss. Their mothers were there, except for Val's. My mother was somewhere in Boston, well-dressed and with her true love, but otherwise miserable. Living in some walk-up apartment in a despised neighborhood of the city, or perhaps she lived in one of the best sections, on Beacon Hill: a whole hill of defiant, lustful women, in Chanel suits and Italian shoes.

I suppose deep inside I'd hoped my mother would attend my concert, although she had no idea I was singing today, had no idea about anything I did. How much of her leaving us was the fact of her lesbianism in such unenlightened times, and how much the fact that motherhood or us, her children, simply didn't interest her?

I would never seek her out. Nor her me.

Twenty years later I would attend the concert of my own daughter, and at the sight of her coltish, bean-pole body clothed in lime-green velveteen, a dress we had bought the day before, I wanted to weep. The braces on her teeth, the pimple on her cheek disguised by my makeup, her maturing face, one moment a teenager's, the next the face of a child—how dare my mother miss this metamorphosis, mine, my daughter's?

To my own spring concert I wore my best dress, which chafed me under the arms, too tight around the chest; underneath was my first bra, crossing my thin chest with a tiny embroidered flower, keeping me in check, mending my poor posture, my broken heart.

Aunt Bobette had taken me to buy the bra, several weeks after Uncle Lake moved out for good, no one knew where, his nose broken personally by my father, who quoted Gandhi as he undertook the chore.

My aunt, furious at what Uncle Lake had done to me, was only too glad to kick him out.

Besides my father and my brothers and their pretty girlfriends,

Aunt Bobette also came to hear me sing, with Sid and Paul, who wiggled in their seats, da-da-ing, ba-ba-ing, pointing and calling out their name for me, Go-Go.

I sang as though born to it that day, harmonizing alongside Val. *"Oh I seem to hear again in dre-e-ams, your melody, your sweet melody. The mandolinas play so sweet, the dancing sound of pra-a-a-ancing feet. Oh could I go back, oh joy complete—Napoli, Napoli, Napoli!"*

I sang until my jaw ached, until my soul escaped. My mother flew out as well, to Back East, land of fog and swans, ocean, mystery: I watched her depart. Soon the blood would fall from my womb, dripping in sorrow for my mother. Like her, I would stain the earth; I would pay for my sins, bear my children in pain and suffering. I sang.

Spillage

MABELLE HSUEH

Kai opened her eyes and looked around her. She was disoriented until she saw the Canadian customs booth in front, with the maple leaf decal on one of the glass panes. She realized she had fallen asleep, missing both the customs booth on the U.S. side and the Ambassador Bridge. Now she and Bailey were at the Canadian border, the first car in the long line of cars, waiting to be questioned by the border guard before proceeding north.

"You had a nap," Bailey said.

"Yes," Kai replied, wondering if she should apologize for having fallen asleep in the midst of their conversation. She glanced at him. He was the palest man she had ever seen: his eyes behind thick glasses, his thinning hair and beard, his freckles. Even his voice that had lulled her to sleep was pale, colorless. He looked like an insect, weak and vulnerable, that had just emerged from its old shell. She guessed he was in his late thirties, ten years her junior.

Now he stepped on the gas and brought the car alongside the booth. The guard, a young woman with long hair and plum-colored nails, asked Bailey what his purpose was in entering Canada.

"We're going to see a Chinese herbal doctor," Bailey answered. "Here in Windsor."

"He's seeing the doctor, not me," Kai chimed in. "I don't need one." At once she felt foolish. The guard hadn't even glanced at her, much less asked her a question.

"Kai Ding here is my interpreter," Bailey said. "The Chinese doctor doesn't speak a word of English, and I don't speak a word of Chinese."

The guard put her hand across her mouth to stifle a yawn before waving them on.

Bailey drove out of the plaza. "I'm glad you're feeling better than me," he said grimly.

Kai was not exactly feeling better. She tugged at the seat belt. She disliked seat belts, especially this one, which seemed like a giant staple nailing her frail chest to the seat.

"...the street," Bailey was saying. "But Dr. Tu and his wife have a two-story house on Wyandotte. Upstairs is the living quarters, and downstairs is the office and shop."

"How many times have you seen this Dr. Tu?" Kai asked. Kai worked in Student Financial Operations with Bailey's cousin. They'd offered to pay Kai for her interpreting work, but she'd said no, it wasn't necessary. Bailey had an inoperable tumor.

"I've seen Dr. Tu twice," he told her. "Once with my meditation group, the second time with a Chinese girl from Hong Kong. She has since returned to her country." He rolled down the window. "I've forgotten Dr. Tu's house number."

Kai was busy searching for her own landmarks. More than a decade ago she and her husband, Ping, and their friends had come here often to eat and shop for Chinese food and groceries. Then just about this time, during the fall season, Ping ran off to New Mexico with his graduate assistant, and their group eventually broke up. Only recently did she realize what she missed most about Ping—not his love, but his presence, a presence to talk to, make connection with.

They were close to Ouillette Avenue when Bailey discovered he had come too far. He turned back and found the place. After parking the car across the street, Bailey led the way to Dr. Tu's house.

The first-floor shop was long and narrow, shaped like a Band-Aid, Kai thought. To the right, along the length of the wall, were built-in shelves crammed with large containers made of glass, wood, tin, copper, bamboo, or cardboard. Kai could see the herbs inside the glass ones. In front of the shelves was a display case stuffed with boxes of pills and powders, and bags of what seemed to be dried mushrooms and ginseng. In the midst of all these things was a twelve-inch long, double-tiered rack lined with red satin, and resting on the shimmering material were several dark objects that Kai could not identify.

The aisles on both sides of the display case were narrow. There were enough fluorescent tubes on the ceiling to light up a room five times the size. Everything seemed to ache under the bright glare.

A middle-aged woman, standing behind the display case, was weighing a handful of dried dates on a tiny scale.

"This is Mrs. Tu," Bailey whispered to Kai.

"*Ni hao,* Mrs. Tu. Mr. Bailey has an appointment to see Dr. Tu," Kai said in Chinese.

At first the woman stared at them without recognition. Then her round face broke into a smile, revealing a mouthful of gold teeth. "Barley, Barley," she cried loudly and hurried to the back of the room.

"That's what they call me, Barley," Bailey said.

Kai nodded. Soon she heard footsteps coming down the stairs, and a man appeared with one hand on his head, patting down the few strands of white hair. "Barley, Barley," he said.

Bailey made the introductions. Dr. Tu, a short plump man, turned his body sideways as he walked down the aisle, squeezing past them, and opened a small door to an office next to the front entrance. The office resembled a closet, crammed with a folding bed and a desk, with a chair on each side. The lighting was no less glaring.

The men took the two chairs. Kai stood in the doorway. Dr. Tu opened the drawer and pulled out a sheet of paper. Kai saw it was Bailey's list of herbs written in Chinese.

"*Shang ci de batie bangmang ma?*" the old man asked.

Kai turned to Bailey. "Dr. Tu wants to know about the eight dosages of herbs he gave you the last time, were they helpful?"

Bailey shook his head. "Not noticeably."

Kai translated.

"Ah, tell Barley he must be patient. Chinese herbs work very slowly."

This man is a quack, Kai wanted to say to Bailey. He's dispensing snake oil by the barrel. Chinese doctors are only good for curing common colds, mild fever, indigestion, diarrhea, and maybe hemorrhoids. Not for anything as serious as a tumor!

As if sensing Kai's agitation, Dr. Tu motioned to her to sit on the bed. Kai told Bailey what Dr. Tu had said, trying to sound as civil as possible, then took her seat. Bailey nodded amiably.

Dr. Tu asked Bailey to put his right arm on the desk, the palm turned upward. Then he began to *hao-mai,* take the pulse. He placed three fingers on the wrist, and these fingers began to move around the area like tiny mice sniffing for cheese.

Kai knew that Chinese doctors used *hao-mai* in all diagnoses.

She remembered hearing about doctors so skillful that they could feel the pulse vibrating through a silk string. This had happened in the last emperor's court, where no male doctors were allowed into the women's bedchambers. Every time a royal consort became ill, she stayed in her room and tied one end of a silk string around her wrist. The servant took the other end and, extending it into the next room, gave it to the doctor to *hao-mai*. Kai always had her doubts about this story.

Finished with the pulse, the old man picked up the prescription sheet and said, "Please tell Barley I am adding two more herbs to this list. His physical condition has improved, so I am making the medicine stronger."

"And will the medicine shrink the tumor, Dr. Tu?" Kai asked, without trying to mask the sarcasm in her voice.

Dr. Tu started and looked at her. "Of course. I adjust the prescription every time I see him. To make sure everything works."

Ah, if everything works, Kai thought. There's the catch.

"Please ask Barley how many portions, or dosages, he wants this time. He knows how to boil each dosage, reduce it to three cups, and drink it every other day." Dr. Tu held up eight fingers for Bailey. "Eight dosages? Yes?"

"Good, that's two months' supply." Bailey clasped his hands in a gesture of thanks.

With the session over, Kai glanced at her watch. "Is this it, Bailey? Can we leave soon?"

"Oh no." Bailey reached into his jeans for the car keys. "Dr. Tu has to prepare the herbs, and that'll take him about an hour. I always go shopping for a special kind of cheese I can't find in Michigan. It was sold out the last time I was here. Want to come along?"

Kai hesitated. What little interpreting she'd done had exhausted her. She realized she was also depressed and did not want Bailey's company. She waved goodbye to him and said to Dr. Tu, "*Wo zai zhe li deng.*"

"Of course, make yourself at home," the old man said.

After Bailey left, Mrs. Tu dragged out a chair from the back room and placed it in the middle of the aisle, right in front of the satin-lined rack. "We have many herbs to weigh and then divide into eight portions for Barley. It will take time," she said.

Kai had not been in an herbal store since she left China more than twenty years earlier. But she remembered the smells: dry and acrid, at times a bit too pungent, other times as delightful as any perfume. She sat down and leaned forward to examine the rack. The Chinese labels indicated that the two small objects were deer horns, the larger one was part of a rhinoceros horn. She had heard that these were some kind of elixir, ground into powder or soaked in wine and sold to old men who wanted to perform in bed like young bucks. There were no price tags.

Dr. Tu was behind the counter. He looked at the containers before pulling one off the shelf, unscrewed the lid, and lifted out one fistful of herbs. As he pushed them onto the tiny scale, the leaves and the stems broke. The remains fell on the counter and on the floor. Unconcerned, he continued to weigh the herbs, adding and subtracting the amount, before dumping them into a brown bag. The process was repeated ten times before he finished with the first item on the prescription.

Kai glanced at her watch. As Dr. Tu brought out more and more herbs to weigh, the area around the scale and the counter became layered with fragments, the air thick with dust. Kai's nose began to tickle uncontrollably.

Mrs. Tu got out eight tinfoil baking pans, badly dented and out of shape, and spread them on the counter. Then she picked up the first brown bag and began to divide the herbs evenly among the pans. Kai watched and wondered why the old man had not weighed the herbs eight times in the first place, thus saving his wife the extra work. He was so slow, so sloppy. He and his wife should have changed places.

Frustration rose like the herbal dust inside Kai. Bailey should have warned her of this long wait. Then she would have brought reading material, crossword puzzles, anything. She got off her chair and took a few steps to the other end of the room.

Here the countertop was stacked with books on subjects that ranged from palmistry, geomancy, feng-sui, kung-fu, and astrology to classical Chinese novels and operas. Next to the books were half a dozen Chinese teacups, cracked and chipped around the edges. She thought they were to be thrown out until she saw the dregs in the bottom. Evidently they had been used earlier in the day. She turned and walked back to her seat.

To her surprise she heard herself say, without meaning to say it, "Dr. Tu, I wonder if you could take my pulse?"

The old man continued to weigh the herbs.

"Will you please *hao-mai* for me?" she repeated louder.

Dr. Tu looked up. "Ah, I did not think I heard you correctly. Yes, of course I will." He brushed his clothing, wiped his hands on a towel, and stepped out from behind the counter.

They went into the office and sat down at the desk. Kai placed her arm on the desktop and felt the old man's fingers on her wrist exerting a light pressure.

The old man closed his eyes. At last he said, "Your body system is not well-balanced. Too much obstruction in the vital channels, thus preventing the flow of energy. We call this condition *xu*." He picked up a pen and wrote the word on the paper.

What else is new, Kai thought.

"You need adjustments in your system," he continued.

Kai pulled the paper closer to her and examined the Chinese word. Dr. Tu was quite a good calligrapher if nothing else. She looked at the desk and noticed the plate glass that covered the desktop. Finally she looked at the old man. On his right cheek were several liver spots. She remembered they were called *shou-ban*, longevity marks. How the Chinese love euphemisms! But there was no euphemism for her.

"I had a mastectomy five years ago, Dr. Tu. They took both breasts."

"Oh, my dear lady," Dr. Tu murmured.

"Last year I had a second operation due to...a *spillage* of cancer cells from...first operation." Without any warning, Kai burst out crying. She covered her face as the tears poured out, between the fingers and down her arms. Her sobs seemed to come from a great distance, inhuman and terrifying. Her temples throbbed as if someone was stomping on her head.

Her aunt had once cried like this—on the night of Kai's fifth birthday. She had come home and told the family that her husband had brought a concubine into the house. Kai had wept along with her aunt, not because she knew what "concubine" meant, but because she was carried away by her aunt's ferocious grief.

Kai realized Dr. Tu was tapping his finger on the desk. "I do not understand the word, ssss..."

"*Spillage.* That's English. I can't translate it."

"Ssss..."

"During the second operation...I had no breasts left then... they continued to scrape and scrape...the wall of my chest..." She could not stop weeping even though she felt it might be a burden to this old man. It was just as well that he didn't understand the word; just as well that they couldn't make connection with each other.

"Use this," he said and thrust something between her hands. Through the blur, she saw it was a man's linen handkerchief, clean and beautifully pressed. Her father had always carried such a handkerchief.

"Please," Dr. Tu urged. "Tell me how to spell it. I have a dictionary here." He reached under the desk and, with both hands, lifted up a big book with *The English-Chinese Dictionary* printed on the spine. "I am turning to the pages of *S*. What letter is after *S*?"

"*P*, then *i*, then *l*..."

"Wait, please. Is *b* after *s*?"

"No, *p* as in Paul."

"Excuse, please. What means *Bau*?"

Her crying stopped as suddenly as it had started. Looking into his face she realized she had confused him. She wiped her eyes with the handkerchief and reached for the book. "Here, let me find it."

"I see. It means *poh*," the old man said when she finally located the word.

"Yes, spillage is *poh*," she said. "Like the herbs that you spill when you take them out of the container and weigh them."

The old man paused and narrowed his eyes. "I see. You think I waste the herbs? No, no. I pick up the big pieces and put them back in the container."

"What about the small pieces and all the particles?"

"I save them also. Behind the counter, on the floor, is a plastic rug to catch the particles. I gather them and brew them into teas for friends."

"Teas for friends!" she repeated.

"For close friends only. Who do not think such a gesture... insulting." He patted the dictionary. "This word *poh*, you must not be afraid of it. Sometimes it is not all bad meaning."

"It's a terrible word to me. I dream of doctors scraping and scraping my chest until they scrape out my heart. Then I become..." She began to weep again. "...a shell."

"Ah," the old man sighed loudly. He lifted a finger and touched a tear on her face. "This is *poh,* also."

Kai watched him close his dictionary and push it under the desk. Then he opened the drawer, took out a tiny piece of flannel, and began to wipe the glass with great gentleness.

"I will give you some herbs to help you sleep better," he said. "They are all tiny pieces, leftovers, so there will be no charge." He smiled for the first time and stood up.

"Do you mind if I sit here for a while?"

"I will turn off the light and leave the door open. Then you will hear Barley coming back."

"Oh, yes, Bailey." She hoped he had found his special cheese. If he was too tired to drive home, she would offer to do it for him.

She leaned back in her chair and saw, even in the dim light, the sparkling glass top. Dr. Tu had wiped it so clean. She thought of the dirty teacups in the other room. Maybe she could find some new ones in a store along Wyandotte, not to replace the old ones but to add to them. She reached for her purse and stood up.

"*Cha-bei gei cha-you,* teacups for tea friends," she said to Dr. and Mrs. Tu. The words sounded nice, as nice in Chinese as in English.

JAMES MORRISON

Stalker

By the third occasion—she couldn't exactly call them "dates"—Mira thought she had him figured out. Before that she had not been able to determine whether he was a crazy person acting sane or a sane person acting crazy. She had met him through the personals. His ad had described him as "energetic" and "ambitious," and had said he liked public radio, long moonlight walks, and quiet times at home. They had moved smoothly enough through the early rituals of acquaintance, though there was an awkward moment after she told him where she worked, when he flushed and confessed bleakly that he had dated someone else who worked there. It was a big company, she remarked, and then changed the subject. Finally his quality of manic inertia had proved too much for her. The reason she had seen him a third time had been only to figure him out. Now that she felt she had done so, to the extent possible or desirable, there seemed little point in continuing. But when he briskly dropped her off at her door and asked in his odd way, "Want to do it again?" she answered cheerfully that he should call her the next week.

Angela had been having trouble sleeping in the week since the phone calls began. At first she thought if she removed the phone from beside her bed, her sleep would be restored. But she resisted the idea of moving the phone because she did not want to have to think she was undertaking any action in her life whatever as a result of the phone calls. So she lay in bed resenting the caller, with his ridiculous, breathy, high-pitched voice, for demanding with his own illicit attentions any of her attention at all, and she stared at the bedside phone as if it were some small, vicious creature curled up in a sleep that mocked her own wakefulness, whose dormant violence could spring back to life at any second. Finally she removed the phone to the extra bedroom, and then she lay staring at the empty space on the bedside table, worrying over her own fear and weakness, and remembering the words of the caller. When she had picked up the phone the first time, she had heard a man's voice screech a stream of nonsense syllables that sounded something like, "You dare for nothing in the least this fine fine sweetness." Taken aback, she had stupidly asked who was calling, as if the speaker of such words could be called to account by the common powers of telephone etiquette. Then he shouted clearer obscenities, and she remembered what you were supposed to do in such situations, but as she hurried to hang up the phone, she heard the caller say, "I'm watching your every fucking move, bitch!"

People at work were starting to notice a quality of distraction in her. She explained it by saying she had not been able to sleep. Often this explanation prompted the intricate elaboration of home remedies for insomnia. She knew that people liked to believe they could cure other people's woes, and she was sure that if she told them about the calls, these same people would offer up a variety of ready-made, makeshift defenses against the sundry threats of violation that were abroad in the world. That would only make it worse, so she decided to keep it to herself so long as he did not call again, and she wondered how much longer she would have to endure her own fear, and listened to her pulse reverberating in her ear as her ear pressed against her pillow. Sometimes the sound of her own pulse comforted her in its familiar regularity, but other times it alarmed her, like the insistent beats of a clock ticking away irreversible time, or as if it were the rhythmic noise of water leaking slowly, drop by drop, from a minute chink at the bottom of a vast but finite reservoir that would one day run dry.

Behind his milky blue eyes gathered a cluster of thoughts and ideas that troubled Mira by accumulation. "People shouldn't believe most of the stuff they believe," he had said, with a broad sneer, "but it's not like there's stuff they *should* believe that they *don't* believe." She had only nodded. How else could one respond to such a remark? The remark had been uttered in the context of what she had thought was a pleasingly circumspect conversation deploring forms of extremist behavior. They had begun by talking about the spate of recent bombings of government buildings, and this led to talk of the rise of private militias in the country, and that in turn led to discussion of the excessive religious fervor or political affiliation that caused such problems in the first place. She had thought they were in basic accord—for how could there be two sides, who would defend the terrorists?—when he made his remark. She had nodded, and quickly turned the conversation to the subject of movie stars who became Scientologists.

But what did the remark mean? It had at once the scary force of an injunction and the open destiny, the laissez-faire attitude, of a shrug. If people were going to give commands, she thought, they could at least be direct about it. Maybe it was a matter of tone. She was aware of men's fondness for giving orders, and she knew that when men tried to be sensitive, the effort resided not in resisting the temptation to give orders but in issuing the orders in patient, gentle-sounding voices. His remark had the blunt tone of an order but the complicated structure of a paradox. She felt deeply frustrated that she was smart enough to recognize the kind of knot he had tied but somehow not agile enough to unravel it. It would not be fair, though, to write him off as crazy on the basis of this utterance alone, however readily its sophistry could be used, in the worst of all possible worlds, to justify the violence of mad bombers. It was what she thought his ideas would finally add up to, one by one, that disturbed her. She glanced down the narrow road of this possible future and saw a wall at the end of the road.

When he called to set up a fourth meeting, she told him she was busy.

Angela was slicing a red pepper when she cut her finger. The pain was immediate; it shot to her core. She dropped the knife on the floor. The pain was so sharp it did not seem to be located in the small, deep cut. It seemed to be elsewhere, attached to something larger. She had not been paying enough attention to what she had been doing. How foolish, how foolish. She looked at the cut. It gaped, and some blood began slowly welling into it, but the cut was very deep, and it would take time for the blood to come. She tried to remember where the bandages were. When the blood came it would be the color of the pepper. She gave the faucet a slow turn. Warm water streamed into the sink. She waited for the blood to come.

* * *

By the middle of the afternoon, the news had traveled throughout the building. Angela, in accounting, had received a special delivery, and she had broken down in the office and been sent home. There were differing versions in circulation of what terrible thing the package had contained, but what was clear was that it had been some sort of small, dead animal with a string tied, noose-like, around its throat. Mira, in marketing, did not exactly know Angela, but they had friends in common, and it had been because of Angela, indirectly, that Mira had recently decided to try dating through the personals columns. Angela had confided to Maureen Hackett that she was trying it, and Maureen had mentioned it to Mira, and that had been enough to fortify Mira's curiosity. If a woman of Angela's beauty could resort to the personals, then Mira, without inordinate shame, could do so, too. Mira had met Angela once at a retirement party a while ago, and on that occasion she had found it necessary to strive consciously to quell her own envy of Angela's beauty, just as now she pushed away the ill-spirited thought that this was what such beauty came to, having angry, wounded men send you dead rodents wrapped up in gift boxes. So much of life had to do with resisting the constant tug of meanness.

That night, Angela swore to renounce her fear. All day friends and family had comforted her, and she had spoken to the police, and they had comforted her as well, with a comfort more hollow but still welcome. But she hated herself for needing their comfort, and she resolved that she would need it no longer. Her resolve was hardened still further by an interview with a murderer that she happened to see on television. Before, she would have changed the channel, but now she forced herself to watch in a state of disgusted fascination. The murderer was a truck driver with a jowly face and placid, quizzical eyes. He spoke of his killings boastfully but affectlessly. He prided himself on the tricks he played on the police, confessing and recanting, or confessing to crimes he had not committed, in order to expose the justice system for the fraud it was. The sight of the murderer, and the sound of his calm, even voice as he spoke of the horrors he had inflicted on women, excited a feeling of loathing in Angela. For a period of years he had gone from town to town, taking women from their homes, or snatching them from phone booths, or picking them up in bars. He was especially brutal with the ones he picked up in bars, he said, because they should have known better. The interviewer asked if he felt any remorse, and the murderer answered that sometimes he felt bad that some of the women were dead, but he could not let himself think about it much. The story of the world was that hatred engendered hatred, and Angela believed the reason she was still alone was because she did not want to be a part of this story, or any of the stories that went along with it, but maybe in the long run she would find that she was able to rise above loathing and feel a contemptuous gratitude to these men, these murderers, for spurring her to be proud of her chosen reclusion, hard in her lonely strength.

Mira glimpsed Angela on the mall at lunchtime, walking with another woman, then settling to eat. The other woman looked like a paler, heavier version of Angela. She must have been Angela's sister, and as Mira watched them she felt a pang of pity for the heavy, pale, plain woman sitting with Angela, pity for having the blessed Angela as her sister. Mira imagined the lifetime of unflattering comparisons such a circumstance would lead to. The afternoon sun was bright, and Angela, smiling and laughing, was wearing designer sunglasses, but her sister was squinting into the daylight, eyes unguarded, contemplatively chewing a bite of a croissant sandwich. It was immediately clear how her sister could make Angela laugh, and it was clear that this ability required no effort on her sister's part. Her sister enjoyed remaining stoically straight-faced, Mira saw, while Angela laughed at her dry observations of the world. Angela offered her sister a stalk of celery, but the offer was refused, and the sister looked away, distance coming into her face, her full cheeks stretching as she turned her head. It was like a little ballet, a stylized pas de deux, thought Mira, an anatomy in mime of a whole history of offering and refusal, advance and withdrawal. She could see Angela's need of the sister; she could see how the sister accepted this need but still drew back, and she could see how Angela hardened, without disowning her need. Then she could see how the whole process started over and repeated itself. The sound of Angela's laughter carried across the mall, so carefree that it bore no traces of recent upset—seemed a laugh always ready, imperturbable, but more expressive of sureness in oneself than of pleasure taken in others. This is my sister, Mira imagined Angela saying, she's the funny one.

At dusk Angela stood at the kitchen sink, carefully and slowly washing a week's accumulation of dishes, when she saw a boy in the street below wearing a white nightshirt and staring upward. Despite having vowed to renounce fear, she might well have felt a rush of fear all the same if she had not seen at once that he was looking not at her, but past her, up toward the roof of the building. Her third-floor window overlooked a shadowed alleyway, and it was unusual to see anyone passing there, and even more unusual to see, in the midst of the city and in the depth of a cold spring, a nightshirted boy who, with his sharp eyes and delicately flared nostrils and high cheekbones, looked as if he had escaped from an English country manor house. He stood stock still in an attitude of frozen concentration. In the briefest second that she glimpsed the boy's face, she saw an intense expression of compliance in it, so that it was clear that the boy was exchanging a look with someone who was looking back at him from above. She thought she saw the boy nod in the instant she looked at him: a brisk, quick nod, barely perceptible, not of permission but of assent, as if he were receiving and accepting some dark command. Too much steam heat was hissing through the clanging radiators of Angela's apartment, so she had cranked open the casement window to let in a little cold air as she did the dishes, and because the window had no screen, she could easily extend her head through it; instinctively she did so, leaned forward out the window, and peered up at the roof to catch a glimpse of whom the boy was looking at, but a twilight glare, bleached and dappled with glimmering black dots, obstructed her view, and when she looked back down at the street, she saw that the figure was moving quickly away. As the figure strode from the effulgent shadow of the alley, rounding a corner into the pale light of the street, Angela saw that it was not a boy at all, but a man, and she saw that what he was wearing was not a nightshirt but a long gray overcoat.

Mira agreed to see Justin one last time, just to confirm her foreboding. On the way to the restaurant, he suddenly pointed gleefully at the car in the street ahead of them. The car sported a vanity license plate, ELVISFAN, and a bumper sticker that said, "God is Pro-Life," but the bumper sticker and the license plate were not the source of his glee. The car contained two passengers, a man wearing a business suit and a turban in the driver's seat, and a woman in an elaborate sari sitting behind him in the back seat. Mira and Justin could see only the backs of their heads, the man's regal headpiece, the woman's shrouded head. Justin laughed and repeated, "Check it out, check it out!" He was clearly delighted by this spectacle of subordination. Abruptly, he grew more serious and said, "Last time I looked I thought it was already going on the twenty-first century."

This time, Justin seemed more consistently self-assured than he had seemed on their previous meetings, but he still shuttled between the dizzyingly bipolar characteristics of the emotionally backward, the bashfulness and the insouciance, the sullenness and the unpredictable, fickle exuberance. As before, he would indulge in occasional half-crazed monologues on arcane topics and then fall silent with an air of stagnating embarrassment. Mira smiled at him across the dinner table with waspish, pseudo-benevolent forbearance in order to encourage this embarrassment, which appeared to have the effect of warding off, or at least postponing, the monologues. Because she knew she would not see him again, she felt expansive and lighthearted as she gazed at his wide, chary face with his too-small eyeglasses, their arms straining to the sides across his temples in their effort to encompass the breadth of the face, to reach the big, far-off ears.

Unexpectedly, Justin embarked on a new monologue that occupied the rest of the meal, souring Mira's mood. If you don't have theories about things, Justin believed, then you are leading the life of the blind, so Justin made it a point of honor to have a theory about everything, and one of these theories was that you should not talk about relationships right away in a relationship but if you do not talk about relationships early on in a relationship, it is a very bad sign for that relationship. He wanted her to know of his past, but she could not know of this unless she understood that he still loved the few women he had loved in his life. He hoped this would not disturb her. He still loved them, and he knew that he would always love them, and he was glad of this, for he believed, he sincerely believed, that if it is the case that love, real love, can die, then it must be the case that life has no meaning. His mother had often spoken, he told Mira, of a man, another man she might have married if she had not married his father. She had once loved this man, and she spoke of him often with a quality of humorous, teasing regret to get a fond rise out of his father; then, after Justin's father died, his mother had met this man again, and she realized after all those years what she had really known all along, that she no longer loved the man. When she told Justin this, she had expected him to feel some kind of relief, as if the memory of his father were being properly honored, but instead he had felt furiously disappointed, disillusioned, enraged. If his mother could stop loving this other man, then how could he be sure she would never forget his father, or even that she would always love Justin himself? If love had an end, how could one be sure of anything?

"I'm going to tell you something I think you already know," said Justin. "*No two people are ever in the same place at the same time.* And what that means is, is that in any relationship, one person is always ahead of the other. They can be ahead in different ways, and at different times, and maybe one's ahead in some ways and the other's ahead in other ways, and it, like, switches around and stuff, but one is always ahead of the other, no matter what. I'm not telling you anything you don't know already. I know you know it. I know from stuff you've said, because even though we're just starting we have this simpatico thing going and we basically think alike, and in any *human* relationship, and I'm talking *human* here, not just romantic-type stuff, but every time you're with anyone else, it's basically about giving and getting, giving and getting, and it's basically this back-and-forth thing, either you're giving and they're getting or they're giving and you're getting, and for there to be something really mutual there, to be giving and getting *at the same time,* is just very very very rare, and when that happens you should never ever let it go because if it was real in the first place, and I mean really real, then it's always going to be still there. I just want you to know this up-front so there are no surprises later; I'm just a really up-front kind of person."

He began a detailed history of several past relationships, breaking off from time to time to ask if he was boring her. When she answered that she was not bored, she thought she was being truthful, since she was conscious only of growing increasingly scared, but she realized with a dulled sensation of slow discovery in the course of the monologue that fear and boredom were not incompatible states. She tuned out for only a moment to consider whether it would be easier to excuse herself and flee or to wait out the rest of the evening in careful silence. When she rejoined his discourse, he had somehow moved from the subject of his old girlfriends to that of popular misconceptions about leprosy. She interrupted gently to tell him she was not feeling well and wanted to leave. He looked thunderstruck for a second, then he neatly folded his napkin and placed it on the table in front of him. On the way to the car, he said nothing, but he walked so fast that she had to break into a run every few steps to keep up with him. She had wondered earlier why he had parked on the same street where he had parked last time they had gone out, even though the restaurant they had gone to then had been several blocks in the opposite direction, but she had concluded that this reflected the staunch commitment to habitual behavior that marked a certain type of obsessive personality. Now, though, as he opened the door of the car for her, Mira noticed that he was looking with steely directness at a window, a particular window, in a row of apartments down the block. As Mira got into the car, she followed with her own eyes the direction of his gaze, and she saw what she thought was the silhouette of a figure moving quickly past the window. Then he slammed the door.

All that week the pattern had been the same, a sharp, unexpected thought registering in Angela's brain just at the decisive moment of sleep's onset, as if its prevention were an urgent need. Usually the thoughts were trivial, their ability to wake her mysterious, and Angela sat up in bed wondering at her continued failure to achieve the condition of sleep, a state formerly accessible without effort, without the thought of achievement, or of failure, or, for that matter, of success.

This time the thought that jolted her—intrusive, violent, stealing into her mind like a mugger lurching into a dark alleyway, shocking her awake—was surprising not for its insignificance but for its magnitude. What if it *was* someone she knew—someone she had dated, or even someone who worked in her office? Suddenly she recalled the face of the last man she'd gone out with. His face had been sharp-jawed, the features severe, and his skin was pale, and cast in a delicate shade of pink, the color of blush wine. The color of the skin looked like a blush, as if he had just been fondly teased and was mildly, pleasantly embarrassed, but the blush never went away, and it gave him an aura of vulnerability despite the hardness and sharpness of his features. Around the edges of his face, at the line of his straw-colored hair, was a thin border of skin of a different color, barely perceptible between the red and the straw, closer to the more ordinary tones of white skin, and this border made it appear as if he were wearing a mask, and the mask was a blush.

It had been nearly three months ago that they had gone out, and she had seen him only a few times, but she had slept with him the last time, and then they had never called each other again. They had not called each other even though, as they were parting after sex, they had each whispered that they would call the other the next day. The very fact of whispering had implied a newfound intimacy. But the next day had passed with no call, and then a week went by, and a month, and with time she knew more completely what she had already known then, even as she had whispered in the darkness to the man she had just slept with, that the intimacy was not real.

She tried to recall the man's voice, so she could imagine his voice speaking those awful words, but she could bring to mind only the way his voice sounded when he whispered. Then she remembered that she had seen him, or someone who might have been him, in the food court of a mall a few weeks before. She had been with her sister, and he had been with an overweight woman who had a star-shaped bruise on the back of one of her hands and was ravenously eating a pizza. Angela said nothing about it to her sister, but she imagined a flicker of recognition and rebuke in the man's eyes. If it had been him, he had changed in the short time since they had dated. He was wearing thick eyeglasses and a gaudy earring, and a thick clump of hair sprouted from his chin and pointed down at the ground. These features were new, but even from a distance and under the mall's artificial light, she could see that the color of his skin was the same and the border at the hair that made it look like a mask was the same. Still, she had concluded that it was not him, but as she and her sister were leaving the food court to go on with their shopping, she had seen the man slowly begin to scratch his forehead with a deliberately extended middle finger as he seemed to gaze at her, a gesture of ambiguous contempt. She had hurried her sister away, and in spite of a moment's alarm, she had not spoken of the incident.

Some of the alarm she felt then returned as she remembered the event. Perhaps the man had felt betrayed by her failure to call him after they had, if not achieved genuine intimacy, at least approached it, achieved the semblance of intimacy, done what was necessary to achieve it. But why then did she not feel, in turn, betrayed by his failure to call her? If he had done so, she would have seen him again. She would probably even have slept with him again. She had not been attracted to him, but she had slept with him because of his gentleness, and because she did not want to hurt him by refusing him. She herself had lived with her own beauty for all of her thirty-one years, and creeps who had seemed nice at first always claimed it was her beauty that drove them to creepiness, so she knew how unexpectedly gentleness could depart. As she'd gazed at his body, she experienced a distant, vague stirring of repulsion. The skin of his chest was very white, marked by many imperfections, and in the hollow of his chest were several ruddy creases, like the grainy wrinkles in sand that an ebbed tide leaves behind on a beach. She resisted the feeling of repulsion, and the meeting of her receding, muted disgust with his eager sweetness produced a rush of tenderness in her that subsided as she undressed. He looked and looked at her after she undressed, and she could see the emotion in his blush-red face, but she could not tell if he was moved by her beauty itself, or by her willingness to give herself to him. "I knew you were beautiful," he said; and because of the way he emphasized the word "knew," she had thought he was going to finish the sentence by saying something like, "But I never dreamed you were *this* beautiful." He did not complete the thought in this manner, though. Instead, he had whispered, "I am seeing you in a different way"; and she had replied, also in a whisper, "I'm still what I was."

* * *

Justin left three messages on Mira's answering machine over the next two days. The first was solicitous, wondering how she was. The second contained a subdued note of sarcasm, observing that if she was out, her sudden illness could not have been serious, since she was already back to work. The third was direct: "Look, I'm not the kind of person who's very good at playing games, okay," said his voice, muffled by the bad sound quality of the overused tape. "So if you're not going to call could you kind of let me know instead of just leaving me totally hanging?" Mira was stunned: He wanted her to call to tell him she was not going to call. It was some completely new form of passive-aggression, yet to be catalogued by the experts. She was listening to his message again in continued disbelief when the phone rang. It was Justin.

"So were you just not going to call or what?" he asked.

"I don't know," said Mira. "I don't respond well to hostility, I know that much."

"Are we just, like, *off* or what?"

"I think," answered Mira, "we are just, like, off."

"Can I ask why?"

"I don't know if I can give you answers. I don't know if I really want to get into it."

"Oh, well, that's just great. Isn't that just typical. I mean, you women: You're always, like, 'Men just can't communicate and it's just so terrible and blah blah blah blah blah,' and so here I am trying to communicate and look who's the one that doesn't want to communicate."

"I don't really know," said Mira, "if I would call this trying to communicate."

"I'm sorry. Okay? I'm sorry." Mira heard him taking deep breaths. Then she heard him resume in the voice she recognized, his earnest, sad-sack voice, only now she saw that this voice, too, was filled with rage, a kind of rage so perpetual that it goes underground, lurks there, learns to imitate reason, waits to break out. "I really am sorry," he said. "Can I just ask you what it was that I did wrong? I think it would really help me to know. I mean, for the future."

The resort to cliché, Mira speculated, might prove to be the quickest way out. "It's not you," she said. "It's me."

"Because everything seemed to be going good, you know, and it really seemed to be building, and like developing, and I was getting to know you, and you were getting to know me, and you really seemed to like me."

"I'm sorry," said Mira.

"So if I could just know what I did that was wrong."

"It wasn't anything you did." Mira decided she would try one last gambit. It was a risk, she knew, for although most maniacs do not recognize their own thoughts when those thoughts return in altered form to beset them, some maniacs do. "Let's just put it this way," she said. "In any relationship one person is always ahead of the other; so why don't we just say you're ahead of me, and leave it at that?"

She knew the risk had not paid off and the silence that followed was an angry silence when he said in a withering voice, "I see." Then he went on: "Well, I guess the shoe is really on the other foot now, isn't it? All that talk, all that talk about men not being able to commit, but when it comes right down to it, we can see exactly what that's all about, now, can't we, and you know what it's all about? *Hypocrisy,* that's what. Hypocrisy, pure and simple."

"Please, Justin," she said wearily. "I never said men can't commit. Why don't we just say goodbye now? I don't want to have to hang up on you."

"But you will have to," said Justin. "Okay? You'll have to. Because I'm not going to. So go ahead. Hang up. Hang up. Go ahead. Turn the last screw."

Mira waited only a second before she hung up.

The hard rain that had fallen all day turned suddenly to snow at nightfall, big wet flakes wafting downward slowly. Driving to the store for milk and cranberry juice, Angela saw a handicapped man crossing a street. One of his legs listed wildly to the side as he walked, the sign of some neuromuscular affliction, and Angela, stopped at a light, regarded him in the moment before she drove on with a combination of pity and gratitude. Imagine living in such a condition, where the simplest task demanded the most daunting work, where every few steps required the effort it took to execute a gauntlet. She took the man's laborious trek across the street as a reminder to appreciate her own comparative good fortune. On the way back from the store, she saw the same man standing a little farther on from where he had been, in the middle of the street, in Angela's lane of traffic. Although it was dark, the snow lit the night, so she saw him in plenty of time to stop, but the road was slick, and as she braked she felt the car slide before it came to a stop. Her heart quickened. She shouted to the man, and as he turned in an antic pirouette to face her, she realized that he was not handicapped at all, but drunk. His tongue was sticking out, gathering snowflakes, and there was a look of scorn in his face, of intoxicated derision. He smiled at Angela malevolently. In his smile Angela saw the drunkard's recognition, which she knew from having shared it when she herself was drunk, that everything is absurd except oneself, and oneself is kept from absurdity only by virtue of being a self, a self that, distilled, is somehow still one's own. All these separate entities, a multitude of oblivious monads, each subscribing to the absurdity of all the others, and the essential rightness of itself: What kind of a world was that? She shouted to the drunk man that he was standing in the middle of the street, and he said it was all right because there was nobody else there. "But I am," Angela cried, "I'm here."

"Keep going," said the man, "and get gone, and then you won't be."

Mira avoided going into Maureen Hackett's cubicle at work because its aura of smug domesticity felt oppressive to her. Maureen Hackett's desk was cluttered with plastic stand-up frames containing photographs of her husband and her two children in a variety of dispositions, from the diurnal pleasure of ordinary life to the posed ritual of special occasions. Alongside numerous posted slogans, comical philosophies of the workplace, more photographs were pinned to the industrial-tweed covering of the cubicle's walls, kids blowing out birthday candles, family groupings in exotic vacation spots, forthright displays of the conspicuous consumption of happiness. The photographs gave Mira the willies. Though she did not doubt that the happiness they chronicled was real, the amplitude of its evidence made her think of it as a greedy happiness. The whole family was cursed with big-toothed smiles that showed their bright, pink gums. Their gaping leers of happiness in the photographs spoke to Mira of unquenchable voracity, insatiability, as if they wanted, the lot of them, to hoard happiness, to squirrel it away, even if it meant others might not get any; as if they would not hesitate to lap up, hoggishly, as much as they could of this scant resource. Mira had to get Maureen Hackett's approval of a memo before she sent it out, and as she signed off, Maureen murmured the lowdown on Angela. The package was not all there was to it, it turned out. There had also been phone calls, and Angela felt she was being followed, watched. Once she thought she had been followed in the parking garage.

It was Justin, Mira knew immediately; it was Justin who was stalking Angela.

Once she had articulated this to herself, the wonder was only that she had not done so sooner. It made cold, lean sense. It fell into place with sharp precision, like the clean-edged segments of a thousand-piece jigsaw puzzle. The varieties of a family's happiness can be verified because there are photographs, millions upon millions, to commemorate every one of them; the fact that no pictures document the grubby thoughts of lone, rapacious, antisocial men who spend their time in festering solitude hatching insidious plots does not refute the certitude with which those, too, can be known. They had answered the same ad, Mira and Angela; he said he had dated someone else from her office. Angela had seen him once, twice, maybe three times, and then she had refused to see him again, and he had felt this as a profound rebuke to him. Mira knew that Justin was the kind of man who would interpret Angela's beauty as a form of arrogance, and he would see her rejection of him, because of her beauty, as a crime of the spirit, as evidence that she, like other beautiful people, felt herself exempt from the decencies of ordinary life. He had wanted to know what he had done, but there had been nothing that he had done, and once he understood this, then he knew that if it was not anything he had done then it was he, *he himself,* that was the problem. It was not his outward action, but his inner essence, and this could only be overwhelming to him because he had to know it meant he could never be acceptable, for one can perhaps change one's action, but one can never alter one's essence.

The hurt was as profound as his very self was now felt to be immutable, but he would never be able to let go of it, to put it aside as he would surely see himself as having been put aside.

No: She had hurt him, and now he would have to hurt her. It was a matter of giving and getting.

So he went on dates with other women, and he parked on her street each time, and glared up at her window, thinking to parade these other women before her, to show her there were women who did not find him profoundly, immovably unacceptable, to show her he had moved on but that she would never in turn be able to elude him. He called her with tidings of assault. He followed her, he sent her horrors through the mail. Maureen Hackett spoke of these things quietly. In no sense did she appear to be afraid for herself. Her tone was one of measured concern, tinged with gossip's lurid curiosity. There was no telling, she said, where it would end.

At a movie with her sister, Angela, bored with the film, slipped away into the lobby. She whispered to her sister that she would be right back. Absorbed in the film, her sister looked startled, and in the second it took her to comprehend that Angela had said something ordinary, not something startling, her hand darted out protectively for Angela's hand; after that second passed, she drew her hand away and nodded to acknowledge her understanding. The lobby was empty, the hulking computer games blinking in silent, colorful disbelief. Ushers pushed popcorn-devouring sweepers across the hard carpets. All of the many films at the multiplex were underway in their separate enclaves, and any stray patrons who wandered out into the lobby were suspect because their presence there signified discontent. It meant they were constitutionally unhappy, dissatisfied with the film, unable to accept direct pleasures or to defer random needs. These patrons clearly sensed that whatever lack their presence exposed lay within themselves, for they shuffled through the lobby with their heads bowed in shame. Angela refused to play that game. She stepped up to the candy counter and voiced her request loudly. Her sister had reached for her hand; then, as she had drawn her hand away, she had done so with what seemed to Angela a quality of shamed recognition of something that was deep, full, but evanescent, too small to be spoken of. The older, Angela had been her sister's guardian when they were children.

She remembered pushing her sister in a swing, how her cries of joy could so easily be heard as screams of fear. The moment of shamed recognition, Angela saw, implied a feeling of rueful commiseration in her sister, kept from pity by force of will, that her sister thought she should resist. Now, between them, Angela's safety might always be at issue. She wondered if she were more vulnerable to the assaults of unknown men or to the consolations of those who loved her. Her sister did not look away from the film when Angela returned to her seat.

Mira could not find Angela's address in the company directory, and her telephone number was unlisted, but even though she had never been to his apartment, she knew where Justin lived. His building was wedged into a busy corner, a corner in the city where five streets came together in a treacherous intersection. The building, with brick the color of an underripe peach's flesh, was shaped like a narrow-tipped triangle in order to fit into the severe bight of the street corner. There was a drugstore on the first floor, and there were apartments on the second and third floors. In the vestibule Mira scanned a row of six mail slots, doors of tarnished copper with circular, barred clefts in each door showing what the little chambers held. None of the slots was locked, and Justin's yawned open carelessly. Such indifference to security did not surprise Mira. She knew that intruders into the lives of others seldom consider their own susceptibility until the moment of their victimization, when their sense of indignity is boundless. As Mira shuffled through Justin's mail, she imagined his outrage with amused satisfaction. Standing there in the open, she smiled, flouting secrecy, adopting an artless, genial watchfulness as an antidote to caution. Anyone who happened upon her would never mistake her for a trespasser.

Mira did not know which window was Justin's. She did not know which floor he lived on. From her car, parked on a near side street that afforded a wide view, she scanned the rows of windows. Some of the windows had latticework covering them, imitating a European style. Others had rusted air conditioners hanging from them like guts protruding from under the shirts of beer-bellied men. In one of the windows, only her face visible, stood a woman with a kerchief tied around her head. She was looking downward, pensively content, engaged in an unseen task, chopping vegetables or preparing meat. In another window that was covered by a translucent shade, a light blinked on and off at irregular, convulsive intervals. Mira looked at the letter she had kept out of Justin's mailbox. It had a return address from the weekly paper where his personal ad had appeared. It was only an instrument; she had no curiosity about the envelope's contents. That was no more the point than it was the point that the task at hand was a test of her courage. She would leave ideas about bravery to the invaders, the pursuers, the warriors of infringement. They were the ones who thrived on such ideas. She was interested only in justice.

Just when she was starting to think her mission would be fruitless, Justin appeared on the stoop, blinking under the dim light of a street lamp. He was carrying a satchel, its leather scarred and bruised. He hoisted its long strap over his shoulder. He walked in Mira's direction, passed very near her car, and got into his own car parked farther down the street. She followed him downtown to a street near the city market. He parked and got out of the car, and pulled on the door's handle to make sure it was locked. After he had started away, he suddenly turned back and pulled on the handle again, to make doubly sure. What fortune was he taking such trouble to protect? Mira watched him cross the street and disappear into a storefront with big glass panels painted black and with three white letters, A-I-M, painted across the door. She did not know what the letters stood for. Mira peered into the back seat of Justin's car. A rumpled coat and scarf, a thick, dog-eared map that bore traces of the frustration of someone who had tried to refold it, a lone tennis shoe. She lifted one of the car's windshield wipers. It felt brittle and fragile, like a skeleton's arm. She placed the letter under the windshield wiper. At first he would think it was a parking ticket. When he had come so close to her car, she had felt something rise in her, a thrill, something she felt that she wanted at once to resist and to follow to its apex. If he had chanced to notice her, she would have looked back at him evenly, without defiance. Standing next to his car, she tried to feel what she knew he would feel, the clandestine tremor of nearness. But she could not incite this feeling in herself, it was nothing she could share.

The first call came that night. No speech: just a long, crackling silence, meant to threaten.

Angela had stopped seeing a man she'd loved many years ago after she discovered he kept copies of his letters to her. He wrote beautiful letters to her, and she loved them. Then one day he told her he had been unsure of the date of something so he had looked it up in the letters. "But how could you?" she asked. "*I have them.*" "I keep copies," he answered. "You keep copies of your letters to me?" "Oh, I keep copies of all my letters." Some weeks later she broke off with him. The letters reminded her of him. Like him, they were usually matter-of-fact but sometimes took sudden flights into lyricism. They had made her believe he had given her something, but he had not. He had kept it.

From the bar, Mira watched Justin and another woman at a table across the restaurant. The place was a big, open room, lit dimly, and Mira sat at the far end of the bar so she could face their table. She wanted to be seen, but Justin sat with his back to her. He had parked in the same place, on the same street, looked up, Mira was certain, at the same window. It was a cycle, and this was another round of the cycle. The woman who was with him had black hair and thick black eyebrows. She did not appear to be uncomfortable, but that was because she could not know. Sometimes Justin leaned toward her across the table, grimly attentive, but most of the time he leaned back and looked distractedly around the room. Their interaction had the air of an unsuccessful audition. The cycle would go on and on until Mira did what was needed to end it. She drank two scotches as they finished their dinner. As they were leaving, she walked right in front of them, and looked into Justin's face, unblinking, but if he noticed her, he did not react.

When the phone rang that night, she listened to the silence for only a moment before she spoke. "Do you think I don't know who this is?" she said. "I know exactly what you're doing. But it's going to stop now. Do you understand me? You're going to leave me alone, and you're going to leave her alone. Do you hear me? *Just leave her the fuck alone.*" She had managed to speak calmly, but when she hung up she was overpowered by a rush of deferred feeling. She would change her phone number the next day. The decision to protect yourself, once taken, is easy enough to put into practice.

They met in the women's room. Angela remembered Mira dimly. It had been a long time since they had been introduced. She said it was good to see her again. Angela was about to leave when Mira stopped her. She said she was sorry, but there was something else she had to talk to her about. There was a man, a certain man. Did she know him?

Mira said his name. Angela's face emptied for a minute, then it filled up again. She had been afraid that this stranger was going to offer her more heedless consolation, but now she understood. She bit her lip and looked away for a moment. The row of mirrors reflected them: two women, standing side by side. She nodded.

Mira thought she'd heard something outside the door. She waited in the hallway. She saw that she had forgotten to draw the curtains. That meant she might also have forgotten to lock the door. Midnight blustered, cold, outside the cold, exposed windowpane. For long minutes the doorknob did not turn. There was nobody there. She knew she was alone. She was in a specific place, but she imagined abstract distance. In her mind she saw gray hills rolling in a vast mist. It was pain that gave rise to understanding. You do not feel the need to understand until after your fullest want has been denied. If that was true, then maybe something, too, would bloom from this fear. She stood fast in the hallway. Light came in the window. She might have felt revealed, but her solitude seemed secure. Her hand went to her mouth.

ANTONYA NELSON

Palisades

I am a good confidante, and I'll tell you the secret: never offer advice, merely listen. You may repeat, ratify, sympathize, query, even divulge a tidbit or two, whip up the objective correlative, but you must *never* give an opinion about what your friend should do next. Never, never, never.

The summer of my separation from my husband, I became the confidante of two different people, Sarah Siebert and Joel Metcalf. I met them at a Spanish language performance of *Much Ado About Nothing*, the translation of which was *A Lot of Noise for No Reason;* the two of them zoomed in on me as if my skepticism were emitting sonar signals. Sarah was a reporter for the tiny local newspaper that Joel edited. In fact, they were the paper's sole employees: owners, distributors, founders, writers, et cetera. It came out once a week; the two of them covered every event in little Palisades, Colorado. They came at me from opposite sides of the park, sniffing through the crowd until I'd been found. I was accustomed, those early days there that summer, to being observed. The town would have to learn how to befriend tourists, I thought, how to lure rather than frighten. Palisades was like someone desperate for a date, that hardly veiled hunger and awkward leer in its face.

I suppose the town had not changed much since I'd first seen it, twenty years ago, with my parents. I'd come back because I held the memory like a beloved locket, inside of which was preserved a tiny distorted image of happiness. For five years, at the height of my parents' best time together, we had summered in Palisades. There was a bar called Fool's Paradise, still in operation, where they'd posed for a legendary family picture, my father squashing my mother in his arms like a duffel, as if to throw her onto the back of a truck, her shirt rucked up, sandal flying from her foot, breasts hoisted under his chin, where my father showed his smirking teeth as if just about to take a bite out of that plump flesh. My parents look slapdash, negligent, debauched, certainly not like parents. Where was I, their little girl, while they were out drinking and yukking it up? Roaming the woods, I thought, a habit I hadn't yet forsaken.

"This is awful," said the tall woman who'd approached on my left. But she seemed pleased by the performance's awfulness, as I was. Sometimes bad art made me laugh, other times it made me want to throw a tantrum, as if it implicated me, as if I, too, were bad art.

"Terrible," I agreed enthusiastically. On my chest I wore my six-week-old daughter, whose dusk fussiness had sent me walking the dirt roads of Palisades. We were joined by another cheerfully irritated presence. My first impression of Joel Metcalf and Sarah Siebert was that they were longtime rivals, competing for something, like siblings for a parent's love. But it turned out they were married to each other, a good fifteen years older than I—the age of my husband, more or less. Their marriage, like all marriages longer lived than my own, seduced me with its caginess. They sniped, they baited, they did not flinch. Their humor was bitter. They seemed worn out and stringy like the old animals at the zoo, the mangy lion, the weary wolf. Many avoid the zoo lifers; you might prefer the young animals, the ones who don't yet know precisely what they're in for and keep bounding to the fence. But I was attracted to jadedness, preferring to think of it as wisdom. Precocious, I had always looked to my elders for instruction.

They were overly glad about my Ph.D.—Palisades was a town about to explode into a fancy resort, full of real estate agents and skiers, developers and bimbos, everyone with what Sarah called well-defined "thigh meat." Joel made a circle with his finger near his ear to indicate general dingbattiness, widespread unworth. *A Lot of Noise for No Reason* was put on, he told me, as a nod to the Mexican construction workers who, during the day, laid brick and blew up tree stumps, while at night had nothing to do but drink and graffiti the alley dumpsters. But nobody I noticed at the performance was speaking Spanish except the actors themselves.

"We're from New York," Sarah informed me.

"L.A.," I responded. The two snotty coasts, represented here in an alpine paradise, a dearth of intellect. That was okay by me; I was tired of talking to people intelligently. My husband had sent me away for the summer. "I *have* to be alone," he'd pleaded. He forgot to eat, often did not sleep, could most frequently be found staring at his own thoughts. Or he cried, which made me helpless with fear. He flexed his thick hands and boxed his own ears, a convincing piece of anguish. Other times, he was simply indifferent, living in the same house like an intolerant tenant, besieged by rather than bonded to his baby. So I took the motherhood leave my office offered and returned to the site of my finest childhood memories. My feelings were hurt; I claimed my daughter's hurt feelings along with my own since she was too small to suffer them. How could he bear to do without her? I wondered as I stroked the hot moist lump of her on my chest. It was not to be understood.

"I walk," I told Joel and Sarah when they asked what I did with myself all day. "I walk everywhere." As a child, I had followed on my parents' expeditions in search of butterflies in the Palisades mountains. My parents adopted hobbies together, and it was in this spirit that I'd suggested to my husband that he come with us, me and his new daughter, to collect flowers or observe birds, camp even. He'd looked at me scornfully, pitying my Pollyanna tactics. He sneered at the photo of my parents, the sexy way my father strong-armed my mother aloft, the nearly palpable swear-word between my father's teeth, just above those succulent breasts. It was true that having a baby had made me soft; I was not the cynic he'd married, not the cigarette-smoking anorexic anymore, my frenetic prettiness lost along the way to a slack healthiness my husband had encouraged by being older, by adoring me, by broadcasting his good luck. His sudden estrangement was like a slap; I appraised my lapsed beauty in mirrors with a fastidiousness I thought I had safely put aside after marriage. My husband had grown both restless and bored, trapped by the very domesticity he'd once claimed to have sought. I counted on him to know what we were doing, and now he was at sea, floundering, sending me on a summer holiday as if to spare me the details. I rented my cabin by the week, set up Lily's portable crib beside my single bunk, and waited to be summoned home. When I lay awake at night, I listened to a silence so profound I could detect my own idling blood.

By day I walked. Hence began my intimacies with Sarah Siebert and Joel Metcalf, avid walkers themselves. The nervous energy of

New York was no match for placid Palisades; they had navigated every trail, taken in every waterfall, stood on every precipice, crawled into every cave—in short, knew everything there was to know. Each had a preferred route, and I alternated days in their company, Monday, Thursday, Saturday with Joel, Tuesday, Friday, Sunday with Sarah, Wednesday alone because that was when their newspaper came out.

On Wednesday they also met their lovers.

Joel drove to Durango, eighty-five miles southwest of Palisades, to get the paper printed. His lover was a degenerate boy named Seth, a pierced, tattooed felon who had a master key to the Fort Lewis College dorms and lived like a scavenging animal pest on the campus. Seth the Rat, I thought of him. They coupled on the bare mattresses of dorm rooms, snacked from candy machines, eluded security. "I haven't been so thrilled since seventh grade shoplifting," Joel told me giddily. "There's not one redeeming part to it. He's the baddest bad boy I ever met." I felt sure the rat was taking money from Joel, but Joel's pleasure in the shabbiness prevented me from feeling sorry for him. He seemed to have erected a force field around his heart, made himself bulletproof by a tough stance, by an attitude of doomed expectation. He knew it could not end well, this tryst, but he seemed to look forward to the fallout. He was in it purely for the sex, and it was purely nasty sex.

"Look at this," he instructed one day, lifting his shirt to show me a puckered red scratch the length of his rib cage.

"Good God! What is he, a pirate?"

"Bedspring," Joel answered proudly, appreciating his wound. "There was blood all over the mattress."

You wanted to spread news like this; I wanted to use it to illustrate to my husband that I was still interesting, having found the most outrageous characters in all of Palisades to hang around with. We could have a baby, these stories would indicate, and still be in the vicinity of the cutting edge. But my husband never answered the phone. He'd changed our outgoing message on the machine, giving my Colorado number to anyone looking to find me.

Joel Metcalf was endearingly neurotic, compulsive, fearful, paranoid. He was terrified of AIDS and had insisted that the boy in Durango go in for a blood test. "But I'm such an *idiot*," he wailed as we trudged through the beautiful aspens, whose trunks watched us with their black-lined blind eyes, whose shaking leaves sounded like maracas. "I made him get a test *after* we'd already hooked up."

"'Hooked up'?" I said. "Is that a euphemism? I feel very out of touch."

"Fucked," he clarified. "But what kind of moron waits until *after*?"

"Most morons," I assured him.

"Fortunately, he was clean, but what if he'd been HIV-positive? I just can't get over how insistent passion is, how irresponsible it makes you. I mean, I'm not a careless guy. You've seen me—I double-tie my laces so I won't trip. I've got a house full of safety devices because I can imagine every conceivable disaster, you can't believe my imagination, smoke alarm, radon detector, lead monitor, a cellular phone in the car, vitamin pills, I've been told I'm a hypochondriac, I get to the airport two hours before all of my flights, and yet I was willing to just forget all of that, completely go against character, for a moment of passion."

"It defies explanation," I said. It did, really. It was spectacularly desperate.

He was shaking his head at himself, but I suspected he was a little proud of his indiscretion. Didn't it prove he was spontaneous? Brave? Unpredictable? Capable of surprising himself? Maybe the ability to surprise oneself was the most necessary of tools as time marched on. I posited this to Joel, who nodded thoughtfully. Every now and then I said something that made him glad I was his companion, his confidante.

"She's so quiet," he said of Lily, offering a rare acknowledgment of my ever-present burden.

"She doesn't need much," I said, kissing the fuzz of her scalp.

"Ha," said my skeptical friend, he of the wretched, degrading needs.

Unlike her husband, Sarah was a romantic. Her lover lived in Palisades, was married himself, an alleged friend of the family, and had had a heart attack not so long ago. "April fifteenth," Sarah said, "just after we'd made love."

"That's Lily's birthday," I commented. My husband had been

waiting in line at the post office when she was born, our taxes in his hands while I had been stoically turning down painkillers, pushing Lily through a ridiculously inadequate aperture into the world. Here in Palisades, Sarah had been frantically driving through a spring blizzard, her lover breathing heavily in the seat beside her, on their way to the local health clinic, him praying, her inventing a story to tell the doctor on call.

"It was absurd," she said as we walked together in the July sun, "me giving him just the simplest plot line. 'You were hiking, and you suddenly had chest pain, and then, by coincidence, I came along and helped you down the mountain.' It was absurd and shameful, at the same time, me worried about getting caught, about losing him because of exposure. It was only after the firemen drove him off to Durango in the ambulance that I realized he might die. It's funny how the mind gets so sidetracked. I'm the one who told his wife," she added a moment later. "She's beautiful, but deaf. They haven't had sex in years."

"Years?"

"Well, maybe now and then they sleep together, like on their anniversary."

Once upon a time, statistics like this would have appalled me; but by then I'd been married four years, and although we made love eighty-two times our first year together, for the last sixth months my husband had not touched me. I asked Sarah, "Why do they stay married?"

"Why do most people? They have kids, it's comfortable, they make a good partnership."

A partnership. Comfort. This was why Joel and Sarah stayed together, I thought. They had their newspaper to run; they liked each other's company. Sarah needed Joel's biting intelligence; Joel needed Sarah's conventional presentability. Where would either be without the other? That night I sort of admired my husband's reluctance to acquiesce to a business arrangement, to get too terribly comfortable, to worry about presentability. He'd claimed he wanted to continue choosing our relationship. "I don't want to just love you," he'd said. "I want to be *in* love with you." Still, he baffled me. I loved Lily to distraction, and I mean that literally. Every week my new friends and their lovers spun into their different alliances—hiked into the woods, sped to the dorm—while I wandered the quiet dirt roads with my baby. I loved that baby. I loved the clarity of our relationship. I loved the single-mindedness of my thinking, that summer. Her father would either come back to us or not; his decision was out of my hands. The only thing *in* my hands was this baby, whose desires were clear, pure, essential. Tabula rasa. Loving her was a pleasure. It was a verb I could do all day long.

When she slept, I slept; when she woke, I attended. On the rare occasions when she slept and I sat restlessly waiting for her to wake and need me, when my exhaustion had been sated, when there were no dishes nor clothes to wash, no phone call to make, no book to read, no television to watch, well, then I looked up at the beautiful mountain out my window and let myself be the baby, cry and cry.

They knew nothing of each other's lover. They shared a kind of disdainful blindness to, and lack of respect for, the other, and could believe no one else would find their spouse attractive enough to bother seducing. "I wish Joel would just admit he's gay," Sarah said one day after a particularly toxic fight they'd had the night before. "He told me my reporting was lazy and my prose was hackneyed, all because he couldn't get it up in bed."

"That's what makes you think he's gay?"

"Oh, that, and other stuff." Her vagueness let me know that she didn't seriously believe he was gay. My omniscience was tantalizing, limited as it was to this couple and their sexual peccadilloes. I had only scant knowledge of their other facets—and, it seemed to me, less information on my own sexual urges. Those had been back-burnered by my husband's weepy renunciation, by the fact of Lily—her inception, development, birth, and now our sequestered summer in the mountains. Sometimes when she nursed I felt erotic current zip briefly through my solar plexus, there and gone, tiny electric shock, not enough to hurt, just enough to scare.

Joel was never quite as blunt about Sarah to me—perhaps he understood that my real allegiance was with her, one heterosexual romantic female to another.

Joel preferred the dramatic hike, and Sarah favored the steady one. I was in it mainly for the gainful use of time, and alternated trails willingly. With Joel I climbed steep Wrigley Trail that went upward, upward, upward, both of us breathing so hard we could not really talk until we topped it, forty minutes later, and then descended through the aspen grove, over the quaint wooden bridge, through the fairy tale forest, and down the more gently sloping path of the other side. Joel's hike was a loop; you did not have to retrace your steps. You could go at it backwards, ascend on the more stair-stepped side, then descend at a steeper rate, but that felt dicey to us both, him with his bad knees, me with my sack full of baby. His hike took exactly eighty-five minutes.

Sarah's hike was into the Sheep Creek Preserve, a former mine road now closed to motorized vehicles. It rose the identical number of feet as Joel's hike—twelve hundred—yet you completed the climb much more casually, walking as if on a vaguely inclined treadmill until you reached the top, where you would find a stunning waterfall, straight off the Coors Beer can. Sarah and I would sit then, soak our feet in the shockingly cold runoff, and eat a snack. Joel did not hike with food; he didn't even carry water, just a pack of cigarettes, Zippo lighter, and chewing gum. He smoked at the summit of our loop—another of his guilty bad habits that Sarah was not to know about—then quickly came down. But Sarah liked to bring along treats, brownies or biscotti, cheese and apples, a thermos of coffee or a sport bottle of wine. She was a sensualist, often standing absolutely still beneath the rippling tree leaves, eyes closed, fingers pinching the air like castanets, smiling serenely. Our hikes were more languid than mine with Joel; I bared my chest and nursed Lily with my feet in the stream, sunshine illuminating the fine blond down on her skull, faithful pulse of her fontanel. We identified birds, revealed our childhoods, passed back and forth food and drink and disclosure. Sarah, I felt on those days, was my true friend, and Joel a curiosity, a lost strange soul I might aid. Sarah had a better sense of humor, listened more attentively, and although was engaged in a most torrid love affair, took time to inquire after my problems now and then.

"He's depressed," she diagnosed my husband. "Midlife crisis stuff."

It was polite of her. Women you could count upon to reciprocate, to at least feign an interest in your life.

Joel, on the other hand, probably had no idea what was going on in my marriage. If he did, it was because Sarah told him. It occurred to me more than once that summer that I would have been a natural subject of conversation between them, perhaps a safe and salving one. They could have convinced themselves that I was their project, the odd young woman who, although abidingly intimate with the landscape, had not one friend in town other than them to call upon. What if I needed a ride to the real hospital, eighty-five miles away, some dreadful night or other? What if the baby became ill? They were looking after me, in my version of their version of our mutual entanglement. I was their good deed.

One day when I was walking home from the market I noticed a commotion at the entrance of the Wrigley Trail. Two police vehicles were parked there, the four officers all standing against one of the jeeps, staring up, passing among themselves a pair of binoculars trained on something. I looked where they were looking. The sky was cloudy yet bright; it was nearing dusk, and the air was cool. Lily slept on my chest, and a plastic sack of groceries hung from my hand. Up on the cliffs stood a man. I had to blink, so bright was the glare, so small the figure. What was he doing? Why were the police watching him do it? And did I have time to go retrieve my own binoculars, set down the groceries, get back, and watch?

I stood there waiting, like the others. Soon another car pulled up, this one occupied by a young man and woman. The man was out the door and running toward the police before the car had properly stopped. Friend of the jumper, I thought. He spoke to the cops, then ran back to his car. "Radio," I heard him say to his companion, who hadn't left her seat. Off they sped. Other traffic passed slowly, people glancing up because I was, because the police were. Up high on the cliff, the man wandered into the dark spruce trees behind the red rocks, then out, onto the cliff, then away from it. This activity might have been nervous, or it might have been meditative. It was hard to tell. At one point, he pulled off his shirt. That made my heart thump; it seemed preparatory to action, and I wanted action. The baby was hot and damp against me, like the package of internal organs she was, and the straps of my grocery bag were cutting into my palm—the weight of milk and juice and water, fluids.

When the man removed his shirt, a second figure stepped into view, someone who'd been in the trees, perhaps accounting for the constant motion between the spruce and cliff of the first figure. What were they doing? Both now stood at cliff's edge, beside each other. Were they holding hands? They were gesturing in some way, not frantically, not randomly, either. Down on the ground the tension was extremely high; a third police vehicle had arrived, and one of the first two had driven off, as if for some sort of rescue device, but what? To get to those two people would require the same long hike they'd made—and, since I'd been many times on the trail just under their cliff, I knew that they'd had to do some dramatic scrambling to arrive where they had. Their perch was not on the beaten path. A helicopter could have reached them, I supposed, one with a rope ladder. Nothing less. Nobody appeared to be dashing up the trail, and the sky, aside from the bright clouds, was free of interruption. Now the two figures retreated once more to the trees behind them, and the tension on the ground lessened. I found myself impatient, checking my watch. Come on, I thought, get on with it. Jump. You found yourself saying that sometimes, didn't you? *Jump already.* You had other things to do, your eyes were watering terribly from looking into the glare of the sky, your baby was heavy, your favorite show was going to start soon on TV, and it was cocktail hour, and despite the hot load on your chest the air was growing a bit nippy out here without a jacket... But you couldn't look away, either. We observers were not together, below, separate witnesses to the mysterious drama above. I wondered what the others were thinking, if they, too, had admitted their desire for the couple to jump. Or maybe they honestly didn't share my desire. I reminded myself that there weren't many people to whom you could just say exactly what you thought, anyway, never mind that what you thought was not what most people thought or admitted to thinking, besides. I could have spoken to Sarah this way, as I had during *A Lot of Noise for No Reason,* but it was my husband I missed suddenly. The emptiness seemed abrupt, as if he'd been abducted just now from my side, against both our wills. "Come on," I murmured angrily, "jump."

Were they stretching up there? Praying? Practicing tai chi? In the throes of a mushroom trip? Were they aware of their audience, the cops and rubbernecks? Was the second figure a woman? A young boy? Was it a suicide pact? A marriage ceremony?

I never found out. You couldn't stand all evening craning your neck. Lily woke, the police drove away, I walked home.

On my next hike with Joel, I told him about the figures on the cliff. We were passing just beneath where they'd been. Of course there was no sign of trouble. Nature rarely betrays our skirmishes on its surface. Joel had heard nothing of this event, which meant, I supposed, that nothing definite had come of it. No wedding, no death. Joel listened in a gratifying silence; he was a conversational snob, generally, and you had to say something interesting or he would interrupt you with a wholly non-sequitous observation, as if he'd quit attending to your dull insight long ago, had gone wandering down his own thought path, and now had this to say. I didn't find it rude, although others might have. Rather, his style seemed to suggest that he would do you the favor of preventing your becoming tiresome. He would rescue the chat, should you have gone astray.

"Another man?" he asked, predictably. He was intrigued at the notion of a gay couple on the cliff.

"Possibly. I couldn't see. The one had his shirt off, the other seemed smaller, either a woman or a boy."

"Hmm," he said. Then, unable to contain his news, he rushed on, "I was so late coming home last Wednesday, I had to tell Sarah I'd dropped acid. I told her I couldn't drive home right away. I had to wait for it to wear off!"

"That is quite a lie," I said, impressed with its idiosyncratic precision, its air-tightness.

"She couldn't complain, of course."

"Of course."

"I thought it was brilliant."

Sarah's most recent transgression was also stunning. She'd left Joel in their bed at three in the morning, climbed onto her bicycle, and ridden to Jonathan's, where they'd made love in the garage, in his pickup truck.

"What if Joel woke up and found you missing? What if the wife came to the garage?"

"I don't know. I wasn't thinking. I just needed Jonathan. And he was awake when I got there, sitting in his kitchen with the lights off, thinking of me, he said. I can't tell you how amazing it was to look through his kitchen window in the middle of the night and see him looking right back at me, so sad, so in love."

Not long after, I met Jonathan. I wished I hadn't, because he was an uninspiring love interest, much better left to the imagination. Older than Joel, he was also balding, running to fat, and wore a constant insipid smile beneath a defeated yellow mustache. He seemed a fool; the rest I might have forgiven. It was hard to feature Sarah distraught over his mortality, dashing to him in the middle of the night, loving him as much as she claimed she did.

We ran into him and his wife on Main Street, the deaf woman with her hand tucked into the crook of his elbow. She was pretty and meek, deferential, and when she released her husband's arm long enough to gently touch the sleeping infant on my chest, I was struck with guilt. Was it fair that I not only knew that her husband deceived her but that she had sex just once a year? And smug Sarah, grinning and fulsome, couldn't I wipe that smile off her face? I had the fleeting urge to clear the air, which was also maybe to brandish my arsenal of information, say something to the wife, her husband, his lover, watch three expressions distort and crumple as if gunshot.

"Cute baby," Jonathan's wife said in the odd voice of the deaf.

"Pleasure," Jonathan said, of our meeting, touching his eyebrow as if tipping a hat.

"Corny, isn't he?" Sarah said excitedly as we made our way up Sheep Creek. "And she's such a mouse!"

On Wednesday she and Jonathan hiked this same trail—except that at a crucial juncture, "up ahead, beyond that rock that looks like a sleeping cow," they swerved off the road, waded across the stream, and journeyed into the trees on the opposite side. "We have a blanket there," she said, "tied up in a waterproof stuff sack, hung from a branch."

"Very romantic," I said. "I'm impressed."

"Jonathan *is* very romantic," she confessed, pleased that I thought so, too. "He's the most unsarcastic man I've ever met. It's refreshing—you know *Joel*, you know what I mean, he's such an absolute *Grinch*. But Jonathan's innocent as a lamb. Do you know what else? He prays. I don't know anyone who actually prays, seriously prays to a serious God, but Jonathan does."

"Church on Sunday?"

"Yes, that, too. See? Here's the turn." She pulled aside a small mountain ash to show me the way she and her lover went every Wednesday. We paused, as if to observe a moment of silence, then proceeded, her step slightly quicker, as if the glimpse into her love nest had inspired her. I'm sure it had. I nuzzled Lily's head with my lips, to keep from... What? Judgment? Or jealousy? The naïve devoted wife—deaf, she was—troubled me. "He's terribly Catholic," Sarah said chirpily. "It will probably be our downfall, his guilt."

"You always think you can circumnavigate deep character traits, don't you?" I said, speculatively.

"Oh, definitely. I pooh-pooh his religion, and next thing I know he'll be crying over the telephone, breaking up with me out of guilt, ready to confess everything to his wife and my husband. Confession is such a Catholic cornerstone." But she didn't sound concerned, not really. She actually believed she could derail his faith, that their love was larger than his Catholicism. Love was beautiful, I thought, the way it made you dumb.

My employer phoned me in August to see how motherhood leave was going. He was awfully delicate about my situation, not asking about my husband, not even broaching a question that would indicate I'd ever had a husband, let alone left him in Los Angeles. I was a legal secretary, and good at my job. The office missed me, as I knew it would, and Frank, the partner now on the line, missed me especially. At home, I was his confidante, in a formal, executive way. He used me to test his own instincts, nodding when his opinion and my own matched up, validated. Although traditional in his demeanor, Frank didn't particularly play by the rules of hierarchy at the firm. Every now and then we had lunch together. For Christmas bonus, he gave me pieces of art instead of additional money. I liked that. And I liked the art, which proved that we were friends—either we shared the same taste, or he knew me well enough to make intelligent guesses about mine.

"You'll be back on the first of September," he reminded me after we'd caught up on business.

"That's right. At the latest."

"And you'll bring Lily in to visit us."

"I will." I was touched that he knew her name, that he could say it so naturally. My husband called her *the baby* when he called her anything.

"Okay, then," Frank said. This was his signature phrase, said with a sigh. Okay, then.

"Bye, Frank," I said, abruptly nostalgic for his good manners, my job in his lovely office, my old life, the city of noisy angels he was standing in as he spoke to me. "Thanks so much for calling," I added, a burst of sentiment that would make him awkward but I didn't care. I was going to cry, I thought, I was *not* "Okay, then," and I needed somewhere to discharge a piece of emotion.

It was after a whole summer of listening to Joel and Sarah discuss their infidelities that I finally figured out my husband's. It would have been obvious to somebody who wanted to see it. I was walking with Joel, who was despondent after having taken incredible pains to meet Seth in Santa Fe for a night, only to have Seth cancel.

"I'm afraid I'll never see him again," he said, unable to rise wryly above the scene, incapable of attributing his fear to paranoia, inept at seeing the humor. He was scared, and all whimsy and sarcasm had left him as he realized the extent of his affection, the depths to which his worst-case scenario could reduce him.

Sometimes insight hits you like a hailstone: icy ping to the skull. I recognized in Joel's state a familiar despondency, and knew suddenly that my husband had had an affair himself, contrary to his claims. Furthermore, it was the woman, whoever she was, who had called it off. I could almost mark the day, if someone had given me a calendar, not long after I'd become pregnant. That was when she kissed him goodbye.

"Are you in love with someone else?" I'd demanded eventually of his moroseness and tears.

"No," he'd sighed, "but I understand the desire to be in love with someone else." He went on to say that though he displayed symptoms, he was not planning to take the next step into adultery. It was too predictable, he said, an affair. He loved me, he said. He was unhappy with himself, he said. He needed *time* and *space*, those one-size-fits-all abstractions.

In fact, I'm sure he *was* unhappy with himself. I had no doubt that he was still unhappy. I knew he loved me, in some way, although not the way either of us would prefer. "I want to be *in* love with you," his voice spoke for the thousandth time on the merciless reel-to-reel in my mind. I had been attending to that line in order to ascertain the inflection, as if it were the key. I *want* to be in love with you. I want to be in love with *you*. He'd been *in* love with someone *else,* and that explained everything. And when even his baby's birth hadn't particularly rallied his love, that lack must have been the unbearable convergence of guilt and despair. Our summer separation now made sense to me. He was willing to miss the first few months of Lily's life in order to save his own.

My husband came clear to me there, but my own situation seemed instantly a swirl of murk and confusion. Why was I a thousand miles from home, standing on top of a mountain, listening to a man I'd only met two months previous telling me about the state of his sore anus and broken heart?

"I feel faint," I said, unexpectedly. "Would you take the baby?"

Startled, Joel immediately began helping me unstrap the front pack. We both were surprised at my assertive neediness.

"I have to sit. Careful with her neck." I lowered my head between my knees, attempting to gain back my peripheral vision, my requisite oxygen, my sense of balance. I stared at a tick as it crawled onto my boot. Lily cried in Joel's arms, but I couldn't worry. For the moment, for the first time in months and months, I was thinking only of myself.

I replayed my pregnancy like some beloved mysterious film, the highlights, the major scenes, the tender moments and the surprising ones, and then I revisited the small incidents, and all the minor players. Now, I was trying to guess who my husband's lover had been, what young girl or old flame.

It incensed me that he'd had a lover, he who'd had dozens before we married, he who was supposed to have sown his oats, he for whom I was in line to be the second trophy wife. His first marriage was supposed to have been the messy one, the one where he got things wrong, the test run, the mistake. I was still in my twenties, for God's sake; if anyone was going to commit adultery, oughtn't it have been me? But mostly I just suffered the humiliation of having been duped, betrayed, left alone with a faith in our happy life like the lone member of an abandoned religious order, its pathetic last nun.

I hadn't felt quite this alone since my parents had died. Orphaned, again.

I decided I wasn't going to wait for my husband to want me once more. I would go home regardless. I said goodbye to Sarah Siebert and Joel Metcalf. Never had I met two people more adamant about retaining those separate last names. They were sad to see me leave, their confidante, their audience, their dramas as yet unfinished. I bought a subscription to their newspaper, which I would read religiously, once home.

I took with me a baby who could hold up her own head and who smiled dazzlingly, faithful as a light switch, whenever she saw me. I had a good tan and calf definition. I had new knowledge, gained at the rare intersection of isolation and exposure, focus and leisure, a four-cornered limbo. It was captured there in my parents' picture, embodied in my friends' secret love lives, manifest in my husband's misery, waiting in my own future fate. You wanted two conflicting things. You wanted to be sitting in a comfortable leather recliner sipping fine wine and reading a passage of exquisite prose to your wise spouse for your mutual amusement, and you wanted to be having demeaning drunken sex in a seedy dorm room with a gorgeous, soulless youth. You wanted a savvy, possibly unscrupulous business partner, and you wanted a devoted fool to pray at your feet. You wanted something solid; you wanted something fluid. They could not be reconciled except by a giant leap of faith. Between them lay the great paradoxical gap, the miserable marriage.

The image of Palisades I'd carried with me for so long, my parents in their racy embrace, was swapped for this year's model. Now, when I thought of that small mountain retreat, I would remember the couple I'd spied on the cliff, my secret desire to see them take each other's hand, and sail off.

STEWART O'NAN

Please Help Find

Why was it, Janice thought, that everything took longer than you wanted? Like life. It was the last day of summer, their last day together, and all the way upstate her mother went on about Cornell—the boys she dated, the friends she made—going "oh," and "oh!" over the radio until Janice's head went completely blank, buzzed emptily like when she skipped her Mellaril. They'd eaten at the travel plaza Roy's (her mother ridiculously ordering a salad), and Janice could still taste her onion rings. Outside the world ran by, bright and hot and sharp as a paper cut.

Of course Lonnie had to come, sitting between them on the front seat like a rug, reeking of flea dip and panting so hard his tongue dripped on the carpet. He was old, a cocker with bags under his eyes like someone punched him. Her mother tipped the air-conditioning vent to blow right on him so the whole car stunk. She couldn't leave him at home, even though she knew Janice couldn't stand him. He was her father's dog, except her father's new wife, Marion, was allergic to his dandruff. Janice hadn't liked him before that. He was sneaky, and growled when you cornered him under a bed. When Janice said, "Stupid dog," her mother dismissed her with a laugh.

"But he *loves* to ride in the car," she'd said. "And this way I'll have company on the way back."

Now they cruised up the Thruway in the slow lane, the Mohawk glittering in the heat. Monday was Labor Day, and traffic was bad, tons of construction. In the fields, cows knelt under scrubby trees. Her mother was going on about Cayuga's Waters and the bell tower chiming every quarter hour, and Janice concentrated on the radio.

They weren't going to her mother's beautiful Ithaca, just dumb, ugly Utica. It was punishment, Janice thought, for trying to kill herself. She'd missed a large part of senior year after the attempt, and her grades were only good enough for a SUNY. Utica was the farthest one from Bellmore and their empty house, and she accepted bitterly, sure her mother wouldn't let her go. But she had. Since October, the Mellaril seemed to be working, or that's what her mother thought. It had been a quiet spring, a quiet summer. There were no episodes. This morning when she opened her pill reminder and ate Sunday's, Janice wondered if it could be true, that it really was the drugs.

It was usually summer when she thought of killing herself, she didn't know why. Something about the long, airless days, the empty streets and hot yards. It had been September last year; though no one ever said, the anniversary was coming up. It had been a day like today, the sun glinting off the parked cars. She walked through the house turning the air conditioners off one by one until she reached her parents' room. Her father had been gone for years, but her mother still kept his dresser, inside it a few shirts pressed from the cleaner's, stiff with cardboard. Janice turned off the air conditioner and let the heat settle before going through the medicine cabinet, choosing. After she took everything, she lay down on her mother's bed and closed her eyes. It took longer than she'd thought, and after a few minutes she got up and stood at the window and watched a boy ride by on a three-speed, a baseball glove impaled on his handlebars, the tassels flying from his grips. She was holding on to the gauzy curtain, feeling the grittiness between her fingers. Little waves of heat shivered on top of the cars. She felt she could reach out and pinch the cars between her fingers and squish them like lightning bugs if she wanted to. If she wanted to, but she didn't. She didn't want anything anymore, and she felt good about making that clear. How satisfying it was to finally say what she meant. The sun felt good on her arms, the stifling air.

And then, after she was dead, she woke up with a hose in her mouth, choking on it. The vomit was hot in her nose, and there were faces flying above her, gloved hands, the noise of voices.

"There you are," a doctor said, huge, hovering. "I'm afraid you can't leave us just yet."

And then the questions, the psychiatrists, her father coming back from Seattle to see if she was okay.

"I'm okay," she said.

"No you're not," her mother said.

Even now Janice had never given her a real explanation for it, or as close to one as she'd figured out herself. What could she possibly say to justify it? I'm lonely. I don't love anybody. I'm tired.

"For God's sake," her mother said, "you're eighteen. You haven't even lived yet. Give it a chance."

And she had. Wasn't this proof, today, going off to college like someone normal?

But it's all fake, Janice thought. It doesn't mean anything.

She looked down and saw that Lonnie had slobbered on her jeans. "Oh, nice," she said, and found a napkin on the floor to wipe it off with. Overhead a sign flew by.

"What did that say?" her mother asked.

"I didn't see it, I was cleaning up this slobber."

"We must be getting close. See if you can find it on the map."

"Find what?"

"The exit. There must be a number."

"What number was it?" Janice asked.

"I don't know—something. Just find the one we want."

Janice flapped the map open so she couldn't see the road, and Lonnie sighed.

"I think that might have been it," her mother said.

It made Janice look up, but there was nothing to see, just a Cadillac passing them. She would have noticed if they were close, she thought. She got the number from the map and folded it away.

"I'm sorry, honey," her mother said. "It just came up on me too fast."

"It's all right," Janice said, and it was. Another hour or two, and she'd be in her new room, her mother caught in traffic above the city, Lonnie sprawled across the front seat, his head in her lap. All summer Janice had been planning for this, making lists of what to bring, buying soap and deodorant, shampoo, new towels. Now she wanted to enjoy her escape, but the hot car, the dry fields slipping by—none of it seemed as sweet as she'd pictured it. It didn't feel like a release. It was still the three of them cruising along in the Buick the same as any road trip, as if they might bypass Utica completely and end up at the cabin at Blue Mountain Lake, her father already there, waiting with a stringer of crappie. It was so bright out, so green, that it seemed like there was a lot of summer left. But no, this was it.

"There," her mother said, and pointed at a sign too far away to read. "What does that one say?"

She slowed, and Janice automatically looked behind them, but there was no one.

"What's it say?" her mother said.

Thirty-one, the sign said.

"That's it," Janice said. "That's the one we want."

The ramp took them west into the city, dropped them on Genesee Street. On the map it was the main drag, but most of the buildings they passed were abandoned, the windows soaped, doors boarded over with plywood and posted with sheriff's notices. Fluff from some tree floated over the road. After being on the highway so long, it seemed like they were crawling. Huge weeds grew in the supermarket lot. The city was deserted, in a park only a boy her age practicing foul shots at a netless backboard. It looked like Hempstead.

They climbed a long hill, hitting every red light, and by the top the neighborhood had changed, the buildings giving way to three-deckers, porches strung with laundry. A panel truck missing a wheel sat propped on cinder blocks, its side crowded with graffiti. Still, her mother said nothing.

They came upon the gates of the college, two brick pillars with a wrought-iron arch above them. A campus cop in a blaze-orange vest motioned them in, pointed toward the dorms. With every speed bump, Lonnie puffed and grumbled. Since she'd received the brochure, Janice had gone over the map so many times that she knew what every building was. By the old stone dorms was a confusion of minivans and Explorers pulled off onto the grass, and parents unloading trunks and desklamps, plants and stereos. It reminded Janice of the first day of skating camp, all the fathers in Bermuda shorts. Another cop had her mother ease the Buick up over the curb and shut it down. Ahead stretched a small quad, complete with a three-story Gothic bell tower sheathed in ivy. When they'd come in March, it lay under a foot of snow, the crisscrossed walks carved out by plows. Just like Cornell, her mother said. Now the grass was brown and bare in patches, a scraggly pack of boys playing Ultimate under the bell tower.

"It looks very nice," her mother said. "Don't you think?"

"Yeah," Janice said.

Her mother set a bowl of water down beneath a tree for Lonnie. He sniffed it and lay down in the shade. They started unloading the trunk. The building didn't have an elevator, and Janice's room was on the fourth floor. The stairs were marble, and echoed. A sign on her door had her name on it, and her roommate's: MARLA RAY. She wasn't here yet. There was an RA who gave her her keys and helped them bring a load up. Janice hadn't wanted to look like a dork in shorts; now she wished she'd worn them. So many clothes. Books, her Mac with the little troll who stood on top of the monitor. She didn't remember packing so much stuff.

"Which bed do you want to be yours?" her mother asked when they'd gotten it all up.

"It doesn't matter," Janice said. "We'll decide when she gets here."

"Is there anything else you need?"

Janice couldn't think of anything. She felt like lying down, letting the whole ride up here drain away.

"If you do," her mother said, "I noticed a phone in the hall there. I took down the number in case I think of anything on the way home. I'm sure I will."

"Oh, I'm sure."

Her mother looked at her and tried to smile—that smile that said, I'm trying, will you try, too? Janice never knew how to react to it. Mostly she froze, tried not to give in to it. It was unfair, her mother asking her that, as if Janice would always disappoint her. Maybe it was true, but why did she always have to do it?

"Are you sure you're going to be all right?" her mother said.

"Yes."

"Okay," she said, and gave her a hug, a final kiss goodbye.

Janice trailed her out the door. Now it was advice time. Get your rest. Eat. Take your medication. When you drink—because I know you will—just have two of whatever it is. And let me know how things are going. Use the calling card.

"I will," Janice said, already wondering how long she'd wait. She could see Marla hollering from the pay phone, "It's your mother again."

On the stairs her mother stopped and looked back at her. "Do you think you're going to like it here?"

"Yes," Janice said, maybe too hard, because her mother looked hurt and said, "All right," softly.

Christ, Janice thought, just go.

Outside, the quad was filling up with cars, a black lab chasing the Ultimate game. Under the tree where they'd left Lonnie, the water dish had tipped over. He was gone, nowhere.

They both stood on the stoop, shielding their eyes. Besides the lab there was a golden retriever circling a family in a Wagoneer. No Lonnie.

"Stupid dog," Janice said.

"He's around here somewhere," her mother said. "He can't get far."

They split up, each taking a side of the quad, walking toward the bell tower, calling and calling. Her mother could whistle with her fingers so loud it hurt, and people turned to her. Janice asked one of the players—a tall guy in a tie-dyed Phish shirt—if he'd seen him. Her mother stopped an RA with a clipboard. Nothing.

They headed back to the stoop, calling. Her mother wiped the dish out with a paper towel; she'd brought some treats, and she put those in the dish and sat on the stoop, then a minute later walked over to the cop and came back with a phone number. "Just wait here," she said.

Campus safety couldn't do much for them. It was a busy day; most of their people were on traffic or issuing parking permits. They'd put something out on him, but they were stretched a little thin. It was the best they could do.

"Do you believe that?" her mother said. "Honestly. How much are we paying for this?"

It was nearly five now, the sun taking on a soft orange light, like in a commercial. Her mother tossed her keys from hand to hand. She stood up. "Let's drive around a little and look for him."

"I'll watch here," the RA offered.

Backing the car onto the road, her mother scraped the tailpipe. "Just great," she said. "This is just what I need."

Janice navigated with the campus map. Her mother hunched over the wheel, peering down alleys, dead-end parking lots. They went by the observatory, the engineering center, the fieldhouse. It only took half an hour.

"Not a very big campus," her mother said, as if unimpressed.

"Maybe he's back at the dorm," Janice said.

Her mother said nothing, just wheeled the car around. "I'm not leaving till I find him," she said, and it sounded like a threat, like this was her fault.

Back at the dorm, Marla Ray had arrived with her family. She was tall and pretty and wore a print dress, her hair in cornrows. Her father was built like a football star and carried her trunk on his shoulder. Marla's mother came down—the whole family was tall—and Janice's mother introduced herself, explaining about Lonnie running away, waving her keys at the quad. "What a day," she said, and Janice went upstairs.

"Oh no," Marla said when Janice told her.

"I know," Janice said. "We've had him for ten years."

Marla's father was a lawyer; her mother didn't work but loved to garden. They were from Pittsburgh.

"I should go take care of my mom," Janice said. Marla understood. It was good, Janice thought; she really liked her.

Her mother was still talking with Marla's, who seemed glad to see Janice.

"Well, we should go get Marla settled," she said. "We have to get back tonight."

"They're nice," Janice's mother said when they were alone.

"They are," Janice conceded.

"I'm going to get a motel room tonight, if that's all right with you. I think what we should do is put up a flyer around campus. Do you think that's a good idea? We can use the number of the phone in your hall, that way people can reach us. Did you bring any pictures of Lonnie, or just pictures he's in?"

"I'd have to look," Janice said, though she knew she hadn't. She hadn't brought any pictures. Her mother kept a big one of Janice on the mantel in the living room; it was the winter she won Regionals. She stood there at center ice in the Coliseum, holding a bouquet of roses, slightly bowing to the crowd. The picture was eight years old. Sometimes she wanted to switch it for one of her in the ER, the doctor shoving the rubber tube down her throat.

"Let me go look," she said.

Upstairs she said goodbye to Marla's parents.

"I don't," she said when she came down.

"That's all right," her mother said. "People know what a cocker spaniel looks like, that's one nice thing about the breed."

They went to Kinko's, which took forever, then to Wal-Mart to buy a stapler and staples, a roll of double-sided tape. The flyers were fluorescent yellow and said PLEASE HELP FIND, and then all the information and their number at the bottom. The reward was $100; Janice didn't say it was more than Lonnie was worth. They walked around campus in the dusk, Janice handing them to her mother, her mother stapling them to trees, taping them to poles. They'd made a hundred of them. When they were done, her mother asked if she was hungry. And how about Marla, did Janice think she might like something to eat? Janice would have to stay and watch the phone in case someone called.

"Is your mom okay?" Marla asked. They'd chosen beds and were lying there talking.

"She's just upset about Lonnie. And me. Everything. You know."

"I know."

"She's not going to have anyone to boss around anymore," Janice said, and thought of the house now, dark, not even the porch light on. That's what her mother was going back to, and Janice thought of that day last September when it seemed there was no one else in the world except her. The empty streets, the sound of insects all day long. Across the street a sprinkler turned slow arcs, darkening the sidewalk. She felt the gritty curtain, rubbed it like grease between her fingers. And then she was dead, she had left, and that had made her happy. How could she ever hope to explain that to her mother? It seemed another failure.

The phone rang in the hall. She looked to Marla.

"It's got to be for you," Marla said.

It was. It was a frat house. The guy read their address in Bellmore off Lonnie's tag.

"He just wandered in here around dinner. I don't think he can see very well."

"Where are you?" Janice asked, and the guy told her. It was all the way across campus; she knew it from the map.

She ran downstairs. Just as she was coming outside, her mother pulled up across the street, the Buick rocking over the curb and onto the grass. Its lights dimmed, and her mother's door opened. For a second nothing happened, and then her mother slowly climbed out, hitching her purse on her shoulder. She leaned in across the seat, then ducked back out with a pizza box, and the purse fell off her shoulder, hit the box, and flipped it so it landed in the grass.

From where Janice was standing, she could see her mother sag, her hands cover her face. They were supposed to have split the driving, but at the Roy's her mother said she wasn't tired, and so she drove the whole way. Now she seemed exhausted, kneeling to pick up the box, then plodding across the road with her head down. She was talking to herself, muttering something, and Janice was glad she had good news, that for once she could make her happy, and as she waited, brimming with it, she realized that this was what her mother wanted for her. It was this same concern, this wish to save her from unhappiness that her mother couldn't give up. That was love. How helpless she must feel, Janice thought, and promised, that instant, not to disappoint her again.

"Mom," she called, "they found him."

"They did?" Already she was trying to smile for her.

"He's fine."

"Oh, good," she said, and Janice reached across the pizza box to hug her. She couldn't remember the last time she'd actually wanted to do this, but it seemed right now, natural. She didn't really hate her, she had to know that, didn't she?

Her mother seemed more relieved than happy, and Janice wanted more. But wasn't this exactly how her mother felt, always telling her to buck up, to smile? It was funny how they'd changed places.

"I *am* happy," her mother said. "It's just been a long day. I'm happy you like it here."

They drove over to the frat and picked up Lonnie. He was fine, the dummy, they'd even given him dinner. The guy didn't want the reward, but her mother insisted, writing a check to the whole house.

On the way across campus, her mother said she'd drive back tonight. She didn't have a reservation yet; it wasn't that far. "And it doesn't make sense," she said. "You want to be with your new friends."

"Aren't you tired?" Janice asked.

"I'll roll down the windows, that should do it."

She didn't park the car. They said goodbye at the window, Janice leaning in, the pizza box on the roof. Lonnie sniffed the air.

"Call me when you get home," Janice said, "okay?"
"You call me if you need anything," her mother said.
"I will."

They both said I love you, and then Janice lifted the box off the roof and took a step back and let her drive off, watched her taillights out the gate and into traffic, headed back through Utica toward the interstate and the city. It was almost night now, the last of sunset dying beyond the quad. Swallows dipped and turned, chittering. The bell tower was lit, and as she paused a minute, breathing in the cool air, the bells chimed, a high, light ringing like Sunday, like the cities in Europe she always wanted to visit, and Janice thought of her mother and what had happened today, how it was a mystery, how it had changed everything between them, and this was the feeling she would remember just a few months later, before her last, successful attempt: how badly she'd wanted to be happy here, and how it had seemed, for one still and perfect moment, almost possible.

HILARY RAO

Every Day a Little Death

I liked Gretchen better when she wasn't trying to kill me. Here's what she used: a Colt .38; a heavy-handled hatchet; a pair of powder-blue knitting needles (one in each ear, a quick thrust, and I'd be *gonzo*, Gretchen said); and a gleaming silver-tipped syringe, its cylinder filled with something thick and yellow.

This was the summer of 1969. Gretchen was twelve, I was eight, and one morning Mother and Dad shoveled our clothes into five paper sacks and dropped us at Nana's house. They'd packed the '63 Oldsmobile convertible with Dad's Indian print shirts and blue jeans, Mother's ankle-length peasant skirts, a bulletin board with pictures of Gretchen and me, and a box full of demo tapes. They'd handed the keys of the Disc Den, their used record shop, to their only employee, Willis Ferguson. They kissed us all—"You take care of my wild things," Dad said to Nana before they pulled from her drive. "We'll send for you guys soon," Mother called. "California doesn't know what's coming—we're gonna slay them." They waved and slid on their wire-rimmed sunglasses. Then they headed to the coast to become stars in the music industry.

The first death happened right there, before I'd stopped waving goodbye. Suddenly I felt Gretchen's finger poked up behind my ear. "Feel that?" she said. "That's a needle knife. It's a weapon so thin and so sharp I could push it through your brain and it would come out on the other side in less than three seconds."

"Leave your brother be," Nana said and gave Gretchen's hand a nudge.

"Don't forget," Gretchen whispered, so close I felt the soft spray of spit in my ear. "I'm watching you every second, Danny."

Every day, Gretchen renumbered Nana's wall calendar, covering the real date with a dense slab of black Magic Marker and writing in something new: the number of days since Mother and Dad had left. We all lived by this calendar now: twelve days, twenty-seven days, fifty-nine days. Gretchen would store the marker in the drawer under the calendar, so she wouldn't have to look for it the next day. Then she'd come looking for me.

"It's your fault," she said the day of my death by hatchet, kind of early on, day seventeen. A postcard had arrived from Mother and Dad that morning, and Gretchen carefully leaned it against a lamp before turning to me. They were crashing with friends in Haight-Ashbury, Dad had written. It was a wild and wonderful place. They missed us madly. "I woke up with a sore throat, and you've been snotty and disgusting all week," Gretchen said. "You're gonna pay, Danny."

I shrugged. I'd stopped arguing with Gretchen after the first few deaths. They weren't so bad, really. They seemed to make Gretchen almost cheerful. Besides, my stutter had gotten worse since we moved to Nana's. Sometimes I got so stuck chugging over the same syllable that I just gave up talking altogether.

Gretchen laid my head on the hassock Nana used to hold up her feet while she watched the TV, and held her hand high. "This is the heaviest hatchet in the world," she said. "It's not too sharp, so it's probably gonna really hurt when it hits you, but it's so heavy it'll chop your head clear off your neck."

As the blade descended, I didn't even shut my eyes. The worn leather crackled against my cheek. The bridge strung with lights on our parents' postcard reshuffled under my sideways gaze. It looked like a lit dinosaur's back. Or the crown Mother made for Gretchen's last Halloween costume. It looked like a brilliant, tipping ladder.

Gretchen and I slept in Dad's old room. Lying in the lower bed of Dad's bunk, I watched the blue curtains puff out over the windowsill and flatten against the screen. I can't say why, but my stutter left me in that bed, and in the dark I replayed memories of Mother and Dad while Gretchen scratched in her journal above me.

"Remember dancing to 'Born to Be Wild'?" I'd ask Gretchen. It was Dad's favorite song, and he'd spin us across the living room floor, singing, *"Getcher motor RUN-ning, head out on the HIGHWAY."* "Remember Mother playing 'Pop Goes the Weasel' on the piano?" It was better than TV, these pictures in the dark—I could hear Mother tweedling the piano keys. I could smell the lemon lozenges on her breath.

But Gretchen didn't want to hear it. "Danny," she said, "if you don't stop talking right now, I'm going to *kill* you." Gretchen didn't like me talking about Mother and Dad, but as far as I could tell they were almost all she thought about. I'd snuck a look at her diary one afternoon while she was picking zucchini flowers for Nana to fry. Three times, Gretchen had started writing letters to our parents. On one left-hand page she'd written DAD DAD DAD DAD from top to bottom, and on the facing page she'd done the same with Mother—though she wrote MOTHER MOM MOTHER MOM MOTHER MOM, as though she didn't remember what to call her. I didn't see the point, and Gretchen must have gotten tired of writing the same thing over and over; she'd penciled big dark X's over both pages.

Mother and Dad called as often as they could. Gretchen drew little green phone handles on the calendar when they did, with loops on the bottom to represent the cord.

On day thirty-nine, they told us they had a weekly gig at a coffee bar in the Haight. They were sending us a flyer; we should look for it in the mail. They were calling themselves Gredan, after Gretchen and me, a name that their audiences found mysterious and cool. "You thought *we* were hippies," Mother laughed. "You should see the folks on the other side of the mike."

Gretchen and I stood with the phone receiver between us. Mother and Dad both talked at once, so they must have been doing the same. I pictured them standing at a pay phone in a magical neighborhood, miles away from our house in Cleveland. The place was filled with people who looked just like Mother and Dad, their hair swinging down their backs, all of them humming and rapping out rhythms on their knees.

Gretchen nodded seriously at the space in front of her while Mother and Dad talked and told them she loved her swimming lessons at the municipal pool—an outright lie.

My own mouth started before my head caught up with it.

"Ww-w-w-w," I said. Gretchen elbowed me. It mortified her when I stuttered. But I'd gotten going and couldn't stop.

I leaned into that *W* until I broke through to the sentence on the other side: "When are you coming back?"

No sound came through the line.

Nana peeled my fingers from the receiver gently as she pulled the borers off her tomato plants.

"Stu-pid," Gretchen whispered to me. "You are so stupid. It won't work asking them that way." I didn't know what she was talking about.

Later, she tied my hands behind me with Nana's nylons. She held the black Magic Marker in her hand. "This is a needle," she said, "a big thick one, it's called a 'syringe.' I've filled it with this special mixture—only I know how to make it. It's yellow," she said. "You like yellow, don't you, Danny?"

I nodded yes. Gretchen looked almost sad. "You won't really notice it, Danny, I promise. I'll poke it in your arm, and the yellow mixture will glue up everything inside you, and then you'll just stop breathing and talking and everything. Okay?" she asked.

"Okay," I said, no stutter at all. She pressed the marker gently to my arm.

It was hot that summer, and Nana took us on the bus to the municipal swimming pool three or four times a week. I liked those days: we saw kids from our old neighborhood, and Timmy Walston and I flung ourselves into the pool like cannonballs. After her swimming lessons, Gretchen talked to her girlfriends, all of them huddled together on terry-cloth towels. Sometimes, especially when the girls were eating in bunches around their mothers' chairs, their moms doling out napkins to catch the plum juice sliding down their chins, Gretchen sat next to Nana, slurping a frozen lemonade, her bangs falling over her eyes. She looked like Mother herself then, with her black hair reaching nearly to her waist.

One day, Peggy Judson's mother asked Gretchen how Mother and Dad were doing. Gretchen and Peggy were sitting on the concrete beside Mrs. Judson's pool chair playing Slap-Jack. Their freckled hands flew as they whacked the cards. I sat at the base of Nana's chair sucking a root-beer pop.

"They're on a business trip," Gretchen said. She slammed her hand on the pile of cards and swept them to her.

"A business trip," Mrs. Judson said. "They must have big plans for the Disc Den."

"Gretchen—" I said, and she shot me a look. We both knew she was lying. Since about a week after I'd asked Mother and Dad when they were coming home, they'd been sending mail nearly daily. Sometimes the letters were long—descriptions of the Golden Gate Park and Bridge, stories about all the musicians they were meeting. Other times they were shorter—poems or lists of their sets Dad scrawled on the back of a napkin from the club where they played. In one envelope was the flyer they'd made to advertise themselves. In its center was a grainy picture of Dad on a stool, leaning over his guitar, and Mother singing with her head flung back, her hair flying out behind her like Nana's sheets on the laundry line. The flyer said, *Come hear Gredan: We're a sound like no other.* On the back, Mother wrote: "Do you guys miss us as much as we miss you???"

"My father's going to start working in the insurance business," Gretchen said. "He's gonna be a big executive. He's got the suits already."

I hurled my root-beer pop at Gretchen, and it landed against her bathing suit with a soft crushing sound. What was she doing lying about our mother and dad?

Eventually, Nana was able to pull us from the pool with Mrs. Judson's help. I was still shouting *Big fat liar* at Gretchen, and she was crying and spitting out unintelligible things at me.

None of us spoke on the ride home. Nana stomped down the steps at our bus stop and didn't look back at either of us. But I wasn't so mad at Gretchen anymore. She'd chewed on her hangnails the whole ride, and by the time we were home her finger ends were chomped and purplish.

I thought Gretchen might have an extra-complicated death for me, and I hung around the yard, waiting for her. But she just walked up to our room and lay on the top bunk. Nana crashed pans in the kitchen and muttered, "Fools. Fools." I asked who she meant, but she didn't say.

On day sixty-four, Mother and Dad called, but Nana didn't let us talk to them. She sat at the kitchen table and scribbled a tangle of black circles on her grocery pad while she said, "Yes, I know," into the phone. When she saw Gretchen and me in the kitchen door, she pointed us to the living room. As we backed away, Gretchen ratcheted her elbow around my throat and said: "Know how easily I could snap your neck?" I didn't move. She swung her arm away. "Never mind," Gretchen said. She scuffed off to our room and clicked the lock shut.

Nana cooked an enormous dinner that night. She laid placemats at one end of the table and neatly piled her magazines, bills, and all the letters we'd received from Mother and Dad at the other. While Gretchen and I sat, she stacked eight hefty pork chops onto her serving platter and dribbled her special orange-juice gravy over them. She heaped mashed potatoes onto our plates, spooned up peas and carrots, slid thick tomato slices from her garden next to the other vegetables.

Mother and Dad tended toward spaghetti and salads. I dug in. The pork juice ran rich in my mouth. Gretchen didn't pick up her fork.

"Kids," Nana said, "let me tell you a story about your father."

I sank a hole in my potatoes and poured a little swimming pool of gravy in the middle.

"Danny, you're a pig," said Gretchen.

"Ever since he was a baby, he loved music." I didn't listen too closely. It seemed I'd heard this story a million times. Music was the thing that comforted Dad from the earliest age; it was the passion of his life, just like it was for Mother. Music was even how they took care of Nana after our grandfather died: Mother brought over a different record from the Disc Den every day—Sinatra, Perry Como, Patsy Cline—and they all sat in the living room and listened and hummed and cried until finally, months later, they didn't need to cry so much anymore.

Gretchen picked up a pea and held it up to her eye while Nana said the same old family stories. She rolled it between her thumb and first finger. I never knew a vegetable could be so interesting. Maybe she was planning to choke me with a fistful of them later.

"Anyway, how do I say this?" Nana asked. "Sometimes things don't always go the way you mean them to." Gretchen put her pea down and laid her head on the table.

"Do you see what I'm getting at?" Gretchen stayed still, her head flat on her arms, and closed her eyes. I mounded carrots onto a spoon.

"Your folks needed to try this thing before they got too old, like your old Nana here."

I sucked on a piece of tomato. It gushed sweet and ripe on my tongue. I didn't know why Nana was telling us all this. Mother and Dad had said the same thing to us the night before they left. They were following their dreams, they said. We'd have dreams, too, one day, everybody does. We'd all be together, real soon, just like before (only famous, only rich, only stars).

Gretchen lifted her head. "They're not coming back, right?" she said. "And we're not going out there before school starts."

Nana wiped her lips carefully with a yellow napkin. She didn't need to, I noticed, because like Gretchen she hadn't taken a bite.

"No, Gretch, you're not."

Gretchen dropped her head to the table. I placed my fork on my plate. The pork bones, picked clean, were piled on one side of the dish, and bits of shredded meat and hunks of tomato were mounded beside them. An odd ringing started in my ears, as if a train were approaching from a distance. All of a sudden my stomach lurched on me; I must have eaten way too much. Nana held a cool cloth to my head and whispered words I couldn't hear while I heaved up all she'd fed me into the kitchen sink.

Later that night, as we lay in Dad's old bunk bed, I talked to Gretchen in the dark.

"I don't get it. When are we gonna see them?" The mattress creaked above me while Gretchen rolled over.

"How do I know?" She sounded mad.

Dad's room looked familiar and odd at the same time. For more than sixty-four nights I'd looked at the shadowy rectangle looming above me. I knew just the arc the light would take when a car passed and its headlights swooped around the far wall. It had felt like a kind of home to me before, this room and this house, but now it seemed the strangest place I'd ever been.

"Danny," Gretchen said, when she heard me chuffing for breath below her. "Danny, Danny, Danny, Danny." She snaked her hand over the side of her bunk and down to me. I held her fingers with both hands. Before I fell asleep, Gretchen raised her arm up through the dark and didn't even say a word about all the snot and tears I'd smeared on her.

I heard the howls first. Next, the crack of Nana's doorknob against the wall and her feet thudding down the stairs.

By the time I reached the kitchen, Nana was flinging water on the table. Her wall calendar lay on the floor over a heap of ashes, its edges charred all around. A candle and a box of matches had rolled under the kitchen table. Gretchen had been trying to burn the calendar when she'd lit up Nana's mail—all those letters from Mother and Dad, too. Orange flames shot up from the papers.

"Gretchen," Nana said, louder than I'd ever heard her speak. "Hell, what a mess." She threw another potful of water and doused most of the fire. Some postcards skidded off the table and continued to flare on the floor.

"Don't you tell me anything, Nana," Gretchen yelled, "don't you even try to tell me anything," while Nana hollered back, "You just stop now."

But Gretchen wasn't done. She grabbed Nana's sewing shears from a kitchen drawer—the ones with the zigzagged edges—and began cutting up what remained of the calendar. She sat against the kitchen door, across the room from Nana, snapping the scissors shut fiercely. The charred paper fell to dust with every snip.

Nana bent over the sink and rested her head in her hands. Her shoulders looked curved as a question mark. It struck me then that our Nana was an old person. "What will your parents say?" she said to the window over the sink.

Gretchen pulled a big hunk of hair away from her head and shut the scissors down fast. I hopped by her side from one foot to the other. Nana whirled and raced to us, but most of Gretchen's hair was gone by the time Nana reached her and wrestled the scissors out of her hands.

Nana laid the scissors on top of the refrigerator and got down on the floor with Gretchen. She pulled her into her lap as if Gretchen weren't a twelve-year-old girl, but a baby, and rocked on her knees. Every now and then Nana lifted a hand to rub my calf. It wasn't hard to reach me; I'd plastered myself against her side.

After, Nana sat us at the table and boiled up hot chocolate, even though it was summertime. We blew into our cups while she mopped the floor and swept up the long skeins of Gretchen's hair. Gretchen looked ragged and strange. She'd missed a spot, and a long panel of hair fell behind her. The hair on the sides of her head was all torn up and jutting wildly over her ears. There was a blankness to her eyes, a flat look I'd never seen before, not even when she was trying to kill me.

"Hey, Gretch," I whispered. I leaned over the table and tapped on the tops of the fingernails of her left hand with my own finger, one by one. This was a habit of Mother's, something she'd do absentmindedly while she was talking to one of us. Gretchen didn't say anything, but eventually she stretched her hand out to mine and began doing the same to the hand I wasn't using: she lightly touched each nail. We sat like that while our cups of chocolate cooled between our outstretched arms. We touched, we lightly tapped, as persistently as if we were drumming out Morse code messages to each other.

Finally, Gretchen said, "Just don't tell them, okay, Nana?"

Nana was by the sink, ringing out the mop. For a minute she didn't answer, but stood looking out to her yard and garden behind the house. Without turning, she said, "All right, Gretchen."

The next day, Nana dropped me with Timmy Walston and his mother at the municipal pool. She took Gretchen to the fanciest hairdresser in town, and when they picked me up, Gretchen's hair was cut into wispy, flyaway layers. She looked years older than she was.

Nana kept her promise and never told Mother and Dad about what happened. Not in the next phone call, when she reported how we'd started school in her district, or in the ones that followed through the fall. Nana didn't even tell the story that winter, when Mother and Dad finally did return. They'd called in December and said to get ready: they were coming home. Their weekly gig had never turned into anything bigger. "Besides," Mother said, "this is getting crazy. We go to sleep every night holding on to pictures of you guys—we want the real thing!"

They arrived a few days before Christmas, the roof up, the car packed with all they'd taken plus presents for us. When they came through the back door and saw Gretchen and me, Dad dropped to a crouch and held out his arms, and Mother covered her cheeks with her hands. They both cried when they hugged us. Mother sat on the steps in the corner of Nana's kitchen, pulled Gretchen and me onto her lap, and sniffed the backs of our necks. Dad stood and held onto Nana.

"I can't breathe," she finally said, and Dad laughed and released her. Nana brought her hand to his cheek, and Dad gave a small laugh and shrugged.

"We tried," he said.

Nana nodded.

"What do I smell?" Dad cried, and we all crowded around the kitchen table, while Nana sliced a lamb roast and filled our plates with food. She had lighted candles and laid down a pale green tablecloth to make dinner a formal celebration. Mother and Dad kept reaching across the table to touch Gretchen and me while they told us stories about California. They touched our hands, our cheeks, our shoulders and wrists. Dad turned on the radio and fingered the air along with Hendrix. When we were finished eating, Mother rose with her plate. As she passed, she tousled our hair—first mine, and then Gretchen's. "You look so different, sweetie," Mother said. "But I like it short."

Gretchen and I eyed each other sideways.

"Yes," Nana said, brushing the tablecloth clean, "she looks right this way, doesn't she?" She placed dessert bowls in front of us, empty and gleaming in the candlelight.

"She does," said Dad, "but I still miss those braids. Are your friends cutting their hair short?"

When Gretchen squeezed my knee under the table, I didn't know if it was a warning or a plea. It didn't matter, though. All I did was say what happened. "No," I said to Dad and Mother. "It was her own idea."

ELWOOD REID

Buffalo

Murphy calls, says he wants to meet me down at the Chagrin River after work. "Fish and talk," he says. I can hear machines in the background, people shouting.

"When's after work?"

"Punching the clock now," he says.

"And?"

"And I have a favor to ask."

I hang up, give the radio ten minutes to play something good. Then I leave.

On the way I buy a bottle of Dickel white label and a sack of crushed ice, even though I'm trying to taper back a bit.

In the parking lot, I wait, engine on, radio off, staring at the crisp paper seal on the bottle. The Chagrin River flows through the exposed shale valley on its way to Lake Erie. The water is full of poison. Nobody eats the fish anymore, not even the homeless who camp out under the bridge in summer and who fish with willow branches and shoelaces. The bums in this town wear tweed sports jackets and high-top sneakers with duct tape on them. Sometimes at night I see them standing alongside the road scrounging for returnables.

I watch as cottonwood blossoms drift out into the brown river and stick in the current. Behind me, under a large green-shingled pavilion, city workers are installing the Frontier Days signs, pounding in log posts and tree trunks for the musket sharpshooting contest and axe throw.

Then I see Murphy's van pull in.

I wave and grab my rod out of the truck bed, reach into the cab, and tuck the bottle into the bait bucket. He nods and gets out.

We walk to the river. "How's the factory?" I ask.

Murphy cocks his good ear toward me—eighteen years at the same press, and he's deaf in his machine-side ear. He's got gray skin, thin sand-colored hair, and a bright red face that makes him look angry all the time.

"Still there," he says.

I point at the bottle. He doesn't say anything, just looks at my hands to see if they're shaking. Steady as a rock.

We go to the concrete embankment that overlooks the dam and set our gear down. He runs a worm on a hook, and I do the same, before we drop our lines into the foam. With the poles propped against a rusty girder, we let the sound of the river breaking over the dam fill us.

Ten minutes later I show Murphy the bottle. He breaks the seal and pours the whiskey into two coffee mugs.

I'm trying to quit, you see.

Murphy knows this, says it's a good idea, but won't tell me I shouldn't have one with him. He works—knows how it is, how a little sip or two takes the edge off, rounds off the day.

I've done the meeting thing, listened while some ex-drunk recounts his life story with a Styrofoam cup of coffee trembling in his hands. Sometimes they make me wear a name tag when I'm looking jammed up. Afterwards when everybody herds together to shake hands, hug, and stack fold-up chairs, I just stand back against the wall until one of the old-timers shuffles over to me, slings an arm over my shoulder, and asks me to join in. All the touching and goodwill makes me want to jump out of my skin, especially when they tell me how I gotta fight the good fight and count the days.

I work alone and don't go out much. I fish and brood.

Murphy grabs his rod a minute and then sets it back down.

"Thought I had a nibble," he says, sipping from the mug. "Thanks for coming, last minute and all."

I wave him off.

"This is good," I say.

And it is. Even the river looks nice. Not like the fall coho run when the river is so full of snaggers you feel like dying.

I wait until Murphy looks the other way before taking the first sip.

He turns back around, and I hit him with a question, so he won't start on me about meetings and how he's happy I'm making the effort.

"How's Jeff?" I ask.

Murphy nods. It's the same nod ever since Jeff head-on-ed a

telephone pole on Lost Nation Road three years ago. He was drunk, just coming home after making last call at Delaney's Sunset Inn. There was black ice. He hit the brakes and took out some mailboxes, before the telephone pole. They pried him out of the car. The police said he was going twenty over the limit and that he was lucky to be alive. But there was a closed head injury—one of those wait-and-see things, and he hovered in a coma for a week. When he came out of it, Murphy called me from the hospital to say things were looking up and asked if I could stop by.

But Jeff wasn't right, the bleeding did a number on his brain. Doctors filtered in and out of the room. One of them looked at me and said something about God rolling the dice, and I wanted to smash his white teeth.

Jeff got fat after the accident. His hair grew back in wild white and brown patches where they'd stitched him. During the day Jeff watched television and stared out the window as cars passed by.

"They got him on new pills. Big as my thumb," Murphy says, flipping his worm into the current, where it disappears alongside mine. "And they had a nurse come out to the house to tell me I have to put him on a better diet."

"Better diet?"

"More fiber. Less fat. They want him to live to be a hundred."

Down river a couple of teenagers dressed in rotten sneakers and cutoffs start skipping rocks at a flock of ducks. Their laughter echoes off the shale cliff as the smell of burnt hot dogs wafts over from a noisy family picnic happening under the cottonwoods. And it's a family photo: Dad doing battle with the yellow jackets, while Mom watches her three children run along the tops of the picnic tables throwing water at each other from red plastic cups.

"What's the favor?" I ask. For a minute I think he's going to ask how my meetings have been going, and I steady my hands against the concrete.

He clears his throat and fiddles with the drag setting on his reel. "Well, Jeff saw one of them stupid ads on the television for Frontier Days. They got these spots with a bunch of guys running around the woods in buckskin pants and long rifles. They're on during the Tribe games. In between innings—you've seen them."

"I guess I haven't," I say.

"Well, Jeff likes them," he says. "Keeps telling me how he wants to go, wants to see the axe toss and buffalo stampede."

"I thought the mayor nixed the buffaloes this year."

"I don't think so," he says. "Anyway. I've got to work this Saturday."

Just then one of the kids from the picnic table approaches the embankment and tosses a hot dog into the water. The hot dog eddies in the current before sinking and leaving an oily trail of mustard floating on the water. The father murmurs an apology, but Murphy waves him off.

"Can't you call in sick?" I ask.

Murphy shakes his head and checks his line. Most of his worm has been nibbled off.

"We're short as it is. Betty Brownlow quit and got married. Can't get the God squaders to work the weekends, and foreman Frank's pissing and moaning about meeting some deadline. Hell, I promised them."

"So you need me...," I start.

"I wouldn't ever ask, but I tried Mrs. Evers already."

My hands tremble as I watch Murphy bait his hook again.

"I'll have to put off a little job I got going," I lie.

Murphy licks his lips and runs his fingers through his thinning hair then. "I know it's a lot to ask," he says, "but he's got it in his head to see a live buffalo. It would mean a lot to him."

"No problem," I say. "Does he remember me?"

"Sure he does," Murphy says excitedly. "Just don't touch him, remember that."

"You sure about this?"

"You'd be doing me one big favor," he says.

I don't say a word. The river hisses and snakes around logs and rocks, kids scream in the distance, and after a few minutes it's just us fishing again, and everything is normal. Then the sun starts to go down. Damp air drops off the hills, and I know that I don't dare have another drink in front of Murphy. So I fill his mug, screw the cap back on the bottle, and tuck it into the bucket where I can't see it.

"You can pick him up in the morning," Murphy says.

"No problem," I say, pulling my line against the current and then letting it drift free for a moment before it thuds to a stop.

* * *

When Saturday rolls around, I haven't had a drop in three days. My face feels like it wants to peel off. My hands hurt. I pull on my clothes and stir together breakfast. Murphy calls me from the plant. I can hear the presses in the background. He has to shout. Says he wants to remind me that Jeff knows I'm coming and that it was all he could talk about last night. He tries to thank me again, and I tell him to forget it, that it'll be fun and everything will be okay. A promise is a promise and all that.

The last time I went to Frontier Days was with this woman named Marie who got drunk on peach schnapps and threw up on the Roto-Twirl. I was out of work then and crazy from sitting around on my hands, waiting for the phone to ring. I never saw her again. Then I got work and was too busy to even think about her, just the money fluttering in from the jobs and the promise of a drink after the tools were put away. I had life in a box. There was no future, just each day, one at a time. I started kicking things around, looking at my options, like some sort of high noon of the soul. Instead of charting a course I spent a lot of time deciding what I didn't want to be, drinking toasts to this and that, getting by. But then nothing happened. I am still a carpenter, still waiting.

At the meetings this old guy named Baron tries to make me feel welcome. He tells me stories about how he helped build city hall back when they did all the figuring in their heads. He says he used to drink two bottles of beer after work and felt good about where his life was going. Then it was six, and from there it was a hop, skip, and a jump to twelve and the bottle. He asks me if I keep count. I pretend not to hear.

I drive over to Murphy's. It is a small two-bedroom bungalow with a nice dogwood tree in the front yard. The only evidence of his ex-wife, Katrina, are a few patches of flowers left over from her sudden gardening binges. Since her departure Murphy has managed to neglect or mow over most of the once burgeoning flowerbeds, leaving only a few yellow daylilies and anemic gladiolas.

I ring the bell and wait until the door swings open. Jeff stands behind the glass storm door, staring at me blankly for a moment like a bank teller. He's tall and pear-shaped, and his hair looks as if somebody else has combed it. I wave, and he smiles before opening the door. I forget and extend a hand for him to shake. He looks at me and puts his hand behind his back.

"Can I go now?" he asks. He shuffles closer. "Dad says I go see buffalo right now."

"Sure," I say.

"Right now."

His brown eyes, still crusted with sleep, stare at my mouth and then at my hands. Not so steady with those three days. I get nervous and clap a few times and tell him to saddle up. He jumps up and down, patting his hair down and shifting his weight from side to side.

He settles and then goes to the door, opens it carefully, and peers outside, as if snipers are waiting for him.

I point at the truck. "You still want to go?" I ask, hoping he'll shake his head no and that will be it. Favor extended. Favor refused. But I've already sunk three days into this for Murphy, so I point at the truck again.

"Sure, yeah," he slurs. "Very cool, very cool—I go."

I step out into the sunlight and head toward the truck.

I buckle his seat belt for him. He stiffens when I touch him and sits staring out through the windshield as if he's remembering his accident all over again. Then I show him how the radio works. He punches the buttons from station to station. "I like them all now," he says, his voice flat and spooky. Before the accident, he was just another young thug, learning to drink and lie, generally up to no good with no strong feeling either way on criminal behavior. And now he's got nurses coming over, feeding him pills, talking about his diet.

I let him roll down the window and stick his head out like a dog. The wind pulls his face into a smile, and for a moment he's pure joy. Suddenly he pulls his head inside. A large wasp is tangled in his hair. It flexes its wings a minute before shooting out the window to freedom.

"We're going to Frontier Days," I say, trying to put some party in the line.

"Dad told me. Buffalo, they going to shoot the buffalo, and I'm gonna watch."

"They won't shoot the buffalo," I say. "They're for people to look at."

My hands are shaking again, and I'm talking too loud.

"You say, whatever," he says as we dip into the river valley and turn off at the Daniel's Park sign. A huge banner that reads FRONTIER DAYS has been strung across two elm trees. Jeff stops punching the radio button and stares at the banner as a policeman in an orange vest points his flashlight, directing us down a dirt path to a line of parked cars. Several families waddle by armed with fold-up lawn chairs and coolers. Groups of children scurry past the truck carrying unlit sparklers and miniature American flags in tight pink fists. Jeff watches the people, and I wait for something to come across his face, a smile or frown. Nothing.

We park. Jeff stretches and stares at the sun. Off in the distance I can hear the echo of gunshots and cheers. A fat man in a buckskin jacket crashes out of a blue Port-a-John, buckling his pants. Jeff stops stretching and stares.

"Davy fucking Crockett," he says, pointing.

The man glares at us, his eyes full of beer and maybe too many hours of work. He's got hands like a welder and one of those I-ride-a-Harley beards.

"Problem?" he says to Jeff.

Jeff freezes, crazy smile plastered across his face.

"He's...," I start.

The man nods. "I understand," he says, walking away. Jeff makes a gun with his fingers and shoots the man in the back, laughs, and then falls silent again. He wanders over to the river and stands there on the muddy bank, head bowed.

That's when I start looking for the bright blue and yellow of the beer garden tent.

"We can come back and look at the water later," I say, hoping he doesn't jump in after something and drown.

He gapes at me, and for a moment I realize he has no clue who I am—just this guy hustling him away from the river to get to some beer.

I walk back up through the crowd, and he follows me to the beer tent. I buy a string of tickets and order a beer, sip off the warm foam, and give Jeff two tickets. He carefully takes them without touching my hand and orders a Coke. He gulps it down and burps loudly. The counter girl looks at me and smiles. She has hickeys on her neck and stringy dirt-blond hair that falls across her narrow face.

"More," Jeff says. She pours him another, less ice this time. He drinks it down and leaves.

We move through the crowd. Nobody steps in front of Jeff. One look at his checked-out expression, and people move the other way and whisper.

Jeff follows the gunshots and comes to a small field lined with a brown snow fence. The air is thick with black powder and wet grass. Families sit on wool blankets and lawn chairs. The children watch as men and women dressed like pathfinders load muskets on rickety plywood tables. A chubby woman in an old-fashioned lace dress stands on a riser, waving her handkerchief at the shooters.

"Gentlemen," she says. "Load your weapons."

Two old-timers dressed in pinstriped shirts and derby hats stand near the targets, ready to tally scores on a marker board. Jeff gawks at the guns a minute before making his way to the front of the crowd, yelling "Excuse me" in people's ears. I follow him, apologizing in his wake, knowing there's not enough beer in the world to make this any easier.

Somebody whoops and throws an empty beer cup onto the field as the rifles fire and gray-blue smoke drifts out over the crowd. The old-timers go to the targets and dig around with pencils and yell out who hit what.

When I catch up to Jeff, he is pressed up against the yellow divider rope and snow fence, watching the men in buckskin slip ramrods down into their rifles. A woman dressed in a coonskin cap and shooting gloves with long ribbons of brown fringe looks at us and says, "Howdy."

Jeff says howdy back, just long and flat enough for her to suspect that something's wrong. She looks at me like I'm his father and smiles politely before loading her gun.

"Shoot," Jeff yells. He laughs and pats his hair.

A little girl dressed in a Mickey Mouse T-shirt and yellow shorts points at Jeff, shaking a piece of watermelon at him. Her mother leans over and tells her to eat the melon and not to play with it. The girl stomps her feet and throws the wedge of melon on the ground. Jeff stares at the melon in the dirt until the crack of rifles breaks his attention.

We watch the contest. Lady Buckskin hits a bull's-eye and bows to the crowd, blowing kisses. Two other men take aim with mirrors over their shoulders and fire. Afterwards, they hold the mirrors up to the crowd. Jeff cranes his neck to see himself in the mirror, pushing his belly tight against the rope as I drain the rest of my beer.

This is easy, I tell myself.

Just as I start thinking about another beer, the little girl in the Mickey Mouse T-shirt approaches Jeff again and taps him on the knee. He freezes and starts yelling, "Hot, hot, hot, hot!" His arms shoot down to his sides, and the girl runs away crying.

"Sorry," I say to the girl's mother. I give her some parental shorthand that tells her Jeff is not right.

Jeff stops screaming when the lady in the dress calls out for the shooters to shoot and the loaders to load. I think about Murphy punching the button on his press, worrying about Jeff and sweating the time clock.

"Want another Coke?" I ask Jeff. He nods and begins walking toward the beer tent, yelling "Excuse me" loud enough to shake up this old couple having a go at some cotton candy.

We make the beer tent and stand in line. Jeff rocks back and forth, one foot then the other, humming.

A woman bumps into me from behind. I turn around and look into eyes so brown my heart stops beating for a minute and my throat goes dry. She has long hair the color of fresh asphalt and slight bags under her eyes, which make her look tired and sexy.

"Sorry," she says, placing a hand on my shoulder. I can smell the beer on her breath and try peeking down the front of her white muscle T-shirt. There's nobody with her, and I start thinking about getting lucky when Jeff turns around and burps at us.

She laughs.

"Yours?" she asks, tapping an empty beer cup against her hips.

"Sort of and not really," I tell her.

She bites her lower lip and laughs again. "Which is it?"

"I'm doing a favor for my buddy." I lean into her so Jeff can't hear. "He was in an accident. Scrambled him some."

She nods and looks at me over her empty beer glass.

"You want another one?" I ask.

"If you're buying," she says.

"All day," I say, showing her my string of tickets.

"You bet."

Jeff sees the tickets. "Ooh," he says, rubbing his stomach.

I hand him a few.

"You look familiar. You ever go to meetings?"

"Depends what kind," I say. "And who's asking."

"Wanda," she says. "And you know what I'm talking about."

I nod. "I go sometimes."

"I thought I recognized you," she says.

"My name's Dan," I say, extending a hand for her to shake.

"We're not supposed to be doing this," she says, pointing at the beer glasses. "But my divorce papers just came through, and I live just up the street, and you know what?"

"What?"

"I got tired of hearing the people having fun. It was making me sad. It was either this or listen to music all by myself and get depressed then spend the night looking for a meeting. So I said what the hell—how many times you get divorced?"

"Not many, I hope."

We watch Jeff order another Coke. He carefully places two tickets on the counter and jerks his hand away before pointing at the soda machine.

"How come you never talk at the meetings?" Wanda asks. "Me, I just let it all out, and I don't give a damn what they think."

"I don't really have a problem," I say.

"Sure," she says. "Neither do I. I just like going to meetings in smoky basements."

"It's not like that."

"Don't worry, I won't tell. Me—I'm kissing three months goodbye, and I've never felt better. What's the longest for you?"

"I already told you it's not like that."

"We can play that game."

"Deal," I say.

She pauses, rolls her eyes, and I can see she's had too many.

"You ought to talk more at the meetings," she says. "People are beginning to wonder about you."

"That's okay with me."

"The mystery man," she says, shaking her hair.

I buy her another beer, and when I turn around to hand it to her, she says, "Your friend—he just walked off."

I search the crowd looking for his slump shoulders and crazy hair, and it's as if he's vanished.

"Did you see where he went?" I ask, trying not to panic.

"He took off that way when you weren't looking. C'mon, we'll find him," she says, taking my hand and leading me through the crowd.

We check the axe and hatchet throw, the midway. No Jeff. I start thinking about Murphy and begin jogging. Wanda follows, apologizing as I race over to the corn-roasting pit. By the time we hit the midway again, I'm running. Voices blur into a beery chowder as game tenders yell out for suckers—Three Darts Three Balloon One Buck, Dunk the Clown, Guess Your Weight.

We walk back to the river, and still no Jeff. Wanda glances at me, and I can see the fear registering in her eyes, making her sober.

"This wasn't supposed to happen. I'm responsible for him. I promised his father."

"Maybe he went back to the car?"

"Where are the buffalo?" I ask her.

"Over there," she says, lifting a few damp strands of hair from her neck.

I take her hand and lead her through the crowd. Overhead, the Tilt-a-Whirl casts a band-shaped shadow across the trampled grass.

We smell them first, a sun-baked stew of wet carpet, dead dog, and buffalo shit. Several people rush past us with worried looks on their faces. When I hear one of them say something about a man chasing buffalo, my tongue drops back into my lungs.

Wanda sees him first. She gasps and points at a group of rent-a-cops and a police officer circling a small herd of dusty-looking buffalo. One of the officers has his revolver drawn while the rent-a-cops brandish flashlights. More people dash by, others point cameras at the spectacle.

Then I see Jeff, standing inside the pen surrounded by the animals, his red Cleveland Indians T-shirt visible against the dirty brown fur. A man dressed in buckskins talks through a bullhorn at Jeff, his words breaking in choppy amplified waves I can't make out.

I push my way to the front of the crowd and see Jeff waving his arms, as if he is orchestrating some private dance with the buffalo as they mill around him. I hop the fence and pull Wanda over. Her shorts catch on a stave iron and tear.

"Shit," she says, dark, sweaty hair cascading around her face as she steadies herself against me. "Just my luck."

"He's going to get killed," I say.

A rent-a-cop intercepts us and points a heavy steel flashlight at my chest like a gun. "Please remain behind the fence," he says.

"His name's Jeff," I tell him.

Wanda nods and grabs my hand, lacing her fingers through mine and squeezing. The rent-a-cop lowers the flashlight, his hands shaking slightly.

"Are you with him?" the rent-a-cop asks, pointing out to the animals.

"He's not right," I say.

"What was your first clue?" he says. Sweat boils out of his pores, running down his neck and soaking his tight collar.

I glare at him and clench my jaw.

"I'm sorry," he stammers, tossing his hands into the air. "It's just we've got a real situation here."

One of the police officers steps away from the ring of onlookers and approaches us. "You know that man?" the officer asks, pointing at Jeff. His face is webbed with broken vessels, and his nose looks as if it has been broken more than a few times.

I nod. "He's with me."

He squints. "Well, he started yelling, said he was going to shoot or something. We think maybe he's got a gun."

"He doesn't have a gun," I say, tightly.

"I don't want to be the one to find out," the officer says. "And I don't want to get stampeded or anyone else for that matter."

"He just wants to see the animals."

"Yeah, but that don't fix our problem now, does it? He gets himself hurt, the city's liable. Are you gonna take responsibility for that?"

"I'll get him," I say.

"As long as nobody gets hurt," he says. "I don't want to have to start shooting buffalo and upset the kids."

I walk out to where the buffalo are pinched into a tight herd.

All the grass has been worn away from their hooves. The noise of the crowd drops away like I'm in some sort of box. Jeff sees me coming and starts waving.

When I'm near the outside edge of the herd, I put my hands out in front of me and close my eyes. I wait until the ground stops shaking before opening my eyes. Three feet in front of me stands one of the larger buffalo. It shakes its mane and stomps, causing the whole herd to shift about nervously. I take a few more steps, figuring there are only two ways to come out of this mess: dead or injured.

I move slowly, touching the animals on the sides, guiding them away from me until one of them leans its rump into me and I can feel every muscle in its body quiver.

Jeff wades farther into the brown mass, daring me to follow him through the animals. Several of them lower their horns as I pass by, touching their dirty flanks. I glance over my shoulder to find Wanda, but I can't pick her out of the crowd.

When I get within ten feet of Jeff, a pair of buffalo step in front of me and lower their shaggy heads as if they are protecting him from my advance.

"Go now," Jeff says, patting an animal on the back as it leans into him. I edge around to the other side, and again the animals react and block my path.

"Don't shoot them," Jeff says.

"It's Dan," I say. "Nobody's going to shoot anything."

He shakes his head, and one of the animals starts licking his leg. Jeff's face lights into a grin, and suddenly I see how delicate the whole thing is, how maybe he moves too fast or hits one of them and the whole herd charges the fences, trampling trash barrels, scattering pylons, and crushing children.

But he doesn't.

He lets the animal lick him, and I work my way through the last wall of animals until I am standing beside him.

"Steady," I say. Jeff looks at me and shakes his head. I can hear the crowd now. Little children screaming and pointing; drunks yelling out advice. I shut my ears and put out a hand for Jeff. The buffalo at his side stops licking and looks at me. Jeff stares at my hand. I hold my breath and inch toward him as if I'm going after somebody stuck in the ice. The breeze picks up and lifts the stink of animals away for a moment, allowing the scent of warm summer river water and cotton candy to drift across us. The animals shift nervously, and before I know it, I am surrounded by them, my chest filled with the sound of their hooves pounding the ground. I force myself to move closer, and just as I'm near enough to touch him, he wraps his arms around one of the buffalo. For a minute I expect the whole herd to move in one merciless brown swarm, tramping me like grass. But they don't.

The animal stands there as Jeff presses his face into its neck and smells. I touch his back. He ignores me and keeps on hugging. The animal's eye rolls in my direction, and for a moment I don't know what to do. I take my hand off Jeff. The bullhorn cackles more words I can't understand. Muskets crack and split the air in the distance. Jeff looks at me, his face covered with fur and dirt, and for the first time today I recognize someone in his eyes—a flicker of the person he might have been. He squeezes harder and harder, his face buried against the animal, and when he looks up his face is blank, the moment gone.

As the animals begin nudging and pushing me out of the circle, closing ranks, I start thinking of Murphy and what I'm going to tell him as Jeff's arms tighten around the buffalo's dusty neck. His body is soft and helpless against the thick brown of the buffalo. I wonder if I look the same or worse to the people in the crowd. A man afraid to move. A man frozen among the animals where touch is everything. The only thing.

JOAN SILBER

Commendable

Marcia's parents, who still lived in New Jersey, were truly happy when she came to live in the East again. Her father said, "Hey! That's more like it," when she first told them she was moving to New York. "About time!" her mother said. Nobody mentioned the years when they had been so bitterly against her. Her parents were old now, and the fights were over long since. And what had they fought about? Sex, Marcia would say. Sex in various forms. And who had asked them to be so nosy? Marcia had lived with some men who were not great people, she had danced in a topless club, she had been in one dirty movie that very few people saw. But it had never been her idea to share this news or to try to make it intelligible to them. Her poor parents, how raging and mean they had been. And the whole thing had been one spell of time for Marcia, among many, and not the most regrettable. For years now she'd been a regular person who worked at a job, and her parents said, "Sweetheart, you are so gorgeous," when they saw her, and, "Don't be a stranger," when she left.

Now that Marcia was living nearby, she could see that her parents had changed quite a lot. They had once been sociable people, bridge players and party givers, but now they hardly went out. Her father was convinced that the teenage boy next door was casing the house when he walked around in his own backyard, and her mother believed that someone was stealing gravel from their driveway. They gave their dire reports with foxy satisfaction; oh, they knew what was going on, they were well-aware. "It's a different world," they said, correctly, although its difference made them read it wrong, Marcia thought.

They were still in the same house where Marcia had grown up, a roomy Colonial that got good sun. And the town seemed remarkably the same, Marcia decided, when she came for a weekend and was sent out to shop. Mitchell's Hardware was still there, only with a new sign, and Garfield's Fine Footwear was in the same spot on Franklin Avenue. Even the shoes in the window looked eternal—patent Mary Janes for little girls, brown oxfords for men, pointy pumps for women.

On the other hand, where the Sweet Shoppe had been was a store that sold exercise equipment, and next door was a Caffe delle Quattro Stagioni, which smelled deliciously of espresso. The Caffe was all chrome and tile, sleekly authentic, but the woman coming out of the door, as Marcia went by, could have been one of the mothers from her youth. She had a look of breezy competence that Marcia had almost forgotten about, a modest but sturdy expression; she wore a blouse and Bermuda shorts, and she had her hair in a short, tidy cut (like a little cap, Marcia's mother would have said). "Hello, hello," the woman said. "What are you doing here?" She was definitely speaking to Marcia.

"Visiting the old homestead," Marcia said. "How are you?" She had no idea, not a clue.

The woman chuckled, a little spitefully, and said, "You don't know me, do you?" but from that dark chuckle Marcia did know. It was Kaye Brightley, older sister of Ivy, who had been Marcia's best friend in junior high.

And what was Kaye doing here? She lived here, had always lived here; she had a job at the pharmaceutical company on the highway, and she had her own house out by where Heiling's Ice Cream used to be. "How's Ivy?" Marcia said.

"In London still. She likes it. You know she's divorced? Her kids are fine, they're old now. She's good, she's living with someone. How are *you* doing?"

Marcia said she was just now on her way to buy tomato plants for her mother.

"I wouldn't get them at Mitchell's, if I were you," Kaye said. "The really good place is the nursery in East Brook. That's where Jimmy gets his, and he has an amazing garden."

"Jimmy McPhaill?" Marcia said.

Was nothing changed here at all? Jimmy had been Kaye's constant companion all through high school. For a while they'd had a romance (of some kind, Ivy and Marcia had done a lot of wild guessing about what kind), but this had fallen apart soon, and after a brief cooling-off period they'd gone back to being buddies. Marcia thought later that Jimmy was probably gay. An opera lover, a sports hater, an impassioned fan of Emily Dickinson. Although now when she thought of him, he seemed corny and avuncular and hearty, someone whose jokes would be all wrong in most gay circles.

She and Ivy, the young pests, had hung around Jimmy as much as he would let them, pale and unhandsome though he was. He had been quite nice to them. He lent them books and made them listen to Gilbert and Sullivan. He took them out for sundaes, with Kaye, and acted tickled by their greed for chocolate, their crushes on the counter guy. Marcia and Ivy were goofy, feverish creatures then; by the time they were more composed, he was gone. Kaye was always shooing them away—"Hey, kidlets, go take a short walk off a long pier"—but she put up with them better than most older sisters would have.

"He's a stupendous gardener," Kaye said. "Every square inch of his yard, back and front, has something sprouting out of it. Every year there's more."

"Say what you will," Marcia groaned, "New York does not have real vegetation. They chain down the saplings."

Marcia went on so long about New York's pathetic, scraggly ginko trees that before she knew it, she was agreeing to go see Jimmy's place. "He can tell you everything you need to know about tomatoes," Kaye said. "He's the one who knows. And then you can get a quick view of the garden, which you really have to see."

Marcia followed Kaye's car out of the town's old center, onto a road with a little mall of newer stores, into the hillier, wealthier, more countrified expanses where Jimmy's parents had always lived. The parents were both dead by now, Marcia had just been told, and he was in their house alone.

Even from a distance you could see that these grounds were like nothing else around them. Marcia's first impression was of an illustration from a Victorian children's book, with roses on trellises and sweet peas clinging by their tendrils to a fence. Everything seemed lush and innocent. And that was only the side of the house. When they parked in the back, they walked out into something more formal and rhythmic—beds of red and pink and blue, trailing arches of lavender and white, and even a sculpted bramble in the shape of a spire. Marcia, who did not know the names of many flowers, was dazzled by the cunning, intricate shapes, the bell-shaped cups, and the open, flat blooms, big as cymbals, and the cascades of frothy white bushes. Sitting on a bench was a large person in a striped shirt and khakis who was Jimmy.

"I didn't know you were coming!" he said to Kaye. He got up to greet her. He was better-looking as a grownup, more evenly proportioned. He'd become a broad-faced man with a beard, quite substantial. Still a little soft around the edges, maybe. When Marcia was explained to him, he said, "Well, well, well."

He thought she didn't like him. He thought she still found him clumsy and unimpressive. Once, when he was home from college, he had taken her out for ice cream, and she had acted quite superior with him. Marcia had forgotten all about this part of it.

Kaye made Jimmy give a tour of every petal and leaf in the garden, which Marcia was genuinely thrilled by. "What do you think?" Kaye said. "Unbelievable, right?"

"You're amazing," Marcia told Jimmy. "I'm amazed. This is too much, this place."

"Right," he said.

"This is a whole kingdom here. You must work your fingers to the bone, just to get the tea roses like that."

Marcia was gushing, but he was hard to talk to, and it was often her instinct to flatter men. She supposed she wanted to stop this; maybe not.

"I've never seen a private garden as incredible as this."

"Shucks," he said.

"No, really."

"I could show you the potting shed," he said. "That's what makes it easier, that I had that built here. The hideaway."

"She doesn't want to see that ratty piece of architecture," Kaye said. "Let her sit down."

Uh-oh. Marcia sat down, just in case Kaye thought she was after Jimmy.

"Do you like root beer?" Kaye said. Jimmy was sent inside to bring them some.

"This place *is* incredible," Marcia said, one more time.

"Every night when I come over, he's playing in the dirt," Kaye said. "He wouldn't do vegetables for a long time, but I talked him into it."

Jimmy was back with the root beer in glass mugs. "The Kaye does not believe in ice cubes for this beverage."

If they weren't a couple, they managed to sound like one. And they matched: the primly casual clothes, the streaks of gray in their hair. But perhaps they were both thinking that Marcia looked foolishly juvenile with her bleached ponytail and her short sundress. They wanted to hear about whatever she'd been up to. A long story; Marcia stuck to the here and now. She had a little, little apartment in New York—the size of a gym locker—and she was a program counselor at Planned Parenthood.

"I see a lot of teenage girls," she said. "You would not believe some of the outfits. They're a cute group. And quite hip. We didn't know about getting our own birth control at that age."

"Speak for yourself," Kaye said.

"Why, Kaye," Marcia said.

"I mean boys knew to buy condoms. Another idea that's come around again."

"Car fins are next," Jimmy said.

"We didn't have the risks," Kaye said, "that they have now."

Had Kaye had sex in high school? Marcia had never imagined her doing any such thing—Kaye with her boxy body, her flat voice. When things got wild in America, Kaye was already out of school. Marcia, who was only five years younger, thought of herself as from another generation, on the boat Kaye had just missed. But who knew what Kaye had been up to? Perhaps she and Jimmy had ventured into those waters, and then turned back.

"Condoms aren't the only things we send people out with," Marcia said. "It depends."

"Better than having them on welfare, right, Jimmy?" Kaye said.

"I'm not against freedom for anybody," Jimmy said. "I just wish they had husbands so the taxpayers wouldn't have to marry them."

"Those stubborn girls," Marcia said, "turning away those eager husbands."

They probably thought she sounded bitter, which she was not, or not about those things; heartless desertions hadn't been her problem. She liked men still, she still cooed and trilled around them, and when would this end? She hoped before it became ridiculous.

Jimmy said, "Okay, blame the boys. Go ahead." On that last trip out for a sundae with Jimmy, she remembered now, he had turned caustic when she'd said she was going to be very, very busy the next few days. "Thank you for your time this afternoon," he had said. And she had not told Kaye, although she had tried earlier to brag about things like that to Kaye.

"Jimmy gets stuck on one idea," Kaye said. "Who could believe that husbands are the answer?"

"I couldn't, personally," Marcia said. "I've had three. One of them isn't quite done yet. You ever have one?"

"Not me," Kaye said.

"Me, neither," Jimmy said.

"I got to see things, at least, because of them," Marcia said. "I lived in Mexico, and before that I was in Senegal for a while."

"I've only been to England," Kaye said. "To see Ivy."

"Where I'd like to go someday is Japan," Jimmy said. "I'd be interested to see the gardens."

"Me, too," Kaye said. Jimmy had money. What was stopping them?

"Asia," Jimmy said, "is great for games." He went and got his mah-jongg set to show Marcia; the tiles were antique ivory. Marcia said the set was beautiful, but she begged off on joining their tournament, which had been running for years, according to the score sheets. Actually in Mexico, where she'd had a lot of leisure, Marcia had been quite a passable mah-jongg player.

By the time Marcia got advice about the tomato plants, she decided it was too late to drive over to buy them in East Brook. When she called home to explain where she was, her mother didn't seem to mind. "I've been hanging out with Kaye Brightley and her boyfriend," Marcia said. "Remember Ivy? Kaye's the sister."

"I know who she is, she's been around here for years. Boyfriend who?" Marcia's mother said. "I thought she liked girls."

It was Marcia's first summer in the East in many years, and she had underestimated how hot New York could get. The wiring in her building was too old for air conditioners. She took dips in the municipal pool on Carmine Street, remnant of a nobler civic vision and safe even now, but so crowded it was like swimming on the subway. As a child, she had swum in Russell Pond in Russell

Park, a few blocks from her house. The pond's bottom was as muddy as ever, she found out one weekend; the water was warm and smelled like tadpoles. Local children were surprised to see her there; adults almost never went in, and most of the morning you had to be a kid taking a class to use it. Several times Marcia swam there in the late afternoon, when the light was bright and dappled.

Neither Kaye nor Jimmy would go with her. Too public, and Kaye had once seen a leech in the water. (So had Marcia, but not lately.) But whenever she could, Marcia stopped in at Jimmy's garden before she went home, and had gin and tonics with the two them; the root beer, it turned out, was only for before three. "Greetings, thirsty voyager," Jimmy would say. Marcia was still stumped on the question of whether they were a couple or not. They seemed to spend together every minute that Kaye wasn't working. (Jimmy lived off what he referred to as family holdings and seemed to have quite an open schedule.) They went out for movies and dinners and drives to the country, and their conversation was as full of old stories and minor bickering as any couple's. Marcia had never seen them embrace, but they were Episcopalians, as Marcia's mother liked to point out, and not young. But then why did they live separately, why wouldn't they marry each other? Kaye's house—small and ugly, in a new development—was bare and provisional inside, as if she were waiting to see about it, although she had lived there for years.

On weekends Kaye did go off without Jimmy for a few hours, to play basketball with a group of women, and it was this—and her square-torsoed, no-nonsense sturdiness—that had given Marcia's mother her ideas about Kaye's sexual preference. "And her manner," Marcia's mother said. She found Kaye gruff and unaccommodating. "A person who is not trying to be pleasant."

"Mother," Marcia said. "Nobody goes through the day being girly and sugary anymore. Kaye has a responsible job. She wears a suit and bosses people around."

"I heard. She makes a nice living," Marcia mother said.

"They all have to now," Marcia's father said. "Am I right?"

Marcia could not imagine Kaye having sex with another woman (something she had watched in person, in fact, more than once), but she knew that watching was unnatural, and so anyone was almost impossible to picture swept away in the mechanics.

Marcia herself had never much liked mirrors; she liked to close her eyes. So perhaps Kaye had known unspeakable splendors. And Jimmy was a whole other set of secrets.

Neither of them seemed at all miserable. Kaye liked her job, as far as Marcia could see. She talked about it with a possessive irritation, a pride in its vexations, always, Marcia thought, a sign of love. She complained about how she always had to check every little thing her "people" did without making them feel like nincompoops; she was probably good at all this.

One night Kaye telephoned Marcia at home for advice about what to wear to a company awards banquet. "A swank affair," she said. She must have been to this kind of thing before, but she probably knew that her type—the dowdy woman of great integrity—wasn't what was wanted for corporate display; she was a respected throwback. "Dark red silk would be good with your coloring," Marcia said. "Spend money." But they both knew Kaye would look like Kaye, anyway.

Otherwise they never spoke to each other outside Marcia's visits; neither Kaye nor Jimmy showed the slightest interest in setting foot on the island of Manhattan. Marcia could go for a few weeks without thinking about either of them; her job was busy and packed with other people's crises, and at night she had long, ill-advised phone conversations with Alejandro, the man she had left her husband, Mike, for, and also with Mike, who was now living with a twenty-five-year-old but was balking about the divorce.

Marcia was glad for her solitude, with its peace and freedom, but she was sorry she was never going to sleep with either Mike or Alejandro again. And perhaps with no one else, either; she knew lots of people—men and women both, her age and other ages—who did without. She could see the advantages, but she had lived a good part of her life trying to be faithful to the currents of desire, sworn to that, if to nothing else. At nineteen, in the topless bar, prancing around on that little catwalk stage, she'd thought she was dancing out the most urgent truth, repeating what everyone knew, only more prettily, with her smudged eyes and her rouged breasts; what a vain girl she had been and how caught up in one single idea. And even later, when she couldn't stand to be anywhere near the Carnival Club, nothing had seemed clearer to her than the primacy of sexual feeling. But maybe her own fate was that she had passed now into another stage, another state. She could imagine it, or almost. But she would have to move to another line of work, where she wasn't all the time explaining to teenagers where their cervixes were.

In a general way, she was fine now, with her tiny apartment, her ambling routines, her touristy pleasure in the noise and sociability of the New York streets. She had a few old friends here from other places, and a few cronies at work whom she liked. In autumn the weather was clear and pleasant; Manhattan (she told Alejandro) was a handsome city, garbage and all.

In the brightest part of October, Kaye called to ask if Marcia wanted to come spend a weekend with them in the country, in a house Jimmy's father had owned, near the Delaware Water Gap. Another relative used it in the summer, but Jimmy wouldn't leave his garden then, and Kaye said they liked it in the fall. "Come be a leaf peeper," Kaye said. "We don't do anything more strenuous than that, I promise."

"You always missed the autumns in the East," Mike said, when she told him she was going.

On Saturday morning she took the train to New Jersey, where Kaye and Jimmy met her at the station, and they rode over highways whose bordering trees were suddenly blazing with color. All that miraculous color, the backlit leaves glowing against the sky, made Marcia fiercely homesick for Alejandro and for Mike, for things over and done with.

The house, which had been quite isolated when he was a kid, Jimmy said, was now on a road dotted with new chalets and A-frames. In the afternoon, joggers of all ages went past and waved to the three of them on the porch; they sat sipping bourbon and sodas, Kaye's drink of choice for the season. The hillside behind them was dazzling.

At dusk they went inside, and Kaye brought out a Scrabble set. "Don't let Jimmy try his fake words. He's ruthless," she said. They were clever players, both of them, good at placing their letters on the high-scoring squares and reusing q's and x's; Marcia was beaten badly. "The Kaye is unstoppable tonight," Jimmy said.

In the kitchen, Kaye stood at the stove, with a bib apron over her wool slacks, and made them what she called a lazy dinner, chicken baked in some sort of salad dressing, not bad. "Children," she said, "you may pick up your drumsticks. We're in the country."

Would Kaye have made a good mother? You could say she had the life of a suburban matron, without the family to go with it. Had she been cheated of her best fate, or would she have been one of those sour, hotly resigned mothers of Marcia's childhood? If Kaye mourned the road not taken, it didn't show. And she did have Jimmy, who at the moment was gnawing away intently at his bone. "You can't get a better bird than this," he said. "Not if you shot it yourself." They were three middle-aged adults without children, although Marcia had at least done things you wouldn't want kids along for. Not that anyone was handing out medals for that.

"In Senegal the chicken, when you got any, was as tough as shoe leather," Marcia said. "At dinners, conversations would hit these long pauses while people were chewing." She noticed she wanted to brag about herself, where she had been and with whom.

"I'd like to go to Africa," Jimmy said.

"He doesn't even have a passport," Kaye said.

"Actually, mine is expired, too," Marcia said.

"Really?" Kaye said. "This shocks me, about you."

"Oh, boy," Marcia said. "My current life would really shock you, then. I don't do a thing."

"What qualifies as a thing?" Jimmy said.

"Don't ask," Marcia said. He looked sly and laughed his old laugh, a hawing guffaw. Marcia felt very racy, not happily. It might be harder than she'd thought, spending a whole weekend with the two of them.

But then Kaye brought out the dessert—do-it-yourself sundaes, with fudge sauce and Reddi-wip and shredded coconut and a jar of walnuts in syrup. "You don't do this all the time, do you?" Marcia said.

"Sure we do," Kaye said.

"Sundae comes once a week," Jimmy said. "Isn't that the idea?"

"I'm in heaven," Marcia said.

Where were Jimmy and Kaye each planning to sleep? That was the question. Marcia's own suitcase had been taken to a dark corner room with sloped eaves, charming in a gloomy way, across the hall from the master bedroom, whose open door showed that somebody's method of unpacking was to dump all the stuff on the floor. When they all went upstairs to bed, Jimmy went into this room, and Kaye stood in the hall saying, "Sweet dreams," and then she went into another bedroom, next door to Marcia's. That's it, then, Marcia thought, I should have known.

Marcia was probably glad, more or less. Lying in the single bed, under a weighty mound of wool blankets, she liked to think of all three of them tucked up in their separate realms, cozy enough. Like children, or like commendable old people in a British novel. To each his own, she thought.

But in the middle of the night Marcia was awakened by a single, soft cry. From Jimmy's room she could hear gasping and short, quick breaths. Ah, well, she thought, let them, but she felt like a man in the audience at the Carnival Club, trapped in his own rapt attention, dumb and hooked and mocked. (*Who doesn't want to watch?* the owner had said. *What else is interesting?*) Then Marcia heard Kaye calling, "Jimmy, Jimmy," but the voice came from next door, from Kaye's own room. The door opened, and Kaye ran out into the hall.

It was not sex—what was wrong with Marcia, that that was all she knew about?—it was a medical crisis or a bad dream. Marcia was probably not wanted in the second case, and she lay still for a minute—Jimmy's voice, a low monotone, seemed to be reassuring Kaye—and then she got up, anyway. How could she pretend not to have heard? Wasn't she here in the house with them? Kaye turned on the light just as Marcia stood in the doorway, and there was Jimmy sitting up in bed, red-faced and sweating; he looked as if he'd been boiled. His hair and his beard were as wet as a swimmer's.

"Are you all right?" Marcia said.

"I woke you up," Jimmy said. "We should've put you downstairs."

"He has medicine he takes," Kaye said. "Don't worry about it. Go back to bed."

"Sorry," Marcia said, and got out of there.

Oh, Jimmy, she thought back in her room, you could have just told me. How long had he had night sweats? Kaye's face had been heavy with a tight, mournful anger. But they might've kept her away from the house overnight, if they really had wanted to keep all of this private and hidden.

Perhaps Marcia was not supposed to say anything about it to them. As if she didn't hand out pamphlets every day urging people to be get tested in four languages. She wondered if Jimmy had a wild and separate nocturnal life with other men, or a longtime lover he just didn't tell people like her about. Jimmy acted as if he didn't know what year it was, Marcia thought, and yet he must know.

At breakfast Kaye was still angry, or plenty miffed, at any rate. "I tell him to just do the *basics* to take care of himself," she said. "It's the least he could do, don't you think? Does he get monitored by the doctor when he's supposed to? No. Does he exercise at all ever? No. Not him."

"He has to be careful. It can make a big difference," Marcia said.

Jimmy, who was sitting right across from them spooning up his cereal, said, "He has to put up with everybody's free advice."

"What are they giving him?" Marcia said to Kaye.

"That's another thing," Kaye said. "Nitroglycerine pills dissolved on the tongue—that can't be the best they can do for angina. Really. Does that sound like a nineteenth-century treatment or what?"

"The heart," Jimmy said, "is a nineteenth-century organ. I have a quaint, outdated malady."

Marcia saw Jimmy's heart, a sequestered valentine, pulsing in its wine-velvet casing. Apparently she was never going to guess right about it.

"Your *father* took those little nitro pills," Kaye said. "How state-of-the-art can they be?"

Jimmy carried his bowl to the sink and walked out of the kitchen.

"None of my beeswax," Kaye said. "That's his little way of letting me know."

"Is he all right?" Marcia said.

"He's not all right," Kaye said. "He knows he's not."

"You can't make him take care of himself if he won't."

"Who, then?" Kaye said. "Who else?"

Marcia was about to say, *He has to do it himself*, but that was just some California jive; perhaps it was her own jive.

"He just goes on in his merry, pigheaded way," Kaye said. "He leaves it to me to worry. I'm the one. It's my job." Kaye was washing the breakfast dishes as she spoke. Steam was rising from the sink like a staging of her ire.

She went at the counter with a sponge, scouring hard. "He just goes off. And you see how he leaves the kitchen. Look at this crud."

"You could ignore the crud," Marcia said. "That's kind of my philosophy."

"Yes," Kaye said. She went on rub-a-dub-dubbing.

"Do you do this whenever you come out here?" Marcia said. "Clean the house?"

"Well, I have to," Kaye said.

"Mike, my husband, was a great housekeeper," Marcia said. "I think I got neater because of him."

"Jimmy hasn't gotten neater," Kaye said. She was taking a broom out of a closet. Marcia followed her into the hallway, where she began sweeping.

"I'll do something," Marcia said. "Do you want me to do something?"

"You're the guest," Kaye said.

Kaye was raising a lot of dust, attacking the floor with great lunges of the broom. She seemed invigorated by her proprietary housework and her wifely griping. Marcia sat down to watch her and felt left out.

Music came suddenly from the living room. A jolly tenor was telling them that he was the captain of the *Pinafore* and a right good captain, too. "Ah," Kaye said. "He's put that on for me. He's sick of it, but I still like it."

Jimmy came out of the living room then, doing a little two-step to the chorus that was giving three cheers and one cheer more. If it was his way of ending their quarrel, it worked. Kaye knew the words to all the verses. Jimmy held the dustpan for her, and they bobbed around in time. "What movie are we in?" Marcia said.

After this Jimmy went out to get the Sunday paper, and when he came back they all sat in the now dustless parlor and read through every part of the paper. Jimmy and Kaye muttered at the articles and read bits of news aloud every so often, and they did the crossword puzzle together, seated next to each other with rival pencils. What if sex were just taken out of the world? Marcia thought. Kaye and Jimmy were like an illustration from a book explaining how this could be done.

What would you do if you were blind? What if you couldn't walk? People always imagined how their senses got sharpened, their appreciations grew within a smaller focus; less stood in the way of their attentions; they became keen and sharp. Marcia was remembering all this.

"This puzzle was designed by a sadist rogue computer," Jimmy said.

"Anybody want to go for a walk?" Marcia said. "A little pre-lunch constitutional?"

"Jimmy sort of has to take it easy today," Kaye said. "Normally I encourage him to move his butt, but now, no."

This meant that Kaye was not going, either, and when Marcia took off for a quick stroll, the two of them waved to her from the porch. It was not Jimmy's fault he had to rest, but they were both so generally quiet in their habits, not to say pokey. Marcia always felt young and coltish next to them, but she wasn't so young, was she?

The weather was not as bright today—a white sky, a dampness in the air—and the foliage looked less fiery, but still panoramically terrific. Marcia went around gathering up the best leaves, the deepest reds and flashiest combos; she did this for something to do, but also with the idea of sending a few in the mail to Alejandro, who had never seen the leaves change.

When she got back to the house, Jimmy was napping on the porch, and Kaye was inside reading a mystery and looking drowsy; neither of them could have slept much the night before. Marcia showed Kaye her leaf assortment—"to send to a friend in California."

"Press them first," Kaye said.

Kaye didn't ask anything about the friend, which disappointed Marcia; she seemed to want to speak about him. "My friend Alejandro," she said. "Who's never been north of Marin County."

A little flush of affection for Alejandro had crept over her on the leaf hunt. "My pen pal," she said, although really they were phone pals.

"I see," Kaye said. She did her knowing chuckle.

"He's a total Californian," Marcia said. "He's never been to New York."

"I've never been to the West Coast."

"It'll be his first visit. He's coming probably in the winter," Marcia said. "I like the idea of showing him the snow." Why was she saying this? She was making it up.

"Better tell him to bring a lot of layers to wear," Kaye said.

"I told him to wait till spring, but he wants to come after Christmas." Marcia knew it was childish to lie like this, but she couldn't stop. She didn't even *want* Alejandro to come, she was fairly sure. She watched Kaye's expression, which was mildly amused and a little put out that Marcia had been keeping secrets.

"It's so small in that apartment," Marcia said, "but we'll manage." She couldn't help it, she felt better. "The man snores," she said, "and hogs all the room in the bed."

Over lunch, which was BLT sandwiches, Marcia said, "I used to cook more, but I stopped."

"Better produce in California," Jimmy said.

"Alejandro likes to cook. It spoiled me. On camping trips, even, we ate well," Marcia said. "You wouldn't believe I would go camping, would you?"

"There are trails around here," Kaye said. "Somewhere."

"We had good equipment. One of those dome tents, one of those amazing lightweight sleeping bags. It was Alejandro's stuff, actually." Kaye looked amused again.

By late afternoon, it was time to drive back; Kaye and Jimmy didn't like to drive at night. On the highway Marcia was afraid they were going to want to play one of those family car games— count all the signs with *S* in them, that sort of thing—but instead they listened to a tape of *The Mikado*. If you want to know who we are, we are gentlemen of Japan. Kaye insisted on driving, although Jimmy looked much better than he had in the morning.

"Alejandro drives like a nut," Marcia said. "He's good, but he's too fast. It's hold-on-to-your-hat time when he's behind the wheel."

"That's California, isn't it?" Kaye said.

"Are you freezing?" Jimmy said to Kaye. "You look like you're freezing." He took off his cardigan and put it around her shoulders. It was one of those old man's sweaters, droopy and gray, and even from the back seat it made Kaye look like Margaret Rutherford. "Better? Okay?" Jimmy said. What scared Marcia was that she was starting to envy them.

"It's the way Alejandro takes the turns," Marcia said. "Too much."

She was making Alejandro sound pretty dashing. He was actually a fairly quiet person, aside from his driving habits. She didn't think it was Alejandro she wanted to see, but he was the phantom object of desire now, the readiest emblem of plain and definite lust. Even now, Marcia thought she didn't really understand what life was without this, and she hoped she never knew, but in time it was likely she would. How little she had imagined before now, how slender her horizons had been.

"Campers," Kaye said, "I see a Dairy Queen ahead. What do you think?"

"Let our lovely guest decide," Jimmy said.

"Stop we must," Marcia said.

Listen to this, will you? she thought. Incredible. They had her talking like them.

The girl behind the counter at the Dairy Queen wore puce lipstick heavily outlined in brown, and she made Jimmy repeat his order three times. Marcia talked to girls like her all day (you could win them over by just admiring their earrings) and had once been that girl, but Jimmy was rattled. Marcia put her arms around Jimmy and Kaye while they waited. "Hello, three musketeers," the girl said when she came back with their orders.

They took the ice cream—two double chocolates and one vanilla-chocolate swirl—and they each tucked into their cones with a happy concentration that Marcia decided (with some effort, and it wasn't easy) not to see as any sort of erotic pantomime. It seemed to be her job to take on innocence now, a trait she had never admired or had any use for before. And she was doing fine at it. Oh, who would have thought?

"The intrepid travelers find refreshment," Jimmy said.

Spring

Many people in New York City stay up all night. I am one of them. I don't know who the other ones are. Except for Walter, and Walter says things like, "I think my fingerprints are wearing off." Things like that, things other people don't think about.

At two a.m., my phone rings. "Get lost," I say into the receiver. Then I hang up. I close the blinds, not so much because I am afraid Walter is looking in, but because there are times I can't help looking in on him. He lives twenty feet away, across the alley. On nights when I let Walter come over at one or two or three in the morning, he is more often than not the bearer of odd little gifts: a plastic Baggie full of extremely small pieces of chopped-up dried fruit, or those little bottles of lotion that they give you in the hospital, the ones that say not for resale, and once an ugly painting in a beat-up frame, which I had seen in the trash pile outside my building the day before.

"What is this shit?" I'll say.

He'll either shrug or smile. His smile is very beautiful, wide and full. He has an open face. You can't picture him wincing. His eyes just crinkle nicely around the edges. Neither one of us is particularly young anymore, nor is anyone I know particularly young anymore. Walter also brings with him a ridiculous mood. All is right with the world. Life is good. I suspect medication.

I begin work, digging into my bag full of English exams to be graded. I am an adjunct professor at three different schools. Night classes, of course. And I teach a poetry class at the Y.

At two-thirty the phone rings again.

"I said fuck off," I say into the receiver. Again I hang up.

The phone rings again.

"Is that how you answer your phone?" It is my brother, Gary.

"What are you doing up?" I say. With Gary it almost always works to change the subject to him.

"They woke me up," he says on a hiss. "They wanted to stick me with needles, take my blood pressure, and weigh me," he goes on. "They wanted to see how much a skeleton weighs at two o'clock in the morning. Un-fucking-believable."

"Can you try and go back to sleep?" I say.

"How can I," he shrieks, "when my nurse is wearing angel earrings and this totally alarming little angel broach/pin thing?"

Lately my brother has added angels to his list of things he finds intolerable.

"People cannot truly believe they are having encounters with angels," he begins. "I mean, have these people exhausted the potential of their UFO sightings and their alien abductions? It's all part of the dumbing down of American culture, and really the whole chaotic crumbling of Western civilization. Superstition and dumb religion and pathetic, sexless cults and everything just falling to pieces."

"Sexless cults?" I ask, digging in my bag for a red pen. I never use the red pen for the poetry students. Poetry should never be touched by a red pen.

"You know, those bald eunuchs," he says, impatiently, "the ones in California who committed group suicide with their brand-new sneakers on."

"Oh, yeah."

"What the hell is the point of a cult if there isn't some weird, perverted sex thing going on?" he rails.

"Gary, Gary, you know the angel thing is just an aspect of contemporary mythology," I say. "Millennium-anxiety stuff."

"Oh, that's just trash," he spits, "pure trash."

"People who see angels believe in their experiences. They pass lie detector tests, right? What's significant is that we're all having the same dream."

"Well, you can leave me out of the dream, sister," he says.

"What I'm saying, Gary, is that it doesn't matter whether people are actually seeing angels, but it may matter that people believe that they are seeing them," I say. "Has your temperature gone down any?" I ask. Gary has pneumonia again. The bad kind.

"Don't be such a Jungian," he says. "Your anti-intellectual positions are really beginning to bore and depress me. What are you turning into, anyway?"

"Why don't you ask for a shot of Demerol?"

"I'm glad I won't be around to see it all fall down around us,

Libby. I'm not kidding," he says. "I'm glad."

"Can you just calm down a little?" I say. "You're going to set yourself up for a big coughing fit."

"No," he says, beginning to cough, "no, I can't just calm down."

"I think you should call the nurse," I say.

"I can't. The angels," he says, hacking away and gasping for breath.

I hang up and call the nurse's station. I ask Gary's nurse, Mrs. Johnson, if she would mind taking off the angel earrings and the little pin. She is a very nice person and agrees to do it for the patient's sake.

"You have to humor some people," she tells me.

"Don't we know it," I tell her. With Mrs. Johnson, it is best to offer her the juiciness of a conspiracy, one which places her at the center.

Every once in a while I take the sleeping-pill route, but sleeping pills are never more than a temporary solution and nothing to change your life over. Eventually, sleeping pills make you feel funny and look funny, and then you can't do your work or face the world, which are things that might be a problem to start with. Psychiatrists have been no help, because they are in love with sleeping pills, which, from the oxygen-depleted heights of their love cloud, they continue to insist have no side effects, even after you say things like, "I'm hallucinating. I feel psychotic and violent. I might kill someone." Every once in a while I try a new psychiatrist, who may say something new, but depressingly obvious and homespun, like, "Have you tried warm milk? How about hot baths?" As though I wouldn't have tried those things when I have had insomnia since the third grade. As my brother used to shriek at bad drivers, "Drive much?" *Practice medicine much?* But nobody knows very much about sleep. Anybody who says they do is lying.

The phone rings, but I have run out of the will to tell anyone to fuck off. You have to be up for that kind of thing. So I let it ring and turn on the TV. I flip around the dial, looking for something, I don't know what. I used to watch all-night cable reruns of *Dallas* over the phone with my friend Yvette. At the commercials we would talk about our ongoing money problems, what kind of diets we were on, her failure to achieve success as an actress, my failure to achieve success as a screenwriter, and if we had to sleep with a *Dallas* cast member, which one would be the least disgusting. Male and female. We tried to be fair. But Yvette got married and stopped staying up all night. She had a baby and sent me a picture of a glum-looking child, dressed in a fairy costume and holding a wand.

I keep flipping, my hand on automatic, pressing and pressing the remote, watching the light and the color and the faces change, until I realize that I want the television itself to turn into something else. It is like my television is an inflatable doll. It will resemble *it*, whatever you desire, and at the same time it will never come close. It will always remind, and it will always disappoint. My feelings of disappointment begin to cause the physical symptoms you would associate with the bad side of drugs. Headache. Nausea. Sour stomach. Dry mouth. Metallic taste in dry mouth.

I pick up the phone.

"Can I come over?" Walter asks.

"Walter, why do you let me treat you like shit and say mean things to you?"

"Because I know you don't mean it," he says.

"How?" I ask. "How do you know I don't mean it?"

"I don't know," he says. "Can I come over?"

"Walter, have you ever seen an angel?" I ask.

"Seen one? No," he says. "But I have heard them now and then."

Walter arrives with a plastic Rite Aid bag full of yellow Post-it notes. Rite Aid is open all night.

"Walter, this isn't bad," I say, taking the bag. "I can actually use these."

He smiles. It is a wide, foolish smile. Walter's brown hair is abnormally shiny for an adult. It is thick and silky, like a child's hair, but often full of bits of plaster or paint from the endless work he does on his apartment.

He sits on the couch and I pick the pieces of plaster out of his hair. He is knocking out walls over there, or something. Putting up new, different walls in their place. Or maybe he is putting the exact same walls back up. I don't know what he does. His parents are rich and give him money, I know that. He has two psychiatrists, one female and one male, whom he calls Mom and Dad. One of the two of them, I can't remember which, is blind. Sometimes I can see him lifting weights. He has a lot of gym equipment and no furniture. His arm muscles are beautiful. They are the long, sinewy kind of arm muscles. His skin is very smooth. You can trace his veins with your fingers.

"I can't find Tuffy," he says.

"You know Tuffy," I say, still finding hardened, white bits in Walter's hair. "Tuffy is a cowboy. He likes to roam. He'll turn up."

Tuffy is an orange tomcat with chewed-up ears who lives in the alley between our buildings. That's how I met Walter, we were both out there with our little cans of Fancy Feast, feeding the strays. My own cat was dying on a blanket on my living-room chair, and that night I couldn't stand the howling anymore. The strays howl and howl, caterwauling, a raw, desperate sound that scrapes at your insides if you listen to it, and causes your head to throb if you try and block it out. Walter walked me back to my apartment and asked if he could kiss me. I said he could kiss my arm, which he did, for an hour and fifteen minutes. Just my arm.

I smooth out Walter's hair, which is thick and straight, and still shiny, despite the residue of plaster. Walter has the kind of hair that if he bounced on a trampoline would always fall perfectly back into place. Sometimes when I imagine Walter I see him flying up in the air, and then landing, hair flying up and then lying flat, up and down like that. Weeee.

"Sometimes I think my fingerprints are wearing off," he says, looking down at his hands. "Have you ever thought about that?"

"You've mentioned that before," I say. "And, no, I never think about it."

Now it is Walter's turn to do my hair. He brushes and brushes, kisses my neck and calls me "Cupcake Lady." Oh, to be a cupcake. With frosting. To be sitting on a plate, waiting to be devoured. At my age. Just when you're thinking you'll never be a cupcake again.

I lie back on the couch, and Walter lies down on top of me. For the moment all I want is to feel his weight bearing down on me, to feel the sensation of weight, to be held beneath it, and made aware again of weight itself. There is a surprising amount of comfort to be found in the simple fact of gravity. But Walter is a man, after all, and begins to move against me. I would like it if he just lay still, but of course I also wouldn't have it any other way.

Walter slips his hands underneath my back and works them down along my spine until he reaches my hips. He pulls us together with one sudden thrust, so quickly, and with such astonishing ease, such natural expertise at the particular way he and I are meant to fit together, that for a moment I can't speak or think or breathe. It's a form of genius maybe, this knowledge of his. A gift, a talent, *a skill at hand.* I could ask why. I could be foolish and ask why, in this one way, this person is perfect for me. But instead I let him take my clothes off, piece by piece, and then again cover my body with his.

Later, in my bed, I watch Walter sleep. I love the way he smells. He smells of something entirely pleasant, something familiar yet difficult to place, like a particular plant or flower, a summer drink or an outdoor cooking smell, something like that, from childhood outside the city. For some reason I don't ever want to learn what it is. I just want to smell it. I just want to close my eyes and smell it.

Here is the thing about spring: Spring uncovers things you don't necessarily want to look at. For instance, take a garbage can on a street corner, somewhere in another part of the city, something benign and commonplace. In the winter that garbage can would be filled with standard New York–issue garbage, pizza boxes and newspapers and soda cans, and snow. You would be cold, and you would hurry right by, pulling the collar of your coat close against your bare throat, which would be inadequately wrapped against the freezing winter wind. You would have things on your mind.

In spring, the garbage can on the street corner in another part of the city would not be filled with snow. You would be walking along, and you would not be cold or in much of a hurry, and the weather with its pleasant breezes and low barometric pressure would wake up your skin and intoxicate you, and you would not have all that much on your mind. You would notice the garbage can, and realize that once, after a party, a long time ago, you threw up in that very garbage can. Then you would remember the party itself, where a man *and a woman* fought over you, while you, getting drunker and drunker, let them. Then you would begin to remember the rest of your life around that time, your restaurant jobs, the clothing you wore, a favorite pair of beat-up black cowboy boots in particular, the couch you slept on, huddled on, clung to like a life raft, as though the rest of the world were shark-infested waters, the time they turned off your lights, the time they turned off your phone, the time things got stolen because you couldn't remember to lock your apartment door, the danger you knew you were in, the ridiculous good health of everyone around you, and, worst of all, your aspirations at the time, your dreams of something for yourself.

I am on my way to the hospital to visit Gary when I see a man standing on the subway platform who could well be my ex-husband.

Spring has uncovered my ex-husband.

He doesn't see me, and I turn away quickly, realizing I am unprotected, realizing that spring can uncover me as easily as any other hidden thing.

When the train appears, I leap into the car and disappear behind two large women and their giant Macy's shopping bags. When I am safe behind the closing doors, I take a look out the window. He is different, but it is definitely him. He is a balding actor who looks like a balding businessman, and so, used to go around New York to auditions dressed like one, with a suit and a tie and a briefcase. He appeared in dozens of commercials and print ads, always as a balding businessman with a suit and a tie and a briefcase. The whole enterprise showed a lack of imagination all around. He looks different now, or rather he looks exactly the same but is dressed differently, in ripped jeans, a faded T-shirt, and scruffed-up work boots. He has a red bandanna tied around his head.

"I'm not making this up," I say, collapsing with relief on the foot of Gary's hospital bed.

"He has transformed himself from one kind of asshole into a completely different kind of asshole," Gary says.

"Yes," I say, "that is exactly what he's done." Now that Gary has summed up the experience, made some kind of sense of it, I feel I can move off of the bed. I've brought Gary a large bunch of peonies in full bloom. It's their time of year. They smell of our backyard at home in Virginia, and the yard of our next-door neighbor, and the yards of all of our friends and enemies, the green lawns of our childhood.

"Smell these," I say. "Don't they just remind you of everything?"

"Get that shit away from me," he says, waving the peonies away. "I don't want to be reminded of everything."

I remove the offending plant life.

"So what did he have to say for himself?" Gary asks.

"Who?"

"Actor Man," he says. Gary always called my ex-husband Actor Man.

"Nothing," I say, arranging the peonies in one of Gary's many vases. Gary enjoys his crystal. He has always loved his things, separate from any ranking in status they may provide, which, I suppose, is the way to love your things, even though this love of things has always somehow unnerved me, in Gary, anyway. Especially all the crystal. He always kept it all so sparkly. And it was always everywhere, sparkling and reflecting.

"He was jumping onto the subway, and he didn't see me," I say, "but he was carrying a harmonica, I think."

"Stop it. He wasn't," says Gary, beginning to laugh. "Tell me Actor Man wasn't carrying a harmonica."

"He was," I say, deciding on this detail, "and I could just tell the harmonica was part of this new Mr. Dirty Red Bandanna persona."

"You know that laughing makes me cough," says Gary, laughing. "Stop torturing me."

Gary reminds me of how my ex-husband and his actor friends used to sit around talking about Marlon Brando, James Dean, and the Actor's Studio.

"For sheer banality and lack of original insight, you just couldn't beat those conversations," Gary says.

Gary begins to imitate my ex-husband and his friends going on and on about how Marlon Brando played Stanley Kowalski as an ape.

Even though Gary was skinny and effeminate as a boy, the other kids called him "Scary Gary," or just plain "Scary," which he was. He had an uncanny ability for mimicry, in which he would pick out the key details of another kid's physicality, flaws, really, like an almost undetectable speech impediment caused by an overbite, or the slightest little limp from a clubfoot which had been surgically corrected in infancy. He had a talent for bringing the defect front and center, exaggerating it out of proportion until it was all you could see about the person. Nobody wanted to be the subject of one of Gary's humiliating impressions. Gary had his tormentors, boys who would pull his pants off and run them up the flagpole. Stuff like that. There were wedgies and black eyes and the various expressions generally associated with Gary's condition. Faggot, and so on. But gradually, Gary would win over even the tormentors with his hilarious, exaggerated versions of teachers, other kids, and even the tormentors themselves. Gary says his childhood taught him two very important things about life: People were mean, and they liked to laugh.

I have buried my face in the peonies, inhaling again, unable to get enough. They are at the height of their bloom, fanned-out and blossoming extravagantly. Soon they will begin to turn down slightly at the edges and will be on their way out. As soon as tomorrow, maybe.

"Why on earth did I marry him?" I say out loud, and instantly regret this utterance. Gary tends to remember everything I forget. Gary tends to remember everything in general, and in stark detail. He never sifts though details and comes up with a selective account of anything. He remembers times and dates and what was said and to whom, everyone's least noble motivations, weaknesses and needs and endless humiliations. Everything bad and good and inconsequential. And what everyone was wearing, especially him. He can still tell you what he wore to high school on any given day.

"The apartment," he practically shrieks. "You can't have forgotten his duplex on West 70th Street."

"Yes," I say, noting that Gary has let me off the hook fairly easily, because there must have been more to it at the time. There must have been weaknesses and needs. "But I barely remember it now," I say. "I can't even remember how long I lived there."

"Three months," he says, "almost exactly."

"Is that all?"

"You were acting like a zombie," he tells me.

"Probably," I say.

"You met him in the park," Gary goes on. "People used to do things like that, pick each other up in the park. Young people. *Us*."

"Oh, God, the park," I say. "The park in spring."

"And by the way," says Gary, softly, exhausted now, "they were just plain wrong about Marlon Brando. Marlon Brando played Stanley as a cat."

Of course Gary is right, I think, watching him close his eyes. A cat.

I sit beside Gary's bed and read a magazine from the visitor's lounge. It's a woman's magazine with lots of tips. For insomnia you are supposed to try a peanut butter and jelly sandwich with a glass of milk, the combined ingredients of which produces a certain sleep-inducing chemical reaction in the brain. They say.

When Gary has fallen asleep, I head into the hallway to get a cup of ice for my warm Diet Coke and run into Mrs. Johnson, an absolute sight in her canary-yellow clogs and the most elaborate hairdo I have ever seen, stiff swirls of gray and black ringlets, fanned out all over her big, round head.

"I love your hair," I tell her. I always tell Mrs. Johnson this because it allows me a moment to adjust to it, without having to take my focus off of it, which is just too difficult. Her granddaughter is a hairdresser.

"Your brother has been using an awful lot of bad language," she tells me. "He sits in there cussing a blue streak." Mrs. Johnson is a Baptist from North Carolina.

"Oh, he's a bad one," I say, my own Southern-ness rising to the surface, as if to communicate the idea that we are united, just two girls up from the South trying our level best to navigate our way through Yankeeland. Here in the North, both Gary and I have a tendency to become more Southern than we ever actually were in the South.

"That's sick people," she tells me. "They say the nice ones get nicer and the mean ones get meaner."

"Mrs. Johnson, you're a peach," I say, sashaying by her toward the ice machine.

I try to be pleasant to Mrs. Johnson because I actually like her, and because Mrs. Johnson is the one and only member of the hospital staff to have gracefully withstood Gary's typed-up (by me) instructions on how to clean his crystal vases. But there is another reason. Gary seems to have given up his usually successful attempts at getting those in charge of his care to adore him. He has not gone to the usual trouble of flattering them with his keen interest in their families, love lives, or hairstyles.

On the way back from the ice machine, I slip Mrs. Johnson six dollars for the collection plate at her church. For two dollars, Mrs. Johnson's entire congregation will say a prayer for you, a pretty amazing deal. You have choices, like Jesus can forgive you, or bless you, or save your soul. I buy Gary the entire package.

"And don't tell my brother," I warn. This makes Mrs. Johnson wink, her conspirator's version of a smile, and I know I have bought my brother one more week of Mrs. Johnson's extra attention, if nothing else.

I settle back into Gary's room with my magazine and my ice chips. I watch Gary breathe, steadily for now. We are not even forty, not until June, and my brother is already an old man. That's the way this disease goes. Before you die, you get to see yourself grow suddenly old, with hollowed-out eyes and wispy gray hairs framing your pale, gaunt face, the elasticity of youth gone from your skin—the new medications, the cocktails, came too late for Gary—and because Gary is my twin, I get to see something of myself wither, too.

Later, when I catch a glimpse of myself in the elevator mirror, I am shocked to see that the color in my face, the fullness, the vibrancy of my skin and hair, is still there.

Yvette calls out of the blue to update me on her second pregnancy.

"I'm too tired to even swallow," she tells me. "And I had to call it off with Rosario. I'm just too huge for anything but the most unspeakable acts, and I'm too tired for those."

I like having a friend like Yvette, someone who, up until her ninth month of pregnancy, continues an affair with a seriously younger man. A waiter. Italian. *Ponytail.* It's just not the kind of thing most people would think to do.

"I want you to have a baby, too," she tells me. "Then we can play together again. You, me, and our babies."

"I'd need to have a date first," I tell her. "At least." I don't tell Yvette about Walter. I don't tell anyone about Walter. You can't go to a movie with Walter. Walter is not a date. And anyway, between the two of us, the gene pool is an iffy prospect.

"Funny you should bring it up," she says. "You want to go out with a really cool-looking Chinese guy?"

"No."

"He's a really good friend of Artie's." Artie is Yvette's husband, a movie industry accountant who wants to produce. Artie has a ponytail, too. But it is the wrong kind of ponytail. The ponytail, a frizzy, scraggly thing, is the only hair Artie has left.

"No," I say.

"Please. He's a *full* professor."

"I don't like meeting new people. I can't account for myself. I can't account for the gaps."

"You jerk," Yvette says. "It's just the loony bin, for God's sake. It's not like you were in prison. Or something really embarrassing like the Peace Corps."

"Forget it."

"Then you have to take my little cousin out to lunch. She thinks she wants to be a writer, and I need you to talk her out of it," she says. "I'm too tired."

"I can do that," I tell her.

Yvette and I are quiet for a while.

"Now I'm just waiting," she says. "Me and my big stomach, just waiting."

Insomniacs are always waiting, waiting for the bluish light of morning, for night to end, for sleep, for the mind to finally quiet down.

"Me, too," I say. "I'm waiting."

"Libby, it's a good idea to know what you're waiting for," she says.

My doorbell rings.

"Who is it?" I say, making sure it is Walter.

"My name escapes me." It's him.

Walter is standing there, holding a pineapple in front of his face. The pineapple is wearing a pair of glasses.

Idiot. Still, I feel a stab of desire, a need that never goes away, the longing to be touched. I begin to wonder why Walter can't be normal, a dangerous thought, one that can't be contemplated without creeping into other areas of dangerous thought, and so I stop the thought cold, because for now I just want to have my hair brushed and feel his arms pull me in and in and in.

We stand there in the hallway with our foreheads pressed together.

"Libby, I'm worried there is something wrong with the moon," he says. "It's moving around. It's not in the same place as it was last night."

With the light of early morning creeping through the blinds, and Walter's smooth arm curled around my stomach, I finally realize what it is that Walter smells of. It is bug repellent.

Yvette's cousin, Kit, is a twenty-one-year-old Columbia University student who is about to graduate this spring. She takes a seat across from me at a restaurant on Broadway which has opened its outdoor café for the first time this year. There is still a slight chill in the spring air, but the sun shines brilliantly.

I did not expect someone so utterly chic. She is dressed in brown velvet pants that flare at the ankle, high-heeled brown boots, and a bright green thigh-length coat cut to fit close to the body. Her hair is dark brown, and parted in the center, worn straight and flat, as only a very young woman can wear her hair. All I can think of is how *of the moment* and *of her time* she looks, and how she'll look back on her youth one day and think, *I was dressed just right.*

She tosses her good leather bag under the table and takes a seat.

"Hi," she says. "Yvette said I'd know you because you'd look like you're not used to being awake during the day."

"She said that?" I say, alarmed and surprisingly ashamed. I don't usually like people to know about my sleeping habits.

"I think it's cool," she says.

"Poor sleep hygiene is cool?" I say.

"Absolutely," she says. "Very decadent. Very out of sync with the suburbs and minivans and snotty kids and pets."

"I used to have a cat," I say.

"A cat is a cat," she says. The waitress brings us water and asks if we need a few more minutes.

"I could tell you a few things about your cousin Yvette," I tell her, "but I'm a better friend than she is."

"What?" says Kit. "Like she still wears fur and commits adultery?"

"Yvette still wears fur?"

"She also told me that you've been in and out of the nut house, which is where the two of you met." She smoothes her cloth napkin over her lap.

My heart beats madly for a second or two, and I expect my head to explode.

"Yvette usually calls it the loony bin," I say.

"Yes, that's what she said, *'the loony bin.'*"

We order salads with dressing on the side. My body seems to calm itself, and I find that I am breathing more or less normally, and that my head has not exploded, and that everything around me is relatively calm. A couple of little brown birds land in one of the sidewalk trees. The waitress scoops her tip off of an empty table.

I wonder if Yvette hasn't done the right thing, turning her experience with mental illness into another outrageous aspect of her outrageous personality. It's a strategy, anyway.

"It seems I have no secrets," I say.

"So what?" says Kit. "I find that people don't really give a shit about the things we find most embarrassing and personal. I mean, people really just don't care, do they?"

Where did she acquire this wisdom? I wonder.

"I'm supposed to talk you out of wanting to be a writer," I say, "but I don't really feel like it."

"Good," she says, "because I don't really feel like hearing about it."

Our salads arrive.

"I started out wanting to write screenplays," I offer without knowing why, since we've agreed not to discuss it. "I had a couple of good ideas, but later I turned to poetry."

"Me, too," she says, excitedly. "That's what I write, screenplays and poetry." She pulls a folded piece of newspaper out of her coat pocket. I notice her fingernails. They are short and painted a purply-silver color, a color I have only seen on the young girls sitting across from me on the subway, or on a student of mine, a color that hasn't crested yet, that hasn't hit the drugstore chains. I remember that, being young and being a certain kind of girl, and knowing what was happening before someone wrote about it in the Sunday Style section of *The New York Times,* by which time it was surely on its way toward the rest of the country, and then the malls and the high school girls and their mothers, and then all of a sudden over and done with, out.

Kit has me looking at an announcement that says "Three Jungians and Peter Bogdanovich discuss dreams, movies, and the unconscious mind."

"My God," I say, "This is my *thing*. My absolute thing."

"Me, too," she says, excitedly. "It's my *thing,* too. Go with me."

"I can't," I say, folding up the piece of newspaper. "I have to visit my brother. He's in the hospital."

"Isn't your brother a famous screenwriter?" she asks.

Of course, she would know this. Everybody knows this.

"Yes," I answer, feeling a familiar mix of pride and fury overtake me, as it always does, at the mention of my brother's career.

"Doesn't he have a major award?" she asks, teasingly.

"He has two of them," I say, holding out my fingers like a peace sign. Two.

"I'm sorry," she says. "Am I being rude?"

"It's okay," I tell her. "Everybody's interested. It's interesting."

"But poetry is interesting, too," she says by way of begging my forgiveness. And I do forgive her. Most people, people you would least expect, too, cannot control themselves from some shameless expression of the bottomless hunger my brother's success inspires.

"You're just being polite," I say.

"No, I swear," she begs. "I'm a poet, too."

"Let's split a huge piece of carrot cake," I say.

"Yes," she says, and begins to tell me about her plans for the summer.

"I want to be decorous this summer," she tells me. "I want to wear just the right skirt and beautiful, strappy sandals, and I want to go sit somewhere outside and order the perfect summer drink. I want to see if I can be both the subject of my own narrative and the object of someone else's narrative."

"Good plan," I say. I actually do know what she's talking about, arranging yourself to be part of the landscape, but I don't remember having a postmodern take on the subject, or any *take* on the subject. I don't remember *thinking* at all. I remember feeling and behaving, and that my skin was especially thin.

I look up to see Walter making his way down the sidewalk. He looks extremely strange out here, in public, in the daytime, the sun on his shiny brown hair, and then familiar—I know his loping walk so well, and the way he swings his arms—and then he looks strange again. I turn my head and shield my face with the dessert menu, but it is too late.

"Libby," says Walter, standing beside our table, "Libby, I can't find Tuffy."

"Walter, Tuffy will come back," I say. I notice that Kit is looking at Walter's feet. That's Walter. He'll look perfectly normal until you notice the odd detail. In this instance, his shoes, men's brown oxfords, are without any shoelaces. There is also the absence of socks.

"Who is this person?" says Walter, looking at Kit with his big, unblinking eyes.

"My friend, Kit," I say.

"Hello," she says.

"Can I sit down here, too?" he asks.

"Walter, can't you see I'm having lunch with someone?" I say. I can see that Kit looks puzzled by the harshness of my tone.

"It's okay," says Kit, her face now lit with devilish curiosity, "sit down."

"No," I say. "Walter, you should leave now."

I look away, like a child who, before the age of reason, hides her face in her hands in order to disappear altogether, until Walter turns around and leaves, walking back in the direction he came from.

"That guy lives next door to me," I explain before Kit can ask. "We both feed the cats in the alley."

"He's cute," says Kit.

"Weirdo," I say, circling my index finger in the air around my ear in the universal sign for crazy person. "I try to stay away from him."

I find I am extremely tired. Whatever exhilaration I had felt at the novelty of being awake for lunch, and being out during the day, and talking about life is gone. If I lay my head down on the table in front of me, I'm sure I would fall asleep.

The cake arrives. I can't even taste the frosting, which is the main reason I eat this cake.

"What happened to your screenplay ideas?" asks Kit.

"Someone stole them," I say.

I arrive at the hospital to find a priest sitting by my brother's bedside, gathering up a scattered deck of playing cards.

"This is Father Donovan," says Gary. I know the various expressions on Gary's face, better than I know any other thing in the world, and I have never seen the look that is on his face right now. He is beaming. Goofily. "Father Donovan is my new AIDS buddy."

"Oh, really?" I say. In all of his years with the disease, Gary has angrily rejected anyone who has come calling bearing the title "AIDS buddy."

Father Donovan, on his feet now, extends a hand. He is a handsome man of about thirty-five, with dark brown hair and startling blue eyes.

"You must be Libby," he says. He takes my hand in both of his and squeezes warmly, like an old, old friend.

"Doesn't Father Donovan look exactly like Montgomery Clift, in *I Confess*?" Gary says. "Look at that jaw."

"Does Father Donovan know that you often rail against all games as a waste of time?" I say to Gary.

"It's true. It's true," he tells the priest, laughing, merrily. "I do that. I *rail* against all games as a complete waste of time."

"The cards were my idea," says Father Donovan, releasing my hand. "I'm teaching your brother to play poker. He's going to be quite good, I think."

Gary makes a crazy face, eyes bugging out, tongue hanging slack. "Look, it's my poker face," he says. They hoot.

"Did you tell Father Donovan that we were raised by atheists?" I say.

"He doesn't care," says Gary.

"I don't care," says Father Donovan with a shrug. They both burst out laughing like a couple of ten-year-olds.

"So, there is no talk of God or anything?" I say, plopping myself down in a padded armchair. Father Donovan finally returns to his seat. Most men don't do that anymore, stand until the lady is seated. I never knew how much I missed it until this moment.

"Shhh, not a word," says Father Donovan, his finger to his lips.

"Good," I say, "because my brother gets very agitated by spiritual beliefs."

"Not true," says Gary, holding his cards in a dainty little fan. "I get agitated by *fledgling* spiritual beliefs, especially those cobbled together from a mishmash of bogus influences. I don't like the pick-and-choose incoherence of it. I say, 'Choose a religion, a *real* one, and stick to it.'"

"How about Catholicism?" I say.

"There's a fine choice. Perfect. Exactly what I'm talking about," says Gary.

We turn to Father Donovan.

"I'm not saying anything," he says. "Not a word."

"Then what do you two talk about?" I ask.

"Fag stuff," says Gary. "Musicals."

"Love 'em," says the Father.

But the merriment has now exhausted Gary, and Father Donovan begins to pack up his cards, gently lifting Gary's little fan from where Gary has laid it down on top of his rasping chest.

"Please," says Gary, wearily, "let me keep this hand till next time. I seem to be very attached to it."

"Shall I say 'God bless you'?" he asks Gary.

"Libby, you have to hear the way he says it," Gary says, softly. "It's so elegant and sincere, not like a talk show host or some cheesy celebrity, those phonies who go around saying 'Goodnight and God bless.'"

Father Donovan smiles. With his velvety black eyebrows, he does look like Montgomery Clift in *I Confess,* only not as tortured or pained. That dark Montgomery Clift cloud is not hovering nearby, the cloud of a secretive past, and the many sins that must be hidden forever.

"Say it, Father," Gary says. "Please."

"God bless you, my children," he says, genuflecting, and I feel as though I have just witnessed the perfect expression of something too fragile to name.

And then Father Donovan is gone.

"I can see it in your face, Libby," Gary says.

"See what?"

"He's a priest, and nothing is going to come of it, right?"

"Get some sleep, Gary," I say, feeling stupid and scared that this is all I ever have to say anymore.

"But I'm dying, Lib," says Gary. "Nothing is going to come of anything."

I get off the subway and walk toward my apartment with a growing awareness that a crowd is beginning to accumulate in the middle of my block.

When a bicycle falls from a sixth-story window, at first I decide it must have something to do with a movie that has been shooting here and there in the neighborhood. Some trees on our block have been painstakingly affixed with lifelike-looking leaves in fall colors, like brown and orange. People, including myself, stop to touch the leaves, which turn out to be made of surprisingly strong plastic.

The bicycle seems to fall forever, its wheels spinning crazily, while the frame appears to float, suspended there. When it lands, it does so with a comical little bounce. It rides itself down the sidewalk for a yard or two, before it finally careens into a garbage can. It is Walter's bike, I see by now, the one that hangs on the wall of his apartment, and a crowd has begun to gather to watch what else will come flying out of the window. The bicycle is followed by an old record player and a number of record albums which go hurtling wildly in all directions. They fly like Frisbees. They smash into jagged, black pieces.

I watch like everyone else. The police arrive, followed by an ambulance, and people begin to make comments about how somebody forgot to take their medication. Two women behind me wait for the next item to fall while talking about local preschools and Starbucks coffee.

Clothes go flying. Shirts, sweaters, socks. Pants are especially comical, hollow legs flapping frantically as they go. Weight-lifting equipment is not so funny, and neither is a brand-new television, and people scatter, covering their heads with their arms. And then nothing else falls from Walter's window, and the window sits there, open like a mouth struck dumb, waiting for the words to come.

Suddenly Walter appears in the window, naked and screaming.

It is a shock, the nakedness, the white of the skin and the dark of the pubic hair. He screams, shouting out, until he is grabbed from behind and pulled inside. The screaming, the terrible screams, like the cats in the alley when it rains, stops as abruptly as it had begun.

It's not true that I have never thought about my fingerprints wearing off. But then I was told that the belief that one's fingerprints are wearing off is a paranoid delusion, and eventually I stopped thinking about it. It has been years. Finally, it has been many, many years.

Two beefy men in blue escort Walter from the building. He is wild-eyed, barefoot, and dirty-looking, covered only by an old towel wrapped around his waist.

I remember Gary's face when it appeared beside my hospital bed, distorted with concern, but there beside me, recognizable among strangers' faces, more recognizable than my own.

"Walter," I say, as I break from the crowd, lunging forward toward the ambulance, dropping the books and the papers I have held clutched to my chest. I am reaching for his hand.

Do I know this man, they want to know, and I keep reaching out for Walter's hand. Do I know him? they ask.

ABOUT CHARLES BAXTER

A Profile by Don Lee

Charles Baxter can't sleep at night. An insomniac most of his adult life, he takes comfort in Nabokov's claim: If writers don't stay awake thinking about their work, how are they going to make their readers stay awake?

Baxter—the author of two novels and four collections of stories, as well as a book of essays—is, if anything, circumspect about his work, and about pretty much everything else, for that matter. He is affable in many regards, famous for his gentle, dry wit, his modesty, his intelligence, and his generosity with his students. But he likes things to go his way, he likes his routines. As predictable as a clock, his college roommate had said. And when something goes awry, when something intrudes, Baxter will fixate on it—not an altogether bad habit for his writing, he has discovered.

Baxter won't quite admit to being an obsessive-compulsive, but he'll allow that he's "conscious of pattern-making." He writes from eight to noon in a study built over his two-car garage in Ann Arbor, Michigan, and maybe once in a while he'll take his laptop computer to the back porch, but he'll always face east into the morning light. "I think if you are somewhat compulsive or habitual in your ordinary life," he says, "it gives you some latitude to be wild in your creative work."

His childhood, however, was anything but ordinary. Baxter was born in Minneapolis in 1947, and when he was fifteen months old, his father, who sold insurance, died of heart failure. Three years later, his mother married Loring Staples, Sr., a wealthy attorney she had met at the symphony, and Baxter and his two brothers were moved to a lakeside suburb, Excelsior, and plunked down on a forty-acre estate, improbably yet fittingly called World's End. They had a cook, caretaker, nannies, horses, and sheep, but no neighbors. Baxter was the youngest, and as soon as his brothers were old enough to drive, they escaped. "There often wasn't much for me to do except go out into these woods or fields or watch the sheep or read. So I did a good deal of that," Baxter says. Loring

Staples, a forbidding, erudite man who modeled himself after English country gentlemen, had collected an enormous library of first editions. An entire shelf was occupied by a complete set of Nietzsche, about whom Staples would lecture during dinner, which was strictly a coat-and-tie affair. Staples would also recite, by memory, long swatches of poetry, especially Swinburne. "It was *very* disconcerting to hear him do this," Baxter says.

The other side of his family was literary as well. Before his father died, he and Baxter's mother had befriended many musicians and writers, including Sinclair Lewis. "My mother often told me of how she and my father would entertain Lewis late into the evening. He would come over, and my father would fall asleep on the sofa, and she would elbow him and say, 'You can't fall asleep. He's a Nobel Prize winner.'" His aunt Helen's confidants were artists and bohemians as well. Brenda Ueland, the author of *If You Want to Write*, was among them. Whenever Baxter would visit his aunt, Ueland, who was quite deaf by then, would shout at him, "Charles! What are your great plans?" Baxter would mumble that he didn't have any, and she would yell, "You should be ashamed of yourself!" Baxter comments, "I lived, it seemed, in a set of anti-worlds. They didn't combust when they met each other, but this world of older people on my father's side who still lived in Minneapolis and fancied themselves to be artists, and this other strange world on the estate that was more like *The Turn of the Screw* than anything else—they were almost mutually exclusive. They must have affected the way I turned out."

Despite his denials to Ueland, Baxter did have plans: to be a writer, a poet. He went to Macalester College and was the editor of the literary magazine there (he once had to petition the head of the student council, Tim O'Brien, for funding) and reveled in the permissive, politically charged mood on campus. Hard to believe, but Baxter alleges he was a hippie—granted, "sort of a conservative hippie." But the Vietnam War, especially as graduation in 1969 neared, overshadowed everything. "I believed absolutely that it was a bad war, it was madness, and that I was not going to it." He discovered he could obtain an occupational deferment from the draft by becoming a public school teacher, so he taught fourth grade for a year in Pinconning, Michigan. "It was kind of an exotic experience for me," Baxter says, "and I came to feel it was one of the most important things that happened to me in my life. The area where I taught was absolutely flat. It's in the Saginaw Valley, where Theodore Roethke grew up. It looks like the Great Plains out there. They're quite poor. Cash crops are sugar beets and pickling cucumbers. I was enraged at the war and was trying not to bring the war into the classroom and sometimes failed." Once, unprepared for class, he winged it, making up facts on the spot about ancient Egypt and irrigation—an episode that inspired a short story called "Gryphon," in which a substitute teacher tells her fourth graders that angels live in the clouds over Venus and sometimes visit Earth to attend concerts.

At the end of the year, Baxter had a high enough lottery number to feel safe from the draft, and he enrolled in the Ph.D. program at the State University of New York in Buffalo. Donald Barthelme and John Barth were teaching there at the time, but Baxter never took a workshop with either of them, or anyone else. "I had a very thin skin and felt that it was very important for me, as a writer, not to be criticized," he says. "I think I felt that any criticism that I got from these people might have been lethal." In any event, Baxter was writing poetry then, with some success. He published two collections, *Chameleon* and *The South Dakota*

Guidebook, through New Rivers Press before getting his doctorate in 1974.

For the next fourteen years, he taught at Wayne State University in Detroit, another eye-opening experience, his students mostly working-class and blue-collar. In 1976, Baxter married Martha Ann Hauser, who was a teacher at a children's psychiatric hospital in Ann Arbor and who now teaches remedial math and reading (they have one son, Daniel). But around that time, Baxter was having a crisis with his poetry. "I spent an entire summer trying to write poetry, and failing at it. It was as if the knowledge of how to do it had somehow left me, and I found myself ill-equipped to write. I was becoming more interested in sequences, characters, and characterizations, the rickrack of detail surrounding people."

He turned to fiction and churned out three novels, but they were disasters. "They were very abstract, these novels, very schematic, in some sense like bad postmodernism," he says. "Nothing in them felt particularly real, although I didn't realize that at the time. You rarely do when you're working. I thought they were great. I was utterly baffled by the indifference or loathing with which people read them."

One agent was particularly cruel. "I called her and said, 'Julie, what do you think of my novel?' And she said, 'I hate it.' And then she said, 'Tell me why I hate it.' And I said, 'Julie, I don't know why you hate my novel.' She said, 'Oh, you must, you wrote it. Tell me why I hate it. Is it the characters? Is it the setting? I just don't understand any of it. Help me out here. Why do I hate your novel?' It was an amazing phone call. And I kept having experiences like that. This person I knew on the West Coast read one of my novels and said, 'Well, maybe your imagination's poisoned right at the source.'"

Baxter decided to give up. He would just teach and write criticism. He had pounded out hundreds and hundreds of pages and wasn't getting any better, apparently, and he had only one fiction publication in an obscure anthology to his credit, "another sort of historical-postmodern-pastiche travesty." But before he quit, he tried one more thing: boiling down those three novels into short stories. "There was something I wanted to reach," he says, "but like many young writers, I not only reached the point, I kept going past it. That is, I had too much. And so what I took from those novels was a kind of core, and rather than overwriting it, I tried to underwrite it."

He took apart his baroque, experimental style and taught himself craft. In rereading Joyce, Chekhov, O'Connor, Woolf, Porter, and Evan S. Connell, he also learned something else: "that fiction didn't need to be about extraordinary things. It could be about ordinary things, ordinary lives that I had spent my adult life observing." It was a long apprenticeship—his friend, the novelist Robert Boswell, has admitted him into a club called The Slow Learners—but Baxter was disciplined and diligent, and eventually his work began receiving recognition.

His collection *Harmony of the World* won the Associated Writing Programs Award for Short Fiction, judged—in a nice coincidence—by Donald Barthelme, and was published by the University of Missouri Press in 1984. His stories landed in the hands of Charles Verrill at Viking, which swiftly released his second collection, *Through the Safety Net,* in 1985, and his first novel, *First Light,* in 1987. Then Baxter met Carol Houck Smith, an editor with W.W. Norton, which published his next two books, the collection *A Relative Stranger* in 1990 and the novel *Shadow Play* in 1993. Since then, Baxter has come out with *Believers,* a collection of stories and a novella (Pantheon, 1997), and *Burning Down the House,* essays on fiction (Graywolf, 1997).

Each book has produced better and better reviews, and each has further mapped out what could be called Baxter country, portraying, in luminous, precise language, solid Midwestern citizens, many of whom reside in the fictional town of Five Oaks, Michigan, whose orderly lives are disrupted, frequently by an accident or incident or a stranger. Baxter explains that he enjoys contradicting the notion that Midwesterners are not "story-worthy." In one of his poems, Baxter compared living in a landscape with no oceans or mountains to a woman who will not kiss you back. "There's something about the restriction, the glamour of the finality here, that fascinates me," he says. The limits of geography tend to elicit introspection, and when even a small calamity befalls Baxter's characters, they brood over surprisingly large issues of morality and theodicy, grappling with good and evil and the mysteriousness of existence.

A prototypical Baxter story might be "Saul and Patsy Are Pregnant." Saul Bernstein and his wife, Patsy, have lived in Five Oaks for two years, transplants from Baltimore. Saul teaches high school, Patsy is a secretary in an insurance office, and one night, Saul, a little drunk, falls asleep at the wheel and flips their car into a field. Miraculously uninjured, they walk to the nearest house, which happens to be occupied by a former student of Saul's, Emory McPhee, and his wife, Anne. At one point, Saul is left alone in their living room: "Having nothing else to do, he looked around: high ceilings and elaborate wainscoting, lamps, table, rug, dog, calendar, the usual crucifix on the wall above the TV. There was something about the room that bothered him, and it took a moment before he knew what it was. It felt like a museum of earlier American feelings. Not a single ironic sentence had ever been spoken here. Everything in the room was sincere, everything except himself. In the midst of all this Midwestern earnestness, he was the one thing wrong. What was he doing here? What was he doing anywhere?"

Saul becomes obsessed with Emory and Anne, envious of their seeming happiness: "They lived smack in the middle of reality and never gave it a minute's thought. They'd never felt like actors. They'd never been sick with irony. The long tunnel of their thoughts had never swallowed them. They'd never had restless sleepless nights, the urgent wordless unexplainable wrestling matches with the shadowy bands of soul-thieves."

Yet at the end of the story, Saul, while making love to his wife, has a tiny moment of grace. A vision floats in, but quickly drifts away, still ineffable—a non-epiphany epiphany: "He understood everything, the secret of the universe. After an instant, he lost it. Having lost the secret, forgotten it, he felt the usual onset of the ordinary, of everything else, with Patsy around him, the two of them in their own familiar rhythms. He would not admit to anyone that he had known the secret of the universe for a split second. That part of his life was hidden away and would always be: the part that makes a person draw in the breath quickly, in surprise, and stare at the curtains in the morning, upon awakening."

Baxter is acknowledged as a brilliant craftsman whose greatest gift is the compassion with which he reveals his characters, especially his women. He has received countless awards, including fellowships from the NEA, the Guggenheim Foundation, and the

Lila Wallace–Reader's Digest Fund. His work has been selected for *The Best American Short Stories* five times. Yet Baxter still has doubts about his writing. Occasionally he even feels "the fraud police" knocking on his door. He doesn't have writer's block, per se. If he's stuck on a piece of fiction, he'll focus on a book review or an essay or a lecture. "I love that phrase from William Stafford: 'I don't suffer from writer's block; I just lower my standards.' I'll try to get something done, but because of my experiences as an apprentice writer, I do still worry about the fraud police. I think a lot about how evanescent success in writing can be."

Novels in particular still give him fits. "I find them a terrible stretch normally," he says. "What seems apparent to every other novelist is never apparent to me: that is, how to get from one chapter to another. I've rigged up various formulations for myself: Short stories are more often about people acting impulsively. Novels are more often about people making decisions and plans. But it's never scrupulously clear to me that the overarching line of narrative in a novel is available to me." Nonetheless, he has just finished his third novel, *The Feast of Love,* which begins with a "somewhat shadowy character" named Charlie Baxter who meets a friend in a city park late at night. This Charlie Baxter is an insomniac.

He wrote the novel without an advance contract: "They make me feel compulsive, of course, about meeting the deadline." (*The Feast of Love* has just been sold to Pantheon, with a tentative release date of May 2000.) And, to further loosen his schedule, Baxter is giving up the directorship of the M.F.A. program at the University of Michigan, where he has taught since 1989, to go on adjunct status. In the past, he could never teach and write at the same time, too engrossed with his students. At Michigan and also at Warren Wilson College's low-residency program, Baxter has always been careful about what he can promise to workshop participants. "You can't make anybody into a writer. It can't be done. I like the metaphor of tools. You offer people some tools, you show them how to use them, but having the tools isn't the same thing as building the structure. I think teachers have to be very clear about that."

Those tools are sometimes delivered in the form of provocative lectures on craft, many of which were published in *Burning Down the House.* Baxter eschews how-to tutorials on fiction writing—

"I mean, that's very American: self-help," he says—and prefers instead to examine what animates certain types of stories, like fictional inventories. "Lately I've been thinking about the relations between inventories and traumatic experiences and how the Book of Job starts with an inventory. Novels are full of inventories. When you think of three of the most anthologized stories of our time, Tim O'Brien's 'The Things They Carried,' Jamaica Kincaid's 'Girl,' and Susan Minot's 'Lust,' they're inventories. They're essentially about trauma in the form of lists. I've been thinking about that. I'm not telling anybody to do anything. I'm just saying, Notice this."

Baxter isn't always so analytical. He has his playful side, too, such as agreeing to write lyrics for his son's rock band, The School of Velocity, an unlikely but perfect outlet for the ex-poet. (Baxter's last volume of poems, *Imaginary Paintings,* was published by Paris Review Editions in 1990.) He uses the nom de plume of Ponosby Britt, itself a fictitious name for the executive producer of the Rocky and Bullwinkle shows. Some sample lyrics, from the song "Victim of Fashion": *"You're from Banana Republic / You look like J. Crew / You're a victim of fashion / I'm a victim of you."*

And now, especially since he is no longer teaching, Baxter is sleeping better. "I've found the best cure for insomnia," he says, "is thinking there isn't anywhere I'd rather be than in bed. And my other cure is one that I first heard from Stanley Elkin, which is to imagine and then to start reading an endlessly large memorandum from some functionary in the English department."

BOOKSHELF

Recommended Books · Fall 1999

THE PLEASING HOUR *A novel by Lily King. Grove/Atlantic Monthly Press, $23.00 cloth. Reviewed by Jessica Treadway.*

This may be the first time you hear of Lily King, but her debut novel, *The Pleasing Hour,* assures that it won't be the last. With an acute sensibility tuned to the finest details of character, place, and experience, King delivers an emotionally suspenseful story in language nearly as exquisite as the setting itself—a houseboat on the Seine in Paris, where a young American woman named Rosie arrives with one secret and soon after acquires another.

Seeking escape from the pain of a heartbreaking sacrifice she has made for her sister back in Vermont, Rosie takes a job as an au pair for the Tivots, a French family accustomed to a mutable list of *jeunes filles* charged with helping the mother, Nicole, take care of the household. With her distant beauty and low tolerance for mistakes, Nicole intimidates Rosie, who is far from fluent: "I knew if she asked me my own name I would not be able to say it correctly." Despite her deficient language skills, Rosie is quick to discern a lack of communication between Nicole and her husband, Marc. When one of the Tivot children witnesses Rosie stepping into the breach, Rosie flees the family, a fugitive for the second time, and comes to rest in the south of France with Lucie, Nicole's elderly aunt, who provides Rosie—and the novel—with poignant historical context for Nicole's aloof, mysterious airs.

Though King tells most of the story in Rosie's voice, she also allows a third-person narrator to render each of the Tivot children's perspectives, as well as Lucie's account of Nicole's early life and her legacy of loss. In some hands, such alternating points of view might jar the reader, but King pulls it off masterfully; the shifts feel not imposed on the story's structure but organic to it, and add a layer of complexity uncommon to first novels.

One of the strongest scenes in the book depicts a bullfight in Spain, where the family has gone on holiday. In the space of eight pages, we see how the blood sport affects each Tivot child on a profound level. Guillaume, the nine-year-old who wants to be a priest, prays that the bull will be spared. When the bull, gored, collapses at the matador's feet, "amid the snap of whips, the jangle of bells, the scrape of a body along the ground, a thought surfaced and would not be submerged. It bobbed two or three times before Guillaume acknowledged its arrival: *Perhaps there is no God.* The rest of his mind retreated quickly—he had never, ever doubted before—but the brain is small and there was no place to hide." At the same time, Guillaume's sixteen-year-old sister, Odile, is imagining the letter she will write to a girl, Aimee, with whom, despite her boyfriend and her desire to conform, Odile is falling in love. "*Wasn't there,* she would write, *something nearly comforting about the certainty of death?*" Finally, nine-year-old Lola experiences the pas de deux of the matador and his bull through the vibrations of burgeoning sexuality, though of course she doesn't realize this. "A few rows below her, a shirtless man pulled his girlfriend close for a long kiss, and Lola could see their red wet tongues tumbling over each other. She found herself wishing the matador would go for the sword and then was horrified by the wish.... It was not the bull or the matador or the rolling tongues or the arms around her or the blood in the ring or her own slippery sweat, but it was all these things together. She felt like standing up and walking a long, long way; she felt like bursting into tears."

So *The Pleasing Hour,* like all intersections at which lives converge, belongs to more than one person—but ultimately it is Rosie whose emotional evolution we celebrate, and with it the arrival of Lily King to the world of bright new literary voices.

Jessica Treadway, author of Absent Without Leave and Other Stories, *is director of the graduate program in creative writing at Emerson College.*

THE LONG HOME *Poems by Christian Wiman. Story Line Press, $12.95 paper. Reviewed by H. L. Hix.*

Poets' voices seldom emerge fully formed: first books more often air promise than plenitude, recklessness than resonance. But Christian Wiman's *The Long Home,* winner of the 1998 Nicholas Roerich Prize, speaks with mature authority.

The Long Home starts with a sonnet, "Revenant," that introduces the book's muse, an ancestor of the narrator, one who so loves "the fevered air, the green delirium / in the leaves" and the "storm cloud glut with color like a plum" that she stands in the fields during storms expecting to be struck by lightning, her face "upturned to feel the burn that never came: / that furious insight and the end of pain." But if the storm never speaks *to* her, it does speak *through* her: "spirits spoke through her clearest words, / her sudden eloquent confusion, her trapped eyes."

That prophetic figure in "Revenant" returns as—or prefigures—Josie, the narrator of the spellbinding title poem in which the book culminates. Obeying the principle implicit in James Merrill's rhetorical question "Who needs the full story of any life?," Wiman's "The Long Home" recounts the crucial events from Josie's rich and dramatic life, beginning with her family's departure from Carolina to a Canaan that (as in the biblical exodus) was really "Papa's dream," and that proved to be Texas, continuing through her sister-in-law's suicide, her own multiple miscarriages, and her husband's death, and ending in a final visit with her grandson back to the farm where she had raised her one son. Wiman develops plot and character as a novel might, but with the concision and repletion of verse.

In between those two poems, Wiman treats the reader to a cluster of lyrics as inviting as a blackberry bramble buzzing in summer with drunk insects, as full of sweetness and scars. A poem like "One Good Eye" exemplifies Wiman's mastery. Its pretext makes it seem least likely to succeed. As Louise Glück's *The Wild Iris* must make plausible poems from an implausible pretext (flowers in the garden speaking), so "One Good Eye" must make a memorable and original poem from a trite pretext (boy forced to endure the hugs of an ugly aunt). It achieves its unlikely success through the purity and beauty of its music. The poems begins with this melodious sentence: "Lost in the lush flesh / of my crannied aunt, / I felt her smell / of glycerine, rosewater / and long enclosure / enclosing me, / and held my breath / until she'd clucked / and muttered me / to my reluctant / unmuttering uncle / within whose huge / and pudgy palm / my own small-boned hand / was gravely taken, / shaken, and released." And ends full circle: "Then it was time: / my uncle blundering / above me, gasping / tobacco and last / enticements; / —while my aunt, / bleary, tears bright / in her one good eye, / fussed and wished / the day was longer, / kissed and sloshed /

herself around me, / a long last hold / from which I held / myself back, / enduring each / hot, wet breath, each / laborious beat / of her heart, thinking / it would never end." The sonorous repetition of sounds and the selection of perfect words ("crannied," "clucked," "sloshed") typify the musicality that pervades the book.

No one collection commits a poet unalterably to a style or a set of preoccupations, but *The Long Home* already establishes Christian Wiman as a legitimate heir to Frost. The kinship appears unmistakably in a poem like "Clearing," which reanimates the best of Frost's meditative inner-quest poems, like "Directive" and "After Apple-Picking." But the connection is neither so isolated nor so simple. Wiman is no impersonator among the masses mimicking Frost's mannerisms, but a voice possessed of the same rare virtues: independence from poetic fashion, an inviting surface transparency over turbulent depths, shared thematic concerns (home and family, for instance), and an ability to make regional speech representative and individual lives universal. Such exactitude as *The Long Home* embodies, syllable to syllable and line to line, makes Wiman a medium, allows spirits to speak through him, their cadences haunting and their stories true.

H. L. Hix's translation of EugenijusAlišanka's City of Ash *will be published by Northwestern University Press in 2000. Among his other books are a poetry collection,* Perfect Hell, *and a book of criticism,* Understanding W. S. Merwin.

LAST THINGS *A novel by Jenny Offill. Farrar, Straus & Giroux. $23.00 cloth. Reviewed by Fred Leebron.*

Jenny Offill's stunning debut novel, *Last Things*, captures the crucial years in the life of a young narrator trying to choose between a conventional but remote father and a mesmerizing but insane mother.

In the mid-1980's, Grace Davitt is a seven-year-old living in a small Vermont town, only child to Jonathan, a high-school chemistry teacher, and Anna, an underemployed ornithologist at the local raptor center. While Jonathan is prone to pragmatism, Anna continually lives in a world of skewed invention, inspiring her daughter with a new alphabet and an array of knowledge that attempts to make sense of a random and arbitrary world. Both the reader and Grace must respond to these moments by trying to understand what appear to be anecdotes, but are actually bursts of stories within the larger story of the novel. Throughout, a seamless, compressed lucidity characterizes the prose, which is at once descriptive and philosophic: "I sat on the edge of the bathtub and watched my mother put on her face. Outside, the trees were breaking themselves into pieces. Ice tapped against the glass. My mother went to the window and rubbed away the steam. 'Listen, Grace,' she said, 'I think someone's speaking to us in code.'"

Surprising details are so frequent they become the norm, yet the plethora of such discoveries is never numbing. Short declarative sentences like "I had once seen my father eat a raisin-and-mayonnaise sandwich when there was nothing else around" are almost instantly followed by only more enlightenment: "Once, when my mother went away for a weekend, he read me an entire book about the evolution of squirrels." The storytelling is a wondrous mix of the associative and the chronological, with linear aspects so tied to the diverse elements of this novel of ideas (the meaning of life, the nature of the universe, the problem of family) that the effect is simply dazzling.

It comes as no surprise that Grace's favorite book in this engaging mayhem is *The Encyclopedia of the Unexplained,* nor that her genius babysitter should sit in a chair "reading a book called *The Story of Stupidity.*" Offill delivers a light cynicism with feather strokes of language, and even in moments of dramatic fracture, where so much is omitted that in the rush of time she offers only glimpses of the domestic drama, the dramatic arc unravels with a compelling and engaging sense of fulfillment. When Grace begins to understand that she must choose between her father and her mother, her despair escalates to danger and—as in all the bits of stories that her mother has told her in these years—to the crucial sensation that she has learned many things but does not know which are true. "I thought of the Amazons who lived in the jungle and cut off one breast so they could shoot a bow and arrow as well as a man," Grace says as her mother begins to lose grip. "I went into my mother's room and got the camera out of her bag. I held my foot up to my face and took a picture. When it came out, I wrote the date on the back and put it in the drawer."

Last Things is a delightful novel, rich for its voracious eye onto real and imaginary moments of quandary in the lives of its characters and in the larger life of the universe, and richer still for the resilient fashion in which it explores alternatives to any simple answers.

Fred Leebron is the author of the novel Out West *and the co-editor of* Postmodern American Fiction: A Norton Anthology. *His new novel,* Six Figures, *is forthcoming from Knopf.*

BAD JUDGMENT *Poems by Cathleen Calbert. Sarabande Books, $12.95 paper. Reviewed by Victoria Clausi.*

Calbert's second book, *Bad Judgment,* is a searching, sometimes seething look at the traditions of love and marriage, revealing a strong voice adept in the use of irony. These poems frequently open onto a world poised between the surreal and the real, between loss and fulfillment, where the dominant voice vacillates between wanting the "dream / of wedding veils, floating higher, turning blue / in a world made of colors and marital sex" and disdaining them. "In my night sky, I have only men, harmonizing: / *There was a serpent who loved to sing, there was, / there was, hiss hiss. Thus, he forsook his serpenting / because he was in love, he was.*" Another poem, which was included in *The Best American Poetry 1995,* discovers a woman's love for things reversed "until she was loved by trees and appliances, from toasters / to natural obstacles, until her ceiling shook loose to send kisses" and "until everything living and unliving wonderfully collided."

Calbert seduces readers with satiric collisions from the start, even within the table of contents: "The Nights Were Full of Sex and Churches," "The Woman Who Loved Things," "My Dead Boyfriend," "Dream Babies," "The Vampire Baby," "Dead Debutante," "Lunatic Snow," and "The Last Angel Poem."

With an elegance reminiscent of Whitman, these poems celebrate the singer as vigorously as they do the song. The result: lyrics that are witty, cynical, sharp-edged, stunning. Although some critics might take exception to Calbert's extensive use of catalogue, they'd have to concede that she is very good at the technique—so good, in fact, the reader is more likely to see herself reflected in the poem than she is to feel manipulated by the poet.

Mimicking the disassociation that loss can cause, "After the Tragedy" begins: "We put away the dishes. / Someone changed the sheets. / Windows were opened, then painted blue, and painted shut. / We wrote lists and threw the lists away." After a transition that forces the mourners to claim, "We watched ourselves weep in the mirror to see how ugly we could be," the speaker turns inward—to a wilder, darker, reflective list: "We slipped a sliver of faith into the lining of a checked apron. / We slipped a sliver of faith into the veins at our wrist, wondering if it would work its way to our heart. / We sang 'Sweet Bird of Youth' and 'Sweet Mystery.'"

In "Beyond the Power of Positive Thinking," Calbert's well-tuned device of repetition is combined with sardonic little slaps at positivism gone bad. "I've stopped holding on to negative energy / and no longer need academic poverty. / I am radiant and free, calm and serene. // It's okay to have a green Mercedes. / I can accept a green Mercedes. / A green Mercedes is okay with me."

Part of the pleasure of reading Calbert's poetry is watching her play: with language, with sound, with tradition, with the reader. *Bad Judgment*? Hardly. This is a wise book: sexy, witty, irreverent, and filled with moments of brilliance, carefully crafted by a poet who loves "the sweet suck of consenting molecules" so much she can't help revealing the comic absurdity and beauty of the resulting collisions. *Bad Judgment* delivers poems that are, in Richard Howard's words, "so cool, so speculative, so disabused, so warm."

Victoria Clausi teaches poetry at O'More College and in Bennington College's July Program. Her limited-edition chapbook, Boarding House, *was published this June through Bennington College's M.F.A. in Writing Alumni Chapbook Series.*

EDITORS' SHELF

*Books Recommended by
Our Advisory Editors*

George Garrett recommends *Someone to Watch Over Me*, stories by Richard Bausch: "Twelve new stories by one of the most gifted short fiction writers alive and writing." (HarperCollins)

Maxine Kumin recommends *Dead Men's Praise*, poems by Jacqueline Osherow: "A stunning collection. Many of these poems come out of Hebrew Psalms, improbable as that sounds, and are often wonderfully humorous and down to earth." (Grove/Atlantic)

Philip Levine recommends *Reign of Snakes*, poems by Robert Wrigley: "Robert Wrigley has been a fine poet through four previous books; his last, *In the Bank of the Beautiful Sins*, was a finalist for the Lenore Marshall Prize. In this new book he has become someone else, someone who has wandered into a ferocious cave of the natural world and suddenly sees his life, and ours as well, in bold and undreamed of colors. It's almost as though the veil has been lifted from his eyes, and the glorious and terrifying truths have been revealed in poems that are at once majestic and personal." (Penguin)

James Alan McPherson recommends *Who's Irish?* by Gish Jen: "Very funny stories about domesticity." (Knopf)

Chase Twichell recommends *Ocean Avenue*, poems by Malena Mörling: "This is a remarkable first book—taut, often egoless poems that subtly nudge the reader into territory that's wholly original yet also familiar. Each poem creates a minor shock of recognition." (New Issues)

Dan Wakefield recommends *City of a Hundred Fires*, poems by Richard Blanco: "A stunning first book of poems by a young Cuban-American writer of awesome lyrical talent. This book tells the story of the Cuban-American experience as powerfully as a novel, and speaks to all who appreciate personal insight, irony, and love of language, both English and Spanish." (Pittsburgh)

EDITORS' CORNER

*New Books by
Our Advisory Editors*

Leonard Michaels, *The Diaries of Leonard Michaels, 1961–1995*, a memoir: This frank, resonant collection of journal excerpts reveal more than a man, but also an era, going from Greenwich Village, where Michael's first wife, Sylvia, committed suicide at the age of twenty-four, to upstate New York and Berkeley. (Riverhead)

Alberto Ríos, *The Curtain of Trees*, stories: In nine moving tales, Ríos brings us small-town life along the Arizona-Mexico border. The collection presents a dark worldview, but it resounds with Ríos's characteristic tenderness, compassion, and power. (New Mexico)

Dan Wakefield, *How Do We Know When It's God?*, memoir: Ten years ago, Wakefield, then an atheist, had a religious reawakening, which resulted in *Returning: A Spiritual Journey*. He follows up on his spiritual progress in this heartfelt, important book. (Little, Brown)

POSTSCRIPTS

Miscellaneous Notes · Fall 1999

COHEN AWARDS Each year, we honor the best short story and poem published in *Ploughshares* with the Cohen Awards, which are wholly sponsored by our longtime patrons Denise and Mel Cohen. Finalists are nominated by staff editors, and the winners—each of whom receives a cash prize of $600—are selected by our advisory editors. The 1999 Cohen Awards for work published in *Ploughshares* in 1998, Volume 24, go to Chris Adrian and Herman Fong. (Both of their works are accessible on our Web site at www.emerson.edu/ploughshares.)

CHRIS ADRIAN *for his story "The Sum of Our Parts" in Winter 1998–99, edited by Thomas Lux.*

Chris Adrian was born in 1970 in Washington, D.C., and grew up in Florida, the youngest child of an airline pilot and a flight attendant. "I started writing in high school," he says, "after I realized that I had no talent for painting, and that I had better give that up before I hurt myself or someone else with my sloppy, gruesome studies of malproportioned nude women." After high school, he spent a year in Germany as an exchange student and did a great deal of writing, then went to the University of Florida, where Padgett Powell was his mentor. "He taught me, thank goodness, the difference between good writing and bad." After Florida, he received a fellowship to the Iowa Writers' Workshop and studied with Marilynne Robinson. Also at the University of Iowa, he worked as an assistant in a clinical pathology lab and an obstetrics-gynecology research lab. Since 1996, he's been a student at Eastern Virginia Medical School in Norfolk, Virginia.

Besides *Ploughshares,* Adrian has published stories in *The New Yorker, Story, The Paris Review, Zoetrope,* and *The Best American Short Stories 1998*. His first novel, still untitled, is due out next summer from Broadway Books.

About "The Sum of Our Parts," Adrian writes: "It's based, more or less (but certainly less than more), on my experience working in a pathology lab very much like the one described in the story. I was walking down to the neonatal ICU one night, on my way to draw blood from an infant, when a stray and apparently sourceless groan came wafting down the hall. Early the next morning (I worked the nightshift), I happened to see a little girl practicing at a piano in the atrium. The groan and the girl stayed with me in a way that was sort of horrible, and in order to be rid of them, I started a story which gradually drew upon other elements of the nightshift lab experience—receiving brains in Tupperware bowls, gossiping about a patient who leaped off the top of a parking garage, drawing and analyzing our own blood just for fun. Over successive drafts, a female ghost snuck in, replacing the sentient blood-analyzing machine, and commandeered the narrative, and the story came more and more to be hers.

"The final story bore about as much resemblance to the real experience of working in the lab as Batman does to a bat. In real life, there were no ghosts, no multiple transplants, no overheated love polygons. It's full of medical inaccuracies. But I hope the story reflects some of the terrible strangeness of the hospital, how it seemed not unreasonable, at three a.m., that a dissatisfied, ambivalent ghost might be wandering the halls, visiting friends who didn't know her and looking for a way out of life."

HERMAN FONG *for his poem "Grandfather's Alphabet" in* Spring 1998, *edited by Stuart Dybek & Jane Hirshfield.*

Born in Los Angeles in 1963, the fifth of six children, Herman Fong was raised in the San Fernando Valley. Each of his parents' families had fled Canton for Hong Kong, where his father and mother met and married. They immigrated to the U.S. in 1956. However, his family history in the U.S. began decades earlier, when his paternal grandfather labored as a busboy and then a cook in Chinese restaurants on the West Coast; he served as a U.S. Army cook in Europe during World War II, then returned to Los Angeles and opened his own restaurant, The Far East Terrace, which had become a landmark by the time he died in 1985. Fong's father was himself a chef at The Far East Terrace until 1986, when the restaurant was closed.

Fong originally wanted to study architecture, but ended up

majoring in accounting at Biola University in La Mirada, California. After graduating in 1984, unable to find work, he enrolled in a prep course for the C.P.A. exam. "I grew bored," he says. "I would sneak out to the movies, frequent bookstores, or hide out at the Cal State–Northridge library, reading poetry and literary journals." He failed the C.P.A. exam. His next plan was to get an M.B.A. at Cal State–Northridge, but during the first week of registration, he decided he just couldn't go through with it, and transferred to the master's program in English. His first poetry workshops were with Eloise Klein Healy, Lary Gibson, and Dorothy Barresi, who encouraged Fong to go to her alma mater, the University of Massachusetts at Amherst, for his M.F.A. "The idea of living somewhere wholly different and so far from where I had lived my life was wonderfully liberating and terrifying," he says. He graduated from UMass last September after working closely with James Tate, Dara Wier, and Paul Mariani.

His poems have appeared in *The Best American Poetry 1997, The Gettysburg Review, The Massachusetts Review, Indiana Review,* and *Northridge Review.* He has received two awards from the Academy of American Poets, as well as an Associated Writing Programs Intro Journals Award. He currently lives in Northampton, Massachusetts, and lectures on writing at UMass. He is also an events coordinator and publicist for author appearances at The Odyssey Bookshop in South Hadley. He is now in the process of sending out his manuscript for his first collection, *Lightning Field.*

About "Grandfather's Alphabet," Fong writes: "I have written more poems about my grandfather than about anyone else. But my grandfather never read my poems; I didn't know how to show him them, and, in any case, I didn't think of myself as 'a poet' until years after his death. (As was the Asian custom, my grandparents lived with their eldest son, my father, and my grandfather was the looming patriarchal figure while I was growing up. It was his approval we all sought, his disappointment we avoided.)

"Until 'Grandfather's Alphabet,' the writing of previous grandfather poems fell within two periods. The first came during college, when, declining in health and grown impatient, he argued with me about my future. Those poems were bitter. The second was after his death. Weighted with grief, these were poems about the morning he suffered an aneurysm, about yellow chrysanthemums brought as a gift during his hospital stay, his cemetery plot, afternoons packing his belongings and giving them away, and the ghost of him that visited in sleep. Then I stopped.

"About the time that 'Grandfather's Alphabet' was written, I was reconsidering narrative and lyric poetry: how to create a narrative—tell a story, tell a life—without narrative, and how to convey and control emotion strictly through imagery. When I began the poem, I didn't know that I would write about my grandfather. Taking a cue from the title of Olga Broumas's book, *Beginning with O*, which I was reading at the time, I started the poem as a simple list—things that resembled an *O*, things that *O* resembled. Soon I realized that I was naming things belonging to my grandfather. I hadn't wanted to write about him again, but then felt I had to offer something balanced, more embracing: *O* as a whole and as emptiness, *O* as completion and as a continuing cycle."

MORE AWARDS Our congratulations to the following writers, whose work has been selected for these anthologies and awards:

BEST STORIES Aleksandar Hemon's "Islands," from the Spring 1998 issue edited by Stuart Dybek & Jane Hirshfield, will be included in *The Best American Short Stories 1999*, due out this fall from Houghton Mifflin, with Amy Tan as the guest editor and Katrina Kenison as the series editor.

BEST POETRY Tony Hoagland's "Lawrence" and David Mamet's "A Charade," both from the Winter 1997–98 issue edited by Howard Norman & Jane Shore, and David Wagoner's "Thoreau and the Crickets," from the Spring 1998 issue edited by Stuart Dybek & Jane Hirshfield, will appear in *The Best American Poetry 1999* this September from Scribner, with Robert Bly as the guest editor and David Lehman as the series editor.

O. HENRY Sheila M. Schwartz's "Afterbirth," from the Fall 1998 issue edited by Lorrie Moore, has been chosen for *Prize Stories 1999: The O. Henry Awards* by editor Larry Dark. The anthology will be published in October by Anchor Books.

PUSHCART Charles Baxter's "Harry Ginsberg," from the Fall 1998 issue edited by Lorrie Moore, has been selected for *The Push-*

cart Prize XXIV: Best of the Small Presses, which will be published by Bill Henderson's Pushcart Press this fall.

SHELLEY   Tom Sleigh, a frequent contributor to *Ploughshares,* has won the 1999 Shelley Memorial Award from the Poetry Society of America.

MACARTHUR   Campbell McGrath, a previous Cohen Award winner, has been given a $280,000 MacArthur "Genius" Fellowship.

CONTRIBUTORS' NOTES

Fall 1999

JILL BOSSERT was a digger on archeological sites in England, created a comic strip for adolescents, did storyboards for Ken Russell's *Altered States,* and lived at the Society of Illustrators, where she curated exhibitions and wrote books on the subject of American art for reproduction. As the Philip Guston Fellow at Columbia University, she wrote a novel about a suburban woman and an abstract expressionist in 1958. Her story "The Dig" will soon appear in *Ontario Review.*

MICHAEL BYERS is the author of a collection of short stories, *The Coast of Good Intentions* (Houghton Mifflin, 1998). A former Stegner Fellow, he has also received awards from the Whiting Foundation and the Henfield Foundation. He lives in Seattle.

PETER HO DAVIES's work has appeared in *The Atlantic, Harper's, The Paris Review,* and *Story,* and has been selected for *Prize Stories 1998: The O. Henry Awards* and *The Best American Short Stories 1995* and *1996.* He is the author of the collections *The Ugliest House in the World* and the forthcoming *Equal Love,* both published by Houghton Mifflin/Mariner Books. He is a recipient of fellowships from the Fine Arts Work Center in Provincetown and the National Endowment for the Arts.

DOUG DORST is a Wallace Stegner Fellow at Stanford University. He received his M.F.A. from the Iowa Writers' Workshop in 1997. His stories have appeared in *ZYZZYVA, Gulf Coast,* and *CutBank.* He lives in San Francisco.

ROB EVANS has exhibited his work internationally, and his paintings can be found in the permanent collections of many museums, including the Corcoran Gallery of Art in Washington, D.C. His paintings have also been featured in a number of magazines and journals, including *American Artist* and *The Gettysburg Review,* and on numerous covers for books, including Charles Baxter's novel *Shadow Play.* Evans lives near Wrightsville, Pennsylvania, with his wife and two children.

EMILY HAMMOND is the author of a short story collection, *Breathe Something Nice* (University of Nevada Press). She lives in Fort Collins, Colorado, and has recently completed a novel.

MABELLE HSUEH lives and writes in Ann Arbor, Michigan.

JAMES MORRISON teaches film at North Carolina State University. His work appears in *Crescent Review, Florida Review,* and *Prism International,* among many other quarterlies, as well as in the Lambda Award–winning anthology *Wrestling with the Angel* (Riverhead, 1995). He is also the author of a memoir to be published by St. Martin's Press.

ANTONYA NELSON is the author of three short story collections, *The Expendables, In the Land of Men,* and *Family Terrorists,* and three novels, *Talking in Bed, Nobody's Girl,* and the forthcoming *Living to Tell.* She lives in Las Cruces, New Mexico, and Telluride, Colorado, and teaches creative writing in Warren Wilson College's M.F.A. program, as well as at New Mexico State University.

STEWART O'NAN's first story collection, *In the Walled City,* won the 1993 Drue Heinz Prize. This April, Holt released his latest novel, *A Prayer for the Dying.* Next year Doubleday will publish his nonfiction history of the Hartford Circus Fire.

HILARY RAO received a 1998 fiction grant from the Massachusetts Cultural Council. She holds an M.F.A. in writing and literature from Bennington College and lives in Lexington, Massachusetts. "Every Day a Little Death" is her first published story.

ELWOOD REID is the author of the novel *If I Don't Six,* which was published by Doubleday in 1998. His short story collection, *What Salmon Know,* will be published this fall by Doubleday, with a novel, *Golden Heart,* to follow in 2000. He is a frequent contributor to *GQ* magazine.

JOAN SILBER is the author of the novels *In the City* and *Household Words,* which won the PEN/Hemingway Award. Her story collection, *In My Other Life,* is forthcoming from Sarabande Books. The recipient of grants from the NEA, the New York Foundation for the Arts, and the Guggenheim Foundation, she teaches at Sarah Lawrence College and Warren Wilson College's M.F.A. program.

ELIZABETH TIPPENS is the author of a novel, *Winging It* (Putnam/Riverhead). Her short stories have appeared in *Mademoiselle, Cosmopolitan,* and the anthology *Voices of the Xiled* (Doubleday), and her nonfiction has been published in *Rolling Stone, Playboy,* and elsewhere. She lives with her husband, David, and her son, Henry, in New York City.

HOW IT WORKS *Ploughshares* is published three times a year: mixed issues of poetry and fiction in the Spring and Winter and a fiction issue in the Fall, with each guest-edited by a different writer of prominence, usually one whose early work was published in the journal. Guest editors are invited to solicit up to half of their issues, with the other half selected from unsolicited manuscripts screened for them by staff editors. This guest-editor policy is designed to introduce readers to different literary circles and tastes, and to offer a fuller representation of the range and diversity of contemporary letters than would be possible with a single editorship. Yet, at the same time, we expect every issue to reflect our overall standards of literary excellence. We liken *Ploughshares* to a theater company: each issue might have a different guest editor and different writers—just as a play will have a different director, playwright, and cast—but subscribers can count on a governing aesthetic, a consistency in literary values and quality, that is uniquely our own.

SUBMISSION POLICIES We welcome unsolicited manuscripts from August 1 to March 31 (postmark dates). All submissions sent from April to July are returned unread. In the past, guest editors often announced specific themes for issues, but we have revised our editorial policies and no longer restrict submissions to thematic topics. Submit your work at any time during our reading period; if a manuscript is not timely for one issue, it will be considered for another. We do not recommend trying to target specific guest editors. Our backlog is unpredictable, and staff editors ultimately have the responsibility of determining for which editor a work is most appropriate. Mail one prose piece and/or one to three poems at a time (mail genres separately). No e-mail submissions. Poems should be individually typed either single- or double-spaced on one side of the page. Prose should be typed double-spaced on one side and be no longer than twenty-five pages. Although we look primarily for short stories, we occasionally publish personal essays/memoirs. Novel excerpts are acceptable if self-contained. Unsolicited book reviews and criticism are not considered. Please do not send multiple submissions of the same genre, and do not send another manuscript until you hear about the first. *No more than a total of two submissions per reading period.* Additional submissions will be returned unread. Mail your manuscript in a page-size manila envelope, your full name and address written on the outside. In general, address submissions to the "Fiction Editor," "Poetry Editor," or "Nonfiction Editor," not to the guest or staff editors by name, unless you have a legitimate association with them or have been previously published in the magazine. Unsolicited work sent directly to a guest editor's home or office will be ignored and discarded; guest editors are formally instructed not to read such work. All manuscripts and correspondence regarding submissions should be accompanied by a self-addressed, stamped envelope (S.A.S.E.) for a response; no replies will be given by e-mail or postcard. Expect three to five months for a decision. We now receive over a thousand manuscripts a month. Do not query us until five months have passed, and if you do, please write to us, including an S.A.S.E. and indicating the postmark date of submission, instead of calling or e-mailing. Simultaneous submissions are amenable as long as they are indicated as such and we are notified immediately upon acceptance elsewhere. We cannot accommodate revisions, changes of return address, or forgotten S.A.S.E.'s after the fact. We do not reprint previously published work. Translations are welcome if permission has been granted. We cannot be responsible for delay, loss, or damage. Payment is upon publication: $25/printed page, $50 minimum per title, $250 maximum per author, with two copies of the issue and a one-year subscription.

INDIANA REVIEW

Fall / Winter 1999

Featuring a conversation with Li-Young Lee.

Also featuring:

Poetry	**Fiction**
Denise Duhamel	Eric Johnson
Jim Elledge	Paul Ketzle
Lisa Lewis	Karenmary Penn
George Looney	Darrell Spencer
Adrienne Su	

and others

Subscriptions:
Sample copies available for $8.00.
$14 / 1 year (2 issues), $26 / 2 years (4 issues)
Now accepting submissions in non-fiction, poetry,
fiction, and book reviews. Send SASE for guidelines.

Indiana Review Fiction Prize
First Prize: $500
and publication in *Indiana Review*

Final judge: Scott Russell Sanders
Entry fee: $10 (includes prize issue)
Deadline: November 15, 1999
Send entries to "IR Fiction Prize."

**Indiana Review • Ballantine Hall 465 • 1020 E. Kirkwood Ave.
Bloomington, IN 47405-7103**

BENNINGTON WRITING SEMINARS

MFA in Writing and Literature
Two-Year Low-Residency Program

FICTION
NONFICTION
POETRY

Jane Kenyon Poetry Scholarships available
For more information contact:
Writing Seminars
Box PL
Bennington College
Bennington, VT 05201
802-440-4452, Fax 802-447-4269

FACULTY

FICTION
Douglas Bauer
Elizabeth Cox
Susan Dodd
Maria Flook
Lynn Freed
Amy Hempel
Alice Mattison
Jill McCorkle
Askold Melnyczuk
Rick Moody

NONFICTION
Sven Birkerts
Susan Cheever
Lucy Grealy
Bob Shacochis

POETRY
April Bernard
Thomas Sayers Ellis
David Lehman
Jane Hirshfield
Carol Muske
Liam Rector
Jason Shinder

POET-IN-RESIDENCE
Donald Hall

RECENT ASSOCIATE FACULTY
Robert Bly
Lucie Brock-Broido
Karen Finley
Marie Howe
Carole Maso
Howard Norman
Robert Pinsky
Roger Shattuck
Tom Wicker

THE BOSTON BOOK REVIEW

http://www.BostonBookReview.com

The Best of Both Worlds

The Apollonian

The Bostonian

The Dionysian

The thinking person's literary arts magazine with fiction, poetry, interviews, essays and book reviews.

Subscribe to the BOSTON BOOK REVIEW.
Discover the well-written.

In addition, sign up to receive our **FREE** bimonthly email Gazette for info about authors, new articles and reviews, BBR bestsellers and best picks, occasional short reviews, and more. Send an email with **subscribe** in the subject line to Gazette@soapbox.BostonBookReview.com.

SUBSCRIPTIONS: 1 yr. (10 issues) $24.00 plshr
Canada and International add $26.00

Name _____
Address _____
City _____ State _____ Zip _____

Credit Card Payments: No. _____
or call (617) 497-0344 Exp. date: _____ Signature: _____
☐ VISA   ☐ MASTERCARD   ☐ DISCOVER   ☐ AMEX
Or send check to:
THE BOSTON BOOK REVIEW, 30 Brattle Street, 4th floor, Cambridge, MA 02138

DARK HORSE LITERARY REVIEW

Starting Gate Opens November 15.

Submissions Accepted August 1.

Department of English
Texas Tech University
Box 43091 • Lubbock, TX 79409-3091
Leslie Jill Patterson, Editor

SANTA MONICA *Review*

spring 1999

available now

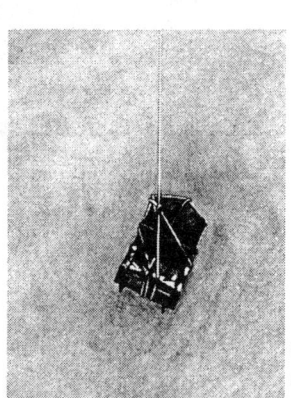

Fiction / Essays / Novel Excerpt

Bernard Cooper / Diane Lefer
Michelle Latiolais
Ben Slotky / Judith Grossman
Peter Carr / Greg Bills / Janice Shapiro
Maria Caruso / Jim Krusoe
Derek Jensen Interviews John Zerzan

$7 copy / **$12** yr. subscription
SM Review / Santa Monica College
1900 Pico Boulevard / Santa Monica, CA 90405

M.F.A. in Creative Writing

M.A. in Writing & Publishing

Located in historic Boston, right on "The Common," Emerson College offers an exciting community for writers and aspiring publishers. Home to the nationally renowned journal *Ploughshares,* Emerson's graduate program nurtures new voices and provides diverse opportunities for study in an environment of discovery and growth. Class sizes are small, with enrollments limited to twelve students in workshops.

Graduate Admission
100 Beacon Street
Boston, MA 02116
Tel: (617) 824-8610
Fax: (617) 824-8614
gradapp@emerson.edu
www.emerson.edu/gradapp

EMERSON COLLEGE

Current Faculty in the Department of Writing, Literature & Publishing:

John Skoyles, Chair
Jonathan Aaron
Douglas Clayton
William Donoghue
Robin Riley Fast
Eileen Farrell
Flora Gonzalez
Lisa Jahn-Clough
DeWitt Henry
Christopher Keane
Maria Koundoura
Bill Knott
Margot Livesey
Ralph Lombreglia
Gail Mazur
Tracy McCabe
Pamela Painter
Donald Perret
Michael Stephens
Christopher Tilghman

Adjunct Faculty include:

David Barber, Sam Cornish, Andre Dubus III, Marcie Hershman, William Holinger, Kai Maristed, George Packer, Martha Rhodes, Elizabeth Searle, Jessica Treadway

Concentrations in:

Fiction, Poetry, Non-Fiction, Screenwriting, Children's Literature, & Publishing

MFA Creative Writing
UNIVERSITY OF MARYLAND, COLLEGE PARK

FACULTY – 1999-2000

Poetry
Michael Collier
Stanley Plumly
Phillis Levin
Reginald McKnight

Fiction
Merle Collins
Joyce Kornblatt
Howard Norman

RECENT VISITING WRITERS

Julie Agoos
Russell Banks
Rita Dove
Patricia Hampl

Robert Hass
Seamus Heaney
Edward Hirsch
June Jordan

Philip Levine
Peter Matthiessen
William Maxwell
Mary Robison

Marilynne Robinson
Tom Sleigh
C.D. Wright
Charles Wright

For more information:
Michael Collier, Stanley Plumly, Directors
Department of English • University of Maryland • College Park, MD 20742
(301) 405-3820

RATTAPALLAX

A Journal of Contemporary Literature
with CD featuring poetry from the journal read by the poets

$7.95

Editor-in-Chief George Dickerson
Senior Editor Judith Werner
Art Editor Arlette Lurié
Publisher Ram Devineni

One Year (2 issues) $14.00 / Two Years (4 issues) $24.00
532 La Guardia Place • Suite 353 • New York, NY 10012
www.rattapallax.com

Ploughshares

a literary adventure

Known for its compelling fiction and poetry, *Ploughshares* is widely regarded as one of America's most influential literary journals. Each issue is guest-edited by a different writer for a fresh, provocative slant—exploring personal visions, aesthetics, and literary circles—and contributors include both well-known and emerging writers. In fact, *Ploughshares* has become a premier proving ground for new talent, showcasing the early works of Sue Miller, Mona Simpson, Robert Pinsky, and countless others. Past guest editors include Richard Ford, Derek Walcott, Tobias Wolff, Carolyn Forché, and Rosellen Brown. This unique editorial format has made *Ploughshares,* in effect, into a dynamic anthology series—one that has established a tradition of quality and prescience. *Ploughshares* is published in quality trade paperback in April, August, and December: usually a fiction issue in the Fall and mixed issues of poetry and fiction in the Spring and Winter. Inside each issue, you'll find not only great new stories and poems, but also a profile on the guest editor, book reviews, and miscellaneous notes about *Ploughshares,* its writers, and the literary world. Subscribe today.

Sample *Ploughshares* online: www.emerson.edu/ploughshares

❑ **Send me a one-year subscription for $21.**
I save $8.85 off the cover price (3 issues).

❑ **Send me a two-year subscription for $40.**
I save $19.70 off the cover price (6 issues).

Start with: ❑ Spring ❑ Fall ❑ Winter

Add $5 per year for international. Institutions: $24.

Name _____

Address _____

_____

Mail with check to: Ploughshares · Emerson College
100 Beacon St. · Boston, MA 02116